"*The Quiet Is Loud* made me believe wholeheartedly in the para-dextrous powers of its characters and their world, so wholeheartedly that at times I forgot that what I was reading was not possible. Garner's is an exciting new voice."

— LIZ HARMER, AUTHOR OF *THE AMATEURS* AND *STRANGE LOOPS*

"Samantha Garner's rich prose deftly weaves together family politics, estrangement, and finding one's own place in the world. A lovely exploration of friendship, and identity, and what it means to be truly accepted.

—LINDSAY ZIER-VOGEL, AUTHOR OF *LETTERS TO AMELIA*

"In *The Quiet is Loud*, Garner builds a world where dream visions, tarot readings, and the existence of the paradextrous are a natural part of day-to-day life. Written in clear-eyed prose that effortlessly weaves in Filipino and Norse mythology, *The Quiet is Loud* is an exciting and sensitive look into the mind of a young woman grappling with the consequences of family secrets, while also coming to terms with her unique talents. It is a powerful debut."

—TERI VLASSOPOULOS, AUTHOR OF *ESCAPE PLANS*

"In *The Quiet is Loud*, Samantha Garner has deftly crafted a world that left me breathless. Getting to know Freya Tanangco's story, watching her weave together the strands of her Norwegian-Filipino identity and the unexpected power she wields, was both suspenseful and filled with quiet illumination. At the heart, the novel is a gripping journey of self-discovery and the family bonds that hold us all together."

—JULIA ZARANKIN, AUTHOR OF *FIELD NOTES FROM AN UNINTENTIONAL BIRDER*

THE QUIET IS LOUD

SAMANTHA GARNER

Invisible Publishing
Halifax & Prince Edward County

Library and Archives Canada Cataloguing in Publication

Title: The quiet is loud / Samantha Garner.

Names: Garner, Samantha (Samantha Kaisa), author.
Identifiers: Canadiana (print) 20210169265
                Canadiana (ebook) 20210169311
ISBN 9781988784717 (softcover) | ISBN 9781988784779 (HTML)

Classification: LCC PS8613.A7667 Q54 2021 | DDC C813/.6—dc23

Edited by Bryan Ibeas
Cover and interior design by Megan Fildes | Typeset in Laurentian
With thanks to type designer Rod McDonald

Printed and bound in Canada
Invisible Publishing | Halifax & Prince Edward County
www.invisiblepublishing.com

Published with the generous assistance of the Canada Council for the Arts, the Ontario Arts Council, and the Government of Canada.

Canada Council
for the Arts

Conseil des Arts
du Canada

ONTARIO ARTS COUNCIL
CONSEIL DES ARTS DE L'ONTARIO
an Ontario government agency
un organisme du gouvernement de l'Ontario

Canadä

For Mom, my first reader and biggest supporter, and for Dad, who taught me the power of a good story.

Something wasn't right. I felt its threads at the edges of my awareness.

The containers from my takeout dinner earlier—they were still in full view of my webcam. The last time I'd left fast food containers in sight, the comments I got in the chat were displeased, to say the least. It didn't bode well that I'd almost forgotten again. I cleared them away petulantly, as if they'd thrown me off on purpose.

I lit a stick of incense, and the cloying smoke made my eyes water as I arranged its little stand on the coffee table. I wished I could go without it, but the sharp scent had brought me back to my senses more than once, and I needed to feel more in control for today's shift.

I took a deep breath, tried to ground myself. I didn't usually work so late, but I couldn't ignore my manager Carol's request to cover another reader's time slot. I needed the money and to score some points with her. Make myself a little more agreeable and available, and maybe Carol would let me expense for an additional camera setup, one that'd let me show my tarot cards as well as my face. It wouldn't be hard to make myself seem worthy of reward—one of the other readers had picked her teeth with the Three of Wands on public chat last week. All I had to do was keep my shit together.

I relaxed into my pre-work ritual of making coffee, the same mug, the same teaspoon of sugar and splash of cream, and soon felt better. I admired the living room as it would be viewed over my shoulder: cozy lighting, couch cleared of personal effects, incense on the table. Perfect. Exactly what they expected.

Coffee in hand, cards ready on my desk, I sat down, switched on my camera, and connected to the Oneira server. I felt a strange little vibration of—what? Excitement? Anticipation? A late-evening Saturday shift was uncharted territory for me. It was a novelty, not knowing what to expect. Evenings usually brought out a slightly different crowd. I wondered why. Lonely people anticipating bad dreams, or waking from bad dreams and unable—or unwilling—to try sleep again? Even if I didn't see any regulars tonight, I'd at least have the chance to give people some guidance or comfort. Hopefully.

My chat room filled up quickly. The names in the chat were mostly unfamiliar to me, but I saw a few I recognized. Good. I may not have to moderate too much. Free chat meant mostly making small talk, but in a way that subtly reminded people I was there to help solve all their life's problems with a paid reading. I had gotten almost too good at answering just enough questions to pique their interest, then snatching my assistance away before I could give them the details they wanted. It didn't always result in a paid reading, but it only had to some of the time.

I watched the messages scroll by, gauging when it was best to let people help each other, and when I could be useful.

wallflower18: Will Steve ever answer me?

IsItMe: wallflower you need to stop giving Steve so much of your energy.

IsItMe: Remember last week when he stood you up and wouldn't answer why?

wallflower18: Ya, I know. I just want closure.

bayoudancing: so i had that dream again last night argh!

> **TaurusTarot [Moderator]:** @wallflower18, closure has to happen within you. You can't rely on someone else to let you move forward. Think of the High Priestess and her message of trusting your intuition.

> **TaurusTarot [Moderator]:** @bayoudancing, I'm sorry to hear that! Was anything different this time?

wallflower18: @TaurusTarot That's so true! xo

bayoudancing: well this time my grandfather wasn't there but i could still sense him, waiting to tell me something

bayoudancing: but i woke up before i could hear it i can't help thinking about it. what could it mean?

wallflower18: Sounds intense, bayou. Maybe you can try meditating before bed.

Glen1979: Hey everyone, is this tarot card girl a veker, do you think?

I winced, as if pinched. As if I'd heard the words loud in my ear. I took a deep, grounding breath. *Just words on a screen. I can handle this.*

> **TaurusTarot [Moderator]:** @bayoudancing, sometimes all you need to do is go outside, breathe the fresh air, get some space. You need to remember who you are and find your role in the world. You're almost there, I know it.

> **TaurusTarot [Moderator]:** @Glen1979, let's keep it respectful around here. I'm banning you from chat for one hour.

Blusprite: Hi @TaurusTarot, how are you? I have a couple of questions about my work. Can we go private?

I hesitated. I was still rattled from Glen1979's comment and could use a few minutes to collect myself before going private.

Then again, chatting with Blusprite would be calming. Her real name was Lucy. She came to me fairly regularly for guidance with her burgeoning photography career. She was uncomplicated in a refreshing way, and she didn't see me as a carnival fortune teller or as someone dictating her fate. I could relax and not get overwhelmed with her.

> **TaurusTarot [Moderator]:** @Blusprite, sure! I'll turn my mic on, one sec. Talk amongst yourselves, everyone else!

Lucy turned her webcam and mic on, and I was immediately reassured by her kind eyes. We made some quick small talk, then got down to business. I opted for a quick and easy four-card life purpose spread. It was something I liked to do for creative types, and people who considered their work and their identity to be one and the same.

"This is promising. Look. The first card I pulled is Strength."

I like the Strength card because you can tell all you need to know about it just by looking at it. A woman is grasping a lion around its jaws, but her hands are relaxed, not clenched. The lion's tongue is lolling out—not an attack posture. He's ready to submit. I held the card up to the camera a moment and heard Lucy's happy intake of breath.

"That's got to be a good card, right?"

I didn't like talking about cards in terms of good or bad. The cards were just themselves, the barest of definitions ready to be interpreted. Every combination of cards could either bode well, encourage caution, or suggest a new course of action.

Lucy's next card was Seven of Cups reversed. That didn't surprise me. The Cups cards are about emotions and expression of feelings. Seven always rippled with excitement to me, its cups filled with a mixture of negative and positive objects: a dragon, a snake, a tower, a wreath. Everything in the clouds, up in the air. Illusions, wishful thinking, choices. Drawing a card that's upside down changes its meaning, adds a different layer of insight or consideration. It sometimes results in an opposite interpretation from the card right-side up. In the case of the Seven of Cups, the reversal means there may be too many choices.

"So, let's review these together. The first card represents compassion and confidence. Strength without violence or anger. The reversed Seven suggests you turn these cups upside down, dump out all the options, and pick one—and Strength seems to be reassuring you that you are able to corral all your creative forces onto one path."

"That's exactly the problem I've been having lately," Lucy replied. "I've been really interested in self-portraits, but I also want to document abandoned spaces. But I've also been having ideas for projects that have nothing to do with either of those. What does the next card say?"

I held up the Magician reversed.

Lucy made a small sound of dismay. "That one reversed isn't always great, is it?"

"On its own, it's not the most cheerful card, no. It can mean uncertainty about an action. Or results you expect but aren't seeing. A lack of motivation to get to a goal."

It could also mean deception and manipulation, but I didn't want to freak her out by putting it that bluntly. Something tugged at me, some dim memory.

"Last time I saw you in chat, you were talking about an artistic partner, right?"

"That's right. My former mentor from college. We've been working together on projects now and then, but—"

Lucy's voice suddenly sounded distant, as if she were speaking through a closed car window.

A memory drifted into place.

Lucy stands in a room, sunlight pouring in through opened windows. Curtains flutter inward. Wind ruffles the ends of her long hair and she tucks an errant strand behind her ear. She leans over a table, spreads out photographs, arranges them. There is another person in the room now, strangely out of focus, her face obscured. She moves just outside of Lucy's line of sight, making deft movements with her hands as she circles the table. A gust of wind blows through the room and the table is covered in sand and ash. No photographs remain. Lucy is alone once more.

It was over in the span of just a moment, a few deep breaths of incense. The recall of one of my dreams that was more than just a dream. I had remembered a vision.

"—just don't think it's wise for her to put us up for a corporate project where we'd have basically zero guidance and a sixty-forty split between us," Lucy was saying, "and only because my partner and their CEO are friends. Hey, are you okay?"

I straightened slightly, pinched my arm under the desk to snap back to full awareness. Put a big calm tarot-reading smile on my face. Relaxing energy, everything as it should be.

"Sorry," I said. "I was just trying to envision the most likely outcomes of what these cards are suggesting based on what you've been saying."

I leaned back and looked at the card in my hands. I liked Lucy and wanted her to succeed. I wanted to tell her straight up that her partner was definitely untrustworthy. But I didn't—I wouldn't be able to answer the questions she'd have in response.

So instead, I cleared my throat and let the card say what I couldn't.

"Yes, this does suggest that you should step back and re-evaluate if something doesn't seem right. At least until you have your own path solidly figured out, as we discussed with the Seven of Cups. Maybe you should tell your partner that you need some time on your own to reflect on your next project. In fact, there's no maybe about it. You very much should. But let's see what the last card has to say about it."

I finished the rest of the reading without incident, and Lucy signed off happy and confident in her next move.

Lucky her, I thought.

Before going back into the public chat room, I turned off my webcam and mic and closed my eyes, took a deep breath.

I was suddenly exhausted. I desperately wanted to go back to my original plan of a bath, a book, then bed, but I had most of my shift left to go. Was my comfort worth the lost bit of income or risking Carol's disappointment?

I sighed and gulped down the last of my coffee. Then I squared my shoulders and logged back into public chat.

The sun streamed bright into Freya's eyes and she held up a hand to shade her face. She blinked against the light drowsily. Was she too late?

She wasn't even sure how she got through her bedroom door. A blur of arms and legs, and all of a sudden she was in the kitchen. Before her were the surprised faces of her parents, their hands poised mid-air, mid-action, frozen.

"Are you okay, Pumpkin?" Mom asked. "Bad dream?"

Mom opened her arms and Freya climbed in, let herself be rocked just for a moment. A kiss pressed firm to the top of her head. She slid back down, her bare feet cold against the linoleum, and brushed the sleep from her eyes.

Only when she took her place at the table did she process the wrapped present, the candle in a cupcake.

"Don't move," Dad said, flicking a lighter at the candle. They sang "Happy Birthday," and Freya didn't know where to look—at Dad's fingers drumming the time against the table, at Mom's eyes starting to fill with tears.

The singing cut short with a gasp when the smell of French toast, too sharp, curled over from the stove. Dad flung himself at the pan as Mom brushed a hand across her eyes. The breath of a laugh.

"I'm sorry, honey." Dad's shoulders slumped. "I burned it. And this was the last of the eggs too."

Freya pretended not to hear him curse under his breath. She told him it was okay, and it was. She had a cupcake and a present. She also had a piece of paper that unfolded into a pencil crayon drawing from her five-year-old cousin Mary in Toronto. The two of them together in Kelowna, with identical sticks of black for hair and triangles of red for dresses. Balloons with green scribbled outside the lines. Okanagan Lake with triangle mountains rising behind it.

"Open your present," Mom said.

Freya tore into the wrapped rectangle and shiny green strips cascaded to the floor. She already knew what it would be, but seeing the book finally in her own hands sent a wave of happiness through her all the same.

"Is that the right one?" Mom asked.

She nodded and began to describe the story around a mouthful of cupcake. Dad scraped his chair back and bent forward, resting his chin against his hand. He reached across space and gripped Freya's cupcake arm.

"I feel so bad," he said. "I know you love French toast. Maybe we can stop at Tim Hortons on the way to Penticton. Which means you won't need this!" He made a playful grab for the cupcake before Freya shoved the rest in her mouth.

"Oh that's wonderful, Brian." Mom scolded playfully. "Let's make our child choke to death on her birthday."

Dad rapped his knuckles against the wooden table. Always superstitious.

Mom wound a length of Freya's hair around her fingers, released it. "My baby. I can't believe you're seven now! I remember when you were seven seconds."

Freya chewed, swallowed, leaned back in her seat. She knew what was coming: the ritual remembrance of the day she was born. She clutched the new book to her chest as she listened to her parents recite their parts. She already knew which specific words they'd use, where their voices would rise and fall, knew they'd both be teary at the end. When she was younger it made her upset to see her parents cry. Now she understood that tears didn't always mean sadness.

In the car, Freya clutched half a box of Timbits, all for her. She luxuriated in the rich sweetness, let the crumbs fall down her shirt. She tried to read her book at the same time, but got the pages sticky with sugar, and she eventually gave up. She began to feel sleepy, drifting on the lull of low voices from the front seat.

"...fun writing now that I've let myself forget about typical sentence construction..."

"...the parts I've read so far. It's a lot of fun to read your almost musical kind of..."

"...ready for a novel like this, but my last one was pretty well-received, so I..."

"...especially the part inspired by that time Freya and I found that poor bird..."

Freya remembered the bird. She remembered it flying upwards in a shaft of light, the bright redness of its head, the horrible sound it made as it repeatedly hit the skylight, desperate to get out.

She hadn't thought about that bird since she was five. She leaned forward in her seat, suddenly curious.

"Daddy," she said. "Did you put the bird in your new book?"

"Sort of. You and your mom and the bird are there, but it's not the same story. Not the true story. It's more of a metaphor."

She nodded in false understanding. How could something be real but not true? Why couldn't grown-ups just say what they meant? She drifted off again, sliding into sleep as the car hummed along the highway.

The sound of her door opening woke her and she stretched, blinking. Mom and Dad swung Freya between them as they walked toward the petting zoo, though she was too big for it.

It was her birthday and they were doing only what she wanted.

She spent the rest of the morning with cupped hands, planting her feet and standing firm as goats, pigs, sheep ate the feed she offered. Their tongues were hot and slimy, they made her want to shriek. She hated the thick smell of the pens as the animals crowded her.

Dad, breaking the rules, held her over the edge of a pen so she could pet a lone alpaca. When Mom noticed and scolded him, he winked at Freya and they laughed.

She approached the ponies side-on, askance, sizing them up. Their tails flicked, muscles twitching here and there on their mottled legs. Taller than she'd thought. She squinted, imagined herself up there, so close to the sky.

Mom slid her arm around her shoulders. "You don't have to do it if you're not ready, Pumpkin."

"I want to, but I don't want to."

"I can walk next to you the whole time," Dad said, "and that man will be leading the pony so it can't run, see? Let's go talk to him."

Freya paid no attention when her father spoke to the pony handler. She was too distracted by a little girl, her cousin Mary's age, who sat at the man's feet with a box full of sun-yellow chicks. Freya imagined how soft they were, like fingers sliding across smoke.

The girl spoke to her. "They like you," she said with a green-eyed stare.

A little kid's talk. Freya straightened her back to show her maturity.

"I promise," the girl continued. "They like me and they like you. But not my dad. They feel prickly if he gets too close."

"Their feathers?"

The girl huffed, frustrated. "No, they *feel* prickly. It comes out of them."

Freya looked up at Mom, who shrugged slightly.

The man with the ponies shrugged as well and chuckled. "She thinks she can feel what animals feel," he said to Mom. He seemed accepting, or unconcerned.

The girl lifted one of the chicks up to Freya. "Want to hold this one? She likes you the most."

Freya reached down but Dad suddenly pulled her away, his grip tight around her hand.

"Sorry, honey," he said. "I just don't think you're ready for a pony this year."

Part of Freya was relieved. Part of her slid slightly out of place, hung there, until it found a name: *lie*. Her father was lying.

"Was that girl a veker?" Dad whispered to Mom when she caught up to them. "She didn't seem right."

"What's the big deal?" Mom whispered back. "She can't control minds or anything."

"Yet."

"Come on, she's just a little kid. What do you want her father to do, lock her up somewhere?"

"Yes! Or at least keep her under very close supervision. For everyone's safety."

"I think you're hungry and overreacting. Let's all get some funnel cake and talk about this later."

Freya climbed onto Dad's back, let her head rest against his shoulder, let her arms dangle. After the funnel cake, he held her over the alpaca pen again, but she kept her hands pressed to her sides. This time, the alpacas looked at her, then their attention floated away. Their shared curiosity was over. Dad lowered her to the ground and she threw some feed over the fence. The alpacas ignored it and Freya wished she could feel what they felt, like the girl and her chicks.

At home, Freya nested in a pile of blankets on the couch. She propped her book on a cushion and sank into her own imagination, letting the images and stories pass like a film over her vision. The world moved past her and she went unnoticed. She made herself unnoticeable.

For dinner, Dad made Freya's favourite Filipino breakfast, longsilog. She loved the crimson-coloured sausage, the garlic-fried rice, the fried egg—the longanisa, sinangag, and itlog that, together, gave the dish its name. Dad's fried rice was always perfect. He even chopped up the charred tomatoes and put them in a small dish of vinegar, just the way Freya liked.

As they ate, they laughed about the animals at the petting zoo, the way a goat almost ate Mom's sleeve. Afterwards, Dad shut himself into his office. Freya went back to her book, and Mom joined her on the couch, disrupting the blanket nest, but Freya didn't mind.

"Did you have a good birthday?" Mom asked.

She nodded.

"And you're sure you don't mind spending it just with me and Daddy? If you want, we can have a small party with your friends this weekend."

"No, it's okay. I like this better. I like it when it's quiet." Freya paused. The thing lying in wait way back in her mind couldn't be patient any longer. "Mom? Was something wrong with that girl? The girl with the chicks?"

Mom sighed, her breath tickling the ends of Freya's hair against her face. "Nothing's wrong with that girl, Pumpkin. She's just different. Her daddy is going to look after her and she'll be okay."

She squeezed Freya in a tight hug, too tight. Her book slid to the floor, its pages fanning against the carpet.

"I have an idea," Mom said. "Let's go drag Dad out of his office right now. Just this once. He shouldn't be writing on Freya Day!"

They burst into the office and began pulling Dad's arms, his legs. Spinning his chair. Freya's world swung as Dad hoisted her up over his head and she screamed with laughter. Then the betrayal, on her own birthday, of her parents rolling her up in the couch blankets like a burrito.

When the laughter died down she stayed in her burrito, contained and comfortable. They sat on the couch, and Dad rescued her book from the floor, smoothing out the dog ears. He started to read aloud from where Freya had left off. She tried to pay attention, but there was the usual problem with his reading voice—it was, as always, for adults, for the television, for the people who bought tickets to quietly sit in theatres and listen to him talk about concepts and theories and things that were real but not true.

Freya had a thought and she wriggled her arms free so she could say it. "What happens to the bird, Daddy, in your new book?"

Dad lowered the book and slid his thumb out from its pages. He looked over Freya's head at Mom.

"It doesn't hit its head on the skylight. It opens a window and flies away."

Freya closed her eyes. She remembered the real bird, driven mad by the unreachable sky, and decided to believe in the open window instead.

It had been a mistake to tell Mary about the deep-fry party—whatever it was. When I'd shared the link from a meetup site with her as a joke, I should've known that she'd take it in her teeth and run with it—she was always encouraging me to be more social, after all. "Don't get cynical," she'd said to me. "What could go wrong?"

I remembered her words as my route took me along the river, on the very road connecting my place in Markland to her house in the nearby town of Solingate. Markland was a small city, just perfect for me. There was enough here to keep me interested, but not so much that I felt overwhelmed. I was glad it wasn't more developed—it's closer to Guelph than Toronto, where the tendrils of expansion crept outwards—but I knew my town wouldn't be a well-kept secret for much longer.

When I got to the party and dragged my feet up the porch steps, I still found myself wishing I hadn't decided to check the meetup site on a whim for the first time in three months. The last event I'd attended was an awkward book club, which only served to reinforce that I was terrible at socializing with strangers. A resolution I'd apparently forgotten. I could be at home right now, comfortable, safe.

I sighed. Maybe Mary was right. Was I too cynical? I'd always considered myself pragmatic instead. Cynicism was something I tried desperately to avoid. But next to my cousin, we were all cynical.

With a start, I realized that I'd been standing on the dim porch for about five years, clutching a container of broccoli and staring into space. I knocked and a nearby curtain was flung open. A man peered suspiciously at me through the window, so I raised my container in offering until understanding crossed his face, and he indicated that the door was unlocked.

I entered and shook his hand, confidently introducing myself the way Mary would do.

"Welcome," he said. "I guess. Our host went to pick up a friend in Toronto and she just left me in charge of her home. She doesn't even know me."

His earlier expression now made sense.

"I'm going out for a cigarette or three," he continued. "Watch the door?" And in an instant, he whirled outside, shutting the door firmly behind him.

I blinked at the space where he used to be. A voice inside said, *Get out.* But then I pictured the face Mary would make if I reported that I only got as far as the front door. I took a long breath in and stepped forward.

A handful of people threw a glance at me from the living room, then turned back to each other, uninterested in the new gazelle at the watering hole. *Introduce yourself, goddammit*, my inner voice said, and it sounded annoyingly like Mary. So I steeled myself to jump into their conversation and walked over.

"Did I tell you," one of the women was saying, "I saw some veker getting yelled at on the bus over here?"

The words traced a cold finger down my spine. I stopped at the margin of the group, holding my breath.

Another person leaned in, his eyes flaring. "What was he doing?"

"Talking to the woman next to him. I think the veker asked her if her cancer treatments were working. And she started yelling at him not to talk to her, she didn't know who he was. But he kept saying he sensed her cancer or something. Then she started panicking and the veker got thrown off the bus."

"Good. I hope he got his face kicked in too."

I did an awkward about-face into the kitchen. It was bright and cheery compared to the living room, from which I could still hear their disgust. I hadn't realized my heart was pounding. I needed to do something banal and distracting—something like taking the photo of the deep fryer that Mary wanted me to take as proof I actually left my house.

A man and a woman stood next to the stupid machine, which was on the counter working away on rice balls. I extracted my phone from my pocket and surreptitiously aimed it. And of course, because the evening was cursed, the camera made the loudest sound in the world.

The pair who ostensibly belonged to the rice balls turned to look at me, and out of instinct I straightened my spine slightly.

"Sorry," I said, "I was taking a picture of the deep fryer for my cousin. She wants to get one like it."

They nodded, satisfied. The man noticed the box for the deep fryer sitting on top of the fridge and moved past me to retrieve it, leaving a clean, scrubbed scent of soap in his wake. He held the box in his hands and smiled at me politely. I had to crane my neck up slightly to look at him. His eyes were glacier blue, with a deeper blue around the edges, and his hair was dark, short, brushed smoothly back from his forehead.

"You could take a picture of this too," he offered. "It has the model number."

As I took the box from his hands, the corner of his mouth tugged into a broader grin. I cleared my throat and looked down when his fingers lightly but unmistakably brushed across mine. I returned his smile.

"Wow," his friend suddenly said. "That girl looks exactly like you!"

I blinked at her, then followed her pointed finger to the box I was holding. In my distraction, I hadn't noticed what was on the other side.

Of course.

It was my own face, ten years younger but certainly mine. I let a long and hopefully quiet breath out my nose. Should I feign ignorance? Or should I explain? There was nothing shameful in the truth, but the thought of claiming it openly felt brambly. So I denied it with a laugh, one I hoped would without offending highlight the absurdity of thinking that I was some random model on a deep-fryer box. Then I quickly excused myself to find the washroom.

What was I doing? Who did I think I was? I wasn't my cousin, with her easy confidence and certainty she dragged up from some indefinable, unfindable reserve within her. I knew she meant well.

I splashed water on my face and watched the drops slide down my nose and cheeks.

Two strikes already and I'd only been there ten minutes. I hastily wiped my face dry and left the washroom, blinders on for the front door.

The man from the kitchen, with that smile of his, stepped in front of me.

"I didn't catch your name," he said.

"Freya," I answered without thinking. I could see the door, tantalizingly close over his shoulder. I could hear the voices of the people in the living room, the ones who were talking about vekers. No, they weren't talking about that anymore. Were they getting closer? Their voices seemed louder.

"...but everyone calls me Ian."

I focused, realized I had been staring at him without listening.

"I don't know why," he continued. "A joke that turned into reality." He looked at me for a moment, his eyes widened slightly in expectation. Or recognition.

My own smile switched on automatically. It did the trick. He returned it.

"Ian," the woman from the kitchen called. "These rice balls are turning out so well!"

He turned his head to his friend. I couldn't see his eyes but I sensed the *not-now* expression he was making at her. When he brought his attention back to me, his look was warm.

It could be easy. I could cross over to the other side of this thing. I could deflect. I could pepper him with questions about himself, react so appropriately that he would forget to ask about me. I could take the grain of myself and fold it into a different truth. I could choose what threads of my life to share with this stranger.

One of the men from the living room accidentally jostled Ian as he moved past him toward the kitchen. He apologized, clapped Ian on the shoulder. Then he looked at me, for the briefest instant, before moving on.

Too close. In that instant, I came back to myself.

"One minute," I said to Ian. "I think I left my car unlocked."

It was the flimsiest excuse, and I caught his confused expression as I turned from him and slipped out the door.

The night was warm and smelled like rain. I walked on autopilot down the porch steps and back to my car. It looked inviting under the golden glow of the streetlight, and I was relieved to get in. I started the engine and opened the window just as the first drops of rain fell, sharp on my face. I looked up through the windshield. The clouds were dark across the sky, at once foreboding and compelling.

As I drove, I tried to think only of the rain, the hypnotizing swish and squeak of the wiper blades. But my relief soon turned staticky, became regret. Had I been too hasty? The image of Ian's face—his kind eyes, his disappointment at my leaving—made me want to pull over and kick myself.

Only after I entered my neighbourhood did my thoughts turn to my comfortable couch, my records, my books, my space. I relaxed into the images. I had client emails to respond to, readings to do. I had the stupid picture of the stupid deep fryer to show Mary. Most importantly, I had proof for her that I could go out into the world—and that my misgivings about it had been right.

Dad was setting up his weird sheet thing where Freya's reading chair used to be. So weird to see the space white, empty. It was already a small basement, and her reading space had shrunk even more. No more curling up with her blankets and her books and letting her parents' footfalls overhead become mysterious aliens, robbers, monsters. Nothing to hang her secret world on.

Freya sighed. Even though she was seven, she craved a tantrum.

Mom squeezed her shoulder.

"I know, Pumpkin. But Dad needs more room to take his pictures. Maybe you two could take some together. He's got all those different backdrops in cool colours."

Dad straightened, grimacing, and rubbed his back. "Want to come help me calibrate things, Freya?"

She didn't know what *calibrate* meant, but based on what came next she guessed it meant making funny faces while standing on that sheet of white paper that was a wall and a floor at the same time.

Dad circled her, clicking his camera, adjusting things, getting close, moving far away. She decided to move too, tried to be too fast for him. She was proud of this, tried to dart away from the shutter more and more, quicker and quicker. She was a mystical forest creature from a story, weaving in and out of the trees.

Then Mom clapped her hands: she had an idea. Together, Freya's parents brought over some books, a blanket, and a cushion. Despite his concern for the paper backdrop, Dad also helped Mom carry over the reading chair. And as he arranged the blankets and cushion around Freya, he said, "This is the first piece of furniture Mom and I bought when we moved in together." He said this whenever he saw the chair. Freya acted surprised.

Freya sat with a book, and the chair's worn blue fabric was smooth against her cheek like old cotton. But the words she read were meaningless, her awareness constantly plucked by Dad: "Tilt your head, move your arm, hold the book like this."

Soon Mom joined in, gathering Freya on her lap like a kindergartener. "I remember nursing you in this chair," she said, pressing a kiss long on her forehead. The sound of the shutter. Mom stroked Freya's hair back from her face as they pretended to read, and Freya almost forgot they were being arranged, observed. Or maybe she didn't care.

Then came the day the photos were ready.

As Freya hoped, most of the funny face pictures were a blur. But something about the pictures of her and Mom made a ping inside her.

"I don't like them," Freya said quietly.

Instead of cooing over the photos, Mom agreed, just as quietly. "We seem a little posed," she said.

Dad scoffed. "That's because you were!"

Mom laughed, but Freya caught her eye and knew that Mom understood. It was their moment, their expressions, caught in a thing Dad was going to present to a stranger. Suddenly, she wanted the pictures private, didn't want anyone to look through that window into their world.

Dad, observing them, spoke. "Well, we don't have to sell those ones if you don't want to. But they're nice quality, aren't they? We can keep them for ourselves. Look at how sweet you both are."

"Freya, could Dad try to sell your funny face pictures? Only if you're sure."

Freya hesitated. Those were only meant to make Dad laugh.

"Who would buy them?" she asked.

Dad shrugged. "Schools and libraries. Places for kids."

"Pick your favourite," Mom said.

Freya liked the idea of making other kids laugh too. Her finger landed on her funniest face, the one where she'd pretended to be a monkey. But when Dad wasn't looking, she slid her real favourite photo out of the pile.

In it she was a blur, head tilted back, teeth bared, like an attacking animal. Freya was drawn to its wildness, wanted it only for herself.

Back in my building's ancient elevator, I sagged with relief against the wall and listened to the soothing clanks and grinds carrying me up to where I belonged.

At least I'd tried, right?

My cellphone rang as I was struggling with my door's sticky lock. I answered it without needing to check who it was.

Mary sounded disappointed when I told her I'd left early. Then something in her voice switched. "Wait, did you go at all?"

I snorted and texted her the picture of the deep fryer. Then I sat back in my armchair.

"Okay, fine. Did you talk to anyone?"

I groaned inwardly, remembering Ian's disappointed face. "Yes. The arm in the grey T-shirt in the background of that photo. Well, the whole guy, not just the arm." I attempted levity. "What are you up to?"

"Hang on," she interrupted. Why did I think she would let me change the subject? "Did something happen with this guy that made you leave early?"

"No, he was fine." *He was great.*

I squeezed my eyes shut for a moment. I could pretend I'd felt ill. Or tell her that the party was all a cover for a sex cult and I just barely made it out unrecruited. But my cousin deserved the truth.

I cleared my throat and told her about the close calls. Of course the veker conversation was the one she focused on the most.

"Holy shit. Those absolute dicks. Who talks like that about people?"

"Yeah. Just my luck." I'd meant it to sound chummy but it came out bitter.

"Oh, Frey, I'm sorry. It's good that you went and I'm proud of you for making an effort. And I don't mean that as condescending as it sounds. I'm just sorry the very first people you encountered were bigoted jerks."

I had intended to act a little more *ha—in your face* about the way the party had turned out, but hearing the sadness in Mary's voice took the wind out of my sails. "Don't worry about it, it's not your fault. People like that are everywhere. Anyway, maybe I'm too old for deep-fry parties with strangers. They're not for rusty old shut-ins like me."

She snorted. "I'm sorry, are we in the thirteen-hundreds? Twenty-eight is old, good smells ward off the plague, we're all wearing arsenic in our makeup?"

I laughed. As usual, my cousin pulled me out of self-pity with her charming snarkiness. "That last one is Victorian, actually."

"Enough out of you, grandma. Look, it's still early. If you're not going to totter off to bed with a hot water bottle, I can come over. Elliot doesn't have to come if you don't feel up to hearing about the dog's latest vet bill."

"I don't want to make you drive all the way over here this late on a work night. Actually, I should see if there's another Oneira shift available."

"Text me if Tarot Tooth Picker is online and I'll log in just to roast her. Promise me you'll take it easy tonight, okay? I'll see you at lunch tomorrow?"

I shook my head as we said our goodnights. Even though Mary was two years younger than me, she always seemed like the older one. Her long-term boyfriend, steady job, and elderly dog only reinforced that.

I shut my eyes for a moment and relished the silence around me. It was nice to be home, even nicer to talk to my cousin, and I felt the knot of the party loosen.

The second and third close calls hadn't been that bad, really. I pictured Ian's face once more and decided to focus on our initial meeting, that glimmer of hope that I could hold his interest.

I could have very easily held the wrong person's interest at that party.

I got to my feet before that thought could take hold and messaged Carol to see if it was okay for me to work. I answered a couple of emails from private clients I'd done readings for earlier in the week, letting myself relax into the work, the ease I felt with these people and their lives and the problems I could help with. The simplicity of drawing a card and following where it led. The way my dreams sometimes showed me how to help them. A few of my clients had been with me for five years, the entire time I'd been giving readings. That had to mean I was doing some good, right?

Ding.

Sure, come online whenever you like! ☮ ~ Carol

I quickly went through my pre-work rituals, focusing on my couch and coffee table area to make doubly sure nothing embarrassing was on display. Satisfied, I set an alarm for two hours' time and took my place at my desk. Oddly, I felt the same vibration I'd felt during my last shift, the tingle of excitement or anticipation. Maybe it was a sign to stop drinking coffee so late in the day.

Public chat moved swiftly and I soon relaxed, looking forward to an easy shift.

seahorse24: i hate that i can't find the job i want. ive done so many interviews

seahorse24: can i have a card pls? will i get the job i interviewed for yesterday?

Russiandoll: What is everyone doing tonight?

gwynethh: Russiandoll Nothing much, just bored!

lovelybird88: I'm avoiding work lol

lovelybird88: Taurus do u do runes?

> **TaurusTarot [Moderator]:** @seahorse24 I can't do specific readings in public chat but I can pull a general card for you.

> **TaurusTarot [Moderator]:** no @lovelybird88, sorry

seahorse24: yes pls

I shuffled my deck, angling it to the camera. I pulled a card at random. Eight of Swords. I tried not to frown. Ace of Pentacles, with its clear message of financial success, would have been better. Eight of Swords was about feeling trapped or restricted. However, there was another aspect to this card that might work. I held the card up to my camera.

> **TaurusTarot [Moderator]:** @seahorse24, Eight of Swords is telling me you may be held back by negative self-talk or overthinking. Job-hunting is stressful and I know it can feel hopeless. Maybe there's another area you could explore, or a person you could turn to for help who you haven't considered.

seahorse24: ok ill try that, thank you!

I tried to keep my expression neutral as I watched the chat scroll by. My interpretation sounded great in my head, but my words on screen looked trite, maybe dismissive. I knew what it was like to not have a secure job—it wasn't like my own gig was the most stable situation in the world. I remembered that floaty, unmoored feeling from before I started tarot reading. *Just think positive* messages would have pissed me off. But seahorse24 was still logged in so maybe they weren't too annoyed.

I tried to hope for the best, that I'd maybe get in a private reading or two. People paid by the minute for those, and though I never wasted their time just to get more money, the money was kind of the point.

Then a message popped up in chat, one that made me worry for a moment that I'd actually spoken my thoughts aloud.

JIsARaven: Hi @TaurusTarot, can we go private?

A name I didn't recognize. I scrolled up quickly through the chat history to see if this person had been talking to others, had said anything to give me some preparation, but nothing. Requesting a blind reading like this, without talking to me or anyone first, was unusual, but JIsARaven's money was still worth the same as anyone else's.

TaurusTarot [Moderator]: @JIsARaven sure thing!

I heard the welcome doorbell-style notification of a private chat starting and I adjusted my posture slightly. I felt that strange little flicker in my stomach again and tried to push it aside.

JIsARaven's window opened beneath mine in the split-screen of the private chat room. Brief graininess as a webcam came to life on the other end. I could make out his features only vaguely. Skin slightly darker than my own, short black hair neatly trimmed. His camera was at a high angle. In the background was a framed photograph of a field of winter trees, and on a low bookshelf, three burning candles.

Candles, seriously? This isn't The Craft. But I put on a smile and said, "Hi there. Can you hear and see me okay?"

"Yes, hello." The voice was clearer than the image, which was lucky. It was hard to do a good reading when I couldn't hear them.

"I see you have more than enough credits in your account for a private reading, so we can start if you're ready. What can I help with today?"

He was silent a moment, staring right into his webcam, and I felt a bubble of suspicion in my stomach. Too many men thought of Oneira as a hippie version of a sex chat room. I was about to insist that he say something when he did on his own.

"Before we start, do you mind if I ask you about your readings?"

I began to relax. His voice was hesitant but kind. He didn't seem like he was going to demand anything salacious.

"Sure. Well, the basics are that I've been reading tarot for about five years. I've always been intuitive, and the cards help me tune into people's vibes, so to speak, and give them advice."

"What's it like, when you tune into the vibes?" He lifted a mug from off-camera and drank from it. Like we were friends having a cozy chat over tea.

What was it like, indeed.

I told JIsARaven the same thing I told everyone else. "It's very calm and peaceful. I make myself open to a person's energy and interpret the cards I draw for them. It's very much a two-way street. The better connection I have with a person, the better the cards can help."

He was silent again, looking down into his mug.

"Does that help you understand?" I asked. He was paying for this reading, but I still found it annoying when people pulled me into a private chat without any idea of what they wanted to ask. I tried a different strategy. "It helps if you have a specific question for me, but I can do a more general reading too."

"So does anything trigger it?" he asked, ignoring what I'd just said. "I'm just so curious. What is it? Is it the cards? Is it something about the person you're talking to? How long have you been able to do it?"

"Able to do what?" I whispered.

And then black spots washed over my vision. My own heartbeat in my ears.

I tried to click the End Call button. It moved and changed colour. Again and again. I chased it with my cursor, bemused.

I laughed. How long had Oneira's site been so funny?

I heard JIsARaven's voice faintly. "What's happening now?"

I wasn't supposed to answer his questions. Never answer questions. That's how they get in. You have to hide in plain sight.

But his voice was so familiar and soothing.

He leaned in close, staring.

A loud, repetitive sound. The most irritating sound I'd ever heard. Where was it coming from?

I looked over my shoulder and could barely make out a blue jay on the balcony railing, outlined by faint streetlight. Its call sounded exactly like an alarm. Was that what a blue jay sounded like?

How fascinating to have one so close. I should record it.

I saw that my phone was already in my hand, and in its dark screen, through the fog of my vision, was my own reflection.

I dropped my phone to the floor.

The smell of coffee curled over Freya from inside the house. The only sounds were the clinking of cups and spoons, the call of a crow or a raven far away.

"Do you know what your name means?" Dad asked.

Freya did, of course, but this was one of the stories she really liked. She folded her legs underneath her on the wooden bench and leaned against Dad's arm to get closer to his words.

"In Norse mythology, Freya is a Vanir, one of the two races of gods, the other being the Aesir. She rules Fólkvangr, where half of those who die in battle go in afterlife. Freya gets to choose first, then the rest go to Valhalla. She has a magic cloak made of falcon feathers, a chariot pulled by two cats, and a big battle pig. After the war between the Aesir and the Vanir, she introduced the concept of seiðr to the Aesir."

"*Say*-der," Mom cut in. "Stress the first syllable."

Freya cracked one eye open, then the other, as the sun passed behind a cloud.

Mom slid Dad's coffee across the pebbled glass of the patio table, nestled in her chair with her mug, and picked up where Dad left off. This was the part she always told. "In ancient Norse society, people believed that there was a type of magic called seiðr. They said it could weave new strands of fate."

Freya yawned. "Tell me about the war again."

"Who, me?"

"No! Dad."

Mom laughed and nodded at Dad.

His voice was eager. "A very long time ago, there was a great war between the Vanir and the Aesir. The Vanir were older, more concerned with fertility and life. The Aesir were younger and more interested in power and fighting. One day, a woman approached the Aesir in Asgard. She was travelling from town to town, casting spells in exchange for shelter and protection. She brought to the Aesir the chance to alter their fates. The Aesir were excited about this. They had powerful magic themselves, but they couldn't reweave fate.

"So they let the woman join them. However, their greed for her fate-magic overwhelmed them, and the Aesir started to fight amongst themselves. They decided the only thing to do was burn her. They burned her three times. And three times she was born again. They called her Gullveig, but some believe she was the goddess Freya."

"Brian, you always sound too excited at that part," Mom said.

Freya wrinkled her nose in mock distaste, but really she felt something thrumming up inside her, some mix of excitement and danger. She felt the same way when Dad told his Filipino folk tales: the sun and the moon as living things with living bodies, gods who came to feast and hunt with people. How thrilling it must have been to be the first Freya, with a cloak of falcon feathers, real magic.

As if by its own kind of magic, the sky grew dark all at once. A cloak drawn across the sun. Coffee sloshed as they raced inside before the storm hit.

"Gold used to be called 'rain from Freya's eyes,'" Mom said in a quiet voice as she looked back outside. She poured herself more coffee, sliding into her spot at the kitchen table, crossword already there to receive her.

In the living room, Dad switched on the TV. "I want to see what the winning lottery numbers are."

Freya ran in to join him. "If we win the lottery you said you'd buy me a horse, don't forget!"

Dad's eyes were distant and he waved a hand at her. She froze and followed his attention to the TV.

"New information has come to light today regarding Gary Quick, the individual formerly known as Alan Y. In 1972, six-year-old Quick manifested an unusual mental ability that inadvertently caused a doctor's waiting room full of patients to become catatonic. This resulted in worldwide panic as a growing number of people with similar abilities emerged. Today, the British advocacy group Solidarity for Humanity League claims they have uncovered evidence proving the Pancek Institute used Quick for unsanctioned medical research. Though the Institute maintains they were merely teaching Quick to manage his condition, the advocacy group is urging local government agencies to investigate."

Freya didn't know what *catatonic* meant, but she knew what *panic* meant. She wanted to ask but Dad's face looked stern, the way it had that time she dropped pizza facedown on the carpet.

Freya turned away to join Mom in the kitchen. She tried to sneak a sip of milky coffee from Mom's mug but Mom pulled it away, her eyes still on her crossword.

"What happened after they burned Freya three times?" Freya asked.

Mom gathered the mug close to her with both hands, as if she could draw its warmth into her. "I don't like hearing you use your name that way," she murmured before telling the story anyway. "The Vanir and Aesir both resented each other for what happened with Freya. Their feelings got so bad that they went to war. The Vanir used magic and the Aesir used weapons. It was a long war, so long that they got tired of fighting, and they agreed to stop. Both sides sent a few of their own people to live forever on the other side to prove that they wanted peace. Freya went to live with the Aesir, along with her twin brother Freyr and their father Njörd, the sea god."

Rain drummed the windows, the roof. Freya sat with the story for a while, turning it over quietly in her mind.

"That's sad," she said finally. "They blamed her for what they did and then it started a war. And then she had to go and live on the other side. It's good that her brother and dad were there, but weren't they scared to be with their enemies?"

Mom lowered her mug quickly to the table and gathered up Freya's hands in her own, warmed from the coffee. "I used to think it was a sad story too when I was your age. But your great-grandmother helped me see it another way. After the war was over, Odin made Freya a very important priestess. Half of the people who die in battle spend eternity with her. She's wise and brave. Some people consider her a war goddess, the leader of the Valkyries. And even if it's true that she started a war, think about how she helped to end it. She brings Vanir wisdom and seiðr magic to the Aesir. She unites them. She changes their fates forever."

Freya frowned as Mom drained her cup and brought it to the sink. She thought of the Vanir Freya, sent away from her home. It made the image of the goddess's falcon-feather cloak and seiðr magic, all that power, seem wasted.

What time was it? I reached for my phone on the nightstand, but the nightstand didn't feel right. I squinted my eyes open. My hand was on my coffee table. The laptop on my desk was open, the screen black. Bewildered, I looked down. I was wearing last night's jeans. My phone was on the floor, halfway under the couch.

I slowly rolled up to a sitting position and pressed the soles of my feet firmly to the floor, forcing my focus on the rug, the roughness of its fibres, its comforting solidity.

My movements stirred up a roil of nausea and my brain clanged with dehydration. Those were the usual signs that, at some point the night before, I'd had a vision.

But had I? I tried to weave back through what I remembered of my sleep but my concentration brittled into nothing.

My stomach wavered. I lurched to the kitchen and chugged a glass of water, trying to remember the day before. The deep-fry party—was that really yesterday? Blue eyes, my old modelling photo, an overheard conversation, the rain. I came home and talked to Mary on the phone. I worked a bit. Oneira chat. I did a private reading. Then...

What?

I drank another glass of water, slower this time, and fished a reasonably fresh pita out of the fridge. I tore pieces off and ate, trying to remember more.

Something was different about this experience. I felt wrong, misaligned.

My nausea started to subside and the feeling of brain desiccation eased. But I still felt only halfway aware of myself, like I had one ear underwater.

A few of my cards had fallen to the floor. I picked them up. The Tower, Death, the Devil. Did they mean anything? No. None of them gave me any clue about what had happened last night.

Despite myself, however, I felt a little twinge of significance. If this were a real reading, a spread consisting entirely of cards from the Major Arcana would suggest major events on the horizon. The Tower, lightning striking its walls, flames, people falling from windows. Death, the skeletal reaper. The Devil, yellow eyes staring from the horned goat's black fur. Newcomers to tarot were always scared by these particular cards, an immediate, almost visceral reaction. For a moment, I saw them in the same shocking light.

I grabbed the deck and went to my bedroom. There, I whipped the tidy blankets into disarray, nestled into bed. I took a few grounding breaths, then closed my eyes. I concentrated down through my fingers as I shuffled the cards, trying to sense out one that would give me an answer.

There.

I flicked it onto the bed and opened my eyes.

The Lovers.

I almost laughed. Everyone loves the Lovers. People always assumed its literal interpretation: success in romantic relationships. Ironic, considering I'd just run like a spooked deer from someone who'd shown interest in me. But no, this couldn't be about that. It didn't feel right.

I traced my thumb along the card's smooth face. This particular deck's lovers had a full-bodied 1970s earthiness. The man's hair was long, his beard substantial. The woman he held in his arms was pale, with long red hair. Lilies surrounded them. It could have been a folk band's album cover—with more nudity. I had to admit it was a sexy card. But more than that, it was about connection, deep relationships of all kinds. Being naked to someone, vulnerable, yet accepted. Searching, finding, being found. Clarifying your values. What you want and what you need. What you stand for.

Searching, finding. Being found.

I turned the card facedown on the blanket. Did I want to be found? Or was I doing the finding? The lack of clarity was unsettling, but there was something glimmering at the edges of my thoughts, something I was missing.

My alarm blared from the living room. *Shit, already noon.* I'd slept later than I'd thought, and now I'd be late getting to Mary's place for lunch if I didn't hurry.

I whirled into fresh clothes, shoved my unruly hair back in a bun, and ran to my car through fallen leaves still damp with last night's rain. It was early October and an invigorating wind was chasing away the southern Ontario humidity.

I felt restored by the time I was on the road to Solingate. It was a short and uneventful drive along the Kirkby River. Actually, it was boring. But a relaxing boredom.

I pulled into Mary's driveway only fifteen minutes late and jogged up the stairs to the porch. Peeking in through the kitchen window, I saw her boyfriend Elliot pulling something out of the oven and my cousin leaning into the open fridge. My stomach growled. Mary claimed to have zero kitchen skills, but she somehow always created meals that were deeply satisfying.

Zeus, their ancient yellow Lab, barked once at my knock, but strolled back to his bed in the kitchen once Elliot opened the door.

I watched the dog's slow retreat. "Mary told me he'd been to the vet recently," I said.

Elliot sighed and ruffled a hand through his short blond hair. "Yeah, he's been having a little trouble with stairs lately. Arthritis, most likely. He's definitely not a puppy anymore."

I sat down at the table next to Zeus's bed and gave him a scratch behind the ears. I hadn't visited in a couple of weeks, and I felt myself settle into the familiar comfort of the home. It was safe here.

Mary and Elliot's house was a small split-level built in the seventies, with the kitchen and dining room on the entry level, and short staircases leading up to the bedrooms, and down to a sitting room and what they called the TV room. Maybe not ideal for an old, arthritic dog like Zeus, but I always enjoyed the cozy, den-like feeling. I wondered if there was some familial zone of protection that extended from my place to my cousin's.

Mary put down plates of food. "Here, let's eat."

Pickles, green grapes, cold prosciutto, chicken soup, some reheated slices of leftover mushroom quiche. I fell upon the food almost before the other two had their cutlery properly in hand.

Mary looked at me appraisingly. "So. Got here late, appetite of a starving pack animal. Rough day?"

I chewed slower, considering how much to tell them. I caught myself arranging my knife and fork carefully next to my plate, lining them up so they were perfectly parallel, and nudged them back out of alignment. Mary would notice my fidgeting.

Might as well tell them the truth. Mary would understand, and Elliot would just have to deal with it.

I told them what I remembered: the emails to clients, going online at Oneira, chatting and doing a single-card pull for someone in the chat. Starting a private reading. Then the question mark.

I cleared my throat, poked at a grape to send it spinning. "I don't actually remember what happened after that. And I don't remember falling asleep. The next thing I knew, I was waking up on the couch this morning."

There was silence, chewing, the politely quiet settling of cutlery.

Elliot asked, "Did you have one of your weird—uh, your dreams?"

I shifted in my seat. Tried to not frown at the word *weird*.

"I think I did. But this time I was awake when it happened."

"That's never happened before," Mary said. "You only see things in your sleep, right? They don't make you black out when you're awake."

I nodded. Someone else might've found it amusing for my cousin to tell me how my own ability worked. But I knew she was just saying things out loud to make certainties of them, to file them in her mind for later. In the large section in her brain marked *Freya*.

Elliot just stared at us, his expression unreadable. I shovelled a large bite of quiche into my mouth and tried to will a different line of conversation into existence.

Elliot must have sensed my cosmic ping to the universe because he changed the subject. "You should tell Freya about your mom's phone call," he murmured to Mary.

"Phone call?" I asked. I couldn't remember the last time Mary had mentioned her mom.

Mary put her fork down, sighing. "She joked about coming here for Thanksgiving next week."

"Did she? But she's never been here before."

"She has, once, briefly. Just after we moved in. I think she was a bit put off by how much house we have. She hasn't internalized the fact that this house is cheaper than a condo in North York. She's been living in Toronto too long."

"She thinks we're millionaires," Elliot said. "On my junior software engineer salary and the big bucks Mary makes."

"Because dance company marketing departments are notoriously filthy rich," Mary said, shaking her head.

"Is she doing okay?" I asked.

"She is. She's got the same job she had the last time I talked to her. And she told me that she hasn't had a drink for over a year. But it's like she calls me just to have someone to rant about her job. I have to be in the right mood for it."

"Not that you would know what else to talk about anyway," I said with the certainty of history. Mary's relationship with her mother was only fractionally better than mine was with my father, thanks to my aunt's shaky relationship with alcohol in Mary's childhood.

As if reading my mind, Mary asked, "Have you heard from your dad lately?"

I huffed out a laugh, shook my head. He'd texted me last month to remind me to get my car serviced. Did that count as hearing from him?

Elliot chimed in. "When was the last time you actually talked? For longer than twenty minutes."

I bristled at his overly familiar assumption and took a deep breath. Elliot and Mary had been together since university and I knew that she told him almost everything. She wouldn't let him get this close if she didn't trust him. So I had to trust him too.

"April, I think. My birthday. He texts me every now and then to say hi. But that's okay. I'm sure he's busy working on a new book."

We finished our meal, and I was so pleased to feel normal again that I could have curled around Zeus in his bed on the floor and gone to sleep.

Elliot scraped his chair back, gathered plates.

"Tea?" he asked.

And in one swooping rush, I remembered.

Tea.

When I'd fritzed into blackness, I was talking to someone holding a mug. Someone who was asking questions about me.

JIsARaven.

Freya stopped in her tracks. There was a faint, thin whine coming from the trees. She followed it, guided through the dark by her ears. There was no moonlight, no streetlights, but a weak brightness seemed to hover above her as she picked her way through the forest. She didn't once consider the fact that she should be afraid or wonder where Mom and Dad were. There was only the sound.

It grew louder, and then she knew what it was before she could see it. A puppy, whining at the base of a tree. It sat there patiently, waiting for her. As soon as Freya approached, it turned and ran, looking back, its tongue lolling. She followed, speeding silently through the forest, darting through the dense trees in pursuit of the puppy. Never in her young life had she felt so fast and buoyant.

Then, suddenly, there was no dog. Freya realized she was the one being pursued. But she was unafraid. She could have run forever, just for the feeling of it.

She was out of the forest and back in her neighbourhood. But wait—no. It was her neighbourhood but different. Rearranged. Instead of the street, the sidewalk, the front yards, the houses, there was a line of low backyard fences as far as she could see.

A light flared in her heart and she started running again. Though she knew her pursuer wasn't far behind her, she had yet to feel fear or panic.

She had all the time in the world.

She ran to the first fence and placed one hand on top, vaulting over it easily. She kept running. The next fence was slightly higher but not at all harder to clear. As she continued, the fences got slightly higher and her leaps got higher too. She felt like she was floating, like each rise upwards might be her last. She might never touch the ground again.

A voice came to her, from far away in the forest: "Freya. Pumpkin. Get up, sleepyhead."

The mist of the forest cleared and the racing of her heart slowed. Freya blinked her eyes open.

Mom was in her room, waking her up earlier than usual. It was the last day of Grade Four, and Mom wanted extra time to try and tame Freya's hair into the elaborate double-braided creation she'd been planning for the big day. Suddenly, Freya was wide awake and nothing else mattered but the last day of school.

Mom was excited too. She tried to be gentle but the brushing, the twisting, the bobby pins made Freya's eyes water. It was worth it, though, to see the look of pride on Mom's face as she examined her finished work.

"Are you sure we can't walk with you?" Dad asked after making the proper oohs and aahs over her hair.

"Dad, no!" She had a vision of them guiding her down the street, hugging her goodbye. She shook her head.

"Well, then at least let me make you a lucky breakfast. Sit there. I'll surprise you."

She couldn't resist a snarky comment. "Dad, you can't surprise me. I can see the stove from where I'm sitting."

Mom chuckled, causing her coffee to miss her cup entirely and splash from the coffee pot onto the counter. "Watch out, Brian," she said, "our girl's finishing Grade Four today. She won't be fooled by anything anymore."

Dad laughed, and Freya did too, but she also felt bad for him. She saw how his shoulders had drooped so slightly. Freya felt like she'd taken away something he was genuinely excited about. So she made a point of sitting still as a statue, covering her eyes, and letting Dad surprise her.

Later, when she left the house to start her last Grade Four walk to school, she felt her spine straighten with wisdom and generosity. She'd noticed Dad's hurt feelings about breakfast because she paid attention. She'd been able to see the invisible.

The late afternoon sun had burned away the clouds and the air was heavy with humidity. Freya was flying. Her lungs burned, her legs were needles of pain, but she was an arrow shot from a bow. She was like an international spy outrunning criminals she'd just caught smuggling diamonds. She was like a cat hunting in the jungle.

She heard the pounding of feet behind her. The fence was approaching fast but she knew she wasn't going to stop there. She put her hand on it and a lifetime passed in the instant her leg muscles tensed and then released. She'd never jumped that fence before but she just knew she would make it. She vaulted easily, landing with a roll in the grass on the other side, and turned her head just in time to see her friend Tasha fly over the fence and land with a squeal next to her. They stretched out starfish style, unable to decide if they should catch their breath or give in to a giggling fit.

"I'm dying," Freya said, though every part of her had come alive.

"How the hell did you do that with one hand? I had to use two." Tasha sat up, brushing grass from her sweaty cheek.

Freya didn't know. In that moment, she didn't know whose idea it had been to race to the low fence at the end of the school playground, she didn't know how she'd shot ahead as soon as Steve shouted "GO," and she didn't know what made her decide to clear the fence instead of simply stopping there like they'd agreed on.

The adrenaline was starting to wear off as they made their way back to their friends, and this time Freya definitely had to use two hands to climb over the fence. The small group that had gathered to watch the race started hooting and clapping at their return.

Freya was suddenly bashful, the tips of her ears reddening. She felt a strange guilt at having won the race.

One by one, the group broke off into clusters to walk home. Steve and Tasha's houses were one street over from Freya's, so they always walked home together.

"Grade Five! I can't wait!" Steve was a golden retriever puppy, bouncing all around, simmering in excitement over the last day of school.

"We still have to get through the whole summer, Steve," Freya pointed out.

Steve shrugged. In his mind he was already another year older, powerful.

"Oh shit, I got grass stains on my shorts!" Tasha whined, swiping at the offending smear, pulling the leg up high. "The last day of school and I mess up my uniform."

Steve pointed and laughed, mocking.

Tasha smacked him on the arm. "You jerk!"

And then Steve and Tasha were off, yelping, all arms and legs in their shifting dance of pursuit and retreat. They called goodbye to Freya as they ran away down the street.

Freya continued on home, reliving the light, buoyant feeling of the race. Was it possible that the best part of her whole year had just happened, right at the end? Maybe it meant that in Grade Five she was going to surprise them all. Freya was always the bookworm, the quiet one with perpetually tangled hair. But look! Freya in her magic falcon-feather cloak, elegant and terrifying as she cuts through the air! What an amazing girl! We must know everything about her!

A car horn made her jump and drop her backpack. It was Mom, turning the car into the driveway.

Freya shouldered her backpack and hurried over.

Mom got out of the car without cutting the engine and wrapped her in a hug. "Happy last day of school!"

Freya stood taller. Could Mom tell that she was elegant and terrifying now?

When they went inside, there was a note from Dad: *Camilla— Checking out the new photography studio. Be back by five. Will get dinner. Wink wink!*

"He actually wrote *wink wink*," Freya said. "He always gets McDonald's for my last day of school. It isn't a secret."

Mom laughed and shook her head. "So how was your last day?"

Freya, already halfway inside the pantry in search of chips, said, "Not yet! I'll tell you when Dad's here." She could just picture their faces when they heard about the race. The pride. Mom would probably get weepy.

Mom plucked the bag of chips away. "Go up and change. Is that a grass stain on your shirt?"

At five thirty, the screen door slammed, and a "Sorry! Sorry!" floated through the house. Freya flung her book down and flew down
the stairs to the foyer where Dad was a crane, balancing as he slid
off his shoes. She took the McDonald's bags from him, warm and
promisingly grease-stained.

Mom's face appeared from around the living room doorway, eyebrows raised. "What took so long?"

"I went to the one on Springfield instead of the usual one," Dad said,
gathering Mom up in a hug. "I had a bad feeling about the usual one."

"What do you mean, a bad feeling?"

Dad shrugged one shoulder. "I just had a bad feeling. It felt weird
on the way there. So I went to the one on Springfield."

Freya clattered the plates and cutlery as Mom and Dad walked
into the kitchen. No eating last-day-of-school McDonald's out of
the cardboard.

"Did something happen?" Mom asked.

"No, it was just—" Dad wiggled his fingers around in the air, as
if that would explain it, "—weird. But no harm done, right? Look,
a feast."

They sat, and Freya and Mom exchanged a Look. Dad and his
superstitions! Freya wanted to bring up the time he'd made her late
for school because he had a bad feeling about her regular route, but
the smell of the food reached her brain and suddenly her whole life
hinged on chicken nuggets. Dad, as usual, got six sweet-and-sour
sauces for her, so she could be as greedy as she liked, scooping
rather than dipping. She liked to start with the more symmetrical
nuggets, leaving the fat boot-shaped ones for later.

"So now that Dad's home," Mom said, "tell us about your last day."

The story about the race came out in a rush. Freya heard herself
sounding a bit too much like an excited child, but she didn't care.

When she got to the part about the fence, heat rushed to her
face—like a blush, but hotter. Her head felt like it was stuffed with
cotton balls. Her vision wavered at the edges.

In place of her parents' faces, Freya saw herself vaulting over
a fence with one hand. But it wasn't at school. There were dense

trees all around her, stars in the sky. And she was leaping higher and higher each time.

A voice came to her from far away in the forest.

"Pumpkin?" said Mom.

She blinked. She was at the table again, Dad's hand wrapped around her arm. A plastic McDonald's cup of Coke was sweating into her hand. Her parents were looking at her expectantly.

"So who won the race?" Dad asked.

"I did!" Freya cried. "And then I jumped over the fence! With one hand!"

Their expressions were exactly what she'd predicted. Mom's eyes grew watery with pride. Dad seemed impressed and a little surprised.

Freya grinned, satisfied at her parents' reactions. She liked the look of surprise on Dad's face the most. But as she folded fries into her mouth, her mind drifted back to the trees, the stars.

She knew where she'd seen that forest before.

At bedtime, Freya tried to remember everything about the dream from the night before.

It was almost like she'd dreamed about the race with Tasha before it had actually happened. Was that possible? Did she know she'd make the jump because she'd already made it in her dream, over and over?

Why not? She was Freya. It was in her name. Maybe all Freyas could weave fate in their dreams.

A knock at the door. It was Mom, there to say goodnight.

"I think I dreamed about today's race last night," Freya said. "Everything was the same. Except I was in the forest, like the one we went to in West Kelowna, and it was nighttime. But I remember running and jumping over fences with one hand. It was so easy. And then today I actually did it!"

Mom sat on the bed, stroking Freya's hand absentmindedly as she spoke. "That's cool," she said. "Maybe your dream gave you confidence today."

Freya pulled her knees up to her chest. She felt relieved at the response, the way Mom accepted it without blowing it up into something big. It seemed almost boring.

Something else was kicking at her, a thought from earlier that she'd pushed aside. "I think Tasha and Steve like each other. I think Steve is kind of a dork, and I don't want Tasha to have a boyfriend yet. Is that selfish?"

"Of course not, Pumpkin. Ten is a little young for a boyfriend. It's okay to want to be a kid for a little longer."

Mom looked at her then, silently, and Freya wondered what she was seeing.

She got up and left, only to return a moment later with something cradled in her hands. "A kid forgot this at the restaurant today. I thought it might be neat so I brought it home for you."

It was a small box of what looked like playing cards. But no, there were beautiful illustrations on it. Colourful, rich. Swords and golden goblets and women with direct stares and long flowing hair.

"It's a deck of tarot cards. Some people think they can tell the future."

"Can they?" Freya whispered, entranced, feeling them slide smooth through her fingers.

"No. But when I first moved to Canada, my roommate used them almost like a game. She would think of something she was having trouble with and then pull a card. Sometimes the card would give her something she could think about. Want to try?"

Freya remembered church and Religion class at school, and felt a little bite of fear. "Is it like the devil or something?"

Mom said no, but then slid a few cards quickly out of the pile. Freya saw a flash of a black goat among them. "These ones are a little scary," Mom said. "Okay, now think of something you want answered. Maybe something about Tasha."

Freya closed her eyes, pictured Tasha running behind her and flying over the fence after her. She pictured dorky Steve and his jokes. She pictured Grade Five, and John Tanaka and his big smile and the way his hair always flopped over his forehead.

Mom shuffled the cards, arcing and gliding them together in a blur, then spread them out over the blanket. Freya picked one, embarrassed and excited.

It showed a boy and a girl facing each other. The boy was giving the girl a large goblet like the one in church, but this one had a white flower in it. There were five other cups and flowers filling up the card.

"Oh, the Six of Cups!" Mom said. She took the card and looked at it for a moment, chewing her lip in thought. "To me, this is a card about friendship. Friends give each other gifts sometimes, right? See? They're being very kind with each other and definitely not being boyfriend and girlfriend yet if it's too soon."

How had her mom known she'd been thinking about John Tanaka? But instead of guilt, Freya felt as if they were sharing a secret joke. So she laughed, and Mom did too. Then she was squeezed against Mom's chest, blond hair cascading over her eyes. She could have fallen asleep right there.

"So you like the cards?" Mom asked.

Freya's nod was dramatic and enthusiastic. "Can I look at them for a while before I go to sleep?"

"Sure, Pumpkin. But don't stay up too late, okay? You don't want to sleep through the first day of summer. Your dad might have something cool planned."

A kiss to Freya's forehead, and another one. A kiss for Freya the elegant and terrible.

After Mom left, Freya nestled back against her pillows, her book forgotten. She could hear Mom and Dad talking across the hall, Dad telling a long story as they walked to the washroom. She could picture him leaning against the doorframe, making Mom laugh as she brushed her teeth.

Freya began flicking through the cards, shuffling them roughly in the palm of one hand, and thought of the rows of backyard fences, higher and higher.

The card she pulled first made her gasp. Written at the top was *The Moon*. All dark blues and greys, water and fields. Two wolves sitting by a stream, looking up and howling at a perfect yellow moon.

There were no trees and no stars, but it made her think of her dream. It made her feel relaxed and peaceful. She was proud of herself, not just for having the best day of her whole year, but for dreaming about it too. Maybe Freya with the magic falcon-feather cloak, somewhere hidden and far away, was proud of her too.

She replaced the cards in the box, except for the Moon, which she slid under her pillow for good luck. Then closed her eyes and drifted to sleep on the sounds coming through her open window: the distant rushing of cars, a breeze fluttering through leaves.

The Lovers card was still on my mind the next morning, its presence at the edges of my awareness as I ate breakfast. I straightened my back, stretched, felt the satisfying clicks of my vertebrae. The Lovers was just a card. Not a suggestion, not a guide, not a condemnation. Not everything was a sign.

I grabbed my cards from the bedside table and settled in for a morning Oneira shift. My music was on, the sun was shining, and the windows were open. There was a distinctly autumnal sharpness in the air, revitalizing me.

No issues in the public chat and a couple of private readings. In what seemed like no time at all, my ever-punctual stomach began reminding me that I had leftover pizza in the fridge. I zoned out for a second, thinking about what I would do later that day. A movie? Maybe a walk, a nice long one. I could try that kare-kare recipe Mary kept bugging me to try. I'd have to go to the Asian grocery store to get more shrimp paste... I returned my attention to work, to the chat. I pulled a general card for someone who had a question about their relationship with their sister. As I began typing my interpretation, I once again felt a weird tingle in my stomach, a sense of pleasant, anticipatory nervousness spreading warmly through me.

A notification in the chat window caught my eye.

JIsARaven has entered the chat.

My fingers hovered over the keyboard, frozen in a jolt. I stared at the notification. What should I do? What if he wanted a private chat again, to ask me more questions about myself? Worse—what if I had another strange hallucination?

The image of the Lovers flashed through me again. Had the card been a warning after all, about being found out?

Silly. I was in control of this. I'd spent my whole life safeguarding myself. I hadn't been found out yet, and I couldn't see how that was going to change from one chat.

Samantha Garner

Samantha Garner

I took a deep breath, reminded myself that it was my chat room. I could just ban him if things got weird.

I finished typing my message, then sat back and watched the chat scroll by. JIsARaven said nothing. He was just sitting there—maybe waiting, like I was. Watching to see what I would do.

I had to admit that, though I was also ready to nip this in the bud, curiosity—a deep, flashing, monumental curiosity—was pulling at me.

The Lovers could signify discovery.

I sent the DM before I could stop myself. I needed to know.

> **TaurusTarot:** Hi! Nice to see you again. I'm sorry our last private reading ended weirdly; I wasn't feeling very well. I'd be happy to do another one for you free of charge right now.

I drummed my fingers on my desk as I waited for a response. I didn't even know what I would say if he accepted my offer. What would I do if another waking vision came on? Would I even realize it was happening?

Then the doorbell notification sound. And there he was.

His webcam image was clearer than last time, better lit in the middle of the day. I studied his face. Black stubble dotted his jawline. His eyes were dark and looking into the camera calmly, as if he were waiting for me to make the first move. So I did.

"I'm sorry again about the other day. I must have been coming down with something."

"That's okay," he said, and then nothing more. He continued to evaluate me.

I waited for the rush of blood in my ears, the spotty vision, but neither came.

I took a deep breath and offered to start a reading for him.

He shifted in his seat and cleared his throat. A muscle in his jaw tensed momentarily. I suddenly felt a swell of empathy. He was nervous. An almost overwhelming concern for him flared in me, then went away.

"I was worried about you after what happened," he said.

"What did you see?" I blurted out. "What happened?"

"You whispered something. Your eyes went glassy, like you'd fainted or weren't quite awake. Then you laughed in a strange, slow way. Then we were cut off."

So I'd been able to end the session before I passed out. That was something, at least.

"I'm glad you're okay now," he continued. "And I think I know how to help you."

"I'm fine. Really. I think I was just overtired."

He fell silent again, considering me. "How long have you been able to do it?"

The memory rushed back. That was the last thing he'd asked me before my brain broke. I sucked in a breath.

This time, nothing happened. I exhaled.

"Like I said last time," I began, "I started my business about five years ago—"

He shook his head. "No. I mean, how long have you been able to do what you do?"

I made a show of frowning in confusion.

He huffed a breath out through his nose, squeezed his eyes shut for a second. "I'm not being clear. This is hard for me too. I'm not trying to freak you out, but I need to know—" He cut himself off, sat up straighter. "Let's change the subject. My name is Javier. But most people call me Javi."

He pulled a water bottle into view and took a long drink. I watched him gulp the water, still pinned to my seat as if by darts. I didn't give him my name in return, and he didn't seem to care.

"Okay," he started again, "I'm going to tell you something and I want you to know that whatever you say will be completely confidential. I'm not recording anything and I'm not going to try and get you in any sort of trouble. I have a unique skill too."

Some animals retreat into shells when threatened. Some squirt ink or poison at their adversary. I tried a joke.

"You mean like carpentry? Or crossing one eye?"

He laughed. "I mean I can sense when I'm around other people who are skilled. That's how I found you."

"How you found—"

He kept talking. "When I was online on Saturday, I was browsing. I do it sometimes just to see who's out there. Don't you ever wonder?"

"Look, if you're not going to want a reading, I'm going to have to end this here."

"No, wait! Have you ever heard of the group called STEP?"

My mouse pointer hovered over the End Call button. "What?"

His next words came out all in a rush, as if he could sense his time was up. "Support Tools Empowering the Paradextrous. You can find us online. We're buried pretty far in Google, but we have to be. It's dangerous to be really upfront. We're not an institution or anything like that. We're just a group of people with skills who help others like us. We even hang out sometimes. It's nice to be around people who get it, you know? We have weekly meetings in Toronto. Your profile says you're near Toronto. You should come!"

Too close. Too close. Too close.

I clicked End Call. His face, his eyes big, disappeared as the split-screen window closed. I logged off Oneira entirely and shot up out of my chair. My nerves zinged with excitement, with nervousness, with no small amount of fear.

I had been found. By someone like me. By random chance.

Or was it? The Lovers. Could the weird anticipatory tingles I'd been feeling have been him, somehow? Searching for me?

It was dangerous. What if he found out my name? What if he found out where I lived?

But what would it benefit him to come after me? If he really was a veker too he wouldn't do that, would he?

I hadn't told him anything, hadn't said a single thing that could make him think I had a skill, as he'd called it. And I'd ended the call before things went too far. He technically didn't want a reading, after all, and Oneira wasn't for socializing.

But if he was right about what he could do, *attune* to me, then I'd already given myself away without a word.

The trill of my phone made me yelp.

It was Mary. "Hi! I'm on my lunch break. Got a minute?"

I could hear voices passing in the background, cars, a bird somewhere far away. Through her I was shot into the outside world, the real one, where people like me only get by in silence and in secret.

"You there?"

"Sorry. Yeah, I'm here. Listen, can you talk?"

A snort. "No, I called you because I'm super busy, you turd. What's up?"

I tripped into my couch and sat down. My nerves stilled, slightly. I wanted to tell her everything about—what was his name—Javier. But I couldn't just tell her the story directly. I could imagine the decibel level of her voice if I'd told her the truth. So instead, I folded a lie around the kernel of it.

"I was just chatting with a client and he made an offhand mention of a group for vekers. Support Tools Empowering the Paradextrous. Have you ever heard of a group like that?"

"No, never."

"They're a mix between a support and social group, apparently. No idea what *paradextrous* means."

"That sounds great!" Her enthusiasm, while not exactly surprising, seemed a bit too immediate. I could have kicked myself for forgetting the basic truth about my cousin: never tell her about something you don't want her to follow up on.

"You think so?"

"It might be good for you to find people you can relate to."

"I have you. And Elliot. Hell, even Zeus."

Mary didn't fall for it. "I love you, but I can't help you all the time. Especially when it's something completely out of left field, like what happened on Saturday."

My stomach twisted.

"What happened on Saturday was a fluke. I just spaced out for a bit, my alarm went off, I logged off Oneira, and passed out on my couch. That's all. I don't need help."

"Freya, come on. Just look into it."

"I don't need to, seriously. I have enough in my life to keep me from getting bored. My job gives me a good outlet for my ability. I'm not hurting anyone. Why ruin a good thing?"

"Did you ever think that you could be missing out on something better just because you're scared?"

"You know better than anyone that I have a very good reason to be scared!"

She sighed, exasperated, and when she spoke again her voice was tense. "I won't always be around to help you. And sometimes I can't help you. You have to let other people in sooner or later. And if you can't trust people who are in exactly the same position you are, then you might end up lonelier than you can handle."

I stood and paced again, tamping down frustration. Why couldn't she just be cool about this one thing? She didn't understand how it was, how it really was. It was easy for her. She got to live a completely normal life, never once having to think about being discovered, or worry about what her brain was doing, or feel like she was some sort of aberration and always would be.

And the most frustrating thing was that if I had just told her the truth about Javier, about his persistence and odd behaviour, she wouldn't be pushing me. I'd fucked it up.

"Can we just drop it?" I asked, deflating. "Everything is okay, I promise."

After we hung up, I still felt like pacing. I decided that I might as well be outside, since it was a lovely fall afternoon, so I pulled on my shoes and jacket and walked to the coffee shop on the corner of my street.

I'd been going there for years. They recognized me now and made me my usual with-room Americano without my having to ask. It made it difficult when I went in with a craving for tea, but I accepted the usual with the understanding that this was what it meant to be a regular. I was upholding the social contract.

I considered staying to read and relax but my urge to move was still strong. So I took my coffee for a walk.

Had I been too quick to dismiss Mary's enthusiasm? Was I being too stubborn? Why was I turning and running from something the moment it challenged me?

The people at the deep-fry party, sneering about the veker on the bus. How easily that veker could have been me. I'd always considered my ability benign—mostly—but what if the wrong person got spooked by it? What good would it do to attract more of that risk?

It's bad enough worrying about what one person might do with your secret, let alone an entire group.

I stopped. Blinked. Emerged from my fog. I'd walked further than I'd realized, almost to the river. A cool wind picked up and tangled my hair. A crow called somewhere overhead. Or maybe it was a raven. I could never really tell them apart.

I looked up.

Wings. A blackness that obscured the sun.

Heat rose through my body. I could feel my blood rushing fast—too fast. I couldn't breathe. I could barely see through the fringes of black snaking their way down from the sky.

Something inside me snapped its fingers, and I ran.

I could hear my own heart, my too-quick breathing.

The sky exploded in stars, and then all the lights went out.

Mom was singing a lullaby.

Even though Freya was much too old for lullabies, she nestled into the crook of her mother's arm and sighed happily. But as the song continued, Mom's voice changed, barely noticeable. A low rasping sound, getting louder and louder.

The air grew cold.

Freya looked up and saw that Mom's face had become distorted and horrible. Her eyes bulged. Lumpy outlines of bugs crawled under the skin. Her mouth contorted and her song turned into a metallic wail. Worms slithered from her hair, her dress, everywhere. They covered her face. Freya tried to pull away, but she was caught in the bony grip of fleshless hands.

Yelping, she shot straight up and opened her eyes. Freya was alone in bed. Her flailing had nearly sent her lamp crashing to the floor. Her heart was racing faster than it ever had and she was sweating.

The room was quiet, familiar. Everything was as she'd left it when she went to sleep. She could hear Mom and Dad talking downstairs. Everything was fine. Her heartbeat returned to normal as the fragments of reality started to creep back in.

Freya was ten—nightmares were for stupid little kids!

She kicked off her blankets, quickly changed out of her pyjamas, and went down to the kitchen. Dad saw her coming down the hallway and pulled out her favourite mug. He gave her a conspiratorial wink as he sloshed in the tiniest amount of coffee with her milk.

"Hi," she said, sliding into her spot at the table.

Mom peeked out from behind the Sunday paper. Frowned. "Are you okay, Pumpkin?" she asked.

Dad slid the milky coffee toward Freya, squinted at her face. "She looks pale." But he didn't seem too concerned and returned to the stove to get their food.

Mom touched the back of her hand to Freya's forehead. "Seems fine. A touch warm, but fine."

Freya couldn't help but flinch at the touch. She remembered the skeletal hands from the dream, the coldness. She dragged her gaze up to Mom's face and for a flash she saw the worms, the outline of her skull, as clear as day.

She opened her mouth, but it still felt too real to share. "I'm okay," she responded, ducking her head and focusing on her pancakes.

"Well, your dad will keep an eye on you today in case you're feeling a bit sick. Okay? I have to go in to work, unfortunately."

"Aw, really?" Freya whined. "But we were going to go see *Hercules*!"

"Again," Dad muttered as he sat down. "Disney's going to make millions off our daughter, you know. It's practically child labour."

Mom whacked him lightly with the Arts section, laughter in her eyes. "I know it's disappointing," she said to Freya, "but Luisa called in sick."

Freya tried hard not to sulk. She had only a vague understanding of what covering shifts and extra hours meant. They were things adults thought about, and she accepted it, but she had been looking forward to the matinee with Mom all week.

"Next weekend, Pumpkin, I promise. But maybe after Dad's done writing for the day, you can both have dinner at the restaurant. Sit in my section. I'm sure I can sneak you a strawberry sundae for dessert."

After breakfast, Freya sat at the bottom of the stairs. Mom sat next to her, putting on the thick-soled black sneakers she wore at the restaurant. She smelled vaguely of vanilla and coffee, the way she always did. Freya felt an overwhelming urge to fling her arms around Mom and hold tight, so tight that she'd be unable to move, would be forced to stay home forever.

It was just a nightmare. It didn't mean anything.

Mom kissed her on the forehead and went out the door. The sun was bright as she got in the car. It glinted off the windshield, obscuring her face.

Freya sat in the silence of the house and considered talking to Dad about her dream. She walked to his office but paused by the open door, hesitant to break the rules. *When I'm writing, don't bug me unless your arm is hanging off by a thread.*

He was leaning forward in his chair, his fingers a blur over the computer's keyboard. He got into these trances sometimes, when he wouldn't move from his chair for hours and the typing was never-ending. Sometimes he even forgot to eat. It had been a long time, but a few weeks ago he'd gotten an idea, and the typing fury started again. She knew nothing about it except for what he'd said to Mom: "A big risk but it'll really pay off." Freya didn't know what could be so risky about a novel. It wasn't like he was a war reporter or anything.

She spent the morning wandering through the house like a ghost: touching the phone to call Tasha, then changing her mind, putting her shoes on to go ride her bike, then deciding not to, picking up a book, then getting bored. She went on like that until somehow it was lunchtime.

As she was getting sandwich ingredients ready, the phone rang. Dad had a strict no phone calls policy when he was working, so she answered it.

It was Dad's sister, Aunt Judith. She sounded mad.

"Are you okay?" Freya asked at her aunt's terse greeting.

There was a short silence. "Yes, honey, I'm fine. Can you please get your dad?"

"I can't. He's writing, and he gets mad if I bug him. I'm sorry."

A sharp inhale, then a pause. Freya could almost feel Aunt Judith's restrained anger crackling down the line and flowing through her own body.

"Can you please give him a message for me then? Please tell him: *Do not continue. I do not give my permission.* And tell him to call me back."

"Okay." She wanted to ask Aunt Judith what the message meant, but she didn't want to be nosy. Besides, her aunt had already hung up. Toronto was long distance, and even though it was cheaper on the weekends, Aunt Judith never stayed on the phone too long. It was too bad—Freya would've liked to talk to Mary. That would've been way more interesting than anything else she was doing.

She abandoned her sandwich and approached Dad's office, hesitating again in the doorway. "Dad?" Her voice came out in a squeak.

Typing.

She cleared her throat. "Dad?"

Dad's hands froze over the keyboard, his shoulders tensing. "Is your arm hanging off?"

"No."

He turned, searching her face. "Are you sick?"

"No. Aunt Judith called."

A scoff, and he turned back to his computer. "Let me guess. She was mad."

"Yeah." Freya took a few steps into the office. "She said, 'Do not continue. I do not give my permission.'"

Dad smacked his hand onto the keyboard, and Freya gasped in alarm. His face softened. He held out one arm and she leaned into his hug.

"Sorry, Freya. Your Aunt Judith is just—she's very stubborn, you know. She's not happy with this project I'm working on. But it's okay, we're not in a fight. She's just overreacting. Thanks for passing along the message." He ruffled her hair. "Now scoot, before I lose my train of thought."

From underneath his arm she peeked at his computer screen and read: *He couldn't believe his own sister could dare to defend Alan Y. Couldn't she see how vekers could destroy?*

Just as Freya and Dad were getting ready to meet her at the restaurant, Mom came home. She looked tired and was limping slightly.

"Are you okay?" Dad dropped his shoes and went to her, guiding her to the couch.

She waved him off but then took the help. "I'm fine. I just hurt myself a little and they told me to come home early. I don't know why they bothered. I could have kept working. It's just a bruise, see?"

She rolled up her pant leg to show them the bruise on her shin. It was big and angry-looking.

Freya curled up on the couch next to Mom, suddenly wishing she'd insisted Mom stay home.

"I'm okay, Pumpkin," she said into her hair. "But I think you'll have to make dinner tonight. Anything you like. Peanut butter and cheddar sandwiches. Lamb with chocolate sauce. Or maybe you'll take pity on me and finally try some of my pickled herring?"

Freya wrinkled her nose, but she couldn't muster a laugh.

In the end, Dad made homemade burgers, homemade fries, and quick pickles, going all out as if an abundance of food would crowd out Mom's pain. She limped out to the backyard with them and they ate under a blanket of humidity. Nobody talked.

Without knowing why—maybe she wanted to fill the silence, talk about something boring—Freya blurted out, "Aunt Judith called when you were at work."

Dad stopped in mid-chew, his jaw tense, and Freya knew she was in trouble. She lowered her eyes and waited for Dad to scold her, but he said nothing. Instead, he looked at Mom, who was looking back at him as if he were in trouble. Freya hated the expression on Mom's face. She looked so sad, and Freya didn't know why.

Then, a burst of inspiration: Freya flew into the kitchen and grabbed the offending jar before she could think about it. Back outside, she presented it to Mom with a flourish.

"I promise I will eat one pickled herring today," Freya said. "Just for you. A really small one."

Mom opened the jar and placed a glistening grey piece of fish on a torn-off piece of hamburger bun. It was squishy and too strongly fishy and Freya almost spat into the grass. She felt herself turn green.

"How is it?" Mom asked, her eyes large with hope.

"Great!" Freya lied. And the burst of happy laughter that came from both of her parents made her feel proud and brave, like a heroine who'd passed through an evil kingdom's trials to prove her strength.

Mom's bruise didn't get better.

Over the next couple of days, the redness spread up her leg. Mom and Dad argued when they thought Freya couldn't hear, whisper-hissing in their room.

"...nothing wrong with getting it looked at..."

"...walking better. I just need to rest for..."

"...being so stubborn for no reason. Why are you..."

"...always so superstitious about everything. It'll be..."

"...been two days now. What if Freya got injured like..."

She would have eaten a whole jar of pickled herring if it meant Mom would be okay.

The next day, three days after her injury, Mom started coughing up blood at the doctor's office and collapsed. After the ambulance took her away, Dad packed a bag and called a babysitter.

Mom never came home.

Dad told Freya later that a blood clot in her mother's leg had travelled up into her lungs.

Freya never got to say goodbye.

One moment, Mom was alive, she was hurting and scared but alive, and then in another moment, she was gone.

What were Mom's last words? When was Mom's last smile? The last hug?

In the stunned, ashen days afterwards, Freya felt like she had died too. She was hollowed out with death. She wanted to find Mom, bring her back, and she couldn't, and she knew why.

It was her fault. Freya had done it.

The less sense it made, the more sense it made. She could feel the truth inside like her unwanted breath.

Aunt Judith and Mary flew out to Kelowna, but only Mary attended the funeral. It was a lovely, sunny, hot day. A beautiful day. Airplanes soared low overhead, and the regular noises of the nearby airport were comforting, because none of it was real. Or maybe Freya herself wasn't real.

Mom's casket was open at the funeral, but Freya didn't want to see. Instead, she hid in the funeral home's coat-check room with Mary.

"I made her die," Freya whispered. "I had a dream about her being dead and then she died."

Mary just stared at her, not understanding, and kept crying as she'd done all day. Freya watched her and wished she could cry too. Everyone around her was crying, but Freya only felt the cold reality of her mother's absence, the cold reality of her dream.

"Oh my god, are you okay?"

A man's face came between me and the clouds. Not much older than me. Huge, scared eyes.

I turned my head. Through his legs I saw the headlights of a car parked at the side of the road. My right arm was stretched out on the sidewalk, as if beckoning to the car.

I sat up, wincing at the throb of pain in my right arm. Then, stronger, a pain blared from my leg.

"You just came running out into the street. You're lucky I was just parking and not driving."

I struggled to my feet, wavered there for a moment. I wanted to get away from him.

I limped away, left him standing there shaking his head. I found a bus stop, slumped onto the bench, and tried to catch my breath. Then I pulled up the torn sleeve of my cardigan and found a cut. It wasn't serious, the blood was already starting to dry. I wanted to look at my leg too, but the narrow fit of my jeans prevented me from rolling them up more than two inches. My leg throbbed the whole way home: as I got on the bus, as I sat staring out the window, as I limped the four blocks home from the bus stop.

Walking into my apartment gave me a strange feeling, almost hollow, like I'd been gone much longer than—how long had I been gone? Only two hours. It felt like an entire day, I was so tired. All I wanted was a nap, but I was distracted by the pain. I dragged my feet to the bedroom and pulled off my clothes, which were covered with grit from the road.

There was a dark bruise along the side of my leg, car fender height. A bump too, red and purple. I thought of the angry-looking bruise on my mom's leg eighteen years ago and tried to not let myself panic over that. I touched it gently and flinched. I was glad the car had somehow missed the bone. How fast had the car been moving? How fast had I been running? Why couldn't I remember what had happened?

After the relative relaxation of a hot shower, the more quotidian functions of my body began to return. I opened my fridge to consider the potential combinations of random assortment of ingredients there, distracting myself with cooking. As I ate, I caught myself reaching down toward the bruise on my leg, searching.

I last remembered leaving the coffee shop. I'd turned left, toward a part of town I didn't normally go to, all maze-like streets and blank 1980s houses. I'd wandered around until I eventually came through to the other side of the neighbourhood, where the 1980s gave way to the 1970s and its more fanciful house designs. I had a fondness for the split-levels, carports, and the ostentatious roofs that extended sharply down over second storeys, upper windows peeking out from a fringe of shingles. I remembered trying to imagine the lives of the people who lived in those houses, now and in the past.

Then what?

Maybe I'd somehow missed some signal from my body or my brain that something wasn't right, lulled by the aimless walk and my own curiosity?

A yawn wrenched my jaw open, followed by another one almost immediately. I couldn't focus. I needed to sleep. Maybe sleep would clear my head. Leaving my barely eaten meal and dishes where they were, I climbed into bed gingerly and slipped into oblivion.

My phone blared me awake.

"Hi!" Mary chirped. "Listen, I've got Chinese food. I'll be there in fifteen minutes, okay?"

I stifled a groan. Of all the days. I could say I was sick or busy. But she had food, and she was already almost here. I'd feel like more of a jerk if I lied to her.

"Sure," I said, "sounds great!"

I hung up and checked the time. I'd been asleep for two hours, but it felt like two minutes. My head still full of cotton, I forced myself into action, clearing away the now-cold soup, finger-combing my hair into some semblance of order.

"Sorry I didn't buzz in," she said as she arrived. "Someone was leaving and held the door for me. That guy who lives on the first floor who wants you, I think. He must remember me."

"He does not want me," I said, accepting the bags of food.

"You know, for someone who can see the future you can be pretty dense. What do you have to drink? Sorry, I didn't think to get anything."

She made herself at home, a blur around my kitchen as she collected plates and cutlery, then rummaged in my fridge until she found a couple bottles of beer. She wouldn't accept any help, so I sat at the table and waited dutifully. When the food was placed in front of me, I realized I was starving, but I resisted the urge to wolf it down. I didn't want Mary to think anything was out of the ordinary again.

Thankfully, Mary did most of the talking. I soon became a captive audience to the latest instalment of a work saga at her ballet company, involving a program for an upcoming performance and all the hoops she was having to jump through. I didn't mind listening. I sometimes envied her: being around people on a regular basis, creating something together, doing interesting things to show to the world. Having funny stories to tell your cousin. Sometimes I encouraged her to go even further into work minutia. How their company intranet worked. What they talked about at meetings. What she ate for lunch. Those things were fascinating precisely because they were so removed from my own life.

We finished our meal and I pushed my chair back, full and satisfied.

"So, listen," Mary said, fidgeting with her cutlery. I straightened my spine and got ready. I should have known she wouldn't have forgotten. "I did some research and I found that group you told me about. STEP."

"Oh?" I wanted to see where this was going before I reacted.

"It wasn't easy. They're on page twenty-six of Google. And that was after I'd tried all the search terms I could think of. Anyway, I think they sound pretty legitimate. Look."

She pulled her phone out of her purse, swiped it on, and handed it to me. I considered handing it back but could see no good end result there, so I took it and read.

Support Tools Empowering the Paradextrous. Don't fear your abilities! We're here to help. No judgement, completely discrete.

I winced at the wrong usage of discrete—one of my dad's pet peeves I'd inherited—and kept reading.

Have you ever thought, felt, or done something you couldn't explain? Something your doctors couldn't understand—or maybe you were afraid to go to a doctor. Maybe you're afraid of what's happening. Have no fear—Support Tools Empowering the Paradextrous is here! At STEP, we're curious about the curious. We're not an official organization. We're just a group of people in Toronto who aren't afraid to peek behind the curtain of reality and examine what's really possible.

If you're curious about a strange new ability you've picked up, have some questions you need answered, or just want to socialize with others who get it, our group would love to hear from you. We're always holding meetings. Get in touch today!

I handed the phone back to Mary. "Another beer?"

"Come on, don't be like that. Tell me what you think."

I sighed. "I told you before. I don't want to get involved with any group. There's no point. I really can't see any benefit to befriending other—"

Blackness. The beating of wings, a raven's wings spreading across the sky, just before the world went dark.

That was why I ran, why I ended up right in the path of that car.

I'd had another waking vision.

A cool hand was squeezing my own. I blinked at Mary's face, her brows furrowed in concern.

"Hey," she said. "You okay?"

"Yeah." I stood shakily and picked up my plate. "Do you want another beer?" I asked again.

Mary pushed her chair back to help me. I wasn't paying attention and walked right into it. Before I could stop myself, I shrieked and dropped to hold my throbbing leg. My plate shattered on the floor, sending noodles and water chestnuts spinning.

"Holy shit, are you okay?" Mary said, fumbling her plate onto the table and grabbing my hands.

I shook her off, but when I didn't get up it was obvious something was wrong.

"Let me look," she said firmly.

I let her roll up my pant leg, and she gasped when she saw the bruise. It was darker now.

"Oh good, the swelling's gone down a bit," I said absently.

"What happened? This looks bad!"

"It looks worse than it is."

"Tell me," she implored, reaching out to grab my arm—right where my other injury was.

I yelped again. She yanked up the sleeve of my cardigan. "Did you cut yourself?"

"I'm fine."

"It doesn't look fine."

I sighed. Mary was a terrier, Dad had said of her once. She wasn't going to let this go. I sat back, closed my eyes, and flattened my voice as I told her about my walk, my vision, waking up in the road after having been hit by a car.

"Bumped. Tapped," I said. "Ever so gently."

Mary took a sharp breath and immediately suppressed what I knew was intended to be a shout. Instead, she said a simple, "Okay." No emotion. She was parsing.

I looked at the shards of plate on the floor and said lightly, "I'm going to be finding food all over this apartment for weeks."

She was on her feet in an instant, standing over me with tears in her eyes.

"Frey, this is serious. You had a hallucination vision and you hurt yourself. You got hit by a fucking car. What if you'd been driving? What if you killed someone? What if you killed yourself?"

"I'm okay. I didn't even hit my head."

"Don't you fucking understand how serious this is?"

I sighed. "I know. Believe me. I've spent all day pretending I wasn't spooked."

She sat down in front of me. "That group. This is exactly the kind of thing they can help with."

"I told you, I don't want to. I can handle this myself. And you're sitting in noodles."

"Fuck what you want and fuck the noodles!" She was on her feet again. "I can't believe that even now, you're more concerned about people knowing about you than you are about your own safety."

"Yeah, it's so easy for you to be sanctimonious about it!" I shouted, lifting my chin to glare at her. "You can do anything you want and not worry about someone punching your lights out or following you down the street shouting at you or, I don't know, sending you to some fucking freak circus to perform like a monkey!"

"Don't be petulant. They don't send people like you to circuses. Do you know why? Because there are people like me who know that people like you are worthy of help and respect!"

I looked down at my arm, my hands. All I could do was sigh.

Mary's hand entered my line of sight as she picked up plate shards from the floor. She threw them out, got a broom. She started to quietly sweep around me, like I was a desk in an office, immovable. I could feel my resistance beginning to melt in her silence.

Was I too afraid to stick one foot out, even if doing so would lead to solid ground? If STEP was for real, people like me would be there, people who had probably all found themselves in a tense moment with a loved one—exactly like this one.

I don't know who we'd inherited our stubborn pride from, but

I cursed that unknown ancestor as I swallowed and said shakily, "You're right."

"Don't do me any favours." Her voice was tinged with bitterness but softer than before.

"I mean it. You're right. But I'm terrified."

She sighed. "I know you are. And I don't know what it's like for you, but I know what it's like for me, watching this happen."

I knew too. In all the years since I'd shared my secret, Mary had only ever cared about keeping me safe. She never once revealed it to anyone, never taunted me with it. It had drawn her closer to me, across the space and distance that divided us for most of our lives.

At the same time, that distance meant that Mary was thousands of kilometres away when my ability first manifested. For most of our lives, she was used to only hearing about the things that happened to me. And now I was having hallucinations out of nowhere. Of course she was scared. She wanted answers, certainty, security.

All I wanted was to hide, to pull into myself. Instead, I stood, brushing noodles off my pants, and got my laptop. Then I sat on the couch and waited. Mary put the broom away and sat next to me. Without speaking, she typed a URL into my browser.

The site that loaded was just one page containing a contact form and the text I'd read off Mary's phone. I read everything again, three times, searching for sinister subtext, a phrase out of place that would signal danger.

"So you'll go to the next meeting," Mary said. It wasn't a question.

"Just to talk. No commitment."

"Sure, as long as you try. It says the woman you have to message about attending meetings is named Cassandra. Fill out the form."

She looked at me expectantly. She really was going to watch me message this person, wasn't she?

I tried not to audibly sigh as I started to compose the message.

Hi Cassandra,
My name is Freya Tanangco, and I

"Hang on," I said, my fingers hovering over the keyboard. "Maybe I shouldn't use my real name."

"Why not?"

"It's a pretty short line from me to my dad. And all that goes along with him."

"I'm sure these people won't care about your dad."

"Maybe not, but I don't want this to be about him, even for a second. I want to be able to relax and focus on myself, not worry about whether anyone's going to run home to gossip to their friends."

"Fair enough. Let's think of a name." Her mood suddenly changed, her voice sparked with excitement. She turned her whole body to face me, legs crossed, like when we used to tell secrets as kids. "How about something like Anne Lewis? Inconspicuous and normal. Or Mary—hey, why not be me?"

Seeing her openness, her chummy happiness, melted the last remnants of my injured pride.

"I could never be Mary Neel as well as you are. I wouldn't do your name any credit."

"Maybe something very flashy then. Outlandish and outgoing. Angelina something. You can use your mom's maiden name. Angelina Dannevig."

"That sounds like a villain from a spy movie—I would be a very disappointing person to carry a name like that. Maybe I should just keep it as simple and as hard to fuck up as possible. Close to my own name." I tapped my fingers lightly on the keyboard as I thought.

I deleted the first sentence of the message and started again.

Hi Cassandra,
My name is Frances Tully

"Frances Tully," Mary read. "I like it. She sounds lovely. Calm and pleasant, but doesn't take any shit either."

"Well let's hope she comes through for me then."

I finished typing and sent the message. My cousin rested her forehead on my shoulder.

"Thanks, Frances Tully," she murmured. And she did sound thankful.

"Hey," I said, "I know it's a work night, but why don't you crash here tonight? We can watch a movie, you can nurse me back to health." I raised my injured leg, a look of mock helplessness on my face. "In the morning we can wake up early and go for breakfast. We haven't done that in a while."

Mary lit up. "Sure! I can go in a bit late tomorrow. Everyone's going to be distracted by rehearsal anyway. And Elliot hasn't had an evening to himself in a while. I'll call him."

In the middle of our second movie, Mary nudged my foot with hers.

"Your cell buzzed. You got a text or an email or something."

Hi Frances,
Thanks so much for reaching out, we'd love to meet you! Our next meeting is Saturday October 10, 2 p.m. at my house: 265 Lincoln Rd East, between Yonge and Mt Pleasant. There will be snacks of course. Hope to see you there!
Cassandra

That heavy feeling lying in wait, the instant between opening her eyes and remembering.

What day was it? The seventh day after the funeral. Thirteen days without her.

Freya swiped the tears from her cheeks and got out of bed listlessly, not sure what time it was. Dad had been letting her sleep as long as she liked lately. Not that she ever felt rested. She didn't think Dad slept much either.

He was sitting in the living room, curtains closed against the light, a cup of coffee in his hands, staring into space.

"Dad?"

He turned to her, and his face looked decades older than it used to. Something pinched in her heart and she hurried over to him, nestling under his arm fiercely, as if he would disappear too if she didn't throw her weight against him.

He set down his coffee, buried his face in her hair. After a moment, she felt tears on her scalp. Freya didn't pull away, didn't try to stop him. Instead she inhaled the coffee smell and remembered Mom. The way she used to drink hers in large mouthfuls.

"Are you okay?" Dad asked, his voice scraping the question out.

Okay. What a strange word that meant nothing.

"I miss Mom," she said, and that also sounded strange.

"So do I."

What was she supposed to do with her feelings, with his? How could she talk about Mom being gone? It felt like a sacred thing. But there was no other way to talk about her. She was no other way but gone.

The moment was broken by a knock on the door. Freya felt a flush of strange relief. Another flower delivery. Dad put the bouquet on the kitchen table with the others, didn't bother to read the card.

"Church in half an hour," he said.

She didn't want to go. She didn't want to stay in the silent house where everything was Mom but neither did she want to go to church with all the dressed-up bright people. She didn't want to hear Dad talk about saints and salvation and she didn't want to hear Mom's name spoken aloud by everyone at the end when the priest requested prayers for her soul. Mom didn't belong to them. She didn't belong to church. She belonged to Freya and Dad only.

But she also knew that Dad needed the ritual, so she went upstairs to get dressed.

On the drive over, Freya fell into a fog and didn't emerge again until the middle of Mass. That was when she realized—even though there was a lot of singing and listening and kneeling and sitting very still—church was a great place to think about your dead mother. You could weep without trying to stop and everyone would just assume that you were experiencing something beautiful, like the comfort of Heaven.

Three months without her. Mom wasn't going to be coming down the hallway, humming absentmindedly, to wake Freya up. She wouldn't be downstairs making coffee. Mom was just gone. Where she was, Freya couldn't know.

Listlessly, Freya showered and got ready for school. She gave a scant two minutes' attention to her hair, which hung in a tangle around her shoulders. Maybe she should cut it, make things easier. She was grateful that she had to wear a uniform to school—the rote, thoughtless process of getting dressed each morning was a blessing.

She went downstairs, averting her gaze from her parents' room at the other end of the hall, and found Dad already awake and in his office.

He turned from his computer as she came into the room. His eyelids were ringed with red and his hair was messy. How long had he been up?

"Hi, honey," he said. He reached out to pat her shoulder.

"Coffee?" she asked, but he'd already turned back to his work. She made coffee anyway, poured out some cereal for herself. The coffee maker gurgled and she watched the coffee drip into the carafe as she ate. She'd made too much. Enough for two adults.

"We're almost out of milk," she said as she put Dad's coffee down next to him.

He grunted his acknowledgement, his fingers unpausing in their flight across the keyboard keys.

"Did you eat?"

Silence.

Freya made him some toast, then slipped out the door to go to school. She pulled the collar of her jacket higher around her neck and wished she lived in Vancouver, just a few hours away but basically another world. In Vancouver, it might still rain in November but at least it wouldn't be nearly freezing out.

Compared to the silence of the house, the street seemed to scream with life. A gull called overhead. Fallen leaves crunched under Freya's shoes.

Just before she reached the corner of her street, she saw Tasha and Steve walking past. Before they could notice her, Freya stopped and became very interested in a pile of leaves, kicking at the nothing in its centre.

Not that they would have talked to her, of course. The girl with the dead mother. After the cards and flowers she had become invisible.

She sighed and shifted her backpack higher up on her shoulder. It was only a few weeks until Christmas break, she told herself. But the thought of the holidays reminded her of the void in her life where Mom used to be. Freya blinked back tears and kept walking.

Dad seemed a little more talkative at dinner that night. He looked brighter around the eyes too. Freya thought he must have snuck in a nap.

He'd made an elaborate chili, something he was very proud of— and rightly so, it was impossible to not have seconds. Freya tried to follow along as he described his efforts to find the three cuts of beef he'd used, all the shops he'd visited and what he'd asked for and what the people had said in response.

Then he stopped talking and looked at her expectantly.

What should she say? What did he want her to say?

She swallowed her mouthful and took a big drink of milk.

"Cool!" she said brightly.

Dad deflated slightly and went back to eating. It wasn't what he'd wanted to hear.

Freya never knew what he wanted to hear anymore. She should have paid more attention when he and Mom were talking. Her parents' flow of chatter, their observations and jokes, merely drifted in the background of her life. She hadn't expected any of it to matter. But now she needed that knowledge, the best way to talk to Dad.

To fill the silence, Freya began to babble about that day's Language Arts project. Dad listened and nodded and made sounds of interest at the right moments, and after dinner he headed straight back to his office.

At bedtime, Freya went in to say goodnight. She found him sitting at his computer, motionless, staring at the palms of his hands. He turned his hands over, then slowly back again, staring as if he had never noticed them before.

He jumped at the sound of her voice and for the briefest moment Freya saw a stricken look on his face. But he covered it up swiftly with a smile that didn't quite reach his eyes.

The sun was high in the sky above Okanagan Lake. From the passenger seat, Freya watched for the low rolling mountains across the lake and the bobbing white masts of the boats docked at the marina.

Suddenly, the lake's water began to churn and boil. A dark shape emerged, rising upward to reveal what looked like a horse's head, but the size of a car. Before the long neck came into view, Freya knew. Her teacher had said the Ogopogo legend was taken from old tales about a lake spirit. A lake spirit wasn't scary. Still, her heart seized in fear as the creature rose up from the water, moving faster than it should, blocking out the sun. The car shuddered and slammed to a halt. Freya was thrown onto the floor, and as she climbed back up to the seat the lake monster roared.

Strangely, Dad seemed unconcerned. He just wiggled the steering wheel uselessly from side to side, grumbling under his breath.

"Dad! Ogopogo's coming! Hurry!"

He didn't seem to hear her either. He got out of the car and walked around it, squatting down to look quizzically at every tire.

"Dad!"

Freya saw people running from the marina, screaming. Dad was kneeling next to the car now, examining something.

"Dad!"

"Freya? Are you okay?"

The next thing she knew, she was being shaken awake in her dark bedroom.

Dad reached over and turned on her bedside lamp.

"I had a bad dream," was all she could manage.

There were dark circles under his eyes. He gathered her in a hug and she melted into it, breathed in his comforting smell of old Irish Spring soap and aftershave and laundry detergent. She wanted to tell Dad about the dream. Dad knew monsters. He used to tell her stories about mythological Filipino creatures: the shape-shifting aswang, the blood-sucking manananggal, the half-man half-horse tikbalang. But those were creatures from the other side of the world and another time, too terrible to be real. Ogopogo was local, immediate.

Dad let her cry on his shirt for a moment. She wanted him to stay but instead he gave her a couple of heavy pats on her shoulder and moved her away. He pulled his sleeve over his hand and wiped her face with it.

"It's okay, Freya, a dream can't hurt you," he said. "I need to sleep now. I have a job interview in the morning."

He paused at the door.

"Lately, I've been praying when I'm scared. It helps."

Then he was gone, leaving Freya alone in a circle of lamplight.

She imagined Dad in his bedroom, pulling back the covers on his side of the bed and getting in, careful not to touch the part where Mom used to be. Maybe closing his eyes in prayer.

What good would praying do? God had taken Mom away.

She wriggled out of her blankets, out of bed entirely. Dropping to her hands and knees, she found the shoebox under the bed, slid it toward her.

The lid was furred with three months' worth of dust, but she climbed into bed with it anyway. Her heart was pounding. For a moment she hesitated, squeezed her eyes shut, shook her head. Then she whipped off the lid and lifted the palm-sized deck of cards out of the box.

They were warm. Warm like Mom's hands, her voice, her smell.

She shuffled them—in the Freya way, not in the complicated way Mom had—then flicked one onto the bed.

Across the top of the card read *Queen of Cups*. The picture of the woman was in profile, her face turned away. She had thick blond hair, like Mom, but it was coiled in a long braid. A high golden crown sat on her head. Her gown was light blue, simple, embellished only by the ruched gatherings of the sleeves and the bands of pearls at the cuff. She was holding a large golden goblet.

Freya was soothed by her.

"Queen of Cups," she whispered, drawing a thumb along the yellow braid.

Clutching the card, she turned off the light, nestled back under the covers, and listened to the quiet.

Freya still couldn't shake the dream the next day. Something pulled at her, a sense that she was missing something, something obvious.

Dad practically followed her around the house as she got ready for the day, buzzing with nervousness over his job interview. He even drove her to school, though it was just a few blocks away, to make sure he wouldn't leave too late.

But despite Dad's jangly energy, Freya found herself distracted all day at school. She didn't hear her French teacher calling on her to answer a question, she spilled juice on her uniform at lunch, and she walked down the wrong street on the way home from school.

She also felt weirdly nauseous. Was she getting sick?

When she finally got to her driveway, Freya paused. Dad's car wasn't there even though he'd said his interview was hours ago. She shrugged and let herself in. If Dad wasn't home, he'd have called Louise from next door to stay with her until he got back.

But it was coffee she smelled in the foyer instead of Louise's strong perfume. She could hear Dad's voice in his office. He wasn't saying much, but when he did talk his voice was pinched, sounding the way it had the time she'd spilled chocolate milk all over the living room carpet. *I'm not mad, I'm just disappointed.*

She slipped her shoes off, lowered her backpack to the ground, and tried to sneak her way past the office to the kitchen. Not to eavesdrop, she told herself, but to get a drink.

As it turned out, she didn't need to eavesdrop at all. Dad met her in the kitchen, a deep furrow between his brows.

Had something happened to someone? Mary? Aunt Judith? Her throat went dry.

"My car's in the shop," he said, brushing past her to refill his cup. "I had a fucking accident."

Freya gasped at the f-word.

"I'm okay, honey. I just missed the interview. Someone blew through a stop sign and almost hit me. I swerved to avoid him and hit a fucking mailbox." He turned back toward his office. "Come get me when you're hungry. I have to make some calls."

Freya stared out the window over the kitchen sink, her eyes fixed as if on a lake, watching a monster loom over Dad's car.

Saturday: the day I was going to meet the members of Support Tools Empowering the Paradextrous.

I couldn't make a useful human out of myself that morning. It was ridiculous. I nearly vibrated off the walls while trying to do a couple of readings. I went for a walk, which did nothing for my nerves.

When I returned to my apartment I realized there was only one thing I could do for this unshakeable restlessness.

I grabbed my laptop and logged into Oneira.

"Javi."

Without meaning to, I'd said his name under my breath, like a prayer. But why? I thought of Dad—his *I had a bad feeling*—and shook my head. Javi wasn't one of the creatures Dad had told me about—like the nuno sa punso, who cursed you unless you chanted a special phrase. He was just a regular guy.

JIsARaven has entered the chat.

I jumped. Holy shit.

A wave bristled through me as I began to type a DM.

>Hi Javi, Nice to

No.

>Hey JIsARaven

Ugh, no.

Then, the doorbell notification sound.

JIsARaven requests a private chat.

I clicked Accept, and there he was. The room behind him was bright and cheery, and he was leaning forward on his elbows at his desk, looking at his camera expectantly. At me.

I wasn't ready for his voice. Not yet. In a few hours I would be in a room full of strangers talking, being questioned, trying to cope and keep calm, so for now I just wanted the comfort of hiding behind my keyboard.

"Do you mind if we just type?" I asked.

Thankfully, he just said a quiet, "Sure," and then I heard his fingers on the keyboard.

JIsARaven: It's nice to see you again.

    TaurusTarot: Thanks.

JIsARaven: I just want to talk, if that's okay.

    TaurusTarot: Are you sure? You paid for a reading.

JIsARaven: I don't mind. Credits aren't too expensive.

I hesitated. Oneira swore up and down that my private messages and readings were not monitored, and logs were kept on my computer only. I tried to remember if the higher-ups had ever talked to me about any of my private conversations. They'd certainly never said anything when random men had flashed me. Still, I almost winced thinking about how Javi had blurted out the name of the group in our last chat, and I wanted to be more cautious. I was only mostly sure readings were fully private—and I didn't know what would happen if I was overheard accidentally revealing myself as a veker.

    TaurusTarot: Okay. I'm here if you change your mind. Also, I just wanted to tell you I'm probably going to check out that group today.

I watched him, hoping he'd pick up on my cue to be vague.

JIsARaven: I could answer some questions now, if you have any.

    TaurusTarot: What's the place like?

JIsARaven: C's been having meetings at her house since the group started a few years ago. Her husband's usually there but he leaves us to our chats, and her kids are teenagers so they never make an appearance.

JIsARaven: There usually aren't too many people there. Actually you'll be the first new face in months. So I hope you're interesting! :)

Despite the smiley face, his actual face remained expressionless.

> **TaurusTarot:** Me too. So what did you want to talk about when you logged in?

JIsARaven: I was just curious what you were up to.

> **TaurusTarot:** Not much. Just did a couple of tarot readings for clients.

JIsARaven: Do you really believe in that tarot stuff?

> **TaurusTarot:** Honestly? I don't know. I don't believe in mystical stuff generally, but sometimes the cards reveal something that's just too perfect to be a coincidence.

I heard a series of heavy clunks before the next message came— maybe the backspace key, erasing his first several attempts.

JIsARaven: Why did you choose tarot?

I thought of Mom. The Queen of Cups. The box of tarot cards I'd dragged out from under my bed over and over, that had never left my life for even one day after her death.

I didn't want to share my life story. Not yet, not until I knew he was safe. So I rearranged a few things.

> **TaurusTarot:** My mom introduced me to tarot cards. She gave me my deck after a kid left it behind in the restaurant

where she worked. She knew a bit about how to interpret them, and she taught me. Now and then we still read for each other. For fun.

I swallowed hard. The image of Mom and I, sitting here in my apartment doing tarot readings for each other, was too vivid. Mom shuffling the deck with that flourish I'd never learned. Our heads bent close together examining the cards. Maybe the blond in her hair would have started fading to white by now. How old would she be today? Fifty-six. She was only thirty-eight when she died.

Only ten years older than I am now.

I coughed. Looked up at the monitor and gave a professional smile.

> **TaurusTarot:** I'm sorry, but I have to go. I'll see you at two.

I logged off, ignoring his look of concern in the instant before he disappeared. I shut my laptop, shaken by how clear my imagining of Mom was. Surprised at how that clarity still surprised me.

Cassandra's house was on a quiet residential street. It looked very normal from the outside, to my relief. In the playground across the street, a toddler was investigating a see-saw with glee. Surely nothing bad could happen in view of a toddler.

I took a surreptitious peek through the front window as I approached. It looked like a very low-key gathering. At the very least, I knew nobody here would casually wish to see a veker's face kicked in.

There was a sign on the door: *STEP—Come on in!* I slipped my shoes off in the foyer and hung my jacket up in the hall closet, as unnoticed as if I were a member of the family. When I poked my head around the foyer wall, a woman glided up from her chair and greeted me warmly, shaking my hand. I guessed she was Cassandra.

"Frances, welcome! It's so nice to have a new person." Her voice was rich and warm, with a slight French-Canadian accent.

Javi sat on a couch along the front window. He stood up to shake my hand—he was taller than I'd imagined. But then again I always thought tall people were taller than I imagined.

It felt both strange and familiar to meet him in person.

"Frances," he said. It felt weird to hear my false name spoken right at me. "You never told me your name. Even though I'd told you mine." He delivered this statement without much of an expression, and for a moment, I felt accused.

I moved to sit in a low armchair next to the couch, the only free seat in the configuration around the coffee table. Across from me, in an armchair matching mine, was an attractive young man with green eyes and dark hair; it was styled long on top and swept back. He looked back at me intently, then gave me a slow grin. I felt my cheeks flare in an infuriating blush.

"This is Shaun Wyatt," Cassandra said.

I said hello. We reached over to shake hands, and it was a handshake I definitely felt.

Cassandra nodded to the large teapot on the coffee table. "Help yourself to some tea, or there's coffee in the kitchen if you prefer."

I was able to calm my nerves by focusing on pouring tea with a steady hand. This was ridiculous. I was supposed to be vigilant, not *blushing*.

"So," Cassandra said, her voice commanding yet kind. That, and the fact that her chair was slightly higher than ours, made me think of the High Priestess card: intuition, wisdom, understanding, hidden mysteries. "Frances, I'm very glad you could join us. I believe Javi told you a bit about the group?"

I nodded. "And your website."

She smiled. Her dark hair was perfectly glossy and her jaw had a determined set. She looked like someone at ease with being in charge.

"So. In your message you say that you have prophetic dreams."

I nodded.

"Before we begin, I'm afraid there's one slightly uncomfortable bit of business we do right away with new guests. Most people who find us do so because they legitimately need help or someone to talk to. However, some people come here for other reasons. Needless to say, that sort of behaviour can turn nasty, and we don't tolerate it. With your permission," she continued, "I'd like Javi to verify that you are paradextrous. I promise it's entirely non-invasive."

I looked over at Javi, saw an expression that was sympathetic but also resolute. I sat forward.

"Okay, go ahead. What does it—"

Suddenly, the air around me felt somehow more dense and I had trouble focusing. It was entirely unlike anything I'd yet experienced. Before I could think about it for too long, though, everything returned to normal. I took a quick sip of my tea to mask my shaky breath.

Javi sat back and gave Cassandra a quick nod. She seemed to relax.

"Thank you. I'll admit using Javi's skill is not very polite, but it's completely effective."

I took a deep breath. I'd been scanned. Like a bag of chips at the Superstore. My voice came out in an embarrassing squeak. "That was weird."

"Sorry about that," he said.

"What kind of reaction do you get from people like me? Us?"

"I sense an aura, kind of. Not a visual one. More like I feel the air around them vibrate at a different rate. It feels a bit like I'm shaking, but under my skin."

I took another sip. "I think I felt it too."

"Some people do seem to pick up a sort of feedback."

Shaun, who was watching my reaction closely, said, "I didn't feel anything when he did it to me, but I could tell that you had a strong reaction. You handled it very well. I'm impressed."

I tried desperately not to blush again.

"So everyone here has an ability?" I asked. It still didn't seem real to me. "How many people like us are out there?"

"There aren't many," Javi said, "but they find us."

"Since I started the group three years ago, we've helped forty-seven," Cassandra said with a proud expression. "There's no official membership. People drop in as they need to, whether things are going well or not."

"What exactly do you do for people who come here?" I asked.

"Let me give you some background. I first became interested in the paradextrous brain when I was a grad student in New Brunswick, in 1997." She paused to sip her tea, then carried on in a clip that showed she'd answered this question many times before. "I was twenty-seven. A friend who knew about my skill told me about an uncle of hers who was doing some work at the Brain and Memory Institute at the University of Toronto. They were looking for participants for a study about long-term memory, but it was secretly also meant to help people like me figure out their skills. I'm no scientist, but for several years I ended up helping them with their research as much as I was able. I met lots of paradextrous people over that time, and I wanted to help them the same way I had been, by helping them to understand their brains and giving them tools to survive. Initially, it was good for my career to be here in Toronto, and the larger population means we have better odds of finding people. So I stayed and founded STEP in 2012."

"Is this the only group like this in Canada?" I asked.

"No, there are others. Though as you can see, we're a small group. In fact, this is the smallest it's been, consistently, for eleven months. Sometimes people need us less, or move away, or want a break. I like to keep the regular meetings, though, even if it's sometimes just Javi and me. It's important that I keep the lights on, so to speak. Unfortunately, smaller population centres don't see even this many people on a regular basis."

"And other groups focus on different things," Shaun said.

Cassandra pursed her lips momentarily but switched to a somewhat strained smile. "Shaun means that some groups focus less on coping strategies and research and more on activism," she explained.

He turned to me. "I think there's a place for activism, don't you? Paradextrous people should be able to openly discuss our skills and demand equal treatment."

"Some people would rather not draw attention to themselves," I offered.

"But after all these years of hiding ourselves away, couldn't that be seen as cowardly?"

I tried not to let the sting of his words show. Instead, I channelled Mary's spirit and lifted my chin to meet his gaze straight on. "I don't think you can decide that about people unless you know what's at stake for them."

Shaun smiled and opened his mouth to respond, but Cassandra interrupted before he could.

"Frances, why don't you tell us a little more about your prophetic dreams."

I took a stabilizing sip of my tea and tried to ignore Shaun's gaze.

"I didn't know how else to put it. 'Prophetic' sounds overblown. But some of my dreams do come true, usually within a few weeks. I don't control them. Sometimes I don't even remember them until something triggers the memory. Anyway, I've been having these visions for eighteen years. I've learned to live with them. But lately, they've been weird, bleeding into my waking life. Hallucinations. I even injured myself during one of them. I don't know why they're happening. That's why I'm here."

Cassandra looked at me for a moment, considering. "Have you ever had a CT scan? To screen out anything anomalous? A tumor, for instance."

"Don't scare her," Javi said.

"No, it's okay," I said. "I hope I don't have anything weird happening in my brain, but I wouldn't mind ruling everything out."

"Leave it with me. I know a guy." Cassandra gave me a wink, then pulled out her phone and started typing on it. "How's tomorrow work for you? Eleven okay?"

"What? Really?"

"Really. He's an old friend. Anyway, if you're having hallucinations, I don't want to leave it too long. I'll confirm with you via text."

I nodded, halfway wondering what I'd gotten myself into.

"It's not that bad, I promise," Shaun said, leaning forward as if he were telling me a secret. "I'm a bit claustrophobic but it was actually okay, and it doesn't take too long."

I smiled, released my held breath. "Thanks."

"See? You've scared her," Javi said to Cassandra. "Maybe we should talk about something else."

"That reminds me," Shaun said. "I have an article I want to show everyone."

The article was actually a tiny sidebar, one narrow column, with the headline *Advocacy Group Seeks Stronger Protection for Abilities*.

"This group is based in Amsterdam," Shaun explained. "Dutch laws for the paradextrous are pretty good, but there's this weird loophole there that actually makes paradextrous people *go on a registry*. The group is petitioning the government to abolish it."

"A registry?" Cassandra asked. "I thought they just had to report it on their census, along with things like education level, race, et cetera. Demographics."

"It's the same thing. The Dutch government wants to know exactly how many paradextrous people live in their country. Who knows what they do with that information? Why does it matter to them? I'd like us to formally support this group."

"You know we don't formally support anything. We're not an advocacy group. We're an informal social group. We don't have political clout."

"But this is really worrying," Shaun said.

"I'm not saying the Dutch government is trustworthy or that there's nothing we can do. Let me think about options, and we can discuss it soon. Shall I make more tea before we continue? I read an interesting story about a man in Ghana who claims he can read car licence plates from two kilometres away."

After the meeting ended, Cassandra shook my hand again, with two hands, and in her warm smile I felt truly welcomed and appreciated. Before leaving, I wrote my fake name and real number down on the STEP contact sheet with confidence. Maybe this wasn't a bad idea after all.

Out on the porch, Shaun breezed past me with a grin and a "Nice to meet you," and turned down the sidewalk before I could respond. I froze, keenly aware of the spot on my shoulder where he'd brushed his fingertips as he passed.

Goddammit.

"Sorry, he tends to do most of the talking in our meetings," Javi appeared beside me, zipping up his jacket. "Did you drive?"

"I'm parked just down the street."

We began to walk together, naturally, as if it were our routine.

"So what do you think?" he asked. "Not too overwhelming, I hope."

"No! Well, yes, at first. But I think I'll get used to it. How long have you been part of the group?"

"Since it started. I met Cassandra about six years ago, when I was three years out of university. Back then, she'd made a name for herself in research on paradextrous people. Mostly because of her own skill. She can remember everything she's ever read and access any fact when she needs it."

"What, like an eidetic memory?"

He scoffed. "Don't let her hear you say that. It's her big pet peeve. She once lectured me for ten minutes about the difference. With eidetic memory there's more of a visual recall of info that only lasts a short time. What Cassandra can do is the real deal. No mnemonic devices or any aids. I've seen her do it."

"I've never heard of her before," I said. Not that I'd ever been anywhere near that world, of course.

"Her reputation is mostly in academia. She couldn't publish in any of the research journals, but she was there, kind of underground, doing her thing. An old professor of mine had heard about her, and he asked my permission to give her my name."

"Did your professor know about your ability?"

"He did, and he was very supportive of it. I'm one of the lucky ones. My family's always known about what I can do as well. And they've always encouraged me to learn more about it."

"Must be nice," I muttered. "My father—my parents aren't very receptive to the idea of people like me. They don't know what I can do."

"That's too bad," he said. There was no pity or condescension in his voice. Just truth—it was too bad.

"Do you agree with Shaun then? That people like us should be more public?"

"I agree that us paradextrous people should stand up for ourselves."

I peeked at him out of the corner of my eye. His gaze was fixed at some point in the middle distance, seemingly lost in thought. We turned the corner and I stopped in front of my car.

"It's cool that you call yourselves paradextrous all the time," I said. "I've never heard that term before."

"Yeah, it's pretty neat, isn't it? Cassandra didn't invent it as a collective name, but she popularized it through her research. Before that we had a scattering of names we called ourselves, not all of them flattering. But she liked *paradextrous* because it was to-the-point. Descriptive. Ambidextrous people are equally capable with either hand—"

"—Or equally skilled in different areas."

"Exactly. Just as we take mental ability above and beyond normal function."

It felt nice, I had to admit. A proper name. I wondered why I'd always reverted to veker, when it was a word other people used with violence, with anger.

I fiddled with my keys. "Why Oneira?" I asked him. "How did you know to find me?"

He shrugged. "I was bored one day and started thinking about psychics. Wondering if there are people out there who can actually tell the future. It was silly."

"But you were right. At least with me."

"It took me a couple of days on Oneira, getting private readings here and there. From one or two other tarot readers besides you, and from people who read runes and angel cards. It's all so silly."

He scoffed, not noticing that I didn't join him, and continued.

"I got the sense that none of them had skills. But with you I suspected otherwise. Especially when you—what actually happened that night?"

Something I'd been holding at bay unspooled, and I let out a shaky breath. I opened my car door, sat down behind the wheel, and put my head in my hands. A breeze came through and cooled my cheeks as Javi quietly opened the passenger door and slid into the seat.

"Sorry," I said, raising my head. "It was just really scary, that night."

I took a deep breath and told him what I could remember. I also told him about the waking vision I'd had after the first one, the one that ended with me running into a car. When I finished, he remained still. We looked out at the car parked in front of us, rusted autumn leaves patterning its surface.

"Okay, this is going to sound super conceited," he finally said. "But what if both visions were about me?"

"You? How?"

"When I first contacted you, you saw a blue jay. The second time, you saw black wings. Jay. Raven. JIsARaven."

I leaned my head back and squeezed my eyes shut for a second.

"That makes perfect sense and also no sense at all. Why would meeting you cause my brain to start malfunctioning?"

"I can give you the number of my last ex and you can ask her," Javi said with a snort, then paused, his expression one of genuine concern. "Are you going to be okay to drive home? I mean, now that you've actually spent time with me in person?"

"I'm sure I'll be fine."

"Great. Then do you mind giving me a ride to Mississauga since I'm in your car anyway?" He laughed at my bewilderment. "I'm just kidding! Sorry, I couldn't resist." He opened the door and pivoted his long legs out. "See you next week, I hope?"

I couldn't resist a small smile. Despite my wariness, despite the strain of my deception, and despite the unnerving possibility that Javi could be linked to my strange hallucinations, I'd actually kind of enjoyed myself.

"Of course," I said. "Next week."

Dad had been in his office for hours doing last-minute media stuff for *Kuya*, his new book. Freya had never seen him so jumpy and jittery. It was like he'd had three pots of coffee on an empty stomach. His office was a mess and the phone kept ringing. She hadn't been able to use the internet for days because constant calls from Dad's agent, the publisher, the publicist interrupted the dial-up modem and disconnected her.

She sighed. She was glad it was summer, at least, and there wasn't any homework to do. In fact, she got to do whatever she wanted. All the books she could read, all the long bike rides she wanted to take around town. And all she wanted to do right then was take her library book down to City Park and stretch out under a tree. It would be so quiet. Well, not quiet, but peaceful. People strolling around, kids playing, dogs sniffing, bikes, basketball, water, overlapping voices. Contentment and calm, at least for another month.

Her stomach tightened. Grade Seven was just one month away. She'd have to talk to people again.

"Freya!"

She jerked back to reality. Dad stood in front of her, framed in the doorway to the living room.

"Didn't you hear me?" he said. "They're replaying my latest CBC Radio interview in a minute."

Freya resisted the urge to roll her eyes and whine. She'd heard it the day before when their neighbour, Louise, who'd come to babysit her while Dad was doing the interview, had insisted they listen to it live. Louise had sat forward in her seat, as if it could get her closer to the studio where Dad was talking in an Important Voice about his brand-new novel. Afterwards, she wondered aloud in a hushed tone if Dad would do a talk with her Wine and Words book club. Freya knew that Louise was also dying to go to the launch, but Dad had been very firm that Freya was not to go, and so Louise had to stay too. He didn't actually say the phrase *no kids allowed*, but

Freya recognized the stern look on his face. Anyway, there definitely wouldn't be any other kids there, so what was the point anyway?

On the second listen, Dad's Important Voice was no less important-sounding. And it wasn't any easier to take him seriously when he said things like, "I'm particularly interested in blurring the lines of genre convention and even the nature of truth itself. Who is anyone to say what's really true? I reject the notion that any one person owns any one memory."

He seemed so different when he was talking to people about this new book. But maybe he'd always been that way. She was eight when his last one, *Only Soaring*, was published, and all she remembered of it now were a few phone calls, falling asleep to his voice on the radio, leaning against Mom's arm.

The memory made Freya sigh. Mom still appeared in Freya's mind when her guard was down. Just then she wanted nothing more than to sit with Mom and talk about Dad, the book, everything. Maybe Mom could help her understand Dad's jittery behaviour, what to do with it.

"That part, I hate that part," Dad shouted. "Why did he have to word it that way?"

Freya realized she hadn't been listening. What had she missed? Better not to ask directly, Dad would just get upset. "I don't remember that from the live interview," she said, not lying.

"To reference the Filipino thing right then," he waved a hand at the radio, indicating whatever the Filipino thing was, "right after I'd talked about my book being a microcosm of struggle on a societal level."

You can't name your book after the Filipino word for brother *and not expect Filipino-related questions*, Freya thought, but didn't say.

"He brings up my background as if we're all here to tell stories of heartbreak or something. As if we can't just have regular lives. We always have to be talking about race."

"But I thought people were racist to you as a kid."

Dad waved a hand, this time dismissively. "Only a few people were actually racist. Anyway, I learned to ignore it. But that doesn't matter because the book isn't about my life! Yes, the main characters are a pair of Filipino siblings growing up in Kelowna in the sixties, but it's not me. Microcosm!"

Freya fell silent, trying to remember what microcosm meant. She had a dim memory of reading it in a book somewhere.

The phone rang, and Dad ran to answer it. Freya couldn't see his face from where she sat in the living room, but she could sense his tension. Soon he was pacing back and forth in the kitchen, still on the phone, passing halfway into view through the doorway, then away again, then back. He was listening. Every now and then, his mouth opened as if to respond, but nothing came out.

Was it a telemarketer? No, he wouldn't be on the phone this long. It couldn't be another interview—he wasn't saying anything at all.

Then he did speak, and she understood.

"Judith, listen. We've been over this. The novel isn't about our childhood and it isn't about you. My whole job is inventing stories, and that's what I did. Do you remember what my second novel was about? Charles Horetzky surveying the Yellowhead Pass. It was a fictionalized account of a real person. But nobody jumped down my throat about that one because I know what I'm doing. Anyway, *Kuya* is in print now. It exists. If you really wanted to object to this you should have done so two years ago. In. Person."

He hung up and stormed back into the living room. Freya pressed herself against the back of the couch and tried to look innocent, not that it mattered.

"Dad?" Her voice was so small, she barely even heard herself.

"Can you believe the fucking gall of her," he exploded. "Doesn't even come to your mother's funeral but decides she gets to dictate what I write about. I've been working my ass off to make a name for myself for fifteen years, and where was your aunt? Fucking around in Toronto with her dickhead of a husband, never once showing a single shred of interest in my work. Did you know the first story I had published, I'd written for her? And she still hasn't told me what she thought of it. I was twenty-two, that's how long ago it was."

He paused to catch his breath.

Freya folded her arms around herself. She was stunned. She didn't know what to say. Everything was a jumble in her mind. Dad's anger at Aunt Judith not being at Mom's funeral. His anger at Aunt Judith in general. Everything that was going on with the book. None of it slotted together. It clanged around, preventing her from thinking clearly. What was she supposed to do?

He was standing so still and so silent. She had the urge to go and hug him, though she didn't know why. But did she need to know why? He was her dad. That should be the only reason she needed.

He cleared his throat. She stayed seated.

"Your mother died and then this happened. And Judith said she's never speaking to me again." His voice came out hoarse, pinched.

That was when she stood up to go to him, but then the phone rang again. Freya froze. She offered to answer the phone for him but he waved her away, and when Dad started talking, she knew it was his agent on the other end.

His voice perked up, again assuming the smooth, competent tones of the professional writer, the public face, the novelist with Important Things to Say.

Freya sat back down. She pulled her knees up to her chest and quietly listened to his different voice, his considered words. Which version of Dad was the real him: the one who talked in interviews about the nature of truth or the one who had just plucked loose the threads of Freya's world with a few words?

I was surprised when Cassandra texted me a few hours after the STEP meeting. I'd thought she'd been bluffing about getting me a CT scan, but no, I was due in Toronto at eleven o'clock the next morning.

I sent her a quick confirmation text and shoved my phone deep in my purse. I decided I needed to shut off my brain in preparation for whatever it was going to reveal.

Cassandra told me I'd need to fast the morning of the scan, so I figured tonight was a good time to do some damage at the McDonald's drive through. Once I got back home, I laid my junk food feast out on the coffee table and settled in for a night of mindless television.

Of course, that was when Mary called. Maybe unwisely, I let it go to voicemail as I started on my first McChicken. I could withstand the torrent that was my cousin's curiosity tomorrow. Tonight, I needed nothing but fat and salt and petty television drama.

Despite my best attempt, my nerves had not strengthened by the next day. My thoughts flitted from *This is fine, nothing but an initiation ritual* to *This is definitely going to be a weird cult* as I drove to Toronto's Annex neighbourhood. By the time I arrived at the clinic, I felt like I was going to disintegrate into a pile of anxious dust.

"Are you sure this is okay on such short notice?" I said to Cassandra, who was waiting for me in front of a short, unassuming yellowish stone building that fit in well with the narrow brick Victorians surrounding it.

"Positive," she said. She pressed a button on a keypad, spoke her name into a speaker. A buzz, a click, and the door unlocked. Cassandra held it open for me. I couldn't help but wonder again why I'd blindly trusted Cassandra—a woman I had only met the day before—to set up a medical procedure on my behalf.

I took three deep breaths and looked around the lobby. It was clean, bright, promising—that is, until Cassandra led us into an elevator and pressed the button for the third floor. The inside of the elevator was barely lit, casting eerie shadows on the planes of her face. The elevator shook and creaked as we went up at a snail's pace. *Weird cult, weird cult.* I took another giant breath in and released it slowly, feeling my heart rate lower a little.

Thankfully, the doors opened to a perfectly respectable hallway. Cassandra led me to a door with a sign on it that read *Richard Day, MD, Radiology.* She opened the door and called out a hello.

It looked like any medical office. There was a small waiting area and a reception desk. A man came halfway around the corner, shrugging into a white coat.

"Cassandra, hi. Just got here myself. One sec." And he was back around the corner.

"Richard is a medical advisor with the Brain and Memory Institute," Cassandra explained to me as we sat. "I told you about him yesterday, my friend's uncle. He's sort of an honourary member of STEP; he's very sympathetic to our cause. So don't worry, none of this will go on any official medical records or anything. It's strictly under the table."

Good thing too, I thought, *because Frances Tully doesn't actually have a medical record.*

"And he's working on Thanksgiving weekend?"

"No, this was strictly a favour. If you've been hallucinating, I don't want to make you wait too long. Funnily enough, it's good timing. He's going out of town tomorrow."

I opened my mouth to ask more questions but changed my mind. I couldn't decide which took precedence in my mind at that moment—guilt for indirectly bringing this man into work on a holiday or a small bit of jealousy at Cassandra for having such easy confidence in the inner workings of a friendship. In the end, I settled on tamping down my anxiety over how close I may actually be to a major brain incident. I surreptitiously rapped my knuckles against the wooden arm of my chair.

Dr. Day reappeared, shook my hand. "Frances. This way, please."

We entered a large room, where my eye was drawn immediately to a large, donut-looking contraption in the corner, with a long table attached to it. To my left was a window into a small room with a table lined with equipment. To my right was another room with a padded, almost dentist-style chair in the middle. A powder-blue hospital gown was folded neatly on the chair.

"Go ahead and change in here," Dr. Day said. "I'll be back shortly."

I entered and he shut the door behind me. My hands trembled as I undressed and put on the thin paper robe, which rustled too loudly in the otherwise quiet room. I perched on the edge of a chair, wondering if I needed to call out or if he was listening for the telltale rustling to subside.

In a minute he knocked at the door and sat down in a smaller chair opposite me.

"So. Hallucinatory visions?"

"That's how I think of them. They look and feel like the dreams I have because of my ability, but overlaid onto waking life."

"Are they prophetic as well?"

"I'm not sure, but they seem meaningful."

"Hmm. Unfortunately, science is still in the dark ages when it comes to studying skills. But we can at least have a look today and see if there's a pathological explanation for what's been happening to you."

"Do you think there could be?"

Maybe he heard the slight raise in the pitch of my voice, because he smiled reassuringly. "It's unlikely," he said.

I wondered if he meant it.

He took my blood pressure and asked me about allergies and my major medical history. I decided in this case it would do no harm to tell the truth. Then we walked out to the CT machine. Through the window into the small equipment room I could see Cassandra, who grinned and gave me a thumbs up. I tried to match her enthusiasm as I lay on the donut-table and Dr. Day began to tie a wide, blue elastic band around my arm.

"I'm going to give you an IV of a special contrast dye, which will illuminate the areas being scanned. You're going to feel it spreading through your body, and it'll feel warm. I do have to warn you that by the time it gets to your pelvic area, it's gonna feel for all the world like you've wet yourself, but I promise that you won't, okay?"

And with that, I released my first laugh of the day. He was right too. I felt the warmth cascading down my body like water, and I couldn't help a startled reaction when his prophecy came true.

He pressed some buttons on the machine, then retreated to the little room. The table lifted me up and inserted me into the CT donut, stopping before my shoulders went through. I looked straight up, breathing slowly, and listened to the little whirs of the machinery. I thought of Shaun's comforting words at the meeting and was very grateful that, on top of everything else, I was at least not claustrophobic.

A few minutes later I was done, dressed, and sitting with Dr. Day and Cassandra in the equipment room.

One of the monitors displayed a top-down image of my brain. Dr. Day moved the image to track the passage of the X-rays through my head. The contrast dye made my veins appear a brighter shade among the greys. It all looked psychedelic, like a flower blooming in water. At one point, I caught a brief glimpse of the orbs of my eyeballs and the outline of my nose.

"I won't bore you with all the medical stuff—unless you want me to. Do you want me to?" He looked at me.

Cassandra chuckled. "I'm sure Frances just wants to make sure everything's okay."

He turned back to his screen. "Short answer: yes. Everything is okay. There doesn't appear to be a pathological explanation for your visions or your loss of consciousness. No tumours, no hemorrhage, no aneurysms. Nothing weird going on with the bone."

"Good. That's good."

It was good. I was glad. But I was also left in the same place I had been this morning. No answers, no solutions.

"Thanks, Richard. I really appreciate it," Cassandra said, shaking his hand vigorously as we left.

"Anytime. You know I'm just happy to help. But next time, please bring me someone with something that I can actually study! Too many clean brains."

I emerged blinking from the yellowish building not a newly minted cult member, relieved to be healthy, excited to go home. I'd had quite enough of big cities and new experiences for a while—I just wanted Toronto behind me, quiet Markland ahead of me. Maybe if I left now, my hunger would leave me alone long enough to get to Mary's. It'd be easier to catch her up on the last couple of days if we were sitting in front of each other, face to face.

"Let's eat," Cassandra said. "Then we can talk about what to do next."

My heart sank, but my stomach roared to life, and I tried not to sigh too loudly as I followed her to Bloor Street. I'd been so anxious about the scan that I didn't even stop to acknowledge I was in my old neighbourhood from my university days. In fact, I knew exactly where Cassandra was taking us when I saw the familiar sight of Future Bakery on the corner of Brunswick Street. The large patio along the side street was almost full despite the fact that it was chilly, and I was glad when we opted to stay inside. It hadn't changed since the days I'd spent hours there with coffee, coconut macaroons, and my textbooks.

The inside of the restaurant was wide open, with rows of rectangular tables in groups of two and four separated by the familiar blue-painted pillars. Against the low hum of chatter were a couple of groups of silent students focused on their work. It was still as comforting as I remembered.

We moved to the back of a lineup, and Cassandra leaned in close: "I've been thinking it over, and there might be something we can try," she said quietly.

By the time it was my turn to order, I was so hungry and shaky that I forgot what I'd ordered almost as soon as the words left my mouth. Thankfully, Cassandra was more attentive than I was. When a plate of the old familiar pierogies, fried onions, and mashed potatoes with mushroom gravy appeared at the pick-up counter, she placed it on my tray. It smelled heavenly.

"Sorry," I said as we sat down. "I tend to go a bit wobbly when I'm too hungry."

"And does that affect your skill at all? Do your visions change in any way?" Cassandra squinted at me scientifically.

I glanced quickly at the tables around us. A couple of elderly women at the next table looked away as soon as I caught them listening, and they began whispering to each other. They made no effort to stop staring at us, however. I moved my chair further away from them and angled myself so my back was to them.

"No, not at all," I replied softly, hoping that Cassandra would take the hint and not broadcast our conversation to nosy strangers. "But being tired does."

She put down her sandwich and leaned closer to me."How much control do you have in your visions?"

"None. I only see them."

"Have you ever tried lucid dreaming?"

I'd heard of lucid dreaming before, where dreamers could make themselves aware they were dreaming and actually participate and control the events. I hadn't tried it myself, and the stories I'd heard were really far-fetched, like dream psychic contests where psychics would try to send an image to the contest participants as they slept. Or mutual dreaming, where people would try to dream the same dream together.

Cassandra continued. "I was wondering if it could help you manage your hallucinations. Since they behave like waking dreams, maybe employing lucid dreaming techniques could help."

I chewed slowly, thinking over the implications of what she'd said.

"You think I could control them as they're happening? Maybe even stop them?"

"That's my theory, yes. But we'd have to do a bit of experimentation. I brought you some research, and stories from people who've undergone lucid dreaming therapy to help alleviate nightmares." She reached into her bag and handed over a small pile of pages.

"Have a look at it as soon as possible. If you decide to go along with it, you can practice it with your regular dreams. And keep a diary for me, if you don't mind? If we see success, then you can try using those strategies next time you have a hallucinatory vision."

The eavesdropping women, their meal finished, stood up, scraping their chairs loudly.

"So what's it like for you?" I asked, lowering my voice even more. "I mean, you seem pretty well-adjusted. You seem to lead a normal life."

"What, and you don't?" Cassandra said, smiling expectantly.

Shit. What had I told her about myself yesterday? Had I told her about my work? Did Javi? What could I tell her? In the end, I went with mostly the truth—it'd be the easiest to remember later.

"Sometimes, when I'm lucky, I'll remember a vision that actually applies to a person I'm doing a tarot reading for. It tends to happen more often with my more regular tarot clients, the ones I have some sort of connection to. I've had visions about total strangers too, but it's more common with people I know."

"How interesting. I wonder how that connection works. Perhaps some sort of activity in the perirhinal cortex." Her gaze drifted for a moment. "But to answer your original question, what's it like for me? Living with my skill isn't easy."

"Javi told me about it. That you can remember everything you read."

"What he probably didn't tell you is that all the knowledge stored in my brain could potentially overwhelm me if the mechanism that allows me to recall information doesn't also allow me to organize it—partition it. That was something I had to really practice at to get right, especially when puberty made my hormones go crazy. Actually, I used to hallucinate too when I was too tired. I got a handle on it by university, though, which was a good thing, because I don't know how I would have survived at all otherwise."

"Do you ever have problems with other people? People who aren't paradextrous?" I asked tentatively.

"Sometimes. I think it helps that my skill is very easy to hide. And it sometimes comes in handy as a party trick. I'm socially acceptable." She smiled with sadness that she didn't try to mask.

"You could be a brain surgeon or the world's greatest scientist or something," I said.

Cassandra shook her head. "Greatness is about more than this one thing that I can do in isolation. I may be able to regurgitate literally any fact or research finding, but what do I do with it?"

"You help people. You already do with STEP."

"I suppose that repays my cosmic debt for spending years on a useless grad degree in anthropology," she said, swirling the dregs of her coffee. Suddenly, something behind me caught her eye. "Shaun, hi!"

I turned in my seat and saw Shaun walking toward our table. He was smiling, and I could have kicked myself for actually thinking it lit up his face.

"Hey," he said. "I'm just going to grab a coffee. I'll be right back." And before anyone could say anything, he was heading toward the counter.

My face was on fire. Was there anything in my teeth?

"I have to go," Cassandra said to me. "My husband's getting the turkey ready but I need to help with the rest. And I need to collect his parents and the girls' friends. Remind me why I thought inviting seven thirteen-year-old girls to Thanksgiving dinner was a good idea. Wish me luck! And don't forget to read over that info I gave you." She stood, swept her jacket off the back of her chair, and waved at Shaun as she walked out the door.

Should I have left with her? I didn't know what Shaun and I would talk about. He'd acted so debate-happy at the meeting yesterday, and I wasn't emotionally prepared for that sort of thing today.

On the other hand, I really wanted to talk to him. About anything.

I stared at the empty chair until Shaun slid into it, holding two cups of coffee.

He pushed one in my direction. "I don't know how you take your coffee. Hope black's okay."

It wasn't, not really, but I felt awkward at the thought of getting up for sugar and cream. "Thank you," I said. "How much do I owe you?"

"Don't worry about it. Consider it an apology for my interrupting your conversation."

"Oh, she just went to get Thanksgiving dinner ready."

Shaun sipped his coffee and shook his head. "Don't tell me I'm going to scare you off too." He grinned, one corner of his mouth lifting, and pushed his dark hair back off his forehead.

Goddamn him.

"No, I'm here at least until my coffee's done."

"Today was your scan, wasn't it?" Shaun asked. "How'd it go?"

"It was fine. Does everyone get one of those? It seems like Cassandra and that radiologist have been doing this a while."

"Not all of us do, but it's nice to rule things out. Did the dye make you feel like you were—"

"Like I was wetting myself, yes," I said, a little too loudly. I clamped a hand over my mouth as a couple of curious heads swivelled in my direction.

Shaun caught my eye and gave me a sympathetic look. I was happy when he changed the subject.

"I'm glad it went well despite that. So what's your plan? For controlling your visions, I mean."

I took a sip of my coffee, winced at the bitterness, and filled him in on Cassandra's theory about lucid dreaming. As I talked, mostly looking into my cup, I felt his gaze fixed firmly on me.

"That could work," he said. "You've never tried it before?"

"It's never crossed my mind. I guess I always thought of my visions as something happening to me against my will. Usually unwelcome." I closed my hands around my cup and allowed myself one instant to think of Mom.

"You should never think that. People like us, our skills are all— this is going to sound corny, but fuck it—beautiful. We're beautiful aberrations." His eyes, his entire being, brightened as he talked.

"I've never heard that word used in a positive way."

"Oh, it's totally positive. You and me, we'll never be like regular people. And it's amazing. What's more unique than us?"

"That assumes uniqueness is desirable to everyone. It's not. To me, it's not."

"Are you kidding me? You can predict the future. That's so fucking cool! I don't know anyone else who can do that. Who wouldn't want that skill?"

I glanced around nervously, but nobody had heard him. Or, at least, they didn't make it obvious if they had.

"I don't want it," I said, "especially not now when it feels like my brain is out of control."

"Well, it's not, I promise you that. I know it probably feels like you're going through a lot right now, but something tells me you can handle it. And anyway, you have us now."

Even though I'd only spoken to Shaun for a lifetime total of maybe twenty minutes, I believed what he said. I wanted to believe what he said. Unsure of what to say, I fidgeted, pushed the sleeves of my cardigan up.

"That looks sore," he said, nodding down at my injured arm.

"Oh," I extended it, looked down at the ellipsis of scabs. "I got bumped by a car a few days ago."

"Hit by a car?!"

"No, bumped. I was having a hallucination. It was parking. But it's fine…" I trailed off as I saw his fingers extend, hover just near the scar, not touching.

I looked up at him, at his dark green eyes glinting with gold. I quickly sipped my coffee.

"What's your ability?" I asked, suddenly realizing I didn't know.

"My skill is actually not too far off from yours. I can tune in to people's true emotions and get a sense of who they are and what fuels their intentions. Based on that, I can sort of predict what they'll do in any given situation."

"That seems very personal."

"It can be. Both for them and for me." He fixed me with another look.

"Are you doing it now? To me?"

He laughed, and I got a good look at a couple of charmingly crooked bottom teeth. "No, it isn't like that. I have to be touching the person, and they have to let me read them."

"That sounds awful."

"Awful?" He frowned.

I'd said it without thinking, and I was afraid I'd offended him. "Not the touching part," I said. "I mean to make that kind of connection with someone. I wouldn't want just anyone to go in my mind and walk around, you know?"

"Like I said, I get permission. It scrambled my brain a little bit when I was discovering it, but once I figured out how to control it, I fell in love with it. It's usually pretty intense, but it's great. What's better than a direct connection, learning so much about someone else, and then helping them learn more about themselves? It feels right."

I looked away, stared at a table of people chattering boisterously on the patio. I'd spent my whole life making sure no one, outside of Mary, could ever get close to me. Not close enough to matter.

What was it like to trust so easily?

I met Shaun's gaze. I didn't not trust him. I didn't trust him either—but I felt like it might be possible.

"I've never met someone like you before," I told him. "I mean, someone with abilities who's so confident and open about it."

"It wasn't easy. I grew up hiding it from my parents and my sister. I was ashamed of it for the longest time. Scared. But one of my teachers in high school put two and two together. She kind of watched out for me. One day, she gave me all this info to read. Alan Y, the ones who popped up after, the discriminatory laws against people like us around the world. Do you know about all that?"

I nodded.

"It's disgusting, isn't it? I couldn't stop reading about it. Especially Alan Y. I still can't. He was treated like he was subhuman instead of the most interesting person to exist in millennia. It makes me angry. But anger is good. It makes you act. You make change. Anger made me prouder of who I am and what I can do. And why not? I'm not hurting anyone. That's what people don't get about us. It isn't like we wield lightning or throw cars with our minds. We just have more developed brains than other people."

I didn't know how to respond. This world that Shaun lived in, where people like us shouldn't have to hide—it was an alien planet to me.

"I'm sorry," he said, as if reading my mind. "I know I can go off on rants sometimes. I promise our next date won't be like this."

"Next date?" I squeaked.

He smiled at me. "Or first date, if you'd prefer. No pressure."

"Dad, isn't room service expensive?" Freya asked. She had to admit, she did want the grilled cheese she'd seen on the menu. But she felt guilty about it.

"Yes, but just this once is fine. That reporter is still here. I can see his car."

Freya now understood why he'd refused a room with a view, asking specifically for a room overlooking the parking lot instead. "Is he the one who took pictures while you were getting our luggage?"

"No, different one. He's not taking any pictures. He's just waiting. Don't be scared. He's not going to hurt us. They just want to talk to me, but they can't do anything if I don't talk to them."

"I'm not scared," Freya muttered under her breath.

And it was true, she wasn't exactly scared—though what she felt, after Dad had told her they had to leave in such a hurry that she forgot to pack her pyjamas, wasn't too far off. But at least the hotel was quiet. She would be happy if she never heard a phone ring another day in her life.

"Anyway," Dad said, "isn't this fun? It'll be like a mini vacation. I don't think you've ever been in a hotel. This one has a pool. Once that reporter goes away we can go."

"Is there a waterslide?"

But he was already on the phone with room service and didn't hear her.

Freya got up and went to the window, crouching down so the bridge of her nose brushed the windowsill. She scanned the parking lot. She couldn't quite remember what the reporter or his car looked like, so she critically assessed every person she saw. A mother bundling a baby into a car seat: probably fine, though the baby could have a hidden mic. A man in overalls leaning into the back of a work truck: he could be a repairman, but then again, anyone could buy overalls. A man smoking and pacing back and forth while talking on his giant, brick-like cell phone: very suspicious.

"Honey, what are you doing?" Dad came to stand next to her.

"Dad, no! He'll see you!"

"Who'll see me?"

"The reporter!" She jabbed her finger at the window.

"Freya, that's not the reporter. That's just a guy."

He looked at her for a moment with an expression that she couldn't read. Then he gently put his hands on her shoulders and led her away from the window. He crouched down in front of her like he used to when she was a little kid, except now that she was twelve, he had to crane his neck up to her.

"Honey, listen. It's not your job to look out for reporters, okay? I'm sorry if I freaked you out. It's really not a big deal. Nobody's going to hurt us. My book turned out to be a bit controversial, that's all, and people want to ask me questions about it. It'll all blow over soon. Now, want to watch cable?" He stood, brushing his palms together with finality—though she caught him sneaking a peek out the window.

She did want to watch TV. They hadn't had cable at home in so long. She scooted backwards on her bed until she was firmly nestled in the pillows and began to flick through the channels. It was dinnertime, so everything was the news. She kept flicking.

Then, suddenly, Dad's face filled the screen.

"Tanangco is under scrutiny for the content of his new book, *Kuya*," the voice on the TV said. "A former friend alleges that some fictional incidents are not—"

Dad snatched the remote out of her hands and muted the TV. Ears red and mouth set in a line, he stared at the now-silent reporter. Then he changed channels until he came to a news station that was clearly American and therefore definitely wouldn't cover the Canadian literary world.

"I'm sorry, but arts critics are full of shit. They didn't like *Only Soaring* because it was too experimental. So I give them a more straightforward Canadian story, and now all they care about is fact-checking? I've already proven myself to the literary world, and this is what they do."

Dad had directed that whole rant at the still-quiet TV. Did he even remember she was there?

Freya was relieved when there was a knock at the door. Dad went to answer it and came back with a room service tray, which he carried to a desk next to the TV. As he silently handed Freya her plate and drink, she wanted to say something to console him, but she couldn't. She was only twelve. She didn't know what to say; it would be useless.

Dad unmuted the TV, and they ate sitting on their beds. The news was boring. Why did the reporters always talk in these serious voices about horrible things happening in faraway places? Why not mix it up with something funny or practical or useful? The news always made Freya feel like hiding in a hole. She turned away from the TV and looked around the room. Ugly bedspreads with a swirled red and purple design. Two lamps screwed into the wall above each bed—Dad would definitely hit his head on his. A painting of some sort of boat, or was it an airplane?

"Dad, what do you think that weird painting is?"

He shushed her, his attention focused on the screen.

"It is alleged that the man had been hiding this volatile mental ability from his employer. His employment has been terminated and he has been ordered to pay restitution to the family he is said to have injured."

"What does *restitution* mean?" Freya asked.

"It means he did something awful to someone and he has to make it up to them. Probably exploded someone's head with his mind or something. I hope they lock him away forever."

Freya shuddered. She put the rest of her sandwich back on the plate, then got up and went to the washroom. She turned on the sink's faucet and sat down on the edge of the tub.

That poor man.

Freya couldn't help but think it.

That poor man.

Maybe it was a misunderstanding. Maybe the reporters didn't know what had actually happened, so they'd just made everything sound mysterious on purpose.

But what if it was true that the man had actually hurt someone? What if the same thing happened to her one day? What if she, somehow, exploded someone's head? She didn't know what her mind could do. Maybe it had ruined Dad's car. Maybe it had killed her mother.

Freya shuddered. She suddenly thought of Mom's old tarot cards. She wished she'd brought them. She wanted to slide them through her fingers, look at the comforting images.

A knock on the door.

"You okay, honey?"

"Yeah, fine. Woman troubles." That always got him to go away.

Freya got up and splashed cold water on her face, watched it drip down her reflection.

One day, would she see her own face on the news?

I didn't have much time to get to Mary and Elliot's house for Thanksgiving. I decided not to stop at home on the way back from Toronto, drove straight there instead. There was heavy traffic on the Gardiner Expressway, but that gave me plenty of time to call Mary and let her burn out her curiosity on yesterday's STEP meeting and today's CT scan.

Over the course of an hour, Mary ran the gamut of her standard responses to big news—shock, loudness, questions, questions, questions, theories, opinions—and it wasn't until I was actually at her door that she hit me with news of her own:

"Mom's coming."

I froze, one foot on the porch, the other in the foyer.

My Aunt Judith, who had effectively cut my dad out of her life and whose relationship with Mary was strained at best. I hadn't seen her in years.

"What, tonight? I thought you said she was joking."

Elliot appeared from the kitchen as Mary pulled me fully inside the house. "She called half an hour ago. She's on her way," he said.

Mary laughed, misinterpreting my stunned expression. "It'll be fine. The turkey's been in the oven for hours already, she won't be able to criticize it."

"Critique it," Elliot said, "and she will anyway. I've just basted it, so it'll be good for a little while before we need to do it again. I'm going to take Zeus to the park for a bit."

"Make sure you're back before she gets here!" Mary said, her eyes large.

"I will be, don't worry." Elliot said. Then, to me: "Glad your brain's okay."

After the door closed behind him, Mary said, "He meant that sincerely. So how are you feeling about everything?"

I stared. "Me? Your mom is coming for Thanksgiving dinner. Why now, after all this time?"

"I don't know, Frey. I can't stress about that right now. I didn't think she would actually come and now I have to make this stupid bibingka and I'm shitting bricks about it."

Bibingka—a cake made with coconut milk and rice flour or, more traditionally, milled glutinous rice—is a staple of Filipino Christmas, but it'd been years since I'd had it. I certainly never thought to make it. "You're making bibingka for Thanksgiving?"

"Don't get hung up on that. Help me. I have just enough time to get this in the oven before she arrives. Can you get the rice flour? I know it's somewhere in that cupboard."

And with that, we put our heads down and got to work. Acting as Mary's sous-chef, I found the rice flour, measured out the coconut milk, grated the cheese, and prepared all the other ingredients. And as I watched Mary mix them all, I felt a traitorous note of excitement over this dinner despite my anxiety over seeing my aunt. Or maybe I was getting high off the aroma of roasting turkey.

Elliot soon returned to complete the happy crowd in the kitchen. All three of us ran around doing last-minute arranging, stirring, basting, boiling, plating. Ours were standard Thanksgiving high spirits—right up to the moment the doorbell rang.

We froze in place and stared at each other.

"Mary," Elliot whispered, "Go, go!"

"I don't want to!" But she went anyway, and before I could prepare myself, my Aunt Judith was standing in the foyer, politely petting Zeus's head.

"He looks so old," she said, frowning down at the Lab.

Elliot went out to greet her, leaving me to watch, paralyzed, through the doorway. My brain whirred like a rusty engine to process the moment.

Then she was in front of me, hugging me. Hugging me. She'd barely ever hugged Mary, let alone me.

"It's been too long, Freya. You never come and visit me!" She frowned, then looked over my shoulder at the detritus of Thanksgiving dinner preparation. "Is that stuffing from a box?" she asked.

In response, Mary fluttered in and spirited us out of the room. "Why don't you two go down to the sitting room? Elliot has this fancy hot chocolate he wants you to try."

A minute later, Aunt Judith and I were sitting on the couch side by side. I had no idea what to say, so I settled for, "How are things?"

"Better," she said. "Things haven't been easy for me but I'm getting by. Work is impossible. I have to train someone who seems to have never touched a computer before. How are things with you? Still doing that psychic thing?"

"Tarot. Yes, I'm still doing that."

"Heard from your father lately?"

"A bit, but not much."

"Good, that's good."

I didn't know what she determined to be good. I didn't ask.

Now what?

I watched Elliot coming from the kitchen with our hot chocolate. He was followed by Zeus, who stopped at the top of the short flight of stairs to the sitting room to lie down.

Sorry, Elliot mouthed at me as he approached, eyes flitting toward Judith.

I accepted the mug with extra-grateful thanks.

"Are you sure you guys don't need help?" I asked him.

"No, I think we're okay, thanks. It's almost ready. Just stay here and enjoy Judith's company." He caught my eye and smirked before turning away.

At that moment, I felt badly for Aunt Judith.

My mom's death, my father's scandalous book—those things should have brought us closer. Instead, even though I'd been living within reasonable driving distance of her since I was eighteen, I'd avoided her as much as possible. I'd told myself I was following Mary's example. But had I needed to freeze Aunt Judith out? I didn't have much family. My grandparents were all dead. My mom's family in Norway wrote her off when she moved to Canada. My dad was my dad. Why had I resisted getting close to my aunt?

And yet, even as I felt a burst of love toward her, an almost desperate need to bring her into my life, there was a kick of resentment: she'd never reached out to me either.

We sat in silence, blowing on our hot chocolates and taking tentative sips. I was just about to get up and go to the kitchen, without caring how rude it seemed, when she spoke.

"I think this house has grown since I've last seen it. Must be nice to have so much space for two people. I bet they're going to start a family soon. Why else have such a big house?"

Was that a rhetorical question? I answered anyway, desperate for something banal to talk about. "There aren't too many small houses in Solingate. People move out here to build McMansions. This place is actually as small as you can get in this town, unless you want a condo."

"See? Living in a family-oriented town."

"She hasn't said anything about starting a family."

"Well. If she hasn't told you," she said, giving me an irritatingly knowing look. "You're twenty-eight and Mary is twenty-six. It'll come up soon, you'll see. Despite what you may think now."

I took another sip of my hot chocolate. It was still odd to me that I knew things about Mary that her own mother didn't. Aren't mothers and daughters supposed to discuss, plan, dream, strategize together?

I wondered what my mother had dreamt for me.

Dinner was ready just before our hot chocolate was finished. I was grateful both for the timing and for the food itself. It was way too much for just four people. Turkey, gravy, cranberry sauce, the vilified stuffing, sweet potato and cauliflower salad, buttery green beans with slivered almonds and, of course, a very large bibingka.

"I know you like bibingka, Mom," Mary said as she brought the cake to the table. "I've been practicing."

Judith levelled a critical gaze at it. "You forgot the banana leaves, but it looks good. If you want more Filipino recipes, I can give you some of my grandmother's. They're great for feeding a family."

Aunt Judith gave me a knowing look. Mary caught my eye, and I shrugged.

We busied ourselves with eating and occasional small talk. I kept a close eye on Mary, monitoring her for signs of strain as she talked with her mother. Judith was being generally pleasant, but passive-aggressive comments still slipped through, like "It's so refreshing to see a basic turkey, Mary. Too many people these days think they need to spend a lot of time on it, but it's good that you didn't think about it too much." However, they were delivered so kindly and casually that I wondered if Judith just had no idea how she came off. Still, I wished I could communicate with Mary telepathically, send reassurance brain to brain.

Elliot, for his part, nearly broke his back trying to redirect conversations onto more general topics: new movies, the weather, his job, traffic in Toronto compared to Solingate, and especially Zeus. Zeus was the great equalizer, and for that I snuck him a couple of large turkey chunks under the table.

By six o'clock, we were all full and finished. To her credit, my aunt ate two generous servings of Mary's bibingka and even asked if she could take some home. As she was leaving, I hugged her goodbye. I felt a strange wistfulness, as if it were certain I wouldn't see her for a long time.

We watched her drive away from the kitchen window and released our collective breaths.

"How are you?" Elliot asked Mary, rubbing her back consolingly.

"Fine. I'm fine." She nuzzled her head into his chest.

"That actually wasn't so bad," I offered.

"Her comment about the banana leaves? Who cares if they're missing, they're decorative. And her implying the turkey was boring. And why does she seem to think I'm hiding a pregnancy from her?" Her voice rose in pitch as she spoke.

"Maybe she's just excited for the future—whatever you decide."

"Oh, we definitely will try for a kid," Elliot said, grinning down at my cousin, "It'll be great."

Mary snorted.

"I meant the kid part, not the trying part." He chuckled. "Go outside and have a cigarette."

She looked up at him. "Are you sure?"

"After the night you've had, I don't mind. And this way I can be sure you aren't actually hiding a pregnancy."

Mary laughed, and our lingering tension slid away. She and I slipped our shoes and jackets on and sat on the porch steps. The light was beginning to fade from the sky, and from the attached duplex next door, I could hear the sounds of clinking cutlery and loud storytelling.

"How much do you want to bet," she said as she sparked her lighter, "Mom is parked just down the street, and she'll run over here right now screaming at me about lung cancer?"

She took a drag and exhaled, and though she blew the smoke away from me, I took a big sniff to catch as much as I could. I hadn't smoked since I was a teenager, but there was something comforting about the smell of Mary's cigarettes. Maybe it reminded me of when we were first out in the world together.

I listened to the cigarette burning away, listened to her breathing. "If your mom can continue keeping her drinking under control, do you think you'd want to see her more? Build a relationship?"

"I don't know. She's always been good about knowing when she has to step back, and I know she goes to therapy. One thing I'll say for her is she worked hard for me after Dad left us. But she never cared about me as a person. She just wanted to have a perfect daughter hitting all the right milestones." She took another drag and let the smoke drift from her mouth. "Now it's too late."

It was my turn to fall silent. The moment Mary mentioned her parents' divorce, I regretted saying anything at all. The divorce happened after *Kuya*. Or, as I knew Mary felt, because of *Kuya*.

I wanted nothing more than to ignore our parents' existence. I just wanted me and my cousin and nothing else. Nothing that needed fixing.

"Do you think Cassandra's lucid dreaming plan is futile?" I asked instead.

"Not at all. It's the first thing that actually makes sense. Are you going to try it tonight?"

"Do you think I should?"

"No time like the present." She took one last puff of her cigarette, then stamped it out. "Wait here."

Mary went back inside the house and closed the door, and I heard her and Elliott talking. They didn't sound happy. After a few minutes, Mary came back out holding a duffel bag.

"I'm sleeping over," she said.

"What?"

"You need me there when you try what Cassandra wants you to try, even if you don't think so. So let's go."

"Don't you think I've been going to this doctor long enough?" Freya asked.

Dad sighed and twisted his hands on the steering wheel. Freya knew the question annoyed him, but she still asked every time.

"We have to see this psychiatrist until your bad dreams are under control. In case it's a more serious problem."

"But it's been two years. If I were going to snap, I would have done it by now."

Another sigh, then silence.

Freya leaned her forehead against the passenger window and let her gaze fall limply outside as Dad manoeuvred out of the medical centre's parking lot and into downtown. They were close to the marina, and as they approached, she forced herself to look at the water.

She still remembered every bit of the dream she had about Okanagan Lake. But the ripples she saw now were nothing but the wake patterns of small boats coming and going. Ogopogo wasn't going to appear. She shuddered anyway.

"So what did you talk about today?" Dad asked, clearing his throat.

"You know I can't tell you that," she said, harsher than she meant to.

"I know that. But are things okay? In general?"

"I think if I were about to pull a Columbine, they would have told you," she said, then winced. "I'm sorry."

But what could she tell him? Shit, she hadn't even told Marcelo, her psychiatrist, everything.

She was getting really good at reading Marcelo, understanding what he'd want to hear and what would make him frown. She liked talking to him. Their sessions always began with five minutes of small talk. They'd talk about movies, or the way Dad's photography side business was growing, or Marcelo would answer her questions about his daughter's experience starting high school.

Then he would ask about her day at school, or what she'd done last weekend, or how she was sleeping. Only then would they talk about her. But he always kept things relaxed, and he never forced her to talk about anything.

"I've been sleeping better," she finally said to Dad.

He turned the radio down. "Yeah?"

"I haven't had a nightmare in a year. That nighttime relaxation routine is... relaxing."

What she didn't tell him—and what she hadn't told Marcelo—was that she was still dreaming, only her dreams had changed. No more nightmares. But now and then she had dreams that left her feeling ill in the morning, with details so oddly specific they grabbed at her attention, even if she didn't remember them until later.

They turned off the main road and passed a block of houses, the old kind Freya really liked.

"When I moved from Winnipeg," Dad said, "this whole area was just fields. I was just a kid. There were barely any other Filipinos here. And when those houses were being built, I wrote a short story about a ghost in the construction site and everyone in my class loved it."

He turned the radio off. They pulled to a stop at the light a few minutes from their house.

"Do you ever dream about your mom?" he asked suddenly. It came out like his throat was trying to stop the words from escaping.

Taken by surprise, Freya's eyes pricked with tears. "Yes, sometimes. But nothing scary. Like, remember how she used to eat those gross pickled herring?"

He laughed. "You didn't like those? I loved them."

"Really? Even when she wrapped them around pickles?"

"Yeah, rollmops. You used to like them, I thought."

"I thought the name was funny. I hate rollmops and I hate pickled herring. I don't know why I dream about them."

"Well, now that you're twelve you might like it better. Little kid taste buds are more sensitive, you know. Maybe we can try it again, have some Norwegian food for Thanksgiving."

"Dad, no. You never have to buy pickled herring ever again."

Dad stiffened. The light turned green and his hands gripped the wheel as he hit the gas.

"I'm sorry," Freya said. "I didn't mean it. I definitely want to try it again. We should get some."

They turned up their street, and the turn signal sounded obscenely loud over the silence.

"It's later than I thought," Dad said as they got out of the car. "I have to call my publisher, and then I have to call that guy about the photography studio space he has for lease, and then I have to go pick up the new camera I ordered. Dinner will be ready in a couple hours, okay?"

A little while after Dad left, Freya was kicked off the internet by a phone call. It was her Aunt Judith.

"Mary wanted to talk to you," Aunt Judith said. "How are you doing?"

"I'm okay." She searched for something else she could say. When had they last spoken? Definitely not since Dad's book came out. "Grade Seven's pretty cool. School's going good."

"Going well. But I'm glad to hear that."

There was a silence.

"Is your father home?"

"No, he's gone to the camera store. Why? Did you want to talk to him?"

"Ah, no. I don't really have time to talk."

More silence. Freya wondered if she should fill it, volunteer something about how Dad was doing. He and Aunt Judith hadn't spoken in months. But she suddenly felt protective of him in a way she couldn't quite understand, and anyway, Aunt Judith was already passing the phone over to Mary.

"Hi, loser," Mary said, giggling.

Freya couldn't resist a laugh too. "Hi, uh, douchebag," she said, trying out something new.

"Ooh, what's that mean?"

"No idea. What's up?"

"Nothing. I'm bored."

"How's Grade Five? How's Toronto? Is it snowing yet? Is the military clearing it away?"

"No, that was in January! It doesn't snow here in October. I've been riding my bike everywhere. Yesterday it was so warm that I got to ride all the way to—"

Mary's voice became muffled, as if she were talking into her elbow. Freya shook her head, blinked quickly.

Mary pedals her bike down a city sidewalk, swerving around small puddles of brown, dirty water, her dark hair bouncing in a ponytail. Mary is walking out of a convenience store, tiny framed in the soaring doorway. The form of the building shifts size, colour. She slings a leg over her bike, and suddenly the bike too has changed, its movements are jerky, strangely undulating. It bucks. Mary is thrown, and when she lands her leg is shaped wrong. She is crying.

When Freya came back to herself, she was hunched over, one arm braced against the edge of the table. She sat upright and let out a long, shaky breath. So that was why she'd felt so weird this morning. She must have had another dream the night before, one that the conversation with Mary had brought back into focus.

"Mary, be careful on the bike. Actually, no. Don't ride it at all. At least not for a few days."

"Why? It's so nice out now!"

"Listen. Do you trust me?"

Something in Freya's voice must have made Mary pay attention. "Yes," she answered very quietly.

"I had a dream last night. You were riding your bike home from the convenience store and you fell off your bike and broke your leg."

"That's just a dream."

"It was just like the one I had just before my mom died."

"Shit, really?"

Freya continued. "It was telling me something. I know it sounds weird but you have to listen. Anyway, if I'm wrong, then you get to make fun of me for a year."

"I don't know."

"It was called Top Choice. The convenience store in my dream."

Mary was silent for so long that Freya thought they'd been disconnected.

"How do you know about that?" she said finally. "It opened on Monday. I haven't even been there yet."

"That proves I'm right, doesn't it?"

"That's freaky. Are you sure I didn't tell you?"

"Promise me you'll stay away for a while, okay? Just a few days."

"Okay... If you're sure."

Then Freya heard Aunt Judith in the background scolding Mary for just standing there and wasting money on long distance.

"I have to go," Mary said.

"Wait! Don't tell your mom about my—"

Click. The line went dead.

"So you're okay with all of this?" Mary asked. She'd been reading Cassandra's notes over and over since we'd gotten to my place, as if she might discover something obvious hidden deep in a sentence. She lowered the pages and absentmindedly chewed on a fingernail.

"As okay as I am about anything," I said. I reached across the couch and took one of the pages from her. "It says here that lucid dreaming is safe. It isn't like sleepwalking." I tapped my head. "Everything happens up here."

"I guess. Anyway, I'll be right here in case something goes wrong. Or do you think I need to be, like, coaching you somehow?"

"I don't see how you could."

"Okay. And this says you're supposed to recognize your personal dream signs, things that you only ever see or that only happen in your dreams. Do you have any of those?"

"If I look in a mirror, it tends to wake me up," I offered.

"Maybe you should avoid that one for now."

"Oh, and I dream a lot about taking baths or showers in public. Not in a sexy way or anything. More like, oh, someone's put a shower in the middle of a room, but okay. I also—" I stopped myself, remembering my first dream. Telling Mom about it. I cleared my throat and continued. "I also dream about jumping over fences."

Focused on her papers, Mary didn't seem to notice my hesitation. "That's good. Hopefully, you'll see one of those signs tonight. And then, once you notice it, you have to try to realize that you're in a dream. If you can do that, you should be able to control or influence the dream. You feel okay about that?"

"Yes, if you're here."

"And you've got a notebook, for that diary Cassandra wanted you to keep?"

"Right by my bed, with a pencil. Should I use a pen instead?"

"Don't get cute. This is important."

"I know, I know. I'm happy you're here. I hope Elliot isn't too annoyed about you staying over so often lately. What did you tell him?"

"I told him the truth. I didn't see any reason not to. The dishwasher will do most of the dinner cleanup. And he's worried about you too. He'll be fine. Now, go to bed."

I stood, not bothering to hide my laughter. Mary didn't need to worry about having children as long as she had me.

"You have everything you need?"

She held up Cassandra's stack of papers. "My light bedtime reading. Sweet dreams."

I hesitated in the doorway of my bedroom, waiting, as if for some sign. The lamp on my nightstand cast a low warm glow on the notebook and pencil next to it. My bed looked tidy and inviting. A book was waiting for me, propped up against the other pillow. All in all, it was a cozy scene.

I shut my door and crawled under the covers, stretching my legs out and feeling the cool sheets against my bare feet. I hoped Mary wouldn't do something silly like stay up all night to keep an ear out for me. Through the door, I heard her speaking to someone on the phone—Elliot, judging by her apologetic and explanatory tone. I felt guilty for being the cause of any argument, but I knew they would be okay. They always were. Even though they were so different, they understood each other. I made a mental note to send Elliot a thank-you gift—maybe a growler of his favourite beer from the small brewery in Guelph I know he doesn't get to visit very often.

I pulled my deck of tarot cards from my nightstand and shuffled through them. I didn't want to focus on any one of them, lest an unwanted message seep in. I just needed their comfort, their familiarity. Their possibility. Then I put the cards away and opened my book, quickly regretting that I'd chosen one so interesting. I flew through forty pages before I noticed the time. I sighed, and it was the loudest sound.

This was no way to fall asleep.

Maybe I should have asked Mary to bring one of Elliot's coding textbooks. One of the really dense ones about a programming language nobody uses anymore. He'd tried to explain one of them to me once after I expressed curiosity, but it was no use. His words just thunked against my brain and crumpled to my feet like wet tissues. I wished I could understand. It seemed so interesting—a new way of communication, using logic instead of sentences. Or maybe the logic was the sentence construction. The only thing that had stuck with me from Elliot's coding explanation was the if/then statement: if a condition is true, then execute a block of code.

All the context in every word, every gesture, all the if/then statements that only go one way.

Our individual contexts, memories shared or implanted.

Illuminated with no logic.

Our individual conditions that cannot be met.

Codes that cannot be executed.

A bright moonlight lay over everything, casting the sidewalks and houses in a dark grey-blue that I found soothing.

There was no sound save for the scuff of my sneakers.

I turned off the sidewalk and down a small alleyway lined by garages, the old-fashioned kind without remotes, you had to open them manually. I turned again and saw endless rows of low fences, some white, some natural wood, a long line of them cut off in a dense forest.

I knew my pursuer wasn't far behind me, but I felt neither fear nor panic. I felt like I had all the time in the world. I jogged over to the first fence and placed one hand on it, vaulting over it easily. I ran to the other side of the yard and leapt again. The next fence was slightly higher but just as easy to clear. All along the way to the forest, the fences grew increasingly higher, but I felt lighter and more buoyant with every leap, like each one might be my last.

I might never touch the ground again.

I did land, though, hard, after the last fence, sending a cloud of dust up around me. Crickets or cicadas, maybe both, made a din that suggested summer heat, but it was still dark, and a cool breeze made the ends of my hair graze my collarbone.

My pursuer was still there, but I knew they were lost, and I would have some time before I needed to run again. I could stop.

Wait.

The fences. This was a dream.

I turned to look behind me and saw the last fence I'd jumped over, looming tall above me. In front of me was the forest. Nothing had changed. I was still here. It had actually worked!

But then the trees of the forest began to grow waterlike, their colours running and bleeding together. I was losing the dream. Quickly—what did Cassandra's notes say to do in this situation? I began to feel the sensation of the pillow against my face.

In a panic, I focused on the trees and ran toward the forest. The colours strengthened. I tried leaping again, as if over one of the fences. Twigs brushed my shoulders.

I entered a house. Small, one room, brightly lit by the sun. A fireplace burned along one wall. There was a kitchen table, four chairs. At the table sat a woman. She was humming a song, but her voice sounded weird. Wrong. She turned to me and her face was skeletal. Lumpy outlines of bugs crawled under the skin. Her mouth contorted and her song turned into a metallic wail. Worms slithered from her hair, her dress, everywhere. They covered her face.

"Holy shit, Frey."

Mary pushed herself up into a sitting position, pulling a hand through her sleep-messy hair.

"I know. I wrote it down. I woke up right away and wrote everything down."

I sat next to her on the couch. Sunlight peeked in through the edges of the curtains. It had taken me hours to go back to sleep after I'd woken up and left the spectre of my mother in that small house. I was stunned—but strangely, not scared. The dream felt familiar. I'd been there before, walked through that territory so often over the past eighteen years. There was no fear for me there anymore.

"What do you think it means?" Mary asked.

"I don't know. Maybe nothing. But I actually had a lucid dream. I almost lost it for a second, but I was able to do it."

"You're right, that's good. A promising start." She gazed at me, considering. "Are you sure everything's fine?"

"Yes, completely fine. Dreams can't hurt me, remember? At least, not the ones I plan on having."

"Elliot and I are going on a hike this morning. Want to come? It'll probably be busy because of the holiday but it'd be good for you to stretch your legs."

I shook my head. "Thanks, but I've got a couple of shifts booked today. Busy is good. I need time to process last night, anyway."

Mary stood up, stretched, and made her way to the washroom with her overnight bag. As she showered, I switched on the kettle and stood at the kitchen counter, closing my eyes to start my usual systems check. Nausea: no. Dehydration: no. Aside from the obvious signs of a night spent in shallow sleep, I felt perfectly fine.

Mary left, promising to check in later. I made myself a quick breakfast and showered so I could at least appear energized for my first Oneira shift of the day. I saw a couple of names I recognized, and I sat and chatted happily with my webcam on.

After my third private reading, I logged back in to public chat and saw that Javi was online. I stifled a smile, almost forgetting I still had my camera on. Suddenly, all I wanted to do was tell him about my lucid dream. He was someone who would understand, really understand.

TaurusTarot [Moderator]: Hey. Want a reading?

One minute later, we were face to face again. Sort of. It was strange to see him through a computer monitor after having spent time with him in real life.

I turned on my mic and said hi.

"Oh, we're chatting normally today!" he said, smiling.

"I thought you might actually want a reading, since you have all these credits and you're lurking in my chat room."

He shrugged. "Sure. I've already had so many crappy tarot readings on this site. Why not?"

I started to shuffle my deck, trying not to take his review of Oneira personally. "It helps if you think of a question you want an answer to. You don't have to tell me. Just keep it in your mind."

He fell silent, apparently in thought, and I decided to pull a simple three-card spread, not assigning any card to any particular thing. I was curious what would come out.

When I laid the third card, I gasped.

"What is it?" he asked.

The reading was all Swords. Three, Five, and Ten. I held them up to the camera.

"It looks kinda cool."

"It's odd. I can't remember the last time a spread was all cards from the same suit."

Not only was it odd, it was sort of worrying. Swords cards pointed to change, obstacles, conflict.

"So are swords going to come flying in through my window now?" he said, laughing.

I didn't share his mirth. "The Three usually signifies a loss of some kind, or major upheaval. The Five is about disagreements and hostility. The Ten is unforeseen tragedy. Betrayal. What question were you thinking about?"

"I thought I didn't have to tell you."

"You don't. But whatever it is, it doesn't look good."

"Hey, aren't tarot readers supposed to put a positive spin on things?" He sounded genuinely concerned, and I immediately regretted how freely I'd spoken.

"You're right, I'm sorry. These cards in combination aren't great, but it's not hopeless. The Three, for example, tells us that this is a loss or setback that can be overcome. The Five can also signify competition, like at work."

I looked at the Ten. A figure laying facedown in the snow, pierced with ten swords, snowflakes falling through the night onto the body. A pool of blood. I shivered. Of course, there was no card that pointed to literal death, but I'd never liked this ten. It creeped me out. I decided to ignore it and slid it back into the pack.

"So what do you do for work?" I asked.

"I work at a language school in north Oakville. I teach English to new immigrants who are looking for work. And Spanish too, for the hell of it."

"In Oakville? So you don't live in Toronto?"

"No, I'm in Mississauga."

"Mississauga! I live even further west than that. Markland. So I actually could have dropped you off on my way home."

"Yes, how rude of you." He smirked. "No, it's okay. I drive to the STEP meetings sometimes, but usually I take the train. It's kind of relaxing on a Saturday. Anyway, I'd only known you for like two hours then."

Which was true, technically. But talking with him already felt natural. Like we'd been doing it forever.

"Can you call me? I think Cassandra emailed everyone my number." Technically I was on the clock, but I couldn't wait. I hoped either Carol wouldn't notice or my relatively spotless record would work in my favour.

Once I had him on the phone, I told him everything about the past couple of days, down to the banal little details. I told him about the CT scan, the surreal look of my scan images, lunch with Cassandra, how Shaun seemed so different away from the STEP meeting. I wasn't sure why I couldn't stop talking, but Javi seemed interested in all of it. I also told him about Cassandra's lucid dreaming plan and how the previous night's experiment had gone.

"So," I concluded, "I know I can do it. I'll need to practice more though."

"I wonder if those dream elements mean anything significant. What do you think that creepy woman in the house represented? Your inner self, maybe? Or the way you see yourself?"

I felt a jab in my gut. I had to remind myself that Javi had no idea about my mother or the dream I'd had when I was ten.

"Who knows," I said. "Anyway, I hope I haven't bored you with all of this."

"No, it's fun to talk about these things. I definitely don't get to talk about my real life with my students. Or most people, actually."

"I know what you mean."

I heard sadness in my voice, and I thought I heard it in his too. The same sadness—perhaps the same loneliness.

"Why don't we carpool to the meeting this week?" I said. "I'll pick you up. And next time you want to chat, just call or text me."

After Javi hung up, I decided to log off for a while. I had only been online for three hours, but I was feeling more tired than expected.

I thought again of my mother.

What of her was in me? I used to think I knew. I used to think I was as self-assured as her. Now I'm not so sure. But maybe neither was she.

So many of my memories were just of the two of us, or us with Dad. We were never a family of socializers. My grandparents came over now and then, and sometimes some of my parents' friends had dinner at our house, but generally it was just us. A complete unit. Maybe she would understand my apartment as my den, my ordered life. Maybe she would have encouraged me as I carved out a protected space for myself. Mom had always laughed and rolled her eyes at Dad's superstitions, the way he worried about inviting trouble by ignoring a sign or omen—but she'd never actually come out and said they weren't valid.

Maybe she'd be nervous at the prospect of me putting so much trust in STEP and people I barely knew, of how fast things were moving.

I almost called Dad. I actually picked up my phone and navigated to his name in my contacts list. I imagined what I would say. *Dad, tell me about Mom. Am I like her? What do I have that's hers?* We could reminisce, share memories of her, refine and correct each other's recollections. Maybe he could tell me stories I didn't know. Their first date, their first argument, their favourite places to visit.

But I couldn't do it. I wouldn't even know where to start.

The phone rang in my hand, and I jumped.

Mary. Of course.

"Hi," I said. "How was your hike?"

"Fine, fine. How are you doing?"

Her voice was so soothing, so familiar. I fell backwards into it.

"I'm okay." I told her about Javi and the conversation we'd just had.

"He was just hanging out in your chat waiting for you?"

"Maybe."

"You are so dense when it comes to men."

"I'm not! He was probably just waiting for someone familiar to talk to—I can't be the only one in the world who feels that way."

A sigh crackled down the line.

"Listen," she said, "I think I should come to the next meeting. I won't say anything, I promise. I just want to make sure these people are who they say they are."

I stifled a sigh of my own. She'd talked me into joining this group and now she'd decided she wanted to vet them?

The Five of Swords, still on my desk, caught my eye. I'd told Javi it was about disagreement—but I knew it was also about regrouping, picking your battles. I decided not to fight this one. After all, what had Mary always been but my protector, standing between me and the world?

Freya was going overboard, she knew it. But she couldn't help it. Mary hadn't been to Kelowna in four years, since Mom's funeral. Freya felt an extra sense of duty to make sure Mary had a good time on this visit.

She vacuumed every inch of their house—or, at least, all the places Mary was likely to go—and washed the extra linens twice even though they were brand new. She was triple-checking the contents of their pantry when Dad came out of his office for coffee.

"We have lots of food, honey," he said. "And guess what— Kelowna also has several fine grocery stores."

"What if she's hungry when she gets here? We won't want to get back in the car and drive to the store. And she'll be so tired. She's flying practically across the country!"

"Mary will like the food we have, I promise. I'm going to make kare-kare for dinner. That's her favourite, right? So it'll be fine. Unless you swept last night though. It's bad luck to sweep at night."

Mary was almost as tall as Freya was. Of course, Mary was twelve now. But Freya was still shocked at the girl, all arms and legs, who came rushing into her arms at the airport.

"When did you dye your hair?" Freya said, weaving a lock of green hair around her fingers.

Mary shrugged. "The other day. Mom didn't even notice."

Dad coughed and took Mary's suitcase from her. "How is your mother?"

"She's okay, I think. She got your email and said thank you."

He nodded, his mouth a tight line, and led the way to the parking garage.

Mary had never travelled on a plane by herself before, and Freya had never traveled on a plane at all, so there was a lot for them to discuss. With Mary around, things felt shockingly normal.

Once they left the airport, Dad became chatty, pointing out every small thing along the way, whether it was actually interesting or not. They drove up to Knox Mountain Park, stopped to look at Okanagan Lake, and almost started driving to Penticton before Freya reminded Dad that it was almost dinnertime.

After dinner, Freya and Mary finally had time to go and talk in Freya's room. Mary sat on a cot opposite Freya's bed, hugging her legs against her chest almost protectively. Despite how much Mary had grown, her mannerisms still reminded Freya so much of the way she was as a little kid. They were fourteen and twelve now. Childhood seemed like a different planet.

"So, listen," Freya said. "Are things really okay? I mean, with your parents and stuff."

It felt weird for her to be the one asking about personal issues instead of the other way around. But now that Mary was here and not limited by long-distance fees—and Aunt Judith in the other room—Freya wanted to know everything.

"It's not really that okay," Mary said in a small voice, and Freya almost regretted asking. "Dad was always working so much, and I kind of got used to him not being around a lot. But it was different when he left. Sometimes I think I'll never see him again."

"I'm sure you'll see him! He's your dad."

"My dad's not like your dad. He and Mom used to scream at each other so much. He didn't really love my mom like your dad loved your mom."

To Freya's surprise, memories appeared. Of the way her parents would brush a hand against an arm in conversation. The impenetrable little jokes and references they inserted into their everyday conversations. The way Dad used to smile at Mom.

It had been so long.

She and dad didn't even live in the same house anymore. The one they lived in now felt too new. She missed their old house, the basement studio, the cozy living room where they watched movies on Friday nights. Where she'd nestle between her parents on the couch, and when they snuck kisses over her head, she would loudly protest. And though they'd always laughed, she now regretted being such a stupid kid.

Freya's eyes welled up. She couldn't help crying and she couldn't stop, didn't want to stop.

Mary slid from her cot and hugged her as tightly as she could.

"I miss my mom," Freya said in a shuddery breath.

"I wish I knew her better."

"Me too. She would be so happy to see you now. We could all be here talking and—"

A roil of sudden anger stunned her. Why did her mother have to go but Mary's horrible dad got to stay? But she immediately felt guilty for thinking it, and let herself have some tears for that too.

Freya woke up the next day in a much better mood than when she'd fallen asleep in, and she gave Mary most of the credit. Now that she'd had a cry and a good night's sleep, she was excited to honour Mary's request to see their grandparents' old house.

"Do you really remember nothing about it?" she asked as they got off the bus.

Mary shook her head. "Bits of things. Grandma pinched my cheeks a lot and called me mestiza. She had a cat and it made me sneeze and it scratched me. That's it."

Suddenly, Mary stopped and began looking around, even though it was close to zero degrees and they were the only ones out walking.

"I need to tell you something," she said. "Before I left to come here, I read a bunch of stuff about people with abilities."

Freya shivered and made them walk faster. "You mean vekers," she said.

"Isn't that a rude thing to say? Anyways, just listen. I found out about a guy called Alan Y. In the seventies, he accidentally made some people catatonic, so they tested him like an animal and then locked him up somewhere. And he was just a kid. Have you heard of him?"

"God, yes. Dad rants about him sometimes."

"Why didn't you ever tell me about this?"

"Because it's scary and shitty."

Mary sighed. "I'm not ever going to let anything like that happen to you."

"Why do you think something would?"

"You had a dream that stopped me from breaking my leg."

"It was just a coincidence."

"Whatever. You know I know and you know I don't care. I mean, I care. But can we just talk about this normally?"

They walked in silence for a moment, Freya trying not to be annoyed that her little cousin had a point. "You don't even know if that dream would've come true," she said, trying not to sound bratty.

"Then maybe you should try finding out what's a regular dream and what's a special dream. Like, take notes or something."

It did sound like a good idea, Freya had to admit. The idea of learning more about her ability—and maybe finding a way to stop it. She slung an arm around her cousin's shoulder and smiled. "You're pretty smart for a little kid."

"Fuck off, I'm twelve!"

"You also swear too much for a little kid."

They'd turned off the main road and were now walking down the middle of a residential street, so lost in conversation that Freya almost walked them right past their destination. When she realized where they were, she stopped so suddenly her sneakers scraped against the pavement.

"Oh my god," she said.

"You're fucking kidding me," Mary added.

The house was completely gone. A skeleton stood in its place.

"I had no idea. Dad hasn't driven us past here in a long time."

Another house she couldn't go back to.

They stood in the middle of the sidewalk and stared in silence at the framing of the new house, bright against the grey winter sky.

On the bus back, Mary leaned against Freya's shoulder and looked out the window. Freya was amazed at how relaxed she was.

This was her life now. She was a veker, like the ones on the news. And a part of her had expected Mary to reject her, call her a freak, despite years of knowing about her ability. But her cousin hadn't.

Of course she hadn't. A strange feeling bloomed in Freya's stomach. This felt so normal. Sitting on a bus with her cousin. Talking about everything openly.

And when Mary went back home, all of that would be gone.

In the end, Mary's week-long visit felt like it only lasted a day. Freya rested her head against the passenger-side window on the drive home from the airport and watched the painted lines of the road blur by. She absentmindedly twisted a friendship bracelet around her wrist, one Mary had made her for Christmas. She'd chosen all of Freya's favourite colours.

"It was a good visit, wasn't it?" Dad asked quietly.

"We haven't had a real Christmas since Mom died," she said to the window.

"I know. And I'm sorry for that. Next year we'll start it back up again, okay? We can make a gingerbread house like we used to. Maybe we can start one or two new traditions too."

Freya turned to him and smiled. "That'd be nice."

"Do you want to have something special for dinner?" he asked. "Maybe we can pick up a pizza and rent a movie?"

"Yes! Bruce Lee?"

"Only if it's not *The Way of the Dragon* again. We've seen that one a million times."

"You're just afraid to do the Chuck Norris fight scene with me again. I always wipe the floor with you."

Dad burst out laughing, and Freya couldn't help laughing too. She was starting to look forward to hanging out with Dad tonight. Her only parent left alive.

"Listen," he suddenly said, turning up the radio. The mood in the car changed.

The news. That morning, in Detroit, a teenage boy with abilities had somehow caused an accident that killed a young child.

Dad swerved into the parking lot of an office building and stopped the car. They were the only ones there, parked crookedly across four spots. His fist was clenched against his thigh.

"A baby," he said shakily. "Why do they let vekers drive cars when they're so dangerous? They can hurt us."

Freya went numb. She didn't know what to say.

When the news switched to another clip, Dad muttered an apology and put the car in reverse.

For the rest of the drive, Freya remained numb to all but her own desperate thoughts. *Dad likes babies. He was sad because we'd just been talking about Mom. He's tired from Mary's visit. That's all.* Something shifted inside, the key to a lock she didn't know existed. She forced herself to look at it.

After the ease of Mary's visit, how openly they'd talked about her secret, Freya had forgotten how things actually were. It had taken Dad, of all people, to remind her that acceptance was a privilege not meant for her—and that she could never make it be otherwise.

My phone rang as I was eating lunch. Probably Mary again. I picked up my phone to answer and stopped when I stared at the word *Dad* on the screen. My finger hovered over the button to reject the call, but then I thought better of it.

It'd been a few days since my lucid dream, and the vision of Mom was still on my mind. As my heart slowed, I decided Dad calling now was a good omen. For what, I didn't know.

"What are you up to?" He sounded surprised that I'd answered.

"Just finishing lunch. What's up?"

"I was just sitting down to write and realized I hadn't spoken to you in a while."

I imagined Dad in the small house we'd moved into after Mom died. It was nine in the morning in Kelowna. His day would've just been starting. Where would he be writing? The two-person dining table? The writing desk in the living room that was too small? Maybe he'd turned my old bedroom into an office, put all of my stuff in storage.

"Did you get my email about having your car serviced?" he asked finally.

"Yeah, I did. I'm going to make an appointment this week."

"Because I worry about that car, you know. It was already old when you bought it."

"I'm taking good care of it, don't worry."

Another silence. As usual, we skimmed the surface, never talking about anything worth talking about.

Tell me your favourite memory about Mom.

"How was your Thanksgiving?" he asked.

"It was fine, I had dinner with Mary. Aunt Judith came too."

It was weird and sad but she's doing okay and she still talks about you. Don't you miss her?

"That's odd. I wonder if she wants something."

"I don't think so. She seemed good."

Why can't you just admit that you were maybe wrong to write about her?

"Anything new with you?"

"Not too much. Just getting ready for winter. Work is keeping me busy."

I can still predict the future through my dreams, Dad, and it's been getting out of control and I'm scared and Mary is scared and I found some other people like me and they're putting time and effort into figuring out what's happening to me. After I hang up with you, I'm going to get ready to drive to Toronto to meet with them.

"Good. Keeping busy is good. I've been busy too. I'm renting a new photography studio. Smaller, but that's okay. I've been writing more anyway. I can't tell you what my new novel is about, though, not yet. It's too new."

"Yeah, I understand."

Tell me something, any little thing. Tell me one character's name. Tell me if she's me. Tell me why I can't tell you anything.

"Well, I'll let you get back to your lunch, honey. It was nice to talk to you. Let me know if the car's okay after the servicing."

"I will. Love you. Bye."

I released my hand to gravity. During the call, my spine had gradually curved into a perfect C. As if I were curling down into myself, trying to escape into the hollowed-out space my body created in the air.

Javi lived in a pale-brick townhouse just off a wide, quiet road in Mississauga, a few hundred metres from a large park that seemed to stretch all the way to Lake Ontario. The small gas station near his house was the only sign of any commercial activity around. I'd heard how boring and uniform the Toronto suburbs were, but I was surprised at how comfortable I felt there.

Javi greeted me at the front door. "You're on time!"

"You're surprised?"

"No, just pleased. Where's your cousin?"

I blinked at him before remembering that I'd asked him if Mary could come to the meeting. She was already in Toronto, catching up with an old colleague, but he didn't need to know that. "She's going to meet us there," I said.

"Come in for one second. I just need to grab something."

He jogged up the stairs and I took the opportunity to look around. The floors were dark wood, and down the hall past the staircase I could see through to the kitchen, where a sliding glass door gave a view of a bright backyard and a decent-sized silver maple tree. To my right was a room I guessed to be the living room. I couldn't resist a peek through its doorway: a white-brick fireplace, a low grey couch, and a wall of built-in bookcases absolutely loaded with books.

Javi came back down the stairs in a rhythmic foot pattern.

"Sorry," he said, "I'm one of those people who always misplaces his wallet. Found it." He held it up triumphantly.

"It gave me a chance to drool with envy," I said, pointing to the bookcases.

"Oh yeah, my life's work, that collection. Feel free to borrow anything you like! First editions don't leave this house, but anything else you can sign out."

"What, seriously? Like a public library?"

"Yes. I did say it's my life's work." A small grin tugged up one corner of his mouth.

"Fair enough. Shall we?"

When we got to my car, Javi had to push the seat almost all the way back to accommodate his long legs. I pulled out of his street and made my way back onto the highway. I suddenly felt very awkward.

"That's a cool-looking park across the street," I said, breaking the silence.

"I'm there all the time. It's great. So close to the lake."

"Is it easy for you to get to work from here?"

"It's not bad. From here to the north of Oakville is fine. The worst is driving in Toronto. Jaywalkers and cars trying to cut you off at the same time." He shook his head. "I grew up here and I like it better. Much quieter. Markland like that too?"

"A little. It's not as big as Mississauga but it seems more like a real city." I winced. I didn't mean to sound so judgmental.

He snorted. "Just you wait. Haven't you noticed how many aging Toronto hipsters are moving to Markland lately?"

"I have. I hope it doesn't change the city too much. I like that people kind of leave you to do your own thing. I like my own space and my own routines."

I realized I couldn't drive and maintain a secret identity at the same time—I was starting to reveal too much about myself again. Best to just keep him talking instead. "I've been meaning to ask. Last week you told me that your family always knew what you could do. What's that like?"

"It's shown up in my extended family before, in Colombia. I'm definitely not the first. When my skill first appeared, I thought I was dying. But my Colombian family stepped in. They were ready with a list of resources and names and favours to call in."

"Resources like what?"

"I went to a specialist in Ottawa my aunt had heard about. My parents moved us there for six months because of it. From him I learned more about what I could do and how to control it. But I hated it for so long. My family treated me like I was some amazing genius. Over-invested in my progress. I just wanted to play video games and read and be normal. It wasn't until I met Cassandra that I stopped being a bitter little prick about it."

He trailed off and looked out the window. Traffic was beginning to slow. Should I turn on the radio? Talk about something else? What did people talk about? But before I could say or do anything, he continued.

"It's an odd thing, this ability to identify people like us. There aren't many of us in the world, let alone Canada. Sometimes I go so long without picking up on anyone else that I wonder if we're all dying off. It can get lonely. I think that's why I like to gather the paradextrous around me."

Now that I'd found STEP, something was sliding into place that I hadn't known was loose to begin with. "I hope we aren't," I said. "Dying off."

For the first time, I was relieved that Mary wasn't in the car listening to all of this. I was learning about Javi in bits and pieces, and I didn't want it rushed or interrupted. And for all her good intentions, my cousin could act like a suspicious television detective.

We drove on, mostly in silence, though now and then one of us would make a comment on our surroundings: the garish billboards on the Gardiner Expressway. A new condo building under construction. A dog in the back of the car ahead of us.

Shortly after we exited onto the Don Valley Parkway, Javi gripped his knees tightly. He closed his eyes and began breathing deeply.

"Javi? What's wrong?" I asked, suddenly panicking, looking for a good place to pull over.

"No, no, it's okay," he said, opening his eyes. "It's just her. In that car." He jerked a thumb over his shoulder at the car matching our speed to our right.

I snuck a couple of quick glances at the driver, a young woman singing along loudly to her radio.

"She has a skill. A strong one. She feels too intense. Feels like an earthquake under my skin."

I slowed down to let the car pass, then changed lanes. Javi seemed to revive, so for the next few minutes I focused on keeping distance between our cars until we had to exit onto Bayview.

"Do you always react like that?" I asked when the coast was clear.

"Most of the time. But I usually handle it better. Whatever skill she has, it's powerful. I really felt like my skin was rippling or something."

"You looked solid to me. Hey, should we have followed her? To, I don't know, recruit her or something? You were just talking about how you like to have paradextrous people around you. And she was cute."

He snorted. "No. It's okay. Not everyone's meant to be found." He went back to looking out the window, and I left him to his thoughts until we got to Cassandra's house.

Mary's jacket was already hanging in the closet when we went to remove our coats and shoes. I took a deep breath before going into the living room. Sure enough, my cousin was on the couch, making pleasant conversation with Cassandra.

"Hi, Fr–ances," she said when she saw me, quickly recovering from her screw up. I was suddenly glad I'd chosen a fake name so close to my real one. At the same time, I realized I didn't know if Mary had planned on using a fake name herself.

"Mary's one of us now!" Cassandra said brightly. "We've been having a great time."

I settled in on the couch next to Mary. Javi shook her hand and sat in the chair to my right. He seemed back to his regular self.

Mary glanced at Javi and raised an eyebrow at me. I ignored it and reached over to pour myself some tea.

"Now that you both are here," Cassandra said, "we can start. Shaun's running a bit late, but that's not unusual."

I hadn't realized that I was looking forward to seeing Shaun again. But then Cassandra turned to me, and I pushed the disappointment from my head.

"I thought we could start with you, Frances. Mary tells us you did some lucid dreaming work this week?"

I reached into my purse, pulled out my dream notebook, and passed it to Cassandra. She opened it and began reading immediately.

"This is great! I can't believe you could do it on the first try. Your synapses must be gorgeous." She sighed wistfully, as if my synapses were something I could show off, like a necklace. "Were you able to do it again?"

"Not since that first time."

"Well, keep at it. I'd like you to eventually be lucid during your prophetic dreams too."

"You think I can do that?"

"I don't think you can't."

She handed me the notebook and I slid it back in my purse.

Cassandra turned to Mary. "I hope this isn't too weird for you."

Mary took a big swallow of her tea. "No, not at all. I've known what Frances can do since we were kids."

"That's good, that's so important. The more people we have around us who we can trust, the more we can work at finding ways to thrive in this world we live in. The one that sometimes hates us."

"Frances tells me your group provides coping strategies," Mary said. "How does that work, exactly?"

"Sometimes we help when people's skills develop beyond their control or comfort zone, like with your cousin. Sometimes we give real-world advice on living in so-called normal society, where doing everyday things can be difficult for them. Sometimes people just want to talk. Or listen. Some people will drop in and not say a word."

"How do you know you can trust those people?"

"How do we know we can trust anybody?" Javi replied quietly, as if to himself.

Mary kept asking questions. "Has anybody threatened any of you? Anybody not paradextrous, I mean."

"People do things to us all the time," Cassandra said, "but if you mean violence—ask Shaun. It's not my story to tell."

She frowned down at her cup, and my heart twisted. Poor Shaun—I suddenly wanted him to be sitting with us, as if I could somehow protect him.

"Do you ever wonder if things would have been different if Alan Y had never happened?" I asked. "Before him, vekers weren't such a huge thing. We weren't targets."

"I don't think it's entirely helpful to wonder things like that," Cassandra answered after a brief silence. "Even if the entire world did accept us, many of us would still lead very difficult lives. The things our brains can do can be hard to manage."

I thought of what Javi had told me of his childhood, about how, in his family, he was respected. People like us were positive aberrations, as Shaun had put it. I had to admit, the idea of respect, maybe even admiration, was starting to sound pretty good to me.

Maybe we shouldn't settle for acceptance.

As if on cue, the front door opened and Shaun called a hello from the foyer. I had to work hard at stopping a grin from crossing my face.

He came around the corner and settled down on the free chair next to Mary. His gaze crossed quickly from her to me, as if he knew we were related.

"Mary," I said, "meet Shaun. Shaun, this is my cousin Mary."

They shook hands and Shaun beamed. "It's so cool that you're here, Mary. Do you have a skill too?"

"Nope, just here for support," Mary said, turning to me at the exact moment I happened to catch Shaun's eye. Mary missed nothing, and I knew she would ask me about it later. I could have kicked myself for framing our coffee date as a mere hangout.

"Sorry I was late. I got a call when I was about to leave," Shaun said to Cassandra. "Remember that Dutch advocacy group I talked about at the last meeting? The one that was trying to get their government to treat the paradextrous like human beings and not put them on a registry?"

"The one we can't publicly support, yes," she said warily.

"I contacted a journalist through a mutual friend and we had a little chat. She has a news site that's very interested in an interview, but they want more people involved than just me. So I told her I'd talk to you all."

"Did you tell this journalist about STEP?"

"Well, of course. Otherwise I'd come across as some lone zealot," he said, smiling affably. "Don't worry, even if no one else here participates, I'll make it clear my views are my own and we're not making an official statement of support."

She squeezed her eyes shut for a second. "You've never spoken to a journalist before, have you? They follow up on everything."

His expression wilted slightly. "Just mentioning we exist isn't going to hurt. I mean, we have a website."

"Which we don't publicize for a reason. Having our name attached to an article like this might damage our ability to help people. If they think we're going around publicly discussing things they've spent their whole lives trying to hide, they might never contact us in the first place. Or the publicity might encourage people with toxic motives to infiltrate us. It's already happened once. I don't want it to happen again."

Shaun flopped back against the chair, arms folded. "I don't see why I can't talk to the journalist on my own. If this is just an informal social group, why do I need to ask permission?"

Cassandra sighed and put on a smile that had no life in it. Her next words came out heavily. "You don't. All I'm asking is to leave the group out of it. And to be careful. You don't know what life this story will take on after it's published."

I stared into my cup and remained silent. I sympathized with Shaun, but I also felt solidarity with Cassandra. They both had good points. I was also struck by the fact they were discussing paradextrous issues openly and frankly, the way others would discuss an election at a family dinner. It wasn't harmonious, but neither was it threatening, or loud, or violent. I'd never in my life encountered conversations like this, about people like me. With people like me.

I'd been looking forward to this meeting all week in a way I hadn't looked forward to a social event in, what, years? I'd even started to feel protective of the others, nervous about what Mary would think of them. Maybe there was something to take seriously here, ideas and beliefs to stand up for.

But not today, not yet. Until I knew exactly how I felt, it'd be foolish to try to stand up for anything.

Freya snapped out of her brain fog when she saw the bus slide to a stop at the corner. She broke into a run, flying through the door just as it started to close. But as she opened her wallet, her feeling of victory quickly evaporated.

She'd forgotten her bus pass at home.

Her high school was a forty-five minute walk away. She'd definitely be late if she missed this bus. She flicked frantically through the zippered pocket of her wallet but she couldn't find the right coins.

"Here, I've got it."

A hand reached across her and dropped the correct change into the fare box.

"Thank you," Freya said.

Her rescuer was Ashley, who sat next to her in music class. She was recorder, Freya was flute. They'd bonded over the hand-trembling levels of nerves they both suffered during practice. Freya had been very grateful when they became friends. Until that point, she'd been feeling unlucky at making new high school friends.

Freya followed Ashley to a seat, trying not to trip over the elderly ladies with their foldable shopping carts. "I'm sorry, I totally assumed I had my pass. Let me give you some money. I have, like, a bunch of fives."

Ashley shook her head and waved Freya's wallet away with a laugh. "It's okay, really."

But Freya insisted, and when they got to school, she ran into the cafeteria to buy Ashley a cookie.

"I hope today goes fast," Ashley said as Freya paid for their cookies. "My family's going to Victoria for spring break. I love it there."

"I've never been there. I'd love to go one day," Freya said.

At one of the tables was a group of Ashley's friends. Freya only knew them a little bit, mostly they'd just said hi, but this time, one of the girls—Freya recognized her from English class—spoke to her.

"So are you pissed," the girl said, leaning in to drop her voice, "that they didn't put your dad's last book in the course?"

"I think Freya's probably tired of talking about it, Brittany," Ashley said.

"No, it's okay," Freya lied.

One of the other girls flashed a smile that was more like a baring of teeth and said, "It's too bad, you could have helped me get an A on it!"

"I'm glad we don't have to read it," another girl said, rolling her eyes. "My mom read it and said it was shallow. Even though there's a veker in it."

"Ew, really?" Brittany said. "Now I want to read it. Is it like a horror novel?"

"No, it's only mentioned. You never see them do anything scary."

"Don't be rude, you guys," Ashley said. "Freya's dad wouldn't be famous if his books were shitty."

Freya pretended to brush a cookie crumb from her shirt, letting her hair fall down in front of her face. She was waiting for Ashley to continue and say "We shouldn't make fun of vekers because they're human beings just like us," but of course she didn't.

A girl at the other end of the table, who'd sat quietly through the whole exchange, gave Freya a sympathetic look.

"It must be so cool to have a writer for a dad," she said. "Is he like really artistic? Does he say cool things all the time?"

Freya almost laughed. Dad? Say cool things?

But this was her chance to fit in—maybe there was something she could stretch the truth about. So she told them about his strict writing rules, how she wasn't allowed to bother him unless her arm was literally falling off. She didn't mention that it had been years since those rules actually applied, and since Mom died he'd been focusing more on his photography business—but why would she tell those parts? It was fun to have these girls turning to her, excited to hear about her life.

She was just about to tell them he was working on a new book when, suddenly, a vision memory came to her.

Ashley sits in her usual spot in music class. The chair next to her, Freya's chair, is empty. Every other seat is filled with people she knows from school. The girls from the cafeteria, a handful of other acquaintances.

Then Freya is in her seat. She can no longer see the others in the room, but she can hear them, a susurrus of whispers. She feels their eyes on her, probing.

Ashley's voice is loudest now, mocking and jeering.

Freya gripped the edge of the table. She stood clumsily, barely hearing Ashley ask if she was okay, and hurried into the washroom across the hall. She didn't know if anyone else was in there but she didn't care, she had to get to a stall. She barely managed to sit down and lock the door.

Moments later, there is a knocking at her stall.

"Are you okay? Did you barf?" It was Ashley, sounding concerned. Ashley, who'd paid her bus fare and chatted with her happily all morning. Ashley, her first real high school friend.

Ashley, who Freya had dreamt would betray her.

It felt so sure, so true.

She was nauseated, a bit woozy.

The bell rang. Ashley knocked again.

"Do you want me to get the nurse or something?"

The concern in Ashley's voice was genuine, and Freya almost stood up and walked out to her.

But then she remembered Ashley's silence during the talk about vekers.

Maybe Ashley didn't want to make a scene. Maybe she didn't know the other girls well enough to say anything. Maybe she'd been waiting for Freya to say something. Or someone else to say something.

But none of those other girls were her friend. It didn't matter what the other girls thought of vekers, but Ashley's silence was deafening.

As urgently as that thought came, another one formed quietly in its wake.

Could she trust Ashley?

How much could someone be Freya's friend if they didn't know or respect the most fundamental thing about her? How much would she have to lie, to rearrange and obscure, to be accepted by people like Ashley?

She put her face in her hands. She was suddenly exhausted.

"I'm okay, Ashley. Really. It's just cramps. Don't be late for class just because of me."

"You sure?"

Freya leaned her elbows on her knees, hugged her arms.

"Yes."

After a moment, Ashley shuffled away, and Freya heard the click of the door closing behind her.

"So which guy do you have a thing going with?" Mary whispered to me as we waited to get our jackets from Cassandra's closet.

"Seriously? Shut up," I hissed.

There was no way he could have overheard, but Shaun grinned at me as he went out the door.

"Need a ride home, Mary?" I asked.

"Please," she said, nodding back at Javi in the living room. "If I'm not going to be a third wheel."

"Stop."

We shrugged into our jackets, said our goodbyes to Cassandra, and filed out into the crisp afternoon. Shaun was waiting on the porch. He hung back so he could walk next to me.

"I'm glad you came," he said with a very disarming grin. "And I'm glad you brought your cousin too. I mean, it's good to see her supporting you."

"Thanks. And thanks." I wanted to say something meaningful, tell him I was glad to see him or show him somehow that I sympathized with him. Instead, I deliberated until we got to the sidewalk and then I just stood there. In the end, the smoothest line I could muster was to offer him a ride home too.

"Thanks, but I need to think about some things and the subway is good for that. Besides, I don't want to distract the driver." And then he actually *winked* at me and walked away.

I watched him for a moment, until I realized I couldn't sense Javi and Mary near me anymore. When I caught up, they were in the middle of discussing Shaun and his interview. Javi was cautiously diplomatic. Mary seemed unfazed by Shaun—to my relief—and appeared to approve of the group in general. She, like Elliot, wasn't one for polite lies. If she didn't like something about STEP, Javi would be getting grilled about it right now.

I sighed out my relief. I didn't know what I'd have done if Mary came out of the meeting angry. I'd only been to two meetings and one extracurricular outing, but I was already getting used to life with STEP.

The two of them continued chattering in the car as we made our way to the highway, discussing newly discovered common interests such as dogs, Alice Munro, and the quiet of living outside of Toronto. I remained silent, monitoring Mary's questions for *This is my cousin's potential love interest* fishing that I would have to nip in the bud.

During a lull in the conversation, Javi twisted around to look back at Mary, then looked back at me. "Are you two at all Filipino?"

Mary caught my eye in the rear-view mirror. I took that as permission to tell as much truth as I felt comfortable doing. If book-loving Javi somehow suspected who I really was, it certainly would have come out by now, and not by him beating so far around the bush by asking us about our cultural heritage. Admitting I was half-Filipino wouldn't make him jump up and cry "A-ha! Brian Tanangco's daughter using a fake name!"

"We're both half Filipino. How could you tell?"

"I had a lot of Filipino friends growing up. I had a feeling."

"Javi's family is Colombian," I explained to Mary. "Maybe we have a shared distant ancestor from Spain and he recognizes us as long-lost family." I leaned on the word *family*, hoping it would throw Mary off any suspicion about romantic interest.

"Lebanese-Colombian, actually," Javi corrected. "And it'd have to be a very distant ancestor. The Philippines was colonized for, what, three hundred years?"

"Long enough for Tagalog to be heavily influenced by Spanish," I said.

"Trabaho!" Mary offered.

"All I can think of are food words," I whined. "Pandesal. Leche flan."

"Chicharon!" Mary called out.

Javi snorted. "I've tasted Filipino chicharon and, I'm sorry, but Colombian chicharrón is so much better."

"No way!" I cried, my culinary patriotism wounded.

"Have you ever had Colombian chicharrón?"

I said nothing, and Mary laughed. "She hasn't, but that won't change her mind. Freya—nces loves Filipino food."

There was a beat of silence, and I stared daggers at Mary's alarmed reflection in the rear-view mirror. Excuses, fast. Maybe a childhood nickname? Maybe when Mary was a baby she couldn't pronounce *Frances* properly and it stuck. I could invent a story as I went along. It would be the most believable lie.

Javi changed the subject before I could say anything. "I remember some of my Filipino friends telling stories about old men who live underground. Have you heard about this?"

"Yeah," I pivoted. "Nuno sa punso. They curse you if you disrupt their little earth-mound homes or trample through their territory. You have to let nuno know you're there first. You say 'tabi tabi po, nuno!' when walking through a forest. I know nuno aren't real, but I always feel a little anxious if I don't say the thing when I'm in a forest."

"That's interesting. My family has its own superstitions. Have you ever heard of the Boraro?"

For the rest of the drive to Mississauga, Javi regaled us with tales of legendary Colombian creatures. Mary and I reacted appropriately at the right times, but I sensed her growing more tense as the conversation continued.

When he was safely dropped off and inside his house, Mary slid into the vacated passenger seat. She began apologizing frantically before she'd even put on her seatbelt.

"You helped me come up with Frances!" I cried. "We chose it because it's easy to remember. Freyances? There's no way he didn't notice that! And now he knows I'm half Filipino. He's probably Googling me right now. If he figures out who my dad is, he'll know everything about our family. I bet he has all my dad's books! He has a ridiculous personal library."

"I know, I know. I feel like an asshole. I'm sorry. I really am."

After a few minutes of silence, during which I considered the repercussions of just pushing her out of the car at the closest GO train station, I accepted her apology. "But we—no, you—are going to have to come up with a plan for if Javi puts two and two together."

"Okay," she said quietly. Then, only slightly louder, she said, "I really like everyone there, Frey. I think it's really helping you already."

I sighed, felt a sliver of my anger peel off.

"I think so too. I think it's the best thing you've ever forced me to do. That's why we can't fuck this up."

"What about that one?" Freya said, pointing at a boy coming out of their high school building.

"He's too short," Erin replied.

"He's not short! Anyway, I don't like really tall guys. What about that one?"

"The one trying to skateboard across the field? His hair's too swoopy."

Freya couldn't help but giggle at Erin's hair judgment. Much as she hated to admit it, her friend was right.

She leaned back on her elbows, feeling the grass sharp against her skin. Lifted her face to the sun, closed her eyes. It wouldn't be warm for much longer. It was nearly October and the late afternoon sky was darker than she liked for the time of day.

Erin sparked her lighter, took a long drag of a cigarette. "I'm so bored of the boys in our grade," she said. "They're all the same."

"Maybe you should try the next grade up."

"Ugh. Forget it. I'll just stop having sex this year until I figure it out."

Her eyes still closed, Freya lifted an arm and gestured for the cigarette. The tip was gross and wet from Erin's mouth, but she ignored it and inhaled. She wanted to change the subject. She had no idea what to say when Erin talked like that. Freya was sixteen and had never had a boyfriend. She felt like a child.

A shadow passed in front of the sun.

"You really shouldn't smoke," someone said.

Freya opened her eyes to the silhouette standing over her. She squinted, could just barely make out his features. Once she recognized him, she sat up straighter. "You're the new kid. Boy. New boy," she sputtered.

"I'm Connor. Hi."

It was a dream. Or so it felt. The fluid way he folded his legs underneath him on the grass in front of her. The way he completely ignored Erin.

"Hi. I'm Freya."

"I know." The corner of his mouth lifted briefly.

Freya began to fiddle with the grass. They were silent for so long that Erin got the hint, took back her cigarette and left with a pointed "Call me later, Freya."

Freya looked up and met his eyes. He spoke but she heard nothing. She smiled.

"But *where* in the Philippines is his family from?" Dad asked for the third time.

And for the third time Freya spat out an exasperated, "I don't know!" She slammed the kitchen cupboard harder than she meant to. She was starting to regret inviting Connor over for dinner. It had seemed like such a good idea at the time. They'd been dating for four whole months, practically a lifetime. Why not have him come over? It was surely what mature adults did.

But Dad was being so intense about everything. Too interested.

Could he somehow tell that she wasn't a virgin anymore? She had an image of Dad opening the door and punching Connor straight in the nose. She shuddered. What had she done?

She wished she had enough time to run to her room and look through Mom's tarot cards. Pull one at random. Maybe it would be lucky.

A knock at the door—too late! Suddenly, Connor was in their foyer, slipping his shoes off. Then Dad was there with a gigantic grin, already vigorously shaking Connor's hand.

Freya had to admit, he hadn't looked so happy in a while.

She hurried over to Connor and hugged him. It was a terse, short hug, and he was careful to not touch her any lower than her shoulders. She didn't blame him—she could feel Dad's stare on her back.

But then Connor sniffed the air and asked Dad, "Is that kare-kare cooking?" and Freya thought Dad was about to knock her over to hug Connor himself.

Freya learned more about Connor over dinner than she had in the past four months. He was happy to answer Dad's incessant questions. Were you born here? Yes. Where were your parents from? Cavite City. When did they come to Canada? Dad in 1979, Mom in 1981. Have you ever been to the Philippines? Twice, when I was one and when I was eleven. Did you like it? Yes but it was too hot. Do you know any Tagalog? Only a few words but I understand more than I speak. What food do your parents cook? A lot of adobo and sinigang and pancit canton. What do they do? They're both tax lawyers.

Why had Freya never asked him these things? When they were together, they talked about their friends, kids who weren't their friends, their classes, music, movies, the world, the future. But never their pasts.

Dad was exuberant. He even sighed happily at Connor's mention of pancit canton, when Freya knew that Dad would have thrown pancit canton out the window. He was a pancit bihon guy through and through—he preferred the thinner rice noodles over the canton's thicker wheat noodles.

"When's the last time you went to the Philippines?" Connor asked around a mouthful of food.

Dad's face fell slightly.

He'd moved to Canada when he was a baby. He had no childhood memories of the Philippines. But he told Freya Filipino stories and cooked Filipino food as if he remembered. She'd always assumed he was mimicking what his parents had done. But looking at his expression now, she wondered: *what if he'd always been trying to construct the Philippines as much as she was?* She'd always felt a bit of an outsider, trying to understand being Norwegian and Filipino and Canadian all at once, split in three but wound together, not exactly knowing where she fit in. She'd never considered the same might be true for Dad. What if he felt too Filipino to be Canadian and too Canadian to be Filipino?

"Not since I was about your age," he said. "One big trip before university. There was no real reason to go. My parents were here and eventually so much of my family had moved to the States. I'd love to go back again. My wife and I had talked about taking Freya but life kept getting in the way. Maybe one day soon we'll go, eh?"

He reached over and squeezed Freya's hand. His face was open in a way she hadn't seen in years. She knew he wished he could have shown Mom the Philippines, all the places that he only remembered as a visitor.

After a moment, Dad frowned, then cleared his throat and stood. "Connor, why don't we all go to see my studio? It's not far."

Freya sighed as she watched Connor buzz around, examining Dad's lights and cameras as if they were covered in gold. How did Dad know Connor cared about photography so much? She certainly hadn't. Maybe Dad could sense it, some sort of sixth sense shared between full Filipinos. *Fullapinos*. The thought made her chuckle and she opened her mouth to tell Dad—it was the sort of corny pun he loved.

But Dad was busy explaining the features of one of his fancy new DSLRs to Connor, so she remained silent.

There was actually a sparkle in his eye as he spoke. When was the last time he'd looked this happy with her? What did they normally do together? Sometimes they went out to dinner, sometimes they went to a movie. They talked. But what did they talk about—really talk about?

Last year was Dad's fortieth birthday, and she'd gotten him a tie because she didn't know what else to do—even though she couldn't remember the last time he'd worn one.

Something twisted inside her.

"Come here," Dad said, waving her over. "Let's show Connor what we do."

Her stomach dropped. "Dad, no," she pleaded.

For a second his lips tightened. Then he smiled the way he did on TV. "It'll be fun!"

The studio was still set up from the studying photoshoot they'd done last week. He guided her to the wooden chair set up behind the rickety old desk, and as she sat, she prayed to nobody and everybody that Dad wouldn't tell Connor how he'd found the desk in front of a neighbour's house, where it was waiting to be brought to the dump.

"Okay, sit there and pretend to read that textbook." He fiddled with one of the lights in the corner, adjusting it in some precise way that only he could really see. When Dad's back was turned, Connor grinned at her, made a lewd expression she couldn't help laughing at.

"Your light's there, honey," Dad said. "Now, read. Look studious."

"Freya's very studious normally," Connor said as Dad's camera clicked. "We spend a lot of time studying. Together."

Dad didn't react. He was so focused that he didn't hear, or chose to ignore, Connor's tone. In any case, Connor stopped talking altogether, and his interest in Dad's work returned. He was more focused than she'd ever seen him.

Freya tried to remember if Connor had ever said anything about Dad's writing, his small fame. He hadn't. He'd never seemed the slightest bit interested in Dad's books, or showed he'd even heard of the scandal they'd been caught up in.

Her shoulders relaxed slightly.

"I have an idea," Dad said, straightening. With his camera still in his hand, he gestured. "Why don't you two move the table over there, and grab that little couch and move it to where the table was. Then you can pretend to study together."

They did, and for the first time since Freya was seven, she was not the only subject in Dad's photographs. He arranged everything: the way they sat, the way they held their books, and of course the position of their heads. Pointedly, he kept their legs and hands from touching.

As Dad spun around them with his camera, Connor offered suggestions to improve the photo. He instinctively found the light. Freya sat still, contained within herself, watching as if at a distance.

When she and Dad took Connor back to his place later, nobody noticed that she'd been mostly silent the whole time. She was an outsider.

Months later, when she found out Dad had gotten permission from Connor's parents to sell one of the photos, and that he was going to do so without asking Freya, even though she and Connor had long since broken up, she was surprised at how little she was surprised.

Someone had installed a showerhead right over my bed. I stood up on the soft mattress and reached up to turn the shower on, and only then realized there was no shower curtain.

And I wasn't alone.

My friend and all of her other party guests were milling about the bed, holding glasses of wine, making conversation. They would all see me.

I looked down at my hands. They weren't right. Blurry, staticky, like my eyes couldn't render them. The dreaming brain can't process hands correctly, my lucid dreaming research said. Of course. I was in a dream—and that meant I could start to take control.

I hopped off the bed and approached the anonymous woman I'd been thinking of as my friend. I circled her. She was talking with someone who was just as much a stranger to me as anyone else here. I moved around the room. At random, I approached one man who looked near seventy and had a kind face. He was nodding politely as he listened to a woman who towered over him. He didn't notice me. Slowly, tentatively, I reached out a finger and gave him an exploratory poke on the shoulder. My fingertip made a dent in the green knitted fabric of his sweater. He felt solid, but I didn't get a sense of warm or cold from the touch. Interesting. I tried a pinch.

He whipped his head around and glared at me. "Can you stop that, please? How rude!"

I jerked backwards. Holy shit, a dream-person was interacting with me! And then I was relieved to note that my shock didn't wake me up.

"Do you know where the cheese is?" I asked.

"Outside," he said, pointing at a wall.

I walked. The wall slipped away and I stood in Cassandra's living room. It was bright, and the details of her house—the foyer, the staircase up to the second floor, the dining room—were blurred and indistinct. I turned in a slow circle, taking everything in, then sat down next to Shaun on the couch.

"Hey," I said.

"Hey," he said, smiling. I reached out to brush the hair away from his forehead.

"You can't read my emotions through dreams, can you?" I asked.

"No. I have to ask for permission, remember?"

"Because you have a code of honour."

"A hero's code of honour."

When he kissed me, it felt soft and warm and real. The weight of his body leaning into me, pressing me into the couch.

I opened my eyes to sunlight.

Goddammit, brain!

I could still feel the ghost of the kiss. I slowly turned my head to look at the other half of my bed, even though I knew I'd find it empty, and decided not to include any of this in my dream journal.

It was a decent enough time to get up. What day was it? I had to think. Wednesday. My days since the last STEP meeting had been fairly quotidian, and they bled into each other.

I threw on some clothes and went out for coffee, shivering as a cool wind drifted around my neck. I should have brought a scarf. Nearly the end of October already. Why did I feel so unsettled? I'd never been one to put much importance in the passing of years. The dull blur of days meant safety.

I pulled my collar closer around my throat. Maybe I was thawing to the idea of a community, of having another way to pass or preserve time.

Halfway home from the coffeeshop, my pocket hummed. I fished out my phone, saw *Shaun Wyatt*, and nearly flung my coffee into the road.

Hey, how are you doing? Do you want to try that first date thing? Still no pressure. :)

Alone on the sidewalk, I relived the full feeling of last night's dream. I did want to try that first date thing. Why not? It didn't have to mean anything, much as I wanted it to. His looks aside, there was something compelling about Shaun that I couldn't put my finger on. I wanted to find out what.

I forced myself to stroll home and calmly take off my shoes and jacket before I allowed myself to reply in agreement. His response came nearly right away:

> Great! Is late afternoon too short notice? I can come to where you are if you like.

This afternoon. Come to where I am. I stood up and looked around my apartment. No. Absolutely not. It was too soon and my space too... me.

> Late afternoon's fine, I replied. I know a park in Mississauga if you don't mind the weather. So you don't have to drive all the way to Markland.

I waited on a park bench by Javi's place. It was cold so close to Lake Ontario. Why hadn't I suggested a different park, or somewhere indoors, where I didn't have to pretend I wasn't freezing to death?

From my vantage point by the parking lot I soon saw Shaun emerge from a car and I waved, hopefully not too eagerly. His eyes glinted when he sat down next to me. He was wearing a navy zip-up cardigan, which was opened to reveal what looked like a T-shirt underneath. Compared to me, nestled in my scarf like a bird, he seemed perfectly temperate.

"I'm glad I brought you this," he said, handing me a paper cup. "It's tea. Earl Grey. That okay?"

"Perfect, thank you." I took the cup and sipped gratefully. "I need this. I'm not used to this weather. I grew up in BC."

"Oh? Which part?"

Shit. Why did I keep fucking up the alter ego thing?

"Tofino." It was the furthest city from Kelowna that I could think of.

"Never been there."

Good. I hadn't been either and was woefully underprepared to discuss Tofino with someone who was actually familiar with the place.

We sat silently for a minute, sipping our drinks.

"Was your drive okay?" I asked just as he said, "Lovely parking lot view." We laughed. Right now he was acting almost as shy as I felt, and in a strange way it relaxed me. Like we were on even footing.

I suggested we take a walk closer to the lake, and we silently made our way down a path. The park was loud with babies crying, dogs barking. A few leaves still clung to their branches.

"So, did you have that interview with the journalist yet?" I asked.

"What? Oh, that. No, not yet. It's been postponed for a little bit. Scheduling conflicts or something." He paused. "I hope your cousin doesn't think I'm a weirdo or anything. If you're introducing me to the family already, I should make a good first impression."

Okay, so much for his shyness.

A V of Canada geese squawked across the sky. Even though I'd brought it up, I wanted to move away from the interview, talk about something less macro. So I began telling him about my lucid dreaming experiments.

"And I, uh, you were in the dream too," I found myself saying before I could stop my thoughts.

He stopped in his tracks and looked at me. "Really," he said, a grin forming.

Why had I said that?

I kept walking and he followed me.

"Not in that way," I lied. "You were just there, and we said hi to each other, and then I woke up."

"Oh, that's boring. I'm sorry Dream Me is so boring."

When we reached the shore, we split off the trail to stand on the boulders along the water's edge. We sipped our drinks quietly again, watching the wind play on the water, like an invisible hand lightly kneading soft dough. I focused on the feeling of him there next to me, his shoulder nearly touching mine. Imagined his steady and even breathing.

"You should try lucid dreaming," I said. "I think you'd like it. It's not as difficult as I'd thought it would be. Rules are different in dreams. Things move around and people come and go and it all makes a strange kind of sense. And in my lucid dreams I get to live in that weird reality. It's like I'm on a different planet."

"Maybe in our dreams we really do go to another realm or something. One where we can live as weirdly or as normally as we like." He turned to me. "Do you feel like it's changed you as a person? This new kind of dreaming, it must have special significance for you, of all people."

A gust of wind picked my hair up and I adjusted my posture, maybe subtly trying to give Shaun a favourable view of the Freya I tried to imagine I was—the strong Freya who could see the future and weave the course of fate.

"I don't know," I told him honestly. "I haven't had time to think about that aspect of it."

"You seem different today than you did the first time we met."

"How's that?"

"You were kind of guarded, maybe even on edge. Today you seem more relaxed. I'd like to take the credit for that but I feel like it has to be something else."

"Well, I was nervous that first meeting. I didn't know anyone."

"I know, but even accounting for that, I see a difference. Maybe it's the lucid dreaming. It's good. I bet this will help you control your skill. Maybe it already is."

"Why do you say skill? I've always thought of it as an ability."

"Look at it this way: an ability is something innate, but a skill is something that you work to master. You understand a skill, you control it."

"Is it an official term?"

"No. We just kind of started using it. It may have been me, actually, who started it. Maybe it's minor, but these kinds of things are important to me—the words we use."

We moved on back along the path. A cyclist zipped past us too close, forcing Shaun to move a step closer to me. The bike moved on but he stayed where he was.

"You're different too," I said. "You seemed stressed that day."

He chuckled. "Yeah, I know. I'm sorry. I can get carried away."

"Do you think it's related to your abi—your skill?"

"How do you mean?"

"You can tune into people's emotions."

"So you're remembering things about me, are you?"

I smiled. "Maybe your skill increases your own emotional state, or sensitivity, or something."

"I don't know. I was always a pretty emotional kid, even before I discovered my skill. Not in a bratty way or anything, but—okay, here's a good example. My parents tried to get me starter pets, like goldfish and things like that, but I always cried for hours when they inevitably died, so no more pets for me." He fell silent for a moment, drumming a finger on the cardboard sleeve of his cup. "I've never thought of that before, the idea that our natures somehow relate to our skill. That's interesting. What about you? Are you a dreamer, naturally?"

"Maybe a little. Or at least, I was. When I was a kid I read a lot. But I also liked concrete things. Building lightsabers out of paper towel tubes, that kind of thing."

"And then who did you fight with?"

"Myself. I'm an only child."

As I looked over at him, I stumbled on a root sticking up from the path. Shaun grabbed my arm to steady me.

"You okay?"

We were the same height, which I liked. I preferred being on the same level as people. When I looked into his eyes, I remembered everything about last night's dream. My gaze flicked down to his lips. Despite his grip, I felt a bit like I was falling backwards. I leaned closer.

Rapid footsteps approached us on the path. Javi stopped next to us with a surprised, "Hey!"

Shaun released me and took a small step back.

"Hey, man," Shaun said. "What are you doing here?"

"I live nearby. I finished work early so I thought I'd go for a run." Sure enough, he was dressed in running gear. "What are you doing here?"

I wanted to disintegrate into dust. Why had I suggested this park?

"We were enjoying a lovely walk along the lake," Shaun said, stepping closer to me again.

Javi looked at him, then at me. "Okay, well have fun. See you Saturday."

We watched him jog away and my stomach sank. I hadn't been able to read his tone at all.

"Did you know he lived around here?" Shaun asked.

"We carpooled to last week's meeting. I remembered this park from when I drove by. I thought it looked neat."

Shaun took my arm and looped it through his own, so our elbows were linked like a proper old-fashioned courting couple. "Why don't we have an early dinner somewhere? I'll drive."

We found a quiet Vietnamese restaurant nearby and chatted over noodles and cup after cup of tea. The restaurant was so small and empty that to me it seemed like our voices rang off the walls, but I didn't mind at all.

It was amazing how different Shaun was compared to the way he was at my first STEP meeting. I decided that though he had been a little brusque, and maybe not the most polite, he hadn't been outright rude. His was just a different personality from Javi's or Cassandra's. And today, he'd shown at least some awareness of how he could come across. To me, that counted for a lot.

After all, I was no sparkling jewel myself. Maybe we were all fucked up, us paradextrous people. Even Javi and Cassandra. Maybe this was what a lifetime of being outsiders did to us.

As we lingered over our tea, Shaun rested his hand against mine, and I let him. This was a rite of belonging—one I finally deserved.

When Rosalie's, a new Filipino restaurant, opened in Kelowna in January, Dad immediately decided he didn't want to try it until after his new book was published in May. A new Filipino restaurant and he of all people wanted to put off eating there for months. Freya couldn't understand it.

Rosalie's was very small. When they first walked in, the front door nearly smacked into a display of Filipino grocery items for sale: soft pandesal buns, packets of spice mixes for kare-kare and afritada and caldereta, bags of Nagaraya cracker nuts—the garlic ones were Freya's favourite. There were even some Filipino cookbooks, likely for the benefit of any non-Filipino customers who might wander in.

A woman smiled at them from behind a one-sided buffet area where several trays of food steamed promisingly. It smelled incredible.

Dad's grin faded slightly as the woman happily greeted him in a flurry of Tagalog. "Oh, kumusta," he said. "I don't know much Tagalog. Patawad."

And with the unfailing chumminess of every older Filipino Freya had ever met, the woman didn't care.

"You have no accent!" she exclaimed, switching to English. "Were you born here?"

"No, actually, I was born in the Philippines. Manila. I moved here with my parents when I was a baby."

"And they didn't teach you any Tagalog?" She shook her head, but her judgement was that of a teasing aunt. "But it's okay. In Canada, it's better that way. Your parents were right to do it." She reached over the sneeze guard to shake his hand. "My name is Rosalie, like the restaurant."

She beamed with pride, and Freya couldn't help but be charmed by her phrasing, the sweetness of it. As if she loved her restaurant so much she'd named herself after it, instead of the other way around.

"I'm Brian. This is my daughter Freya. She's eighteen, and she'll be starting university in the fall."

The woman's gaze fell upon Freya like lightning, and for a brief second, Freya wondered if she had momentarily transformed into the Nordic goddess Freya. Freya the Elegant and Terrible.

Rosalie clasped her hands to her cheeks, then came around to their side of the counter and clasped her hands to Freya's cheeks. "So beautiful! Your skin is so light and your hair is so light. Mestiza?"

Freya nodded against her hands, warm and soft. The fawning over lighter skin both irritated her and made her miss her grandmother.

"Her mother was Norwegian. She passed away eight years ago." Dad's voice was tight.

Rosalie gave Freya a squeeze on the shoulder, then without a word, hugged Dad. Just like that. He'd barely had enough time to register what had happened before she was back around the open end of the buffet. But his smile had returned.

They stepped forward to consider the trays of steaming food. There were only a few dishes she could identify by sight alone. Adobo, of course, and kare-kare. Lumpia and pancit canton. There was a handwritten list of the names of each dish, but she wasn't sure which name corresponded to which dish, or sometimes what a dish even was. There was a tray full of noodles that she wondered about. Was it a kind of pancit? It had the same sort of rice noodles as pancit bihon, but a thick yellow-orange sauce that she'd never seen on Dad's pancit, as well as shrimp, boiled egg, and what looked like fish flakes. She wanted to ask him about it, but Rosalie was talking to him again.

"I live in Vernon," she was saying, "but I wanted to open the restaurant here because it's a bigger town. Do you know Jun Mendoza or Fern Mag-Iba? They come in here all the time."

"No, I don't know them. I know—" he paused, and Freya could see the gears in his brain working, "—Esther and Dennis Alinea."

Freya bit down a smirk. Dad had met Connor's parents once, and had definitely not spoken to them since Connor and Freya had broken up two years earlier.

Rosalie nodded, waited for more. There was no more. She smiled again and pointed at the tray Freya was considering. "Pancit palabok," she said. "It's noodles with ground pork and shrimp sauce. Pancit is traditional Filipino noodles."

Freya looked up at her. "Thank you. Dad makes pancit all the time, but he makes pancit bihon usually. I'll have the palabok, please."

Dad looked at Freya, proud, grateful. "Same for me please."

As they walked to the small seating area with their trays, Dad said, "I've never had this before, actually."

They ate in silence for a few minutes. Freya wasn't sure if she liked the pancit palabok. It was too rich, too saucy, at least compared to Dad's bihon, which he'd spent years perfecting. Still, she felt pleased as she looked around at the small restaurant, at the wooden knife and fork hanging on the wall next to them, the paintings of palm trees and mountains, the photograph of women in bright yellow dresses performing a folk dance.

"What's that called again?" she asked Dad, gesturing to the photograph. "That dance they're doing."

Dad had shown her videos online once. Two people kneel on the ground facing each other, each holding a long bamboo pole. They tap and slide the poles rhythmically and rapidly, while barefoot people dance, stepping and turning between the poles before they can clap their ankles. She'd always thought of it like double dutch, but more badass.

His expression softened and he said in a quiet voice. "Tinikling. My lola used to do that."

He turned back to his meal and chewed, frowning a little.

Freya wasn't sure why his mood had shifted, so she tried to change the topic to something more cheerful. She held up her can of Coke.

"Congratulations again on your book, Dad."

He looked up, and when he clunked his can against hers, he didn't smile. Why was he sad?

"What's wrong?" she asked.

"You didn't read the *Globe and Mail* review, did you?"

Freya shook her head. With only one more month left of high school, she'd been spending all her time worrying about university applications and daydreaming about life in Calgary or Toronto or Vancouver. She realized, with a ripple of shame, that she hadn't even thought about looking at the reviews of Dad's book.

He sighed. He pulled out his wallet and handed her a folded-up newspaper page from inside. The headline read: *Tanangco's overly ambitious new work falls short.*

Freya couldn't help but wince.

She remembered him telling her a bit about *Alphabet for the Nameless* while he was working on it. It was the first time he'd tried to cross genres, blending elements of fantasy with historical fiction. The parts she'd read were good.

But apparently not good enough.

Why was Dad keeping this in his wallet? She tried to hand it back to him but he shook his head and shoved more pancit in his mouth. She read. The reviewer sounded like he'd been personally attacked by Dad's new novel.

"That's not the only one," Dad said. "They're all like that. Did you read the part where he said I've gotten too cocky from my prior fame?"

"He said perhaps," Freya offered weakly. She knew the look on Dad's face. Her shred of optimism wouldn't land.

He shook his head. "Writers are supposed to grow and experiment. We create, that's what we do. But I guess people don't want that. They want us to write the same book over and over."

"What does Sheila say?" She'd only met Dad's agent a couple of times, but he was always talking about how level-headed she was.

"She said that the interviews the publicist lined up proves that people care. But I know this novel isn't selling as well as *Kuya* did. Or even *Only Soaring* before that." He twirled his fork into his noodles dejectedly.

Freya wanted to say something comforting but found herself coming to another shameful realization: she was actually pleased that the book wasn't doing well. It meant no reporters hanging around. No phone ringing off the hook. It meant the world would leave them alone. She hated seeing Dad so wounded, but the feeling of relief wouldn't go away.

They left the restaurant in silence, offering only the most polite "Salamat po!" to Rosalie as they filed past. Freya fiddled with the radio on the way home, trying to dial in some uplifting music. Dad drove in silence.

At home, Freya noticed a large envelope sticking out of the mailbox. She ran up the porch steps and plucked it out.

"It's from the University of Toronto," she whispered. She was trembling. She wanted to barf.

"Open it, open it!"

She did, sending scraps of torn paper cascading to the ground.

"Dear Ms. Tanangco," she read, "Congratulations! It is our pleasure to welcome you—Dad, holy shit, I got in! I got into U of T!"

She screamed and pumped her feet up and down in rapid movements. She felt like she could have danced tinikling blindfolded. Dad squeezed her hands, tears filling his eyes. He pulled her tight to him, crushing the envelope between them. She couldn't breathe but she didn't care.

Toronto.

Next year Freya would be moving to Toronto.

She'd never been further east than Winnipeg. She felt dizzy.

"I wish your mother was here," Dad said, his voice shaking. "I really wish your mother was here."

"Sorry again for the junk," Shaun said as we got back into his car. "I wasn't expecting to have visitors in here or I would have cleaned up a little."

As we drove back to where I'd left my car at the park, I couldn't help twisting around to investigate the books strewn across the back, amidst the parking meter receipts and reusable shopping bags. I stretched to pick up a book off the ground behind Shaun's seat.

"Somehow I didn't take you for a science fiction type," I said, examining the cover.

"I love it. That author in particular is great. She subverts a lot of typical sci-fi stereotypes. And I like the way she explores political themes. It's not overbearing."

"I read one of her stories once and I thought it was just okay. Maybe I should give her another shot."

"Borrow that one, I've finished it. I think you'll like it."

"I don't need to sign it out or anything?"

He shot me a confused look as he pulled up to a red light. "Sign it out?"

"Javi has people sign his books out."

Shaun snorted. "Typical Javi."

"You don't get along?"

"I wouldn't say that. We're fine. I like him. I just wouldn't really spend any one-on-one time with him. I have no idea what we'd talk about."

We turned into the park. It had rained during the couple of hours we were at dinner, and my car was speckled with fat drops of water that glinted in the streetlights.

"Well, thanks for the lift," I said, and immediately felt awkward.

"No problem. I mean, it was my pleasure. It was nice."

"Yeah."

He leaned back against his headrest, and watched me with those damned eyes again, the streetlight's golden glow highlighting those damned cheekbones. Before I could even think about what I was doing, I reached out to brush his hair back off his forehead. He smiled, lifting one corner of his mouth, and leaned toward me.

A little shock went through me. The kiss was exactly like it had been in my dream. The feel of his lips, his tongue, even the smell of his hair.

He grinned broadly afterwards, and it was so genuine, so sweet and lacking in any flirtatiousness, that I could have kissed him again.

"See you Saturday?" I asked.

"Promise. Text me when you get home so I know you got back safely?" He was still smiling, holding one of my hands.

"I will."

I got out of the car with a huge stupid grin on my face. I couldn't remember the last time I'd felt so young—I felt like a sixteen year old. I had to suppress a giggle as I waved to him.

He turned out of the lot, and I found myself next to my car just staring at nothing. I shook myself out of my reverie and dug around in my purse for my keys.

"Frances!"

Javi, no longer in running gear, stood on the sidewalk holding a shopping bag bursting with goodies from the local Mac's.

"You again?" I called back. "Are you stalking me?"

"I'm not the one in your neighbourhood," he said, laughing as he walked over.

"But you keep popping up," I said.

"Yeah, weird how that happens. My skill isn't a tracking device, though that would be more interesting." He held up the bag. "I have this terrible habit of eating junk food after a run. It somehow tastes better. Have you been here this whole time?"

"No, Shaun and I went for an early dinner. Nice Vietnamese place further down Lakeshore."

"I know it. It's very good. Ooh, what's that?" He pointed at the book in my hand, and I showed him the cover. "This is a good one. Have you gotten to the part yet where the—"

"No, don't tell me! I don't know anything about it. Shaun just lent it to me."

"Fair enough. Hey, I've got some more books you might be interested in, if you want to come over and take a look. We're literally just down the street. I'd feel rude not inviting you in."

Wait.

My memory kicked at me: the ride back from the last meeting. Mary screwing up my name in the car. My fear that Javi now knew who I was.

Was I walking into a confrontation? Once inside his house, would I find newspaper clippings of my father all over the walls, pictures of me circled in red pen?

I shook my head. I'd been living in the dream world too long. Javi was acting the same way toward me now that he had the day we met. There was absolutely no proof he knew anything.

"Sure," I said, finally finding my keys.

"I apologize for the mess," he said as he unlocked his front door. "I wasn't expecting visitors."

"That's exactly what Shaun said about his car," I said as I slid my shoes off.

Javi flicked on some lights and considered me. "How long have you guys been dating?"

"That was only our first date. I mean, our second."

"Wow, you don't even know how many dates you've been on. He must be the one."

I sputtered out a laugh. "Our first one kind of evolved into a date as it was happening. It wasn't a set thing."

We went into his library and I became momentarily distracted by the books. Now that I had more time to look, I relished it. Tall white bookcases lined one entire wall, small LED light fixtures dotting the tops. The shelves held a mixture of hardcovers and paperbacks, the books all looked pristine, and some looked expensive. They weren't organized by surname, as I was expecting. The order seemed to follow no logic at all, and groups of books by the same author weren't alphabetized. How they were organized was something I couldn't really parse at a glance.

"Genre first, then chronology, then last name," Javi said.

I turned to him, my mouth hanging open. "Are you kidding?"

"You keep thinking I joke about my books."

Javi excused himself to put his food away in the kitchen, giving me a few minutes to lose myself in the shelves. I wandered over to what appeared to be the fiction section and, instinctively, let my gaze go straight to the Ts.

Shit. Javi had two of my father's books. The one about my family, *Kuya*, and *Alphabet for the Nameless*. The last one. *Alphabet* was ten years old now, and any anticipation for Dad's next novel had largely died down in that time.

I crouched down, slid *Alphabet* from its spot, and flipped through the first few pages.

I stopped at the dedication page, worried I'd see my name.

To Camilla, alive in my heart.

I shivered. I'd forgotten he'd dedicated it to Mom.

Alive in my heart.

Next I turned to my dad's bio. A mention of a daughter but no name. Good. This one, at least, was safe.

I let my gaze drift to what I had been trying to avoid. My father, ten years younger, looked back at me in black and white, eyes just like mine. His chin lifted almost defiantly as he gazed at the camera, an expression that reminded me so much of Mary. How long had it been since I'd even looked at a picture of my father?

"Cool," Javi said, making me jump. "Brian Tanangco."

"Fan of his?" I croaked, my throat dry.

"Somewhat. I only have two of his books. One of them is so controversial I feel guilty for owning it." He pointed at *Kuya* on the shelf. "Do you know it?"

Unable to breathe, I merely nodded.

"The one you're holding came after and it's very different. Like he's trying to start over. I'd be interested to see how he carries on from it, but he hasn't written anything in years. Anyway, you should read that one! I like it."

"Sure," I said. "Thanks."

He proudly gestured to a small notebook on a shelf. It was the famous sign-out book. On the first available line I put the date, the book, and my name, focusing harder than I'd ever focused before to write *Frances Tully*.

"I hope I didn't make things awkward for you," he said.

"What?" I looked up at him, dropping the pen. *Did* he know about me after all?

"When I ran into you and Shaun earlier," he said.

"Oh, no. No, it was fine."

"Honestly, you two looked more comfortable together than I would have expected. He doesn't give the greatest first impression."

I chuckled. "He'd say the same about you."

"Was he gossiping about me?"

"No, nothing like that. I just get the sense that you aren't best friends or anything."

He shrugged. "I try. I like him. I usually agree with him. We don't always agree on methods, that's all. I can't really fault him though. It wasn't all that long ago but I remember being twenty-five, thinking I had all the answers."

He sat on the couch in front of the window, and I sat too, placing my dad's book gently between us.

"Wanna know something weird? I had a dream about him last night and it sort of came true today."

"Is it dirty?" He held up his hands.

I laughed. "No, I promise it's not. I think it was a lucid dream."

I gave him a brief rundown, not shying away from the kissing part but also not going into detail.

"That's great," he said, grinning. "Was that the first time you were able to control your dream?"

"It was. It was exciting. But it also felt strangely normal. Like I could always do it."

"So Cassandra was right when she suspected it could help you."

"I have a lot more work to do but this small step feels fantastic."

I folded one leg under myself and turned to look out the window behind us. Past the black wrought-iron fence that separated the townhouse complex from the street, cars zoomed by on Lakeshore Drive, their lights illuminating the still-damp road, their tires hissing as they slid across. A teenage girl came down the sidewalk with a dog almost bigger than her. A woman whom I took to be the girl's mother walked next to her, their heads bent in conversation. Through the closed window I could hear the girl laugh loudly.

"Javi," I said, and my voice sounded to me as if it came from far away. "I told you once that my mom and I sometimes do tarot readings for each other. I lied. My mom died a long time ago. When I was ten, I dreamed that she was dead. And a few days later, she was."

Why had I told him?

"I'm sorry," he said, after a moment.

I looked at him and waited for the expression of pity, the almost condescending pat on the hand that usually followed the news that I had lost my mother at a young age. But it didn't happen. He was sad, and I could see that, but he was also looking at me evenly, waiting for me to continue.

So I did. Leaving out any identifying details, I told him about the dream, Mom's injury, her death. How scared I'd been, how alone I'd felt. And then I told him the truth about my first lucid dream. "You remember the woman in the cabin? With the bugs? That was my mother. How she looked when I had my first vision of her."

"Fuck. And I made some stupid armchair psychoanalysis comment about her being, what, your inner self or something? I'm so sorry."

"It's okay, you didn't know. Nobody knows about my first dream, actually, except Mary and her boyfriend."

"Not your dad?"

"No, he—no, I never told him. Nothing about this. We're not close. And he has some very strong opinions against the paradextrous. Among other things. I didn't have the support for my skill like you did growing up. I'm figuring it out as I go along, and I'm probably making mistakes."

"Trust me, I'm a rare case. Most people I talk to hide what they can do. The ones who come forward are—well, you know what can happen to us. Sometimes I'm the first one they ever admit the truth to. That's part of the reason Cassandra started the group. For people like you."

I fiddled with the corner of Dad's book.

"Are you hungry?" Javi asked. "I know you already had dinner, but I can't stop thinking about the chips I bought."

"Are you sure? I've already taken up too much of your time."

"No, don't be silly. Come on."

He stood up and motioned for me to follow him into the living room. It was long and narrow, with little room for more than a couch, a coffee table, and a TV in the corner.

"The one tradeoff for the library," he explained. "This is actually the dining room, but I hardly dine, as you can see. The sacrifice is worth it for the books."

Laid out in front of us was an impressive selection of junk food, all of my favourite garbage—even Dr. Pepper, which I'd always felt was woefully underappreciated. Javi ducked into his kitchen, clanged around a bit, and came back with a plate of pita wedges and a bowl of what looked like a soft, smooth cream cheese drizzled with olive oil.

"Labneh," he said. "It's my favourite Lebanese food. You can think of it like a yogurt cheese, but all that means is it's yogurt with the whey drained out. I mixed in some dried mint earlier but it's also great with garlic."

Under Javi's expectant gaze, I scooped up a small amount with a pita chip.

"Well?" he said. "What do you think?"

"It's so good!"

I immediately went in for another scoop without thinking to ask Javi how he felt about double-dipping. The labneh was cold, smooth, light and fresh from the mint, with a hint of sour. It tasted familiar yet enticingly different at the same time.

"I'm so glad you like it. To accept labneh is to accept me." He grinned and sat down. "Want to watch something? There's a good show I've been watching. I've only seen two episodes, though, so I don't mind starting over."

I nodded and he started the show. It was a Swedish police procedural, dark and gritty but very compelling. I settled in and we watched, silent save for the crunching of chips. When the first episode ended, I put down my glass and turned to him. My reaction to the program must have been clear on my face because he immediately started the next episode.

The episode opens with one of the police detectives entering a bar. She sits down in front of the bartender and orders a drink. She stares into her glass when it's put in front of her. A man approaches her and she turns her back to him. She downs her drink, orders another. She has long, blond hair cascading in a straight line down her back. Her eyes are blue and clear. The camera focuses on her and the lighting changes. Now she's speaking in English. Her hair is short and black. Her eyes are brown. Her skin is a light brown. She looks older.

"Hello, Judith," someone says.

My aunt replies, then drinks from her glass. She drinks more. She slurs her words, gets angry.

I slowly turned to look at Javi. His face was glowing from the TV. He looked at me and spoke but his voice was underwater. I looked back at the TV. My aunt was still there, laughing shrilly despite the displeased looks from the people around her.

I looked down at my hands. Blood was rushing in my ears. Black spots encroached on the edges of my vision. I took a deep breath. *This isn't real*, I thought, or said out loud, I didn't know. I stood up slowly, setting my glass down unevenly on the coffee table, and walked out of the room.

I had a memory of being able to wake myself up from nightmares by looking in a mirror. The closet in Javi's foyer had a mirrored door. I went to it shakily and faced my reflection. My face was distorted, my features blurred.

I felt a jerk inside and then I was looking at my normal face again. A bit startled, but clear. Awake. My heart was racing. I put one hand on the door to steady myself, leaving streaks of potato chip grease on the mirror.

"Frances? Are you okay?" I hadn't noticed Javi's hand on my elbow.

"I think so," I said, exhaling. "I just had a hallucination. There wasn't a Filipino woman in that bar scene, was there?"

He let go of my arm. "No. You look spooked as hell."

We went back to his living room and sat down. The show was still on. I wiped my hands on my jeans and took a shaky drink of water.

"I knew it was happening," I said. "It was so weird. It felt exactly like a lucid dream, but I was awake the whole time. My glass was in my hand, then I put it down on the table. I knew that I was in your house and that we were watching TV."

"You had one of your waking visions."

"Yeah, kind of like that."

"Wow." He fell silent for a moment, lost in thought. "I guess we're even then."

"What do you mean?"

"Remember my little freakout in your car? Thank you, by the way. I felt very exposed but you were really cool about it."

It did feel appropriate that he'd seen me vulnerable the same way I'd seen him vulnerable. In a strange way, the thought comforted me.

"What do you think it means, seeing that woman in the bar?" he continued.

I sighed. "It was my aunt, Mary's mom. She's an alcoholic in recovery. But I saw her drinking. Drinking a lot."

"Maybe it's not necessarily prophetic. Maybe it's just a coincidence, like your dream about Shaun. Your subconscious inserting something you may have been thinking about."

"Could be. I saw her on Thanksgiving for the first time in a long time, so she's been on my mind a bit. I don't know. My visions can often be banal, but these waking ones feel different."

"Significant," he said, nodding with certainty. "What are you going to do?"

"I feel like I have to tell Mary. Maybe she could check in with her mom, get someone to keep an eye on her." I looked at him. "What do you think?"

"I've only spent a short amount of time with Mary but I think she'd appreciate the heads-up. Especially because she knows that these things aren't usually nothing, right?"

"Yeah," I said, rubbing my face. I wasn't looking forward to that conversation. How would I even approach it? How long did I have? I felt like I needed a week alone with all my curtains closed before I could even start to process this.

"Are you sure you're okay?"

"I'm fine, see?" I grabbed a handful of chips and shoved them into my mouth.

His expression brightened, then he looked away for a moment, tapping his fingers on his knee. "So, listen. I wanted to say this earlier, after I saw you and Shaun in the park. I really don't want to offend you because I consider you a friend. But—just be careful."

"Why?"

He sighed and leaned back against the arm of the couch. The TV detectives shouting in Swedish provided an odd sort of contrast to the mood in the room.

"Last year, he told Cassandra it was becoming difficult for him to be so exposed to people's emotions, and he wondered if she knew of anyone who could help him. She spent a few days asking around and going through past research projects she'd worked on. But she couldn't do anything for him. He kept pressing her to do more and she got frustrated and told him to get over it."

"Oh," I said. "Not good."

"Not good, no. But Shaun was just hounding her about it. She apologized, but he's never seemed to forget it. He even visited Dr. Day and demanded to know Cassandra's credentials. It really embarrassed her, and spooked Dr. Day too. The doctor isn't exactly doing these scans with the full approval of the College of Physicians and Surgeons, you know, and he thought Shaun was some kind of journalist. It took Cassandra a while to repair the damage Shaun did between her and Dr. Day. I'm not saying don't trust Shaun. Just keep your feet on the ground with him."

I stood up. "I should go," I said.

He stood too. "I hope I haven't pissed you off."

"No, it's not that. I need to go home and figure out what the hell I'm going to say to Mary. Besides, I've eaten so much of your food already. The labneh especially. I think I ate most of it!"

"No worries, it's really easy to make. If you want the full Javier Nasr experience, I need to make you some real Colombian chicharrón. I promise you'll never go back to the Filipino stuff."

I laughed. "Okay, fine, challenge accepted."

"You've got your book?"

It might have been a bit silly, but I suddenly took Javi's book thing very seriously. It was too large to fit in my bag, so I carried the book protectively to my car. I set it on the passenger seat next to me, and put my bag on top of it so it wouldn't slide around as I drove. Then I reached into the back seat, retrieved the book I'd borrowed from Shaun, and put it on the passenger seat too. I looked at the two books lying there, my bag protecting Dad's book, frustrated to find no answer awaiting me in my search for its symbolism.

Mary sighed heavily on the other end of the phone. "I don't know where to start. You're suddenly dating Shaun? You spent yesterday evening with Javi? You had another hallucination?"

"I know. It's a lot."

It was Mary's lunch hour. I heard the sounds of conversation and clinking cutlery from the cafe she was eating in.

"Pretty sneaky of you to start dating the one guy in this group I'm not sure about," she said around a mouthful of sandwich.

"What's there to not be sure about? He's normal. Very sweet, in fact." The memory of Javi's warning came hot on the heels of that thought but I pushed it aside.

"Well. We'll have to see, I guess." She chewed and swallowed. "So what about this hallucination you had? You didn't hurt yourself, I hope."

My throat went dry. This was it. Mary had given me the opening, but I didn't know if I was ready.

"It was about your mom."

"What? My mom? What do you mean?" A note of panic crept into her voice. She knew about my worst dreams.

"It's not life-threatening. But it's not good," I said.

I described the hallucination to her, every detail. She didn't make a sound the entire time I was talking. No chewing, no drinking—possibly no breathing.

"Why didn't you tell me this right away?"

"I'm sorry. I just didn't know how to bring it up."

Mary sighed in frustration. "I have to go back to work. Come over tonight after dinner. Maybe we can strategize. Or something."

I wasn't sure what strategy I'd be able to assist with, given how little I actually knew of my aunt, especially the parts of her life Mary didn't like to talk about.

But I agreed. Of course I did. Because it was Mary. And it was the least I could do, given that it was my malfunctioning brain that had created this hallucination in the first place.

"So." Elliot said, breaking the silence.

"So," I repeated.

"So," Mary said, trying a weak laugh.

"I really don't know what the best plan is," Elliot said.

"What are our options?" I asked.

"We could directly confront her," Mary suggested.

"She may listen to us," he said, "or she may not. Either way she'll want to know how we know."

Mary shifted closer to him on the couch, then turned to me. She looked so sad.

"Or maybe we tell her everything," she said. "About you."

I almost gasped. "Mary, no."

"We have to tell her about your visions. The one you had about me. The one you had about your mom."

"No."

"I know it's scary for you," Elliot said.

"No fucking kidding it's scary for me," I said to him, gripping the handle of my mug so hard I thought it could snap.

"She's my mother!" Mary unfolded her legs from underneath her and turned fully to face me. I could see the lift of her chin, the angry fear blazing in her eyes.

Elliot took her hand and held it tightly. "Hon, come on," he said to her. "We agreed that we'd give Freya time to think about it, remember? She's freaking out a little. Which is understandable."

She scooted back to her original position on the couch, but I knew she wasn't done with me. I took a deep breath. I felt pinned by her gaze, and not for the first time she reminded me of the Queen of Swords. Clear-eyed, cutting right to the truth, no fucking around.

I knew exactly what was going through her mind: I couldn't save my own mother, so why wasn't I jumping at the chance to help hers?

"Maybe," I said, trying to mimic Elliot's soothing tone, "there's some way we can help her without telling her everything. We can say that a friend of hers called you and was concerned about her. We can ask her how work is going, if it's stressful maybe. Something like that."

"Oh?" she said, her voice rumbling with barely restrained anger. "And you think she's going to be okay with that? Because let me remind you it's not you who's going to have that discussion with her. Or you," she jabbed a finger in Elliot's direction. "It's me. You think she's going to suddenly listen to me, let me have a heart-to-heart? Or we can monitor her, fucking follow her around? Bullshit."

"Don't be ridiculous," I said.

"Do you only give a shit about your ability when you're hanging out with your new little group?"

"You pushed me into joining that group!"

"Okay, okay." Elliot held out his hands as if we were advancing on each other. "Take a deep breath, please, both of you."

Mary and I both leaned back in our seats. My heart was racing. Mary hadn't actually said anything vicious, but I couldn't get my mind away from how bad I felt. Did her acceptance of me have limits? Conditions?

"I think I should go," I said, quietly.

Mary said nothing, but I could tell she was holding back tears. Angry, scared, I couldn't say. She refused to look at me.

Elliot stood and followed me to the door. He was silent too. I slid my shoes on as quickly as I could and we said a terse goodbye. When he shut the door behind me, the whole world became cold and small.

As soon as the first sip went down, Freya decided she hated bourbon forever. Still, given that she was eighteen and not legally allowed to drink for another year, she was impressed to have crossed one drink off her list so soon.

Samina laughed at Freya's disgusted expression and grabbed the bourbon out of her hand, replacing it with a more reasonable bottle of beer. "Beer's gross anyway," she said.

Freya gratefully accepted the trade. Out of all her U of T house-mates, she liked Samina the best. Going to this particular bar had been Samina's idea—she knew that the bartenders believed anyone carrying a university ID should be old enough to drink.

"When are Giulia and Angie getting here?" Freya asked.

"Soon, I think. They wanted to go to that dumpling place first." She shrugged. "I don't know why. The food here's better."

Freya nodded, but felt a pang of jealousy as she looked down at her remaining fries. Dumplings sounded really good right now.

Still, it was a nice bar. It looked almost like someone's house, an old one, with lots of little rooms and nooks and a fireplace. Even a cat! After a couple nights of clubbing with her new housemates, she'd quickly determined clubs weren't for her. She much preferred a place like this. She could look around at the people in sweaters and imagine herself living a cozy adult life. What were they all talk-ing about? She let herself imagine. Illicit but sophisticated affairs. Undiscovered philosophers. Art projects involving big ideas and a bit of public deception. It was Toronto. Anything could happen.

Samina's voice jolted Freya out of her reverie. "So how well do you know Giulia? I think I've only met her once."

"She's in my European Colonialism class and she knows a few people from our house. She's from BC too, but Vancouver."

"And that's not close to Kelowna?"

"No, it's pretty far." Freya was amused by how often people in Ontario seemed to think everyone in BC were neighbours. But then again, when she'd arrived in Toronto she thought Ottawa was only a day-trip away.

Angie's voice shattered the low hum of the bar for a moment as she and Giulia came flying through the front door. Freya was glad to see them. She moved aside so they could squeeze into the booth.

Giulia gave Freya a conspiratorial wink as she pulled a plastic container out of her purse. "I thought you would like these. They're as good as back home."

There weren't many dumplings, but Freya was thrilled. She hid the contraband food under her jacket as the server came by to take drink orders.

"Drinks and dumplings day!" Giulia cried, holding her beer aloft.

They laughed loudly, and Freya forced herself to ignore the swivelling heads of the people around her.

The conversation turned to their families, their lives before U of T. Normal things. Freya was a bit let down at first, but she had to admit their stories were interesting. Funny. The third round of drinks helped.

"Okay, what's your weirdest talent?" Samina suddenly asked. "Like being double-jointed or something." To demonstrate, she hooked the tips of her fingers at the top joints, like little Ls.

And with that, Freya's mood changed. Her weirdest talent had killed her mother and would probably get her in trouble if the wrong person found out. She gulped her beer and made something up. "I can walk on my hands."

Giulia downed her drink, and her words ran together when she spoke. "I can regulate my body temperature. I can just sort of like take a few deep breaths and think about if I want to be warmer or cooler, and then after a few minutes I am. And I never sweat, either. I haven't had to wear deodorant since I was like thirteen."

The rest of the table was silent. Freya was stunned. Had Giulia just told them she was a veker? Just so openly like that?

Giulia must've realized it too, by her expression. She seemed to shrink inside herself. Freya had never seen someone look so alone.

Samina laughed, as if Giulia was just kidding, and the conversation moved on.

At one in the morning, her head still spinning from the night out, Freya found herself tossing and turning in bed. She couldn't stop picturing the look on Giulia's face.

Freya hated that look. She knew it. She lived it.

She should talk to Giulia tomorrow.

No.

She couldn't risk it. Freya didn't really know her, didn't know how trustworthy she was. After all, Giulia had just outed her own secret after a few drinks. It was a sign. A warning.

Don't get close.

In the end, Freya decided to just avoid her. Whenever she saw Giulia at a party or on campus, she always found someone else to talk to, swerved to another path. She began arriving late to European Colonialism classes to avoid having to sit by her. It was better that way.

A month later, as Freya was in the common room trying to make sense of her Japanese Film notes, Samina came running in.

"Holy fuck, did you hear about Giulia?"

A cold stab went through her at Samina's words, their urgency.

Samina sat down on the couch, right on top of Freya's notebook. "She went back to BC."

"Why?"

"Someone spray-painted *veker* on her car. Threw a rock through the window too."

"What?" Freya could barely hear her own voice, her throat was so dry. She coughed. "Who knows besides us?"

Samina shook her head. "Half the bar heard it! She's lucky she didn't get worse. Anyways, I have to call Trevor. He's friends with a guy she was dating." She bounded up the stairs, already on the phone.

Freya sat staring in space, bloodless, motionless. The only thing she felt was something she was afraid to admit.

Relief.

It was relief, blooming and spreading. Relief that she had never reached out to Giulia, relief that she was gone, relief that her own secret was safe.

I stood under a hot shower for what felt like forever, waiting for it to relax me. It didn't. Despite the fact I had only slept for about four hours, my brain was running so fast I swore I heard it whirring. My mind kept pulling me back to yesterday's argument with Mary.

Had I done the wrong thing? Was I my father's daughter, putting my own feelings before the greater good of my family? Was my life with Mary over?

I needed to distract myself. I pulled on some clothes without much consideration, then went out into the living room to check my computer. I didn't have any Oneira shifts booked, and no emails needed my attention. A Friday off with nothing to do but think. Hooray.

I picked up my deck and shuffled absentmindedly, cards face up. The familiar images slid past me, and while they didn't calm me, I was drawn to the potential of their comfort. I stopped, as I now often did, at the Lovers.

Connection, being vulnerable, acceptance.

I needed someone to talk to about this, someone who would understand. Someone who would be honest with me and help me see things that I couldn't or didn't want to see.

Someone who wasn't Mary.

I texted Javi, ignoring the fact that it was eight in the morning, and asked him if he was free to talk. Then my stomach growled at me, so I made breakfast.

No response.

I picked at my oatmeal, drank my coffee slowly, washed my dishes, and still nothing. I was climbing the walls. I ran through a dozen reasons he wasn't available—he was on his way to work, or teaching a class, or sleeping in—but I couldn't settle myself to be patient. I couldn't relax. My stomach was twisting into knots and I felt like I was going to vibrate out of my skin.

So I texted Shaun.

He replied within ten minutes.

Morning ♥ Everything okay? Want to call me?

I did.

I smiled as the phone rang on his end. I was looking forward to hearing his voice.

"I hope it's not too early," I said when he answered.

"Not at all. I was awake. Finishing up a project for a client. What's up?"

"I really need to talk to you about something. Please say no to this if you can't, but are you able to maybe come over today? I know it's a long drive and I'll reimburse you for gas. I'll even buy or make you lunch, or dinner. And we can leave it for another day if you're really too busy. Please don't feel obligated—"

"Stop, stop," he said, laughing. "I'd be happy to come see you. Ten thirty okay?"

"Yes, thank you."

By the time Shaun buzzed in at my front door, I had pulled myself together a bit, emotionally as well as physically. And though I knew this wasn't a date, I also couldn't help changing out of my old U of T hoodie into a newer, nicer sweater, in a colour that Mary always thought complemented my eyes.

"Hey," he said when I opened the door. And despite myself, despite the situation, I felt a flush of warmth.

"Welcome to my den," I said, suddenly very aware of the fact that he was in my home. "It's pretty small, I know."

"I like it. It suits you." He planted a small, warm kiss on my lips. Not one of overwhelming, unstoppable sexual desire, but of fondness, familiarity, comfort. Someone who was happy to see me.

I gestured for him to sit in the living room while I busied myself in the kitchen making coffee. I still wasn't sure what I was going to tell him. I was also very conscious of how odd it felt to have a man in my space, among my things. I was no nun, but I didn't make a regular habit of inviting dates back to my place. Had I made a mistake? Was it too risky to have Shaun in my space while trying to maintain a secret identity?

I shook my head. Too late to change that now. I went through my cover story like the pre-flight routine in a passenger jet, took a deep breath. Thankfully, I'd already thought to clear my living room of anything that could reveal my identity or connect me to my dad.

Shaun called to me from the living room. "Do you like the book?"

He was sitting on the couch, holding the sci-fi novel he'd lent me.

"I do, though I haven't gotten very far."

I brought our coffees to the living room and sat on the couch to face him, folding one leg underneath me.

"I had another waking vision a couple of days ago," I said. I took a deep breath and told him about the hallucination. I also told him about the fight with Mary, about her plan to help save my aunt by revealing my skill. But when I got to the part about Mary wanting me to reveal to Judith that I'd predicted my mother's death, I stopped short.

How much did I actually trust Shaun? Did I really want him to know the most personal thing about me? Could telling him about that specific dream lead to unwanted questions about my family? My mind went back to Javi's warning.

Shaun extended his arm. "Come here," he said. I slid under it and he wrapped me in a strong hug, kissed the top of my head. "That sounds very, very, very shitty. I'm sorry that happened to you. But I think this could be good for you."

"How?"

"This is your chance to prove that your skill is valuable and good."

I slid out of his grasp. "What?"

"What's the worst that could happen?"

"My aunt could tell my family. I don't want that."

"Are you all very close?"

I shook my head. That wasn't the point.

"If they can't accept you for who you are, they don't deserve you. Trust me, I know. When I told my sister about my skill, she didn't speak to me for three years. Eventually she came around and now we're fine. We're not best friends or anything, but we're fine." He took a sip of his coffee and set the cup down resolutely. "I can help you with this. But it's pretty major. You can totally say no."

"What is it?"

"Let me examine your emotions."

"You want to use your skill on me?"

"Yeah. I think maybe your emotions are clanging around, mixing rational thoughts with irrational fears. You're having trouble figuring out what's real. I can help you untangle some things."

I paused, suddenly nervous. "Is it like mind reading?"

"No, not at all. I just feel the feelings."

"What does that feel like?"

"Like a smoke that kind of flows out of me. I might have a bit of a headache afterwards, so I hope you don't mind me hanging around here being grumpy for a little bit. For you though it'll just feel like warmth. No pain, just warmth. I've been told it's quite nice."

He smiled, watching me with those green eyes that crackled with a slyness I found so intriguing—it was like he had a secret he was always a second away from sharing. I wanted to know how to be that way, how to feel confident and one step ahead and free.

"Okay," I said.

"Okay what?"

"Okay, I give you permission. Let's do this."

"You're sure?" He rubbed my hand.

"Yes, I'm sure."

He leaned forward and kissed me again, this time deeply, almost urgently.

"It's usually easier if you're lying down," he said.

"What, do I need to I be naked too?" I laughed, more high-pitched than I intended.

"No, it's not like that." He was suddenly serious. "You can sit leaning against something if you prefer. Most people kind of swoon a bit."

"I've never swooned a day in my life," I said, but shifted my position anyway so that I was supported fully by the back of the couch.

He stuffed a couple of cushions next to me, making a sort of nest.

"More comfortable that way," he said, "Oh, hang on a sec." He stood up and jogged out of the room, toward my bedroom.

I thought nothing of it until I realized I'd left dad's book, the one I'd borrowed from Javi, out on my nightstand. But he was back right away, holding one of the pillows from my bed. What were the chances he'd even seen the book? I took a deep breath and tried to relax as he placed the pillow behind my head.

Shaun moved down to the floor and sat cross-legged on the rug, his back against the coffee table. He took both of my hands in his.

"I do this through the hands. We tend to touch and grab things when we're emotional, so hands can have a sensitivity that helps me. It's also good if I can see your face—it helps the connection. Oh, and close your eyes. Your vision might get weird for a while. If at any point it gets too intense for you, tell me to stop and I will, okay? You're the one in control here."

"Okay," I said.

He quickly knelt up and gave me another kiss.

"I'm going to start now. Try to relax."

He spread my hands out flat and placed his palms against mine, wrapping them solidly with his fingers. I did the same and he gave me a quick, encouraging squeeze. I leaned my head back against the pillow and looked at the spot where the wall met the ceiling. There was a small crack there I'd never noticed before. I took a deep breath at the same time Shaun did. I snuck a peek at him. He was looking in my direction, but his gaze was loose, unfocused. He didn't see me.

I began to feel heat coming from his hands, warming my palms and wrists where he was touching me. It was a strange heat, dry, moving in slow churns like cream mixing into coffee. I remembered Shaun's description of how it felt to him—like a kind of smoke— and I was tempted to look down again.

Instead, I focused on the wall-ceiling spot. The white of the paint turned slowly blue, a cold winter sky. The colour swirled, with slight variations in the tone, but always blue. My heart started to flutter like a bird. The blue got stronger. Warmth rushed through me, but not Shaun's warmth. This was different. My insides were a soup, roiling and simmering as every possible emotion clashed and merged and slid together. I could barely identify one before it slipped away to be replaced by another. I couldn't tell if I was sitting still or if I was weeping, laughing, shouting, jumping for joy. Blood rushed through my ears. I closed my eyes, but that made the feeling more intense. I gripped Shaun's hands tighter at the same moment he squeezed mine.

"You okay?" Shaun's voice was strained, but he looked concerned.

"Yeah," I said. And I was. It was a lot to take, but I didn't feel I was in danger. I opened my eyes again. Tears rushed out and slid down my face. It didn't feel like I was crying so much as my body was just reacting, primal. I could see why Shaun wanted to make sure I was well-supported. I definitely felt a swoon or two coming on.

After an undeterminable amount of time, the heat coming from Shaun's hands slowly withdrew. My heart slowly went back to normal. We released our grip on each other. I blinked and started to panic. My vision was still tinted blue.

"It'll clear in a few minutes," I heard Shaun say. Suddenly, he hunched over onto the floor, holding his face in his hands.

"Are you okay?" I asked, putting a hand on his shoulder. He jerked when I touched him.

"Just give me a minute. If you can, maybe get us some water. That'll help both of us."

I peeled myself from the cushions and climbed over the pretzel of Shaun's arms and legs. I didn't trust myself on the way to the kitchen, feeling out with my hands as if I were blindfolded, and fumbled through the process of pouring water into two glasses. I returned to him and placed a glass in his hand, which he drained before I sat back down.

"Thanks. C'mere," he pulled me down on the floor next to him, knocking me slightly into the coffee table. "Sorry."

"You look nice blue," I said.

He leaned his head against mine and took a few deep breaths, swallowed heavily. I was unsure what to do, how to comfort him, if I even should. After a minute, I moved back up onto the couch.

"How are you now?" I asked.

He sniffed and I caught him surreptitiously swipe at his eyes before he looked up at me. "Getting better. You?"

"I'm fine. A bit drained. But weirdly serene."

"And I feel overstuffed. I'm a Thanksgiving turkey. You are— you've got some crazy emotions, you know? Not crazy. That's a terrible word. God, why can't I just fucking talk?" He smacked the arm of the couch in frustration.

I sat up. "Shaun, don't worry about it."

He rubbed his forehead. "Sorry. All these emotions. Mine and yours. They're all mixed up in me."

"Huh," I said. I felt sort of the opposite. Trimmed down, like a neat hedge.

He stood up shakily, like a foal on new legs, and refilled his glass in the kitchen, gulping it all down at the sink. When he returned to the couch and sat next to me, I took his hand.

"So? What did you see? Or feel?" I asked.

"So much fear," he said, almost in a whisper. I wanted to laugh at his dramatic tone, until I saw the sadness in his eyes. "You're so self-contained. I thought you were guarded. But it's fear."

I was silent.

"You don't need to be afraid of your skill," he continued. "You really don't. And I'm not just saying that because I want everyone to be open about their skills. Really. Your skill doesn't hurt people. It helps them."

My emotions were beginning to seep back to their normal Freya positions, like the colours returning to my vision.

"You can't live all hidden inside yourself forever," he said. He must have been returning to his own normal too, because his speech was becoming less scattered, more Shaun-like.

"I hate this. I feel like I'm playing God with my aunt's life. What right do I have to make these kinds of decisions?"

"You have a right to be a complete person, to use the skill you have."

I sighed. "Do you mind if I just go into the other room to think for a bit?"

"Sure, of course. I might nod off for a couple of minutes. A quick catnap and I should be totally back to normal."

I left Shaun to arrange my couch cushions as I walked into my bedroom and fell backwards onto my bed.

What if I just let Mary tell my aunt everything?

I knew Aunt Judith had encountered people like me in the past. One incident especially haunted me. But I was never sure how she felt about the paradextrous. I glanced over at Dad's book on my nightstand. Part of me wished I'd borrowed *Kuya*, the one about our family. I wanted to look through it now for any hints on how Judith might handle my revelation. Did I need to be afraid of her?

The threat of violence from the world at large wasn't insignificant, but Shaun was right. My skill couldn't hurt anyone. It was passive, benign to everyone but me. I'd probably helped more people than not. Like Mary.

My stomach lurched as I remembered last night, how I'd wondered if Mary's support had conditions. In ten years, Mary had never once been anything but completely on my side. A little rammy perhaps, but on my side. Maybe we were being tested, she and I. Maybe this was a sign.

My namesake Freya sent to live with the Aesir to prove she wanted peace.

I sighed. I was going to do what Mary wanted because it would make her happy. I could erase the angry, helpless look on her face from the night before. I wanted to help my aunt too, but I needed Mary back more than anything.

If Mary was the Queen of Swords then I was the Two. Blindfolded, two swords crossed at my chest, the rocky sea and weak moonlight at my back. I was the card of the crossroads, indecision, that held-breath moment as the blindfold slips.

Time to pick a sword.

I slid off my bed and went back into the living room. Shaun was out cold, curled up like a potato bug on his side, his breathing deep and approaching a snore. I found my phone and took it into my bedroom.

Javi had texted me.

Sorry, busy day today. What's up?

If you let me drive you to STEP tomorrow I can tell you then.

I checked the time. Almost noon. There was a slim chance Mary would call on her lunch break, but I couldn't wait. I was excited and terrified by my decision, and I needed to share it with her, no matter how she felt about me at the moment. I dialed her number.

She picked up just before it went to voicemail. Her "Hi" was cold and flat.

"I was scared. But I want to save your mom if I can. You can tell her anything you want to."

There was silence, and for a moment I thought she'd hung up. Then she sighed, a shaky release of breath.

"Okay." Her voice was still strained around the edges, but at least she was speaking to me. "I'd like you to be there with me when I do it."

"Why?"

"Because you can tell her things that I can't. And I'm scared too. I need you."

I need you. She meant it. I had to believe that. "Okay."

We said our goodbyes and I hung up. I felt buoyant.

I went back into the living room and Shaun stirred, cracking open an eye. "Hey," he said sleepily, cutely. It felt good to see him there, vulnerable yet comfortable.

"Hey. Are you back?" I said.

He nodded and sat up slightly, pushing his hair off his forehead. "I'm back. You look different. Relaxed."

"Mary and I are going to tell my aunt everything. I'm just going to have to deal with whatever happens. I'm glad you're helping me."

I crawled next to him, leaning against his solid warmth. My familiar pillow smell mingled with the scent of his hair. He gathered me up.

"Of course," he said. "You can trust me. I'm so proud of you. Everything's going to be better now."

Why had she never travelled before?

Freya stretched out on the bed in her B&B and wondered what had taken her so long. Despite the flights to London and Manchester and the train ride to York, she wasn't tired. In fact, she was so excited she wasn't sure she'd ever be tired again. And now she got to luxuriate in a room on the third floor of a Victorian building; the room had a little table by the window with a kettle on it, and a little basket with British biscuits and Horlicks, which she discovered she loved. Yes, the walls were so thin that she could hear her neighbours coughing, and the view out the window was of train tracks. But it was comfortable, and she found the momentary rush of the trains speeding by thrilling.

She turned on her digital camera to see how her pictures from the train ride had turned out. She'd wanted to capture the fields absolutely filled with sheep, but in the end, she'd taken photo after photo of white smears. She didn't mind. It was cool. Still sheep, still British.

Her phone dinged. A text from Dad.

Are you there yet? Use the phone card and call me.

Freya sighed. She'd forgotten to text Dad after arriving. Should she reply that she was too jet-lagged? Tempting, but he had paid for more than half of her trip. *A gift for finishing a successful first year at university*, he'd insisted.

She hoped he wasn't expecting a call every night.

Freya padded down the steep stairs to the dining room, where she found the B&B owner wiping down the tables of two and four. When she'd first arrived, the owner had asked her, "So what part of America are you from?" but in such a cheerful manner that Freya immediately forgave her.

The owner approached Freya now, her smile as warm as if they'd known each other for years.

"I'm sorry, but is there a phone here I can use?" Freya asked. "I have a phone card, so it won't cost you any long distance."

"Of course! Right this way."

Freya followed her to a small hallway past the staircase, through a door marked *Office*.

"Just over there on the desk," the woman said. "Go ahead."

Freya did. She squinted at the phone card, careful to dial the right numbers.

"What took you so long?" were Dad's first words.

"Sorry, I had to look for the phone here," Freya said, trying to be quiet as the B&B owner hovered behind her, looking at papers in a filing cabinet. "I only got here about an hour ago. The flights were fine. Heathrow is ridiculous, but Manchester is okay. I caught my train no problem."

"And you're at the address you told me? Is this the number where I can call you?"

"No, this is the office number."

"What? I can't hear you."

"This is the office number!" she said louder. The woman straightened her back slightly, clearly listening now. "Text me unless it's an emergency. I don't have a phone in my room."

"What will you do now?"

"I don't know. Find lunch somewhere. Walk around and look at the buildings. Some structures here date back to the Romans."

"How long will you be out? When will you be back?"

"Dad, I don't know." The call was throwing Freya off. She could almost feel the day's magic slipping away. "I don't want to waste this phone card, so I'm going to go."

Afterwards, the owner followed Freya back to the staircase, listing off places to visit as if she'd taken part in the phone conversation. Freya ran up the stairs to get her purse and ran back down, not caring how loud she was. Her stomach was growling. She was excited to check out the tea room everyone told her she had to visit and then do a tour of York Minster. She was already running out of time.

After a few minutes wandering outside, Freya worried the directions she'd written out were wrong. Up one narrow lane, down another—she felt like she was trespassing. But the B&B owner's directions were perfect.

The tension from the phone call unspooled as she walked. She imagined herself as a medieval resident, winding her way through streets and laneways that had been there for centuries. When she entered a large park containing ruins of a medieval abbey, she decided that York was the most interesting place in the world. She could almost feel the lives that had passed through it.

Freya gazed at one ruined abbey wall for so long that people began to stare. She ducked her head and continued on her way.

As she was taken through stunning room after stunning room on her tour of York Minster, her mind kept wandering back to the ruined abbey. Her imagination hadn't pulled her this way in years. She felt worlds away from her real life, her real self, everything that made her who she was. She loved it.

The next morning, Freya awoke to the aroma of baking bread and remembered that she was in actual heaven. She floated downstairs to the dining area where the other guests, already seated at their own tables, gave her polite nods.

The B&B owner seemed to want Freya's every thought about the tea rooms and York Minster but didn't have much to say about the ruined abbey. "Where will you go today?" the woman asked. "You must visit the snickelways, they're famous and very interesting for a student like yourself. Oh, and of course there are the ghost tours. And the National Railway Museum. And the Jorvik Viking Centre. And Clifford's Tower. And the other Bettys Café Tea Room. And a tour of the city walls."

Freya plastered a polite Canadian smile on her face as she died inside.

She did, however, want to visit the snickelways. She was ready to wander rather than go on another guided tour, and a collection of winding narrow lanes and alleys running between proper streets was perfect for that. Some of them were hundreds of years old and it showed. Freya looked up at the second-storey overhangs of the half-timbered buildings, past the modern shops and restaurants below, and imagined people hanging their washing out on lines, leaning out to talk to someone below, eavesdropping on their neighbours. Blood running down the streets from butchers.

The summer sun was hot on her shoulders, contrary to her expectation of nearly constant English rain. She found a secondhand bookshop and bought a yellowed paperback, then found a café that wasn't a famous tea room and had tea and read her book, and let herself be a blip in the millions of stories that had passed through that same space.

Tea finished and the sun in her eyes, Freya stood, stretched, and decided to walk along the city walls by herself. For some reason she thought she'd be stopped and questioned, as if they were still guarded by medieval archers, but they were easy to access. She couldn't stop taking photographs of everything: the signs marking the gateways, the gardens, the backs of people's houses. It all seemed significant, worth remembering.

She leaned against the old limestone, more mesmerized by the backyards than she had been by many other things during this trip. What must it be like to live in such an old house, with such old walls? What would it be like to live here at all, to take all of its history for granted?

Something turned over in her mind, something that had been quietly seeking her attention as she contemplated the past. A more recent history.

The first veker, Alan Y, was from nearby. At least, Freya thought she'd remembered hearing that a long time ago. Was it possible that he'd walked where she was walking now? Was there a secret pilgrimage people like her made, as if his childhood home were a holy shrine?

She suddenly felt too visible. Here, so close to Alan Y's hometown, would people be able to tell what she was?

A little shiver passed through her, and she decided to leave the walls, walk through the city's streets. Find something nice for Mary, maybe browse a grocery store just to see the differences from Canadian ones. Have an early night with Horlicks and British TV. Be normal. Maybe there was such a thing as too much history.

When I picked Javi up for Saturday's STEP meeting, he didn't seem to remember that I'd wanted to talk to him about something. He chattered on and on about that Swedish police show we'd watched at his house. At first I was glad—so much had happened since I'd texted him that I wouldn't have known where to start. But I couldn't focus on his words either, and eventually he realized I'd barely said anything since he got in the car.

"Are you okay?" he asked. I glanced at him. His expression was, as ever, calm, patient, open. I knew it would be. I couldn't believe I'd only known him for two weeks—a month if you counted our first meeting on Oneira.

I decided I didn't want to hide anything from him. I wanted him to know everything.

"I'm okay," I said, turning my eyes back to the road. "You know your Brian Tanangco novel? Not the one I borrowed, the other one. *Kuya*. The controversial one."

"Yes."

"My aunt, the one I had the vision about. She's Janet in that book. Her real name is Judith. Judith Neel."

"What?"

"And my real name is Freya Tanangco. I'm Brian Tanangco's daughter."

"Really?"

"Really," I said. "Go look at my driver's licence if you want. I promise you, it isn't a common name."

He reached into the back seat and pulled my bag onto his lap. When he found my licence, I couldn't resist a peek at his expression: stern, mouth pressed in a tight line. He put the licence and my bag back and was silent, looking out the window.

"Why didn't you tell me?" he asked quietly.

My guts churned. "I don't talk about it with anyone if I can help it. Everything else I've told you is true. Mary and her boyfriend were the only people who knew about my skill until I joined STEP. My dad doesn't know, my aunt doesn't know. You've read that book my dad wrote. That was what I grew up with. He had no problem mining my aunt's normal life and flinging it out there for everyone to read. Imagine what he'd do if he knew about me."

"Do you really think your dad would do that? Expose you to the world like that?"

"There's precedent. I don't want to risk it. He wouldn't understand."

"He might."

I flicked my turn signal handle a little harder than I meant to. I took a deep breath and tried not to get frustrated.

"Your family was open and understanding about skills," I said. "My father is the exact opposite of that."

For the first time in years, I remembered my seventh birthday. I remembered the little girl at the petting zoo, the one who could feel what her chicks were feeling. Dad wanted her locked up. A little girl like me.

Javi looked out his window again.

"My dad also used me as a model for stock photographs he took," I continued. "A lot of them. Have you seen the billboard near Cassandra's house, for that college in Brampton?"

He looked at me, examining my face, and as we came to a halt behind a pickup truck I pulled my hair up the way I'd had it in the photo.

"Holy shit, it's you!"

Somehow that got more of a reaction out of him than revealing the fact that I'd been lying about my identity.

The pickup began to move again, and I turned my eyes back to the highway.

"My own face keeps haunting me," I said. "So maybe you can understand why I like to keep my life close to my chest."

He fell silent again, this time for so long that I started to worry. When he finally spoke, his voice seemed less strained.

"Almost as soon as we met I told you everything about me. I feel like a fool."

"I know. I'm sorry. I guess it's just become sort of a reflex for me, hiding who I am."

I could almost hear Javi counting to ten in his head. "I think I like Freya Tanangco better than Frances Tully," he said finally. "It sounds cooler. Like a Superman and Clark Kent thing."

I snorted. "Yeah, if Superman had crippling social anxiety and let his paranoia cut off all his relationships before they ever got going."

"You didn't cut off our friendship though. You kind of blew it wide open. What made you tell me now?"

I glanced at him and smiled. "I want you to know me. I trust you."

"Ah, famous last words."

I made a face at him and we laughed, and it felt like the best kind of release. It was almost addictive, this feeling of acceptance.

"So where did the name come from?" he asked. "Your real one. *Freya* doesn't sound Filipino at all."

"No, it's Norwegian. My mom was Norwegian. My dad got a little obsessed with Norse mythology after he met her. I think he wanted to write a book about Norse gods in the modern day or something. Anyway, I was named after a Norse goddess. Imagine living that down in high school."

"Well, I like it. It's unique."

Traffic opened up and we began to coast.

"Mary will be glad I told you," I said. "She won't have to worry about blowing my cover around you at least."

"You're not going to tell the others?"

"No. I can't. Not right now anyway. I trust Cassandra, but it took a lot of preparation just to tell you, and now I feel like I could slip into a nice coma for a week."

"What about Shaun?"

Wow. I hadn't even realized I'd left him out.

I drummed my fingertips against the wheel and cleared my throat. "About Shaun. I texted him after I texted you yesterday, and he came over, and we talked, and I let him use his skill on me."

"What's it like?"

I tried to describe it to him, but despite my best efforts, more than anything it sounded like Shaun and I had dropped peyote in the desert.

"Sounds intense," Javi said.

"It was. But I think I understand Shaun a bit better now. I mean, think about it—he consumes the emotions of other people. All of them. The weak ones, the strong ones, the ones from the past, the ones that affect you right now. And I think all that stuff plays against his own emotions."

"You think that's why he's intense one day and charming the next?"

"I think it's why he seems so self-involved. After our session, he was pretty overwhelmed emotionally and didn't seem to care that I could tell. It can't be easy for him, carrying all that around. Maybe we should cut him some slack."

"I guess," he said. But he didn't sound convinced.

By the time we arrived, I was happier than I had been in a long time. It had felt good to hear my real name coming out of Javi's mouth. But the smile quickly drained from my face when we approached the house and saw Mary standing on the porch, holding a cigarette, watching us.

"Hey," I said. "Is the door locked?"

"No, I was waiting for you." Her voice was even but tense. "Hey, Javi," she said, giving him a quick nod. He smiled back, obviously sensing the tension.

"What's up?" I asked, testing her out. I'd resolved to trust her intentions, but the sting of our fight flared momentarily.

She took a drag of her cigarette, exhaled it quickly, and flicked the butt onto the sidewalk. She jammed her hands in the pocket of her jacket and rocked back on her heels a couple of times.

"I want you to come with me to tell Mom. Today."

"What?" I said.

"Frances—"

"Freya," I said. "It's okay. I told him everything."

Mary glared at me for a second, a look that said *we'll discuss this later*. She turned to Javi. "Javi, Freya has agreed to come with me to tell my mom about the vision she had at your place. And I think you should come too. With my mom, it helps to have a few people there so that she's on her best behaviour. And if my cousin trusts you, then so do I."

Javi looked at me, and I was surprised to see no irritation at all. He seemed to actually want to come.

"Okay," we both agreed.

"She's expecting us after the meeting. I told her I made some lumpia for her. I didn't, but that's what I told her."

"Why lie about that?" Javi asked.

"My relationship with my mother is complicated," Mary said. "It'll be easier to trick her, get her thinking it's a nice visit. If I start out telling her we want to talk, we'll lose her."

She turned on her heel and opened the front door, and Javi and I followed. Shaun was already there, sitting on the couch, an empty space next to him. I took advantage of Cassandra welcoming Mary to sit next to him.

"Hey," I said.

And to everyone's surprise, most of all mine, he leaned in and gave me a quick kiss on the lips in response.

"Oh," I heard Mary say next to me.

I sent a quick prayer for a giant cartoon Monty Python foot to burst through the ceiling and crush me to bits.

Mary turned to Cassandra and said, "I'm so sorry we're late. Javi and Frances were trying to talk me out of my disgusting smoking habit."

"Not at all," Cassandra said. "You were right on time. I'm glad you could join us again today. Tea?"

Cups of tea were passed around over a brief round of small talk about the traffic and the weather.

"So there's no set agenda today," Cassandra said eventually. "Does anyone have anything they wanted to talk about?"

Both Javi and Mary looked at me expectantly, and I raised my hand for some reason, like I was a student. At the same time, Shaun said, "I do."

We looked at each other and grinned. Now that the initial wave of embarrassment had passed, I allowed my gaze to linger on him, his laughing eyes, his smile directed at me.

"Please, after you," he said, sliding his arm onto the back of the couch, not quite around my shoulders, but close.

"Well," I said, looking at Cassandra, "I had another hallucinatory vision on Thursday. And I was able to lucid dream my way through it."

She clapped her hands together like a little girl. "Oh, that's fantastic," she cried. "Tell me everything."

I relayed the whole story, letting Javi fill in the parts from his perspective. I could tell he had known Cassandra a long time because his side was peppered with details that only someone interested in scientific research would appreciate. How dilated my pupils were. How my voice sounded. How long the episode had lasted. I handed her my dream notebook. I'd scribbled in it after I'd gotten home, and we waited in silence as she transcribed the salient details into her own book.

"And this woman you saw in your vision," Cassandra said. "Do you know her?"

I held my breath. *Shit.* I hadn't come up with a plan for this. Would a lie set Cassandra off on a path of inquiry that would be less helpful? I decided to split the difference.

"I'm not sure. She looked familiar, but I couldn't place her."

Out of the corner of my eye I saw Shaun tilt his head like a confused puppy, wondering why I wasn't telling Cassandra that it was my aunt I had hallucinated.

She handed my notebook back to me and made some scribbles in her own. "Okay, Shaun, I guess you're up next," she said.

He shot up like a released spring and produced a folded piece of paper from the pocket of his jeans, leaning familiarly into me as he did. He spoke excitedly as he unfolded the paper. "My interview was published today. Here, I printed it out for you."

He reached across the table and handed the paper to Cassandra, who eyed him for a second before beginning to read.

"You didn't tell me you did the interview," I said to him. We were together for hours yesterday. Why hadn't he said anything?

"I'm sorry," he said warmly, squeezing my hand. "I had more important things on my mind."

"How is it?" Javi said cautiously to Cassandra.

She placed the paper down on the coffee table gingerly, as if it were broken pottery. "It's fine."

"I didn't mention STEP. Like you wanted," Shaun said.

I picked up the paper, aware of Shaun's gaze on me. *Toronto man defies "veker" label*, the headline read. It was true, the article didn't mention STEP. Nor did it really mention the Dutch advocacy group. Instead, it seemed to focus more on Shaun himself, his own story, his own skill.

I finished reading and passed it to Javi.

"We talked for hours," Shaun said, looking around at everyone. "She thought a personal angle would be more effective than an aggressive news piece. At first, I thought it was silly. But then I thought of Frances."

My voice came out as a hoarse croak. "Me?"

"Yeah, I thought of what you would do. You don't go at things guns blazing. You're more sensitive."

Javi lowered the paper and shared a pointed look with Mary.

Shaun continued. "The journalist seemed really interested in my story. She wants to get me an interview on TV."

"On TV," Cassandra said. Her voice had lost its usual professional tinge. Now it was flat, grey.

Shaun was either ignorant of the mood shift in the room, or he didn't care. "She thinks one of those news magazine shows would love it. She thinks it could be the perfect chance to reach more people with my story, show them that people like us are human beings like everyone else. And that it would help if more of us would share our stories."

"Shaun," Cassandra warned.

"Don't worry. I don't ever have to bring STEP into it."

He turned to me, ignoring Cassandra's glare. "You'll do it, right?"

I couldn't speak. On TV? Everyone would see it. My dad.

"I don't want to risk it," I said hoarsely.

His eyes flashed, hardened. "I thought you trusted me."

"Can we talk about it later?" I asked.

He furrowed his brow and looked past me to Javi. "Come on, man. Your whole family is cool with this stuff. It'll be easy for you."

"Maybe," Javi said evenly, talking to Shaun but watching me. "Let me think about it, okay?"

"Fine. Whatever." Shaun sat back again and was silent.

I tried to catch his eye, but even without his powers of empathy, I could feel walls going up between us.

Mary's sigh crackled down the line. "It's not fair. You moving to Toronto just as I move away."

Freya wished she could reach through the phone and hug her cousin. She remembered the feeling of moving far away from home, to another province.

"I've been here for two years," Freya reminded her gently. "And you chose to apply to the University of Winnipeg, and you chose to go there when you got accepted."

"What does that have to do with how unfair it is," she said petulantly, but then sighed. "I just miss you. It's weird here. It's so small."

"What, the university? Or Winnipeg."

"Fucking Winnipeg. I didn't tell you I was recognized last week."

"Recognized? How?"

"Oh my god, it's the most infuriating fucking thing. So I'm out getting some coffee, right? And I'm standing there minding my own business and I hear someone calling my name. It's a Filipino girl from my Intro to Sociology class. And she's got a bunch of family members with her. Parents, titas, kuyas, everyone. So she introduces me to her family and everyone shakes my hand. The titos and titas are looking at me weird, I assume because they're trying to work out if I'm Filipino too. You know that look. So I tell them my mom is Filipino and I'm from Toronto. And that's when one of them goes, 'Are you related to Brian Tanangco?'"

"What? How did they know?"

"Freya, you don't understand. The Filipinos here love your dad. Well, they don't love him. They love that he wrote a book about growing up Filipino in Winnipeg. There's eleven copies of *Kuya* in the public library, I looked. They love the story, the drama. Nobody's malicious about it, but still. Fucking tsismis all the time."

"All the Filipinos there can't love it, surely. There are thousands of them."

"Enough of them do. Someone actually asked me if my mom and your dad are still fighting."

"I'm sorry, Mary. That's shitty."

She sighed again, and I could hear her restlessly drumming her fingers on a hard surface. Then the squeak of a chair. She was pacing. When she next spoke she sounded sad, far away.

"Part of the reason I came here was because Mom was born here. I'm from here, in a way. I don't feel connected to the Philippines at all, I feel like this is my homeland. Maybe that's silly."

"It's not silly," I said quietly. Mary hardly ever talked like this about her mom. I wonder if Aunt Judith knew how meaningful the move had been.

The pacing gave Mary a second wind, it seemed, because she turned angry again.

"I wanted to come here and learn about my mom. See where she went to school. Maybe visit her old house. I was going to ask the people who live there if I could look around and take pictures for Mom. But now all of that is ruined."

"Why? Because people recognized you?"

"Yes. Because if I bring up my mom people will just want to talk about the stuff in your dad's book. What happened to her didn't even happen here but it's ruined everything I wanted to do. She told me this is the last place she was happy, you know. I wanted to do something special. Reconnect, build some kind of legacy, I dunno. I thought it would be good for us."

I didn't know what to say. How old had Aunt Judith been when she moved away? I did the math. Eight. Imagine eight years old being the last time you were happy.

I listened to my cousin's level breathing, then the sound of a bus passing outside my bedroom. I wanted to offer her comfort, solidarity. I wanted to tell her that it would be okay and people would forget about her after a few weeks. But I couldn't get out of my head the fact that my cousin was on her own, in another city, feeling like she couldn't be herself and like everyone was watching her—because of something my father had written.

That fucking book would never go away.

"Well," Mary said, breaking the silence from the passenger seat. "That was fucking awkward."

"Yeah, that's one way to put it," I said.

I couldn't shake the image of Shaun's hurt face. I had tried to talk to him after the meeting, but he gently slid out of my grasp, made some excuse about running late, then headed toward the Eglinton subway station without any further goodbye.

"Did you see how stressed Cassandra looked?"

I sighed. I needed Mary to see Shaun's compassion, his concern for me, so I told her about yesterday, how he'd helped me with his skill.

She was quiet for a while after I'd finished. Then she turned to me. "I wish you'd told me about that earlier," she said. There was no admonishment. Just the simple emotion of feeling left out. I felt it too: a pang of guilt and regret, all the more because I was worried I'd burned a bridge with Shaun and that the story I'd just shared would be the last one.

"I'm sorry," I said.

Suddenly I remembered that Javi was there—he had been so quiet. I glanced at him in my rear-view mirror, and he gave me a small smile that felt as comforting as a squeeze of the hand. I smiled back, hoping he'd be able to see it in my eyes.

"So," I said, and my voice stabbed like a knife in the cathedral-quiet car, "did you still want to go see your mom?"

Mary cleared her throat. "Yeah, I need to. Are you still willing to come, Javi?"

"Of course."

If Mary had a game plan, she would have had us run through it on the drive, but we made the short trip in silence. My aunt's North York condo was close to the highway, a Brutalist concrete building that had gone up before the current Vancouver-mimicking trend of all-glass everywhere. I remember Aunt Judith once complaining that her view had become blocked by the newer buildings going up. I couldn't say I blamed her. It seemed like every time I went to Toronto, there were five new condo towers creeping up through the sky.

As we walked toward the building, I saw a familiar figure pacing back and forth by the front entrance. It was Elliot. Mary ran to him and they hugged. I felt a mix of bashfulness and warmth at witnessing this private moment.

"I thought he wouldn't come," she whispered to me as she punched numbers on the entryway keypad.

I couldn't ask for further details because we were buzzed in right away. The elevator was old and the ride up to the twelfth floor was long. Mary gripped one of Elliot's hands in both of hers, but otherwise she appeared cool and collected. Her calm and certainty was likely due to Elliot's arrival. Not for the first time, I felt a mixture of longing for her stable, normal life, and pleasure at how happy it made her.

Aunt Judith answered the door almost as soon as Mary knocked, and let out a surprised exclamation when she saw the rest of us, followed by a polite nod.

"This is our friend Javi," Mary said. "We were giving him a ride home and he wanted to come along. I hope you don't mind."

Javi gave Judith a strained, tight-lipped smile as he shook her hand. Was he pale, or was it the lighting?

"I wish you had let me know," Judith said to Mary. "It's not nice to catch a hostess off guard. Where's the lumpia? You forgot it, didn't you? Well, never mind. We'll manage. Please, everyone, sit down."

She led us to the small dining room, the same oversized table I remembered from the last time I'd been there, years ago. I didn't think this many people had ever sat around it.

The last to file in, Elliot offered to make everyone coffee and Javi jumped up, almost knocking his chair backwards. "I'll help. Actually, where's your washroom?" And before anyone could answer, he veered off down the hallway.

I felt a shiver ripple down my spine as I watched him leave, but it went away once he was out of sight. I shook my head. Maybe it was nothing. I was just nervous.

"Such helpful boys you have," Judith said.

I came back to myself. I was sitting at one end of the table, Judith at the head, and my cousin across from me. The length of the table made me feel almost like we were in a strange corporate meeting. Had Mary brought a PowerPoint presentation?

"I'm happy to see you," Judith said. "I can't remember the last time you came to visit."

Mary was looking down at her hands. She took a deep breath before lifting her chin to look her mother in the face. "We have something to tell you. It's important."

"Oh god, this isn't an intervention, is it? I'm in recovery, Mary. I'm doing fine."

Mary looked at me. My turn. I opened my mouth to speak and realized I also hadn't made any sort of plan.

"Aunt Judith, I have a secret," I said, then stopped. I couldn't figure out what to say after that.

"A secret?" she whispered, leaning forward. "Is it to do with that boyfriend of yours?" She nodded downwards, toward my very empty womb. "Are you—"

"No!" I cried. "No, I'm not. Javi's not my boyfriend. It's not about me. Well, it is, kind of. But it's about you too."

The scent of brewing coffee filled the dining room. I noticed Javi had joined Elliot in the kitchen, and at the same moment I felt another ripple go through me that made me forget what I was about to say.

Mary nudged my foot under the table, and I started over.

"When I was ten," I croaked, "I dreamed that Mom was dead. The next day, she got that injury at work."

Elliot and Javi filed quietly into the room with the coffee things and I stopped talking. I wanted to run.

A cup was set down in front of me and I looked up to see Javi give me a terse, encouraging nod before he sat further down the table with Elliot. The two of them removed, as if they weren't part of what was happening.

"Camilla was a good woman. I regret not going to her funeral, but I was so mad at your—"

"Aunt Judith," I said quietly, staring into my cup. "My dream was prophetic. I know that sounds crazy but I'm not making it up. I've had many more like it, hundreds maybe. I dream something and it comes true."

Aunt Judith sat motionless.

"Are you saying that you're one of those—"

"One of those people with skills, yes. And that's mine. Prophetic dreams. That's the whole reason I got into tarot card reading. So I can help people. Sometimes."

"Sometimes?"

"Sometimes I try to help and it doesn't work, or sometimes I don't know how to help."

"Once she dreamt I was going to break my leg," Mary offered. "When she told me, I stopped riding my bike for a while, and I was fine."

"That's hardly scientific, Mary," Judith said. Then, to me: "I'm sorry honey, I don't mean to sound dismissive."

Honey?

"So you believe me?" I asked.

"It would explain a lot about you."

"My dad doesn't know. Mom didn't know either. Up until two weeks ago, only Mary and Elliot knew. Since then, I've been meeting a group, a sort of a support group for people like me. That's how I met Javi."

"Oh." Judith frowned and looked back at me. She pushed her chair back slightly. "Well, don't worry, I'm not going to tell your father."

I relaxed a little. I had been banking on my aunt's estranged relationship with Dad to save me. I had no contingency plan.

"There's no reason he needs to know," she said. "You're doing fine. Anyway, you know he'd just write a book about you and profit off it."

Now it was my turn to shift uncomfortably.

Mary cleared her throat. "There's more," she said gently, more to me than to her mother.

I took a bracing gulp of coffee. "I had a vision of you recently. Drinking at a bar."

"Do these dreams of yours all come true?" She gripped her cup tightly, frowning.

I looked down into my cup again, at my dark reflection swirling in the milky liquid. "I think they do, if I don't act on them. I don't always get a chance to follow up with people. And sometimes I've had dreams that I knew were trying to tell me something, but I never figured out what."

"So there's a chance this one could be nothing."

"There's a chance, yes," Mary said, trying hard to maintain a level tone of voice, "but I don't think it's nothing."

Judith didn't reply.

I didn't know what else to say. What could we say? We couldn't force her to do anything. She was a grown woman, and one who wasn't especially close to any of us. I had done my part, kept my promise to my cousin. Revealed my biggest secret. I couldn't do any more.

"Mom?" Mary said, her voice small. "What do you think?"

"I don't know what I think," Judith said. Her voice was small too. I felt like we were intruding on something private between them. "It's a lot to take in."

Elliot cleared his throat. "We know you've been in recovery for a while. But if there's something stressful going on or coming up, there could be a risk of relapse. That could be all it is. Just something to be extra aware of."

Judith took a deep breath. If Mary or I had said that to her, we would have gotten a sniff of offended disapproval. At Elliot, she merely nodded.

"We should go," Mary said after another moment of silence. "You probably want to be alone to process all of this."

We all stood up, filed silently to the front door and put our shoes back on.

Aunt Judith grabbed Mary in a big hug and squeezed.

"I'll call you soon, okay? I love you," Mary said, a bit startled.

We made the return journey down the hall, into the elevator, and back out to the parking lot in complete silence.

"I think that went so well," Mary said finally, clasping Elliot's arm. "So much better than I was expecting."

"I can't believe how easily she accepted what I told her," I said. "It was kind of nice, to be honest."

"Thanks so much for doing that, it really means a lot. You too, Elliot—I think Mom was starting to shut us out before you said what you did. And Javi, thanks for—"

"Mary," Javi said, and his voice snapped the air. "I need to tell you. Your mother. I could feel it."

"You could feel what?" she asked, her voice tight and low.

"It was coming off her in waves. Under my skin. Your mom's like Freya and like me. She's paradextrous."

Aunt Judith was ten minutes late. Freya couldn't sit still. She kept an eagle eye on her cellphone, silent on the table next to the latte she'd ordered. She regretted getting an expensive drink instead of just coffee—what if she'd misunderstood her aunt's lunch invitation and Judith wasn't paying for it?

She looked around at the restaurant. It looked like a place where regular people ate lunch. But it was near Rosedale. Not in Rosedale but maybe close enough.

Freya had resolved to see more of Toronto. Two years and she'd gone to museums, bookstores, record stores, coffeeshops, bars, her own little U of T bubble, and out to Etobicoke to visit Mary before she left for Winnipeg, but she still knew so little of the actual city. She felt a bit like a tourist sometimes. Maybe after this lunch was over she'd go for a walk. A good long one to let herself get lost while she explored.

"Freya," Judith greeted breathlessly. "I'm so sorry I'm late. I was coming from North York Centre and I misjudged how long it would take."

Freya frowned. She had a vague memory of where that was, helped only slightly by the word north.

"It's fifteen minutes from here by subway. That's why I wanted us to meet in this neighbourhood. I've never been to this restaurant. It seems nice."

Freya watched her aunt scan the menu and its prices. It was only after Judith ordered without a fuss and asked her to do the same that Freya finally let herself relax.

She couldn't resist asking what her aunt had been doing in North York. Aunt Judith leaned back in her chair and looked out the window for a moment, a sort of wistfulness on her face. She tightened her lips and Freya regretted asking.

"I've been looking at condos."

"For you?" Freya asked. It didn't make sense. Why leave that nice quiet house in Etobicoke with the garden?

Judith drummed her fingers on her water glass. "It's terrible being in that house by myself."

Ah. That explained Aunt Judith's out-of-the-blue lunch invitation. She was lonely.

"But Mary's only been gone for a couple of months."

"Mary will be in Winnipeg for a few years. It's not right in that house without her. It's time for a fresh start. Anyway, I'm only looking at two-bedroom condos, so if she wants to move back in, she can. Though I doubt she will."

Freya swallowed hard. She remembered Mary's bedroom, the Hello Kitty sticker stuck to her mirror, the turquoise wall she'd insisted on when she was fourteen, the vintage mannequin head they'd bought together in a Kensington Market vintage store a year ago. It seemed wrong for that room to change, to be emptied. She knew Mary would hate it. She gulped her cooling latte instead of responding.

"So what's going on with you?" Judith asked. "Are you still in that same apartment? Still working in that bookstore?"

"The campus bookstore, yeah. It's a little boring, but I've been there so long and I get pretty good money. Same apartment too. It's tiny and there's no oven but I like it. No roommates."

Aunt Judith smiled. "Sounds like heaven."

And then a plate of food was placed in front of Freya and for a while that was all she could focus on. Her budget didn't usually allowed for eggs benedict, and the food was so pretty that she almost didn't want to eat it. She tried not to rush through her meal, delicious as it was.

"I remember when I moved here," Judith said. "This neighbourhood felt like another planet. Yorkville too. I always avoided it, as if just walking through the streets could somehow be improper. I always felt too shabby. Oscar and I had a tiny apartment in the Beaches. Or is it just the Beach now? Anyway, I loved it there. It felt so much more relaxed, like its own little world. And we used to go to St. Lawrence Market for breakfast every Saturday. Mary was born when we lived in that apartment."

"She's never talked about it. She must have been very young when you moved to Etobicoke."

"Oh, a baby still. Oscar insisted. I wanted to stay in the Beaches. What a lovely place to raise a child. Near the lake, it would have been perfect. But Oscar wanted Mary to have a yard." She snorted. "As if she were a puppy. I resented him for a long time. To go from the city to the suburbs like that? I was only twenty-five. But I have to admit, Mary did love it."

Freya ate, sipped her latte. She had zero idea how to respond to any of this wistfulness, fondness, bitterness. All this from a woman who, on Freya's last few visits to see Mary before university, would give her a plate of food and then disappear into another room.

She wanted to ask what her uncle was like. She wanted to ask how having Mary had changed Judith's life. She wanted to ask why her aunt had never really tried to get to know her, why she was trying now.

Freya's phone dinged.

Hi loser :D

"It's Mary," Freya said. "Sorry, I'll tell her I'm busy."

I'm having lunch w yr mom right now

Why?!

She put her phone away.

"Have you talked to her lately?" Judith asked.

"We talk every week. We chat online a lot."

"Oh."

There was silence as they ate. Freya knew that Aunt Judith missed Mary too. Maybe that was common ground.

"She's excited about coming home for Christmas," Freya offered.

"Maybe I shouldn't sell the house until after that. It would be nice for her to have the Christmas she's used to. But if I find a good place, I'll lose it if I wait."

"I think Mary would want you to live in a good place more than she'd want Christmas in her old house," Freya said without thinking. She'd meant it as a good thing. Mary as the considerate daughter. But her aunt answered with a frown.

"Well. Thanksgiving is next week. Maybe you and I could have one last holiday dinner there."

Freya agreed, maybe too eagerly. This was a good sign. Maybe she could finally have a relationship with her aunt, woman to woman.

As they got up to leave, Aunt Judith gave her a hug, one so strong they lost their balance and bumped into someone at the next table. It was nice, the feeling of blood, of family. Freya felt warmth go through her as they started for the door.

That was when she heard the laughter. Shrill, high-pitched, coming from the table they'd just left. No, the next table. And then the laughter changed.

A woman was screaming, slapping at her arms. The man across from her stood up and shouted in panic. Then a server approaching their table dropped his tray and began screaming as well, rolling on the floor. "I'm burning!" he screamed over and over.

The man from the table covered his eyes with his hands. "Don't look at me," he shouted, "don't look at me!"

But it was too late. People looked. And when they did, they too began to scream "fire, fire, fire." A small group nearly knocked Freya and Judith over as they ran for the door. "Fire, fire, fire" in the street. Others stood, confused.

Freya didn't see any flames. Her heart was pounding.

Get away, get away.

Quiet fell. A tangible, menacing quiet.

The screaming woman wasn't screaming anymore. She examined her arms, the perfectly whole arms of her sweater, and began wailing, "You lost control of it!"

The server on the floor stood up, soaking wet, horrified. "What just happened?"

The man from the table was trying to escape, knocking chairs over as he did so. His eyes were still closed.

"Move," Judith said, but Freya was already moving.

They ran out onto the sidewalk, where they paused long enough to see a small crowd of pedestrians gathering. She overheard someone say "It's just like Alan Y" in a horrified voice.

Aunt Judith pulled Freya down a side street, only releasing her wrist after some distance. "A veker," she said quietly, her voice shaking.

A cool breeze whipped Freya's hair across her face.

Someone screamed in the distance. The veker still in the restaurant, a trapped bird. Something bad, truly bad, could be happening to him right now.

The cool breeze entered Freya's lungs, spread ice through her veins.

What if it had been her instead?

Nobody moved, nobody spoke. We were frozen, a strange tableau outside of Judith's apartment building.

"Are you sure?" I asked.

"I'm sure." Javi folded his arms around himself guiltily.

We looked at Mary, who was still in a stunned silence, gripping Elliot's arm.

"You had no idea?" Elliot asked gently.

She shook her head. I didn't know if she was going to faint or puke or scream. I opened her purse and fished out her cigarettes and lighter.

"Forget what I keep saying about quitting," I said as I stuck a cigarette in her mouth and lit it.

We ended up going to Javi's place, at his suggestion. "I can't drop this bomb on you and then leave you to go about your days," he'd said. He and I drove back together, and he hadn't said a word the whole way. Neither did I. I could either attempt unpacking the implications of my aunt being paradextrous, or I could keep the car on the road.

I waited on the porch for Mary and Elliot, and after they'd arrived we sat down on the couch in his long, narrow living room. I looked at the TV. It was off, but I was still drawn to it, looking for some afterimage of my hallucination.

Mary didn't say much, aside from commenting listlessly on how nice Javi's place was and how many books he had. I had never seen someone so stunned, and I had no idea what to say. All the times she'd listened to me, guided me, and all I could do was offer to get us a drink.

I found Javi in the kitchen. He was leaning against the counter, holding his phone to his ear. He raised a finger to his lips when he saw me.

"Yeah, next Friday works for me," he said. "Thanks for being so understanding. And sorry again."

"Who was that?" I asked when he hung up.

"Nobody."

"Javi."

He sighed. "Someone I met last week. We had plans to go out for a drink later tonight, but it's okay."

"Javi, you had a date? Why didn't you tell us?"

"It's fine. Something came up with her, and she would've had to leave early tonight. Besides, I'm not really in a date mood anymore." He spoke casually but I wanted to fall through the floor.

"I'm so sorry."

"It's fine. You all coming here was my idea, remember?" he said. "Now go back out there and leave me to it."

To what, I didn't ask. Nor did I remember the drinks I'd gone in there for. But Mary and Elliot didn't seem to notice.

"What's up?" I asked tentatively, as if there could be something else on her mind.

"How did I never know?" she said, staring at her hands. "All the years I've spent learning so much about skills. And my own mother is paradextrous."

"I'm sure we pass by paradextrous people without knowing every day," I said. "Even I do, I'm sure of it. Most of us try to blend in."

She rubbed at her eyes. "What if it's the reason she started drinking? What if it's hurting her? I need to—I don't know what I need to do. I don't even know how to start parsing all of this."

Her voice sounded hollow. She wasn't really talking to us anymore. Elliot slowly unwound his arm from around her and offered to retrieve the forgotten drinks. He went to the kitchen and, after a minute, returned with three bottles of beer.

"Javi's cooking something," he said. "He says it's chicharon, but it looks nothing like the stuff we get at the Filipino store."

Mary perked up, looking like herself for the first time since we'd left Aunt Judith.

"It's the Colombian kind," I said. "He threatened to make it for me one day to prove that it's better. I have to see this."

And so the three of us ended up disturbing Javi's peace in the kitchen, crowding around him and the pan where thick strips of pork belly were frying in water. But instead of answering our incessant questions, he banished us back to the living room.

"It won't take long," he said. "You can watch TV. There are three remotes, but I'm sure you can figure it out."

The process of figuring out the TV seemed to cheer Mary up further, or at least distract her, and we settled in to watch a program about a couple building a tiny house. The smell of cooking food floated around us and I swore I heard all of our stomachs rumble at the same time.

"That smells so good," I said to Javi as he came in to sit cross-legged on the floor across from the couch.

"It will taste so good too." He didn't look annoyed anymore, and the tiny knot in my stomach started to loosen.

"Hey, do you play often?" Elliot asked, nodding toward the video game console tucked away on a shelf under the TV.

"Sometimes. You?"

"Not as much as I used to."

"His little brother's a famous video gamer," Mary said proudly.

"Speedrunner. He's a speedrunner."

"What's that?" Javi asked.

Elliot pulled out his phone and played one of his brother's most recent videos. Speedrunners, he explained to Javi, complete video games using a combination of glitch exploits, intensive knowledge, and other tricks and strategies to skip huge parts of the game and finish in record time. Will knew his game of choice, Super Mario Bros. 2, inside and out. Knew every pixel, every path, every enemy. And he made a decent amount of money off it too, thanks to fans who donated to support their favourite personalities. When Elliot first told me about it, I hadn't seen the appeal. But I had to admit that the more I learned, the more impressive it seemed.

At the beeping of a timer from the kitchen, Javi flew out of the room. "This is the hands-on part," he called over his shoulder. He was in there for several minutes, and I heard the promising sound of meat sizzling. The smell was driving me crazy. It seemed like hours before Javi proudly carried out the chicharrón. We fell upon it eagerly, our faces lighting up as the flavours hit our taste buds.

"This is incredible," Mary said. "You didn't have to go to all this trouble."

Javi waved her concern away. "In my family, food is the best pairing for any emotion you can imagine."

Mary laughed. "Are you sure you're not Filipino? Too bad you couldn't have brought this to my mom's place. It would have sweetened her up."

We all fell silent for a moment, chewing, swallowing, not knowing what to say.

"Mary," I said eventually, "I think we should tell your mom that we know."

"What?"

She was incredulous but not angry, so I continued. "You said you wanted to help her. This would help her, to know she's not alone. Especially now, after hearing that I have a skill too. She must feel like she's finally—"

"Finally got the kind of daughter she should have had," Mary said sadly.

"Finally got a chance to talk about it with people who understand. That's all of us."

Mary chewed thoughtfully. "Not yet. I don't want to scare her off. I need a plan."

Jovially, as if an invisible hand had released its downward pressure on us, we finished our meal. We reminisced about the video games we'd played as kids, which led to sharing other stories from childhood. I'd of course heard all of Mary's stories and many of Elliot's, but it was especially nice to hear from Javi.

His childhood seemed idyllic, made up entirely of long summer vacations, family jokes, and inconsequential rivalries and teases. I was struck again by the openness he grew up with, the acceptance. Once again, I felt a pang of jealousy when comparing his experience to mine—but a sense of possibility swirled beneath it. Maybe, in adulthood, I could have what he had. It no longer seemed quite so unavailable.

Shortly after finishing the chicharrón, Mary and Elliot realized how long they'd been away from Zeus.

"Thanks so much for having us, man," Elliot said as they got up to leave.

I smiled. Anyone would think we were just four friends having a relaxing Saturday evening.

I started following them to the foyer, but a hand on my shoulder stopped me.

"Could you stay for a sec?" Javi said. "I need to talk to you."

Mary gave me a mischievous look. I rolled my eyes and shut the door behind her.

Javi leaned a shoulder against the foyer wall and scratched his chin. "What a fucking day," he muttered. He pushed himself off from the wall. "I've decided I'm going to do that interview with Shaun."

"Oh?" I tried to keep my tone neutral but failed. I'd been trying not to think of Shaun.

"He isn't wrong. Being part of STEP doesn't mean that I can't talk about my own experiences. I think it could be helpful for paradextrous people who might feel afraid and alone. I know what to say and what not to say—I have friends who are journalists. My family is used to journalists."

"Are you sure?"

"What you said to Mary earlier about your aunt needing someone who understands—that's what made me decide. You're right. If this interview might help even one person, it's worth a shot."

I felt a small swell at his words. Pride? Nerves? What was I nervous about? Javi's story was his own. It had nothing to do with me. And Shaun—

As if reading my thoughts, he nodded and said, "And maybe I want to manage Shaun a bit too."

I released a breath. How different was my life now compared to a couple of weeks ago. I'd opened myself up to Javi, and how easily?

I had the feeling that our first meeting on Oneira, the one that'd blasted a hole in my life, was probably the best thing to happen to me in years.

"Okay. That's fair. And good, actually," I said. "Thanks for everything. I'm glad you came with us today despite how things seem right now."

I gave him what I hoped was a reassuring smile and opened the door. It was a cool night, and the sun was already cutting its way down the sky. I was suddenly looking forward to a quiet night at home with a book.

"Freya." Javi's head poked around the door and I paused at the bottom of the porch steps. He was grinning. "You forgot to tell me that Colombian chicharrón is better than Filipino."

I laughed. "Goodnight, Javi."

Hours after her lunch with Aunt Judith, Freya still couldn't relax. She tried to read, but the words swam together in her brain. She considered calling Mary, but she didn't even know what she'd say.

She'd seen a veker out of control in the world, in exactly the way people feared, and had watched people run, heard them scream on the sidewalks. It was terrifying. What would happen to the man? What if it had been her instead?

And then there was Aunt Judith's response. Freya didn't know what to make of it. It wasn't like Judith had ever openly said anything that would make Freya feel unsafe. Maybe there was a spectrum of intolerance, and Judith was on a different end than Dad. Maybe if it never came up in conversation ever again, Freya would never have to wonder about it.

Too close.

Freya put on her shoes and jacket and slipped outside. It was early evening but already getting dark, and for a moment she felt a little glimmer of pleasure at the thought of taking a long walk. She could leave the Annex, maybe walk north and see where she ended up.

Suddenly, anxiety gripped her. No. Too far north and she would be close to the restaurant. Too close for comfort. What if she saw someone who recognized her? She never wanted a reminder of today ever again.

The Spadina streetcar screamed on its rails. She returned home with takeout pierogies from Future's and opened a bottle of wine she'd been saving. Best to stay home in a nest of blankets on her bed, laptop propped up, stack of DVDs wobbling precariously on the uneven nightstand she'd found at the end of her street last summer.

Start with the classics, maybe they'll be boring and relaxing. Breathless. Breakfast at Tiffany's—*oh wait, Mickey Rooney playing that racist Japanese caricature. Okay, a bit more modern. Can't go wrong with some* Ferris Bueller's Day Off. *Stay away from* Sixteen Candles *though—another racist Asian character. Should probably just throw those movies away. Fuck it, put on the* Lord of the Rings *trilogy and stop thinking about movies. Just throw the dinner stuff on the counter, ignore the clock, curl up and let the world slide away. Imagine a world more fantastical, where people with weird abilities are respected, spoken of reverently, in hushed tones, are made members of important councils that make important decisions using unique insight that regular people simply don't have. Where people like me would go on adventures, quests that could change the world.*

Where could she go to escape on a quest of her own? Maybe the Philippines, the one she knew through her father's stories. Humid and hot, land of mythological creatures—maybe she could meet a real nuno sa punso, gain its trust. Or maybe tame Dad's favourite, the half-horse trickster tikbalang.

Or maybe she could go to Norway. The cold wind, the northern lights, the crackling quiet, the land of her mother and her name and her power.

She shifted her legs, felt the air around her change, grow hotter and then colder.

How long had she not been alone?

The shadowy figure in the corner of her small apartment filled her with dread, but also a strange comfort. A sense of inevitability. The stale taste of red wine gummed her mouth shut as she tried to greet it, but a greeting wasn't necessary. The shadows shifted as it moved, changed size. It turned from a half-horse creature into a tiny old man, his long beard trailing on the floor as he moved closer to Freya using a strange crouching hop.

The nuno touched Freya's wrist and she knew she had been cursed. The imprint of his hand flared, recalling the imprint of Aunt Judith's hand as they'd hurried away from the restaurant.

And then he was gone.

Freya tried to move, talk, anything, but she was frozen, curled around her dead laptop, her useless books, the detritus of her waking life.

She wrenched her eyes toward the window, willing her heart to slow. Why was her window so big? Why were her curtains wide open? Falcons soared across her vision. A cloak drawn across the moon. A glittering chariot pulled by two cats. They burned the goddess Freya three times, she remembered, and it was the cause of a war, a war so endless that everyone just got tired of fighting. Freya banished to the wrong side, forever.

She couldn't wake up. The night so long that she saw every Vanir, every Aesir, learned all of their faces. A dream so long that she saw every nuno sa punso in every mound of earth, learned their names and their histories. She wondered if she had become a manananggal, separated from her lower body, flying forever in a desperate attempt to rejoin herself before she was burned by the sun.

But when the sun finally rose, Freya welcomed the fire, welcomed the release from the endless night.

I came down from my bedroom to find my parents sitting in the living room, reading the newspaper together, laughing. I didn't think my subconscious had retained the sound of my mother's laugh, but there it was, clear as life.

I stopped in the doorway, watching them for a minute. Mom looked up and waved me over.

"Hi, Pumpkin," she said. "Sleep well?"

"Very well. Don't you think I'm too old to be Pumpkin? I'm twenty-eight now."

"You'll always be my Pumpkin, even when you're a hundred."

I sat down next to her and she wrapped me up in her arms. I could smell her hair, her shampoo, her skin. Vanilla. For a second, the reality of her overwhelmed me, swirling my brain. But I relaxed, let my mother hug me one last time. For a second, I let myself believe she was alive.

I pulled back to look at her. Funny, she somehow looked the age she'd be now if she'd lived. She was dignified, comforting. Her eyes crinkled at the corners when she smiled. Just like Javi.

"I'm glad you have a friend like him," Mom said, and in dream logic, it was perfectly natural that my thoughts were communicated to her. "He looks out for you and you look out for him. It's good to have someone like that in your life."

"And Mary and Elliot too. I think you'd really like her now."

"She's even cooler than I thought she'd be."

Out of the corner of my eye, I could see the edges of the room flickering like a flag in a breeze.

"Mom, I have to go," I said. "Is that okay?"

"Of course! Next time let's talk longer."

"Do you think there will be a next time?"

She smiled but didn't answer. My father hadn't moved a muscle the whole time.

I looked to my left, and I was on our front porch. It was summer in Kelowna, and a humid breeze brushed the ends of my hair across my shoulders and into the collar of my shirt. I walked down the middle of the silent street, not a soul in sight. I felt a strange happiness, a complete and pure feeling of contentment. I hovered in the stubborn belief that Mom was real, that she wasn't dead and unreachable.

When I opened my eyes to the darkness of my room, I was already crying.

I knew she was dead. I also knew that I had just been with her. Not in the literal she's-in-a-better-place way that everyone in church kept repeating after she'd died. It was so real. It couldn't have meant nothing.

If she were still alive, I knew, I would have told her everything about me, and she would tear down the whole world to keep me safe.

I don't know how long I lied there, letting every emotion whirl through me without resistance. The room grew brighter. What day was it? Telling Aunt Judith my secret felt like it'd happened three months ago instead of just three days. I wondered if Mary had called her yet. My world had been silent since leaving Javi's, so I assumed not. I didn't blame her. How do you even start a conversation like that, let alone with a parent you were more accustomed to avoiding?

I flung my arms overhead and stretched, feeling every muscle in my body shake and come to life. Time to come out of my cocoon.

There was a message from Carol about working an evening shift, but that was hours away. No clients were waiting for private readings. Maybe I could wade into a few social media tarot groups and try marketing?

No. As soon as the thought entered my brain, I deflated. In my current frame of mind, I had no energy to promote myself.

I pulled on my jacket, grabbed my bag, and made my way to the coffee shop at the end of my street. I hadn't been there in a while, and when I walked in I had a sudden craving for the Americano they always expected me to order.

I sat at a table with my coffee and dropped my bag on the floor. Something thunked suspiciously. It was the book Shaun had lent me.

What did it mean that I'd forgotten about the book so quickly? I felt a strange pang when I remembered the look on his face that last time he'd walked away from me. My fault, really, for letting him into my life so quickly. Into my little egg of privacy and comfort, where everything was ordered just the way I liked—where I didn't have to tell him the whole truth. What was so wrong with keeping it that way?

Maybe this was all too much, too fast. Now that I was getting my strange hallucinations under control, maybe it was time to let STEP go. I'd fulfilled every promise I'd made to Mary. I'd found people to help me. I'd helped my aunt. I understood myself better and had discovered that, at least for a moment, I didn't have to be alone. These were all things I could be satisfied with, maybe even enough to put aside. I was ready to let my world be small again.

Then I thought of Javi, and I knew I didn't want to let go of him completely. I would miss him too much.

Let STEP go, let Shaun go, keep Javi. Baby steps. Maybe one paradextrous friend would be enough. The one who took me as I was—the one I'd been able to really be myself with—who was calm and self-contained in his ability, who didn't demand more of me than I wanted to give.

On my way home, emptying my head of everything but the sound of my feet swishing through spilled-over leaf piles on the sidewalk, I began to feel light-headed. I thought maybe I was just hungry, but then the edges of my vision began to waver.

Shit. Not now.

I could see my building, but its shape grew dim against the blackness threading in.

Not here not here not here.

I walked faster. My ears were blocked and my heart was racing. I could feel my face grow cold.

I remembered Javi's face during my last hallucinatory vision. I pictured his face next to mine in the mirrored closet door of his foyer, his hand on my elbow, and the blackness receded for a moment, long enough for me to shakily get into my building and climb the stairs to my floor. The lock on my front door nearly foiled me, but I got through in time, just as the fabric of my sight unravelled.

Shaun was sitting at my tiny dinner table. Sitting across from him, his back to me, was Dad. I couldn't see his face, but I knew it was him.

I quietly took off my shoes and jacket and padded over to my couch, where I could now see Dad in profile. I dragged my gaze to Shaun's face. Both appeared so clear, so much clearer than my vision of Aunt Judith. If not for the telltale sound of blood roaring in my ears and the waviness at the edges of my sight, I could believe they were really sitting there.

"She doesn't have to know it was me who told you," Shaun said.

"How else could I know?"

"There's another guy in our group, Javi. Tell her it was him. He's a big fan of yours".

Dad was silent, considering his fingertips.

"Why?" I asked, and I couldn't tell if I'd whispered or shouted.

Shaun turned to me with a sneer. "What's the alternative, Freya? Hiding forever? You need to see. You need to see."

I stood up, anger lashing through me. "See what?"

"See how useless it is to be afraid of who you are. You have a right to be a complete person, to use the skill you have."

He was quoting himself, from when he'd read my emotions.

"Don't involve my family."

"They're already involved. I'm involved. You involved me. I helped you. But when I asked you for help, you turned away."

"You're being petty and childish."

"It could have been you and me, changing the world."

I was shaking. But he turned away as if I wasn't there, back to my dad.

"She doesn't have to know it was me who told you."

"How else could I know?"

They were repeating themselves. This was going nowhere.

I tried a different approach. "Dad. Don't."

Dad looked at me, and again I had to brace myself against how real the moment felt. "What about my career? Doesn't that matter to you? Your life is rich and interesting. You can help."

"You can't!" I cried.

"You have no right to tell me what I can't do, Freya." Dad's voice was blank, emotionless.

There was a strange sound, a kind of strangled cry. High-pitched and far away. But it wasn't far away. It was coming from me. All I felt was pain, physical pain. I couldn't breathe, I could barely see. An earthquake under my skin. The world was beginning to go dark.

I needed to pull myself out.

I ran desperately into the washroom, looked into the mirror. My face looked distorted and wrong. Black voids where my eyes should be.

And then I was me again.

I tried to bring my breathing back under control but began sobbing instead. I staggered into my bedroom and collapsed into bed.

Someone was knocking on my door. Loudly. Persistently.

The sound was knives through my brain. How long had it been going on? I thought about not getting up. My head throbbed. More knocking. Louder. I forced myself to stand and go to the door.

The face through my peephole was one I didn't expect.

"Javi," I said as I opened the door, "What—"

But he was already inside, gripping my arms. His eyes were huge and he'd gone pale. "Are you okay? Did something happen?"

"What's going on?"

He looked me over frantically, and through my mental haze, I tried to wave him away. He grabbed my hands, examined them. "Look."

Sure enough, there were small cuts all over my hands, pinpricks of dried blood. Red marks that would bruise. So that's where that throbbing had been coming from. But how?

"Holy shit. Did you do that?" His voice was nearly a whisper as he stared at my dinner table, the dented and splintered wood in the middle.

I made a fist. The marks were peppered along the side of my fist leading down from my pinky, as if I had slammed my hands down onto the table over and over.

"It's just particleboard," I said, but somehow that didn't make it better.

We went into the kitchen to wet sheets of paper towel and gently dabbed at the blood. There wasn't much.

"Looks worse than it is," I said, for something to say.

"Does it hurt?"

"A little. But I didn't notice it before." I looked at the table again. "How the hell could I have possibly done that damage?"

"Adrenaline, maybe," Javi said.

I shook my head, came back to the moment. "Why are you here?"

"I was at work," he said, "when I started to get a weird feeling. Like when you're walking down the street and a subway goes under you. But this was stronger and coming from inside. I thought it was my skill at first. Maybe I was sensing one of my students. But then," he shook his head, "I saw you. Like a projection. Or a hallucination. It was brief but clear."

"Like my skill."

"When we met on Oneira, I could sense you stronger than other people. Maybe this is related."

"I don't understand."

"I don't either. But you didn't look normal. You looked terrified. And I felt terrified. I've never experienced anything like it before. I tried to call a couple of times, but you didn't answer. I was really freaked out. So I came over. What the hell happened?"

I tried to tell him as much as I could about the vision. My recall was full of jagged edges, flashes of white light, but eventually I painted a clear enough picture of what had happened.

He responded with a series of quiet curses.

"Shaun knows who you really are," he finally said.

"Maybe. But maybe not. My phone's been silent, which means he hasn't gotten through to Dad yet." I shook my head. "You should have heard him in my vision. He was so bitter. He thinks I betrayed his trust. We formed a bond when he used his skill on me, and in his mind I've destroyed that bond."

"What? Because you didn't feel comfortable outing yourself on TV? That's ridiculous!"

He was right. It was ridiculous. I felt a hot wave lick through me again and I stood up, pacing to try and calm down. I needed a clear head. I couldn't afford to get emotional. I took a deep breath.

"I need to find out what he knows, if anything. And how he found it out. When is that interview you two are doing?"

"What? Oh." He pinched the bridge of his nose and squeezed his eyes shut. "Next week. Wednesday."

"Eight days from now. Not much time."

"What are you going to do?"

"I don't know yet." I stopped in my tracks. "I'm sorry, I didn't even ask if you wanted water or something. Coffee? Are you feeling better?"

I busied myself in my kitchen, feeling more myself as hunger started to gnaw at me. I was halfway inside the fridge reaching for some leftover takeout pizza when it finally struck me that Javi was in my apartment—and it felt normal. There had been no ceremony beforehand, no time to worry, no need to hide anything. He was just here.

I returned to the living room with the reheated pizza and two bottles of beer, and then we sat back and chewed in meditative silence for a while. Meditative for me, at least.

If Shaun did know who I was, could I head him off at the pass, tell Dad before he did? Maybe. But what if I was able to talk Shaun out of it, figure out why he was going to do it? Then I wouldn't have to tell Dad at all.

But would he listen to me?

I recalled vision-Shaun's tense lips, the valley between his eyebrows, his hard green eyes. Untrusting.

He'd locked me out. It wouldn't work.

I stood, paced around the room. Rubbed my hands, wincing at the pain. I must have had that vision for a reason. It was too weird, too explosive, too real for me to ignore its message. But what could I do?

When I noticed the tarot cards strewn across my desk, I actually laughed.

"What's funny?" Javi asked.

"I can't believe it. How perfect."

I picked up the card and threw it down on the coffee table, pointed meaningfully. Javi squinted at it, shrugged.

"The Hermit? What, your plan is to live in a cave somewhere from now on?"

I shook my head, sat down. "Shaun is a guy who believes his way is the best way," I said. "The only way. Everyone has to fall in line or else. And he thinks he's doing it for the good of all paradextrous people. Who, out of all the people in the world, has any hope of getting through to him?"

"I don't know."

"Alan fucking Y."

Javi swigged his beer, dragged the back of his hand across his mouth. He didn't need to think for long. "Impossible."

"But think about it. Alan Y's whole life was ruined because of what was done to him. How do you think he'd feel about Shaun revealing my secret to my dad against my will?"

"Alan Y might admire Shaun for fighting for our rights."

"He might. But I'm betting that his years of absolute shit will win out over all of that."

"You sound almost like you're hoping it will."

"I know. I don't mean to. I know he's a real human being and I don't want to put him through more trauma. But he's the best idea I can think of."

Javi passed his hand across his mouth again, this time in thought. A prickly sound of fingers scraping along coarse stubble. My own foot, tapping against the leg of the coffee table.

"I can't think of a better idea either," he said, finally. "I have to say, though, that this plan sounds like something Shaun would come up with."

My throat went dry. Could I do this without Javi? Could I be alone again, fighting for my safety? Just hours ago I'd imagined my life without him but now I needed him desperately. "Will you be okay with that? Will you be okay with me?"

He set down his bottle. That Javi look I'd come to know so well. It meant consideration, and it meant certainty.

"We need to stop this," he said.

I exhaled, nodded. "The only advantage we have is that Shaun doesn't know that we know. So we need to act fast."

The sound of Freya's ringing cellphone made her jump, and she nearly flung her takeout cup of coffee across her building's hallway. She let it go to voicemail as she focused on opening her apartment door, but it rang again immediately. Then a third time.

She grumbled when she fumbled her grocery bags and coffee onto her kitchen counter and read *Dad* on the screen.

But then she jolted awake. Something must be wrong.

"Are you okay?" he said frantically.

She cleared her throat. "Yes, I'm fine. Why?"

"Did you hear about it? The veker firebombing?"

"It wasn't a firebombing," Freya said without thinking.

"How do you know? Freya, did you see it?"

Her internal alarm blared. *Be careful.*

"No. I heard about it on the news. Why? What are they saying about it there?"

"They interviewed the veker's girlfriend. She said he'd been trying to keep it under control, but something in him snapped yesterday."

"It can't have been that bad."

"Freya, the fire department and the police were called. A little kid broke his collarbone in the panic."

"Oh." She hadn't known. But she also hadn't had much time to look.

"This is serious, Freya. This is Alan Y all over again. I'm booking a ticket to come get you."

"What do you mean come get me? I can't leave, Dad. I have a life here. I'm midway through my degree."

"You can study history anywhere. Do it in Winnipeg, at Mary's school."

"Winnipeg's history program sucks." She wasn't sure if that was true, but she threw her voice behind it. She would make anything sound true to get him to back off.

"I'm coming tomorrow."

"Dad, no. I'm serious. You can't just swoop in here and pull me away. I'm twenty years old. I'm not a little kid. I won't go."

He huffed on the other end of the line. Angry, she could tell, but she could also tell that her own anger had gotten through to him.

"I don't want you going anywhere aside from campus, do you understand? How far away do you live from school?"

"A couple of subway stops."

"No subway. You're too trapped on a subway."

Freya lowered the phone to her lap, took a large breath.

"I'll be fine, Dad, I promise. This isn't the next Alan Y. Toronto is huge. The odds of this happening again here are minuscule."

"Freya, you have no way of knowing that. You check in with me every evening at six your time for the next two weeks."

He hung up. Not even a goodbye.

Freya shook her head. What time was it? She looked at the phone in her hand. Noon. She could have sworn it was three hours earlier. What had she been doing three hours earlier?

She gulped her coffee, stared at the takeout containers on the counter as she tried to remember last night's dream. Or was it a nightmare?

She dragged her gaze over to the corner opposite her bed, now filled with light. No evidence there of either the tikbalang or nuno from the night before. She shuddered. The idea of them seemed juvenile, but the memory filled her with dread all the same. She'd definitely never had a dream like that before, awake and asleep at the same time. No more wine for a while, she resolved—though as she picked up the bottle, she noted with interest that half still remained. She hadn't drunk as much as she'd thought.

She pulled cold leftover noodles out of the fridge and settled at her small dining table with her breakfast and her laptop. Something she'd blurted out to Dad as a last-ditch attempt to get him to calm down had stuck with her.

This isn't the next Alan Y.

Was that true?

How many Alan Ys had there been?

Her phone blared an alarm. *Shit*. A paper for Early Modern Britain class was due in three days and she still hadn't started. But this other research she wanted to do was too compelling. Way more important. The paper could wait.

Her fingers trembled as she went to Google. First, she satisfied her curiosity about the veker from the restaurant. The restaurant owner wanted to press charges for mischief and vandalism, but the man himself remained unharmed, and wasn't in custody. Interestingly, the mother of the kid who gotten hurt seemed to be the only sympathetic voice among all those interviewed about the incident.

Freya couldn't help a cynical thought that crossed her mind: Dad must love how this veker's girlfriend was talking shit about him all over the news.

She started a new search—*Alan Y*—and froze when she saw the black-and-white face. His little kid face from the newspapers in the '70s. She'd forgotten that despite all the things his existence changed about the world, he'd been just a child at the time. Four years younger than she'd been when she first dreamed about her mother.

The man in the restaurant was an adult, fully in control of what he could do—or at least he knew what he could do. But Alan Y— had he even had any idea what his brain was capable of? How had it felt when that power came out of him? Was it scary? Had it hurt?

How had he felt when his parents sold him to a lab, left him to rot?

Freya jumped as her phone dinged again. This time it was a text from Mary.

Hi loser. Busy? :P

Freya swiped tears from her eyes and took a shaky breath. She texted back.

Nope.

Javi and I arrived at Cassandra's just as her family was finishing up their dinner. It was weird to be there on a Tuesday evening. During meetings, her family were usually out or stayed quietly out of the way. Tonight, the house was lively.

Cassandra's twin daughters were tall, already as tall as she was. They seemed like good kids, helped clear the table, even shook my hand. I was impressed. I made some banal joke about them looking exactly the same, the kind of thing they must have heard a thousand times before, but they both bore my banality with grace, laughing politely and excusing themselves before running upstairs to get on with whatever teenager business they'd most likely been thinking about through dinner.

Cassandra's husband was a chatterbox. He wanted to know about our drive, if we were hungry, thirsty, where I lived, how I'd found the group, how I knew Javi, anything and everything. It made sense when Javi turned to let me know that Kevin was a journalist.

I couldn't help but wonder if maybe he could have interviewed Shaun instead of that other journalist. That might've been easier on Cassandra; give Shaun his fifteen minutes of fame while ensuring the story wouldn't go off into uncharted waters.

Eventually, Cassandra's family disappeared, and we were alone. Cassandra placed two bowls of stew in front of us. I felt awkward and guilty even though Javi had called ahead before we'd left my apartment. I'd forgotten how long they'd known each other. She must have been able to sense something in his tone, what he'd said or hadn't said.

I picked away at the contents of my bowl as we began to talk. I confessed everything: my real identity, the reason I'd gone incognito at STEP, everything that had happened with my aunt, what had been going on with Shaun. Javi filled in a few details, but mostly I talked until my voice started to crack.

Samantha Garner

Cassandra was patient, quiet, making appropriate sounds of interest and surprise. Of course she'd heard of my father, but still, her questions were surprisingly few. The dishwasher's repetitive churning sound rounded out the cozy domestic backdrop. The setting was almost comical, considering that Javi and I were trying to convince Cassandra to help us betray Shaun's trust.

She picked up her coffee cup, from which I detected a whiff of Bailey's. Her eyes radiated calm, but I could see the strain she was under in trying not to frown.

"Freya, I have to be honest," she said. "I worry that you're damning Shaun for something he hasn't done yet. Might not even do."

"That crossed my mind." I glanced at Javi, who was leaning forward on his elbows, his hands folded at his chin as if he were attending an important board meeting. "I'm going to make sure I'm right before I act."

"I'm also concerned about your plan to contact Gary Quick."

It took me a second to remember Alan Y's real name.

"Contacting Gary is just a contingency plan," Javi said from behind his hands.

I hadn't seen them speak to each other outside a STEP meeting before. How long had Javi told me they'd been friends? Six years? His tone was so careful, so reassuring. The respect he had for her was touching.

Six years. Javi would have been the age Shaun is now. I remembered what he'd said to me, the night of my date with Shaun. "I remember being twenty-five, thinking I had all the answers." Was Javi like that when he'd met Cassandra, when he'd helped her with her research, three years before she started STEP? If not for her calm guiding influence, would he have turned out differently? Desperate for solidarity, and lashing out when it didn't come?

I felt a momentary pang. The Shaun in my vision, telling my deepest secret to my father, was so real. So deserving of my ire. But Cassandra was right. I needed to be absolutely sure there was no mistaking what he planned to do. Because what I'd planned to do, there was no going back from.

"There hasn't been anything written about Gary in several years," Cassandra continued. "At least, not that I've found. This man's life was ruined because of his skill. You have to tread very, very carefully."

"I have no intention of screwing up his life any further."

"No, I suppose you of all people would be sensitive to that." She finally smiled—a small, tentative one, but a smile all the same. "Just a minute."

She drained her cup, scraped her chair back, and went to the living room to retrieve a laptop. When she returned to her seat, I couldn't help but notice the scene she created: smartly dressed woman, coffee cup at her side, laptop in front of her. She looked like the subject in one of my dad's stock photos.

"The last article I'd read about Gary was written nine years ago, on his fortieth birthday," she said. I expected her to open the laptop, but instead she laid her hands on it, took a deep breath, and closed her eyes. Her fingers began to twitch, move side to side, almost as if she were paging through an invisible card catalogue. Her eyes shifted side to side under her closed eyelids.

Javi was watching my reaction. Check this out, his expression said.

Cassandra began to speak, her eyes still shut. "Still living in England. Small village in North Yorkshire. Doesn't say which one. Respecting his privacy for once. Goes by an assumed name. Working as a guide in Yorkshire Dales National Park. Says he likes the quiet. The peace. Likes not being near so many people. Not many recognize him. Is thinking of retiring soon. Has family in the States. New England. Finds the same peace in the countryside there. Nothing else of value reported. It's a short article."

She fell silent. Then she flexed her fingers a few times, rubbed her forehead in slow circles, and finally opened her eyes. She looked remarkably refreshed and, well, normal. After using my skill, I sometimes felt like a swamp monster.

Javi and I were silent. She waited as if expecting questions, and when we gave none, she opened her laptop, typed for a moment, then spun the screen around to show us a website.

"The good news is there are only a few dozen Quicks in New England. The problem is the list covers three states."

I leaned forward to squint at the list of last names, first initials, and cities on the screen.

"Can we get more details?" Javi said. "I imagine we can't just call all of these people and ask them to put us in touch with Alan Y."

"We could get more details," Cassandra said, "but it might take some time. Why don't you leave it with me?"

"What do we even do if we find him?" I asked. "How do you say to someone who doesn't want to be found, 'Hey, there you are, now help me'?"

Cassandra sighed, drummed her fingers briefly on the edge of the table, "Leave that with me too. I might know someone who might be willing to help."

I peeked at my phone to check the time. It was getting late, and it was a school night. We'd been there for longer than I thought. "We should go," I said to Javi. And to Cassandra, "Thanks for being so cool about this. All of this. I know it's not what you expected when you met me."

She stood up and hugged me, enveloping me in a strong embrace. Those lucky twins. Still pretty much kids, still able to crawl into this hug whenever they need it, confident that their mother would always dry their tears, laugh with them, fight with them, be there when they woke up in the morning.

At that moment, I really wanted my mom.

Traffic on the highway was surprisingly light and we made good time back to Javi's house. I didn't do much talking. I couldn't. I had no energy to think of anything but keeping the car in its lane.

So I asked Javi to talk. I wanted to hear about anything that wasn't related to skills in any way, shape, or form. His eyes were tired too, but bless him, that friend I'd done nothing to deserve: he talked. For the whole ride home, I hung on his words, his stories about Colombia, about Lebanon, about aunts and uncles and grandparents and cousins and people and places and worlds I would never ever have to worry about as long as I lived.

Freya decided she would rather die than listen to people talk about *Metropolis* one more time, but she enjoyed how upset Leo and Ben were getting.

"You can't say a film is overrated just because you've heard about it a lot."

"I absolutely can. Yes, the effects were great for the time, but the acting. The acting!"

"It was a silent film. The standards for acting were different."

"It was cheesy even for a silent film."

Freya slowed her pace, waiting for them to catch up. Despite the chill and the falling snow, Leo and Ben were meandering as if it were a warm summer day.

"Can you guys have your pretentious debate inside?" she asked. "We're nearly there."

They flung open the door to the board game café, and as she blinked in the dim light, Freya glimpsed the other patrons engrossed in their games of chess or Battleship.

Leo's glasses fogged up as he unwound his scarf. "That couch in the back is free," he said, and hurried off to the back of the cavernous room.

"Sometimes I feel bad for trolling him," Ben said, shaking snow from his hair, "but he's fun to argue with. Do you see how red he gets?"

They walked to the bar area and squinted at the menu. Freya knew Ben would get the same thing he always did: black coffee and a cheese quesadilla.

She'd only met Ben and Leo two months before, at the university Classic Film Club's movie night, but she thought she was getting to know them, maybe even forming a connection—especially with Ben. Which was great. She was already in her last year of university and was beginning to worry about how little she went out to meet people.

She was trying to think of something interesting to ask him when the front door burst open again and someone called her name. The other members of Ben's usual group caught up with them. Freya usually found the three of them plus Ben too much to handle for too long—they always seemed so happy—so she ordered two bottles of lager and a couple of soft pretzels and retreated to the back couch where Leo was already sorting out pieces for a game that reminded her of Tetris.

"Thank you," he said, receiving the food and drink. "Don't let me forget to buy you the next drink. Want to play a round?"

"Shouldn't we wait for the others?"

He scoffed and shook his head. "They have catching up to do first. Even though we only saw them a couple of days ago."

Freya looked over at the bar. Sure enough, they all seemed comfortable enough where they were. Ben was already starting on his quesadilla. He caught Freya looking at him, and she hastily turned back to her beer and focused on setting down the first piece on the board.

Freya and Leo ate and drank, silent as they considered their moves carefully.

"Shit, you're good at this game," he said finally, swallowing his last mouthful of pretzel.

"I played a lot of Tetris as a kid."

"Let's hustle the others. We'll pretend to suck, and then at the last minute we'll crush them."

Freya laughed and out of the corner of her eye noticed the sound catch Ben's attention. She cleared her throat. "So, are you looking forward to the holidays? Are you going to see your family in Hamilton?"

"Yeah, I'll probably spend the whole Christmas break there. I don't really want to, but I'm expected to. What about you? Going home for Christmas?"

Freya shook her head. "No. I'll probably see my aunt and my cousin, but I've never gone home for Christmas. My dad and I don't really get along."

"Sorry to hear that. Same with me and my dad. He tries, but sometimes I think we're just not matched for each other, you know? Like, if he weren't my father, I don't think we would have any reason to talk to each other."

Freya fiddled with the label of her beer bottle. She'd never heard it put that way before. The truth of it, the sense of it, rushed through her. "Mine too," she said.

"It sucks. It really sucks."

"It does. I forget he exists sometimes. Sometimes I stop and wonder when we last talked to each other, and I have no idea."

"And then you feel like an asshole because you kind of don't mind."

"Yeah. Fuck."

They each took a swig of beer.

"Hey," he said. "Since you're not going anywhere, why don't you come out to Hamilton one day over the break? I can show you around. It's nicer than you've probably heard it is."

"Honestly, all I know of Hamilton are the factories you can see from the highway."

"Okay, well then I definitely have to show you the cool parts."

Ben slid onto the couch next to Freya. "The cool parts of what?"

It was a small couch, and the space between her and Leo meant that Ben's leg was squished next to hers. She moved minutely to give him more room, but not too much. The others settled into armchairs around the table.

"Leo and I might hang out in Hamilton over Christmas break," Freya said. "He says it's nice."

"We have a mountain," Leo said. "Wait, no, shit, you're from BC. Forget I said that."

"What part of BC are you from?" Ben asked.

"Kelowna. It's in the Okanagan."

"Oh, I know, I've been there. Well, not to Kelowna but close. I lived in Calgary when I was a teenager. Went skiing in Revelstoke once."

"That's not quite the Okanagan, but still, pretty cool."

"Do you ski? If you're from BC you must be really outdoorsy."

Freya couldn't help a laugh. "Not at all. I like being outside and I used to go camping with my parents when I was a kid, but I don't do that kind of thing anymore. I'd like to though."

"Maybe this spring," Ben said, smiling at her.

She smiled back, enjoying the thought of still knowing Ben in the spring.

One of the others, a girl named Charlotte, interrupted. "You're from Kelowna? What're the odds you're Brian Tanangco's daughter?"

Freya's stomach dropped. She hated that look, the slow grin, the gotcha.

"Yeah, he's my dad."

"No way! I loved *Only Soaring*. He dedicated it to you, right? I remember your name because it was so witchy-sounding. It was a cool book. But I think *Kuya* is better."

Too close.

She stood suddenly. "I have to go."

Ben frowned. "What? We just got here."

"I just realized I have a paper due tomorrow. I'll see you later."

She was out the door before she realized Leo had trailed behind her. The shock of the cold winter wind stung her cheeks.

"Are you okay?" he asked.

Freya sighed. "I've been through too much because of that book. I want to forget it exists."

"Never read it. But I heard about it." He shook his head. "No wonder you don't want to go home for Christmas."

Ben popped his head out the doorway of the café, his breath curling in the air above him. "Come back, Charlotte's forgotten about it."

A wave of annoyance flowed through her. "I'm going home," she said.

"Well, let us walk you to the subway," Ben said, pulling his coat on as he stepped fully outside. "It's dangerous after dark. Vekers might be around."

Freya was silent, stunned.

Leo shook his head. "Seriously, dude?"

"Remember that guy from last year, in the restaurant? That guy's fucking brain exploded and he broke a baby's neck!"

"It was a kid and a collarbone," Freya said quietly, "and it wasn't him who did it."

They didn't hear her.

"What happened to that guy was a random accident," Leo said. "He didn't do it on purpose."

"Bullshit. Why are you defending those freaks?"

"Because they're human beings. For all you know, I could be one of them."

"Are you?" Ben shouted.

Leo took a step closer. "So what if I was?" His voice was low, cold.

"I would beat your face in right now."

A crowd was gathering. Concerned voices, questions.

Leo turned his gaze to Freya. Snowflakes gathered on the dark curls of his hair, silently, gently. "Did you hear what he said to me?" he asked her.

Freya couldn't breathe. She was shaking so hard she thought she would vibrate out of her skin. "Stop it," she said to him. With horror, she saw his eyes flame with betrayal.

"Fuck you," he spat. "Both of you. You fucking deserve each other, you bigoted pieces of shit."

And then he was gone.

Ben went back inside. The crowd dispersed. Freya was left alone.

I barely slept. I couldn't stop checking my phone all night, as if Cassandra would call me at three in the morning with Alan Y's home address. When I finally surrendered to the morning, my head was full, spinning. I shuffled into the kitchen to find something to eat.

My phone buzzed with a text.

Shaun.

My throat went dry. As much as I wanted to hide my phone, I also wanted to read the message right away and just get it over with. But he would see that I'd read it. It would seem like I'd been waiting desperately to hear from him.

Oh, fuck it.

Hey. I know it's really early but can we meet? We should talk.

How was I supposed to interpret that?

I tossed the phone back on the counter and paced the apartment. Goddamn STEP. Ever since I began meeting with them, a greater portion of my life had become me doing necessary things I didn't want to do.

I would meet him. Of course I would. I had to. I didn't want to but I had to.

But I wasn't going to just agree to meet outright. I would do some fishing first. I'd learned a hard lesson about showing Shaun all my cards.

What do you want to talk about? I texted back.

Then I paced more, stopping briefly to chew mindlessly on a banana and a stale croissant. I tasted nothing.

My phone buzzed.

I want to explain myself. I don't like how we parted ways on Saturday.

I felt a flare of anger. Saturday. Four days ago. A long time to wait if he were really upset about something. But I tamped it down, and after a few more minutes, replied that I would be free later.

I'm on my way, should be there in an hour, he replied.

No. Nonononono. No more him being in my den ever again. I threw on my shoes and jacket and stomped down to the river. I realized I hadn't visited the river in a long time. I used to visit often, the downtown area with coffee shops and restaurants and my favourite bookstore. It was the same, normal. But I couldn't relax.

I waited in a long line at a coffee shop, considering whether we should meet right here. It was warm and in public. But no, I didn't want people overhearing anything we would say to each other.

Once I finally got my order, I made my way to a park nearby, sat on a bench facing the river. It was a pretty spot, well-maintained and nicely tree-green in the summer. But no, this wouldn't do either. I needed more distance.

I stood up and kept walking along the river.

Eventually, I came across a spot that I rarely visited. It was scenic enough. Quiet. There was a gazebo. There were benches. It was comfortable but not so comfortable that I would risk being lulled into—what? Complacency? Forgiveness?

I texted Shaun and told him where to meet me. Then I sat on one of the benches and looked out across the water to the other side, at the now-bare trees along the bank. In summer, that trail would be full of hikers and dogs and cyclists and even the occasional rider on horseback. But today, it was still, waiting. I'd walked west from my home, closer to Mary. Somehow, I could feel her at her end of the river, and it comforted me.

A few feet away, a young mother and her toddler were feeding some ducks, stubborn autumn holdovers. Maybe I should find another spot.

No. Enough. I'd moved enough. I checked my phone. Twenty minutes to go.

A chill wind blew up from the water, and I buried my face in my scarf up to my nose. I wished that Mary was actually here with me. I wished I'd told her what I was planning. I felt like a parasailer, hanging in the air, attached to forward momentum by nothing more than a cord.

I still didn't know what to say to Shaun.

I stared at the pattern of the wind on the water and determined my safest course would be to be patient, observe, react. Follow his lead, in a way, in order to stay ahead.

"Frances!"

Shaun's voice made me jump. I hadn't even heard him approaching. And he was early too, the bastard.

He sat down next to me. I didn't expect it to feel so weird, seeing him now. There was something different about his eyes. He was smiling at me but it was dampened, polite.

"Thanks for meeting me here," I said. "I hope you don't mind driving all this way."

"No, not at all. It's good to get out of the city sometimes. Besides, Markland's cute."

Cute. Markland was an old mill city, the product of generations of hard labour and determination. He made it sound like a suburb designed by committee.

My own anger surprised me. Was there nothing left of the way I'd felt about him just a few days ago? Or was I just too livid?

We sat in silence for a moment, watching the river, watching the toddler feed the ducks.

"How have you been?" I finally asked.

He took a while to answer, and for a moment I'd thought he hadn't heard me.

"I've been strange," he said. "I mean, things are strange."

Silence again.

"How so?" I asked.

I pictured how we looked, sitting there with our hands in our jacket pockets, backs flush against the bench, staring straight ahead. Nobody would guess that we were on the verge of building something just a short time ago.

"I feel like I'm about to become the person I always wanted to be," he finally responded, "but I also feel like I'm about to become the sort of person I hate."

I swallowed. "What does that mean?"

Another damning, interminable pause. I hadn't seen him like this, silent and closed up.

His lips tensed. "I read so much fear in you that day. It shook me, just how much."

He shifted now, turned slightly to look at me, but I didn't move a muscle. To face him completely, body to body, would be too much.

"My interest in you wasn't for purely superficial reasons, you know," he said. "When we first met, I'd said paradextrous people should demand equal treatment, and your response was that some people didn't want to draw attention to themselves. Do you remember?"

I did. It felt so long ago, but I remembered. He'd sat across from me that first day, had barely spoken a word up to that point. And I'd looked him right in the eye, even though he was a stranger, and I'd stood my ground.

"You'd said people like that were cowardly." I remembered the sting of it.

"A coward is someone who lacks the courage necessary to take a stand, to do brave things. I used to be that way. I try not to be that way anymore."

"What about people like me, who are just trying to live their lives?" I tried to hide the wobble in my voice, keep things level. "Now that you know me, do you still think I'm cowardly?"

"I threw it at you because I knew it would have an impact. But as I got to know you, I changed my mind. You made me understand your point of view. That's part of the reason I was so drawn to you. I liked to hear about your life. I wanted to figure you out."

"And did you? Figure me out?" I knew I was inching closer to the cracks in the ice, but I couldn't resist.

"Yes, I think so. Your whole life is built on fear. It's a shame because you're so special. You have so much power inside you. You could change so much."

"My whole life is not built on fear."

"Prove it."

A pulse of anger. I had to justify my life to him?

"I told my aunt about my hallucination," I said, not caring to hide a note of irritation.

"You did? When?"

"After the last meeting."

The mother and child had wandered off, and Shaun and I were utterly alone.

"I wish you'd told me. I'm really proud of you for doing that," he said quietly.

I scowled. I didn't want his pride.

"Didn't it feel good?" he asked. "To tell her everything? To help her?"

No, it didn't feel good. And whether I'd helped her or not remained to be seen.

"Anyway," he continued, not waiting for my answer, "This proves my point. You're finally moving away from your fear, doing exactly what it doesn't want you to do. Why let your skill be passive? Why manage it like it's a chronic illness?"

"Shaun, you're twisting everything I'm saying."

"I'm giving you another perspective. I want you to see yourself the way I see you. That's why I was so disappointed. I needed your help. But once again, you let your fear rule you."

"You don't need me. You have Javi. He's going to do the interview with you."

Shaun snorted. "Javi. What good will that do? Javi's whole family has always been okay with him. All his story will tell people like us is that you can only have a good life if you're born into an accepting family. What about those of us who weren't?"

My heart was racing. I needed to calm down. Or to run. I didn't know which. "Fine. You're right. I am afraid. But my fear is real. It isn't irrational."

"I know that now. And I keep trying to tell you that it's going to be okay. Your father will understand. He'll respect you."

Oh fuck. Fuck fuck fuck fuck fuck. I couldn't breathe.

"What do you know about my father?" My voice floated up quivering with anger.

"The day I read your emotions, I was trying to figure out why you were so afraid of revealing yourself. I even ended up Googling Frances Tully. Nothing came up, nothing about you. I was stumped. But then I remembered seeing a Brian Tanangco novel in your room. I remembered how he'd revealed really personal things about his family and tried to pass it off as fiction. It was a crazy hunch, but I followed it. So I Googled all I could about Brian Tanangco. And I found an article, not even an article, a blurb, about a Freya Tanangco who spearheaded a high school food drive in Kelowna. And when I saw the photo I knew it was you right away. Your smile. Then everything about your life started to make sense."

He took my hands in his, unwittingly squeezing the bruises I'd earned from striking my table the day before. I winced and pulled out of his grip, slid away from him.

"You researched me and my life and my family, and you didn't tell me before you tried to use me for your interview."

His face fell. "I would never use you. I can't believe you'd think—"

"Don't!" I nearly jumped to my feet.

"I just want you to be honest with yourself. I can help you. I want to help you."

"I don't owe the world my entire life!" I said through gritted teeth.

He turned from me to stare darkly at the river. "I wish you had my skill for a moment," he said. "Maybe you'd would learn to give a shit about me the way I do about you."

"If you really do care about me, you'll respect what I want."

"You don't even know how good your life could be. Things'll be better for you in the end. You need to see."

"It's not your place to reveal anything about me that I don't want to share."

"You have no right to tell me what I can't do, Freya."

I shivered. Those were the exact words my father had said in my vision.

He continued. "Would you change your mind if you could know for sure that your father would accept you as you are? I can talk to him for you."

An icy finger traced my spine. I couldn't believe it.

"Shaun, don't you fucking dare. I mean it."

"You'll never learn to trust me otherwise, will you?"

"You need to leave," I said. "We're done."

He stood up. "You're putting your own comfort before the good of your people. But we have a real chance to change the world. Just think about it."

I stared at the river. The wind snaked around my face as I listened to his shoes crunch away on the gravel.

Freya shivered and pulled her parka tighter around her.

"Why did you want me to come visit you in February?" she asked Mary, who was walking beside her in a thin peacoat, wearing no gloves while smoking a cigarette.

"It's only minus five, you big Okanagan baby."

"I think I'm dying," Freya said. She tried to distract herself by looking at the low brick buildings as they hurried past—Mary had told her this was one of the oldest neighbourhoods in Winnipeg—and was grateful when they finally arrived at the restaurant. It was warm and inviting and smelled like croissants.

"The French toast here is really good," Mary said, excitedly leading Freya to a table by the window. "I get it as often as I can."

Freya laughed. "When I was in second year I could barely afford to eat regular toast at a restaurant, but you're a proper bruncher."

"Winnipeg is a fuck of a lot cheaper than Toronto."

"No kidding. Your apartment is palatial compared to mine."

"I'm glad you like it—we've been spending so much time there. I feel bad, I should be taking you out on the town or something."

Freya snorted. "It's the North Pole up here. I'm happy to be where it's warm."

Mary proudly introduced Freya to the server as she ordered the French toast for both of them. Freya felt a bit like a show pony, but it was so cool to see Mary on her home turf, comfortable, a grownup.

When their coffees arrived, Mary wrapped her fingers around her mug, suddenly shy.

"I've been nervous about telling you this, but I'm seeing someone," she said, grinning wider as she said it. "His name's Elliot. He's a Computer Science major. We met at this stupid Christmas party. It was a costume party. Who has a Christmas costume party? I put on some bullshit cat ears and he wore a T-shirt that he'd written *costume* on in marker. We talked the whole night."

"My god, you're swooning! I've never seen you like this."

"Freya, he's so cool. He's so relaxed and easygoing. But he's not a pushover or anything. He's just—" Mary sighed, and Freya thought her cousin was going to fall out of her chair. "I told him you were coming and he asked to meet you."

"Of course! I want to meet him!"

She breathed out her relief. "Good. Maybe we can go out for dinner or something. Oh, and I haven't told Mom yet so... oh shit." Her last words trailed off as she looked out the window, eyes huge.

Freya whipped her head around and, through the warped glass, spotted a waving hand, nothing else.

Three Filipino women—one about Mary's age, the other two older—came into the restaurant and approached their table. Mary grew pale as she plastered a grimace-smile on her face.

"Mom, Tita Grace, let's go," the younger one said, looking uncomfortable. "You're being weird."

"Rachel, don't be rude," one of the older women said. She then spoke to Mary without taking her eyes off Freya. "Hello, Mary, how are you? Who is your friend?"

"We're trying to have a quiet brunch," Mary said pointedly.

The woman stuck her hand out to me. "I'm Josie. You must be Mary's cousin Freya. You look so much like your dad."

Mary shot up out of her seat. "Okay, that's enough. You have to leave us alone."

"But I just want to say hello quickly."

"Freya, we're leaving. Come on." Mary yanked a fistful of money out of her wallet and slammed it onto the table, grabbed her coat with one hand and Freya's arm with the other, and pushed past the trio of women. Freya barely had time to whip her own coat off the back of her chair before they were out the door.

"Whoa, what the hell?" Freya struggled against her cousin's iron grip, shocked into breathlessness by the icy wind.

Mary dragged her around a corner and only then released Freya's arm. Freya pulled her coat on, but Mary was too fired up.

"I'm still dealing with this shit! With them!" She pointed in the direction of the restaurant. "With that fucking book, all of it." She plunged her arms through the sleeves of her coat and patted her pockets. "Fuck! I left my cigarettes in there." She stomped off, leaving Freya to follow.

"What's going on?" Freya asked quietly.

Mary huffed out an exasperated breath. "I finally read *Kuya*. All of it. Now I know what Mom was so mad about."

"I still haven't read it."

They stopped at a store, where Freya stood and waited while Mary bought more cigarettes. She looked at her cousin, who Freya still halfway considered a little kid, and wondered if she should try to stop her from smoking. But, she reminded herself, Mary was twenty years old. She was fully an adult. And now that Freya had a moment to think, it dawned on her what Mary had done in the restaurant. She'd stood up to someone on Freya's behalf. She'd protected her publicly. Loudly.

Back outside, Mary lit a cigarette. "I'm sorry about brunch. But there's a diner a few blocks away. I have no idea how much money I threw on the table but I have a feeling it was way too much. Let's get some regular toast."

Their boots crunched over the hard-packed snow. Mary's breathing grew less and less angry.

"Thank you," Freya said, her voice shaking. "It must be hard, living with this every day."

"It's okay. It could be way worse. Anyway, it felt good to get mad at someone about it. You really should read that book, you know."

Freya shook her head slowly. "After what it did to our family? Why should I read it? Look how mad you are."

"The things your dad wrote—there's no way he didn't know what trouble it would cause. And every time some bullshit like this happens, I get even more upset about it. But in a weird way, it helped me feel closer to Mom. Even if some of what he wrote is fictionalized, it feels like her." Mary took another drag of her cigarette, exhaled in a snort. "You can read the one I borrowed. Take it back to Toronto if you want, I don't care. One less copy in the library."

After meeting with Shaun, I walked home, got into my car, and drove straight to Mary and Elliot's. I barely had the presence of mind to call ahead to let them know I was coming. Thankfully, I caught them before they left for work.

They sat me down and waited patiently for me to get it all out.

Mary paced the floor afterwards. "Unbelievably arrogant dickhole! Smarmy little weasel of a fucker! Who the fuck does he think he is?"

"He thinks he's helping me."

"Goddamn fucking bullshit!"

More pacing.

"You're going to stay here and I'm going to stay with you," she said finally. "No, don't protest. I know Shaun's probably not going to break into your apartment and murder you or anything, but I won't be able to concentrate on anything if you're alone. Come on. You need to eat and then we can decide what to do."

I followed wordlessly. Elliot gave Mary a goodbye kiss, then gathered me up in the strongest, tightest hug I'd ever received. He'd never hugged me before. The simple, unspoken kindness of it made me nearly weep again, but before I knew it he was out the door.

My cousin grabbed me by the shoulders and marched me to the dining room table. I sat obediently, and soon enough, a mug of coffee was placed in front of me. The sound of something sizzling in a pan, then the smell of garlic, tomatoes, sausage. Mary was talking as she cooked—light, meaningless, almost staccato chatter that I knew was meant only to keep me from going to a bad place until she could get back to me.

From where I sat I could see through the kitchen window, the trees lining the trail across the street. The leaves were gone, and the bare branches waved forlornly at me, their secret nests revealed. I shivered, remembering the chill wind by the river. I felt like it had followed me.

I still couldn't believe the anger in Shaun's eyes, his utter certainty that twisting my life around to suit his own agenda would somehow benefit me. How could I have been so blind to that aspect of his personality? I searched my memory, scraping through every interaction I'd had with him, every word, every look. I felt like the biggest, most obvious sucker ever foisted upon the world.

Mary clanked a plate down in front of me, and the intoxicating smell of garlicky fried rice, egg, and longanisa went straight to my stomach and made me sit at attention. I had smelled the food cooking, but it hadn't clicked that Mary was making my favourite Filipino breakfast, longsilog. I picked up my spoon and fork and took a moment to appreciate the meal. She'd even remembered I liked charred tomatoes and vinegar with it. There was nothing more comforting than the combination of tomato and tart vinegar sopped up by a spoonful of garlic-fried rice. It was a taste from my childhood that was as much a part of me as anything. Mary always wrinkled her nose at it, and her distaste for it made me wonder why Judith never went in for the Filipino fondness for vinegar the way Dad had, the way I had.

We ate silently for a few minutes, enjoying the decadence. I settled into my usual longsilog routine of trying to get a piece of everything onto my spoon to craft the perfect mouthful. Zeus came loping along to sit on the floor, gracing us with a large, pitiful gaze.

"Was I wrong?" Mary asked after a moment, around a mouthful of rice. "When I talked you into joining STEP," she explained. "The night of your accident. I remember the broken plates, food everywhere, me shouting at you. I know I can be that way sometimes. When I'm scared, or I feel like I have the answer and it's so obvious."

"I lost control of my skill and got hit by a car. I needed to find something to help me."

"But I just bowled you over. I didn't even ask you what you thought. And all this ended up happening. I pushed you into something you weren't ready for."

"Trust me. I would have told you if I'd thought you'd been wrong."

A small smile, unsure. We ate in silence for a while longer.

"What do you want to do now?" Mary asked.

I told her about the plan that Javi and I'd come up with, to find Alan Y, and the more I described it, the flimsier it seemed.

"There's no guarantee he'll talk to us, if Cassandra can even find him," I concluded. "With my luck, he'll press stalking charges or something like that."

"There must be something else we can try."

I exhaled sharply and shook my head. There was only one other thing.

"I can try talking to my dad. Convince him not to talk to Shaun. I could tell him that Shaun's a journalist. As far as I know, he still hates the press."

"He might fly here just to break Shaun's neck for threatening you."

"Or he'll want to hear what Shaun has to say. If I harboured a lifelong disgust of vekers and then someone called me up and said, 'Hi I'm a friend of your daughter and she's a veker and I have proof,' I think I'd be curious."

"Frey, come on. He wouldn't."

"Who knows what he might do. I haven't had a real conversation with him in years. The only other person he was ever close to was my mom. And yours, I guess."

Mary sighed and got up to refill our coffees. On the way back, she stopped short. "Maybe we can ask my mom for help."

"Do you really think she would want to talk to him? Or that my dad would listen to anything she has to say?"

"I meant maybe we can ask her for advice on what you can say to him."

I held my tongue. What insight could Judith possibly give us?

But then I remembered reading *Kuya*, those moments that showed just how close my dad and his sister had once been. If anyone knew how to get through to him, it would be her.

"I think it's worth a shot," I said finally. "The worst she can do is say no, right?"

"I'll call her now."

She grabbed her phone, pushed her chair back, and jogged upstairs. Zeus walked up onto the bottom step and slowly lay down, waiting for her return. It was quiet. The ambient house sounds and the dog's breathing lulled me into something resembling relaxation. If I tried, I could imagine I was having a normal day, a normal visit with my cousin.

Mary soon came down the stairs, phone in hand. "Mom's coming over for dinner tonight," she whispered, then went back up.

I leaned back in my chair and closed my eyes. I took a few deep breaths.

The vision of Shaun and my dad had seemed so vivid, so real. I'd spoken to them. Actually had a conversation. I'd never done that before—it was as if I was in a lucid dream. What did it mean? I was learning so much about my skill.

Could that mean I was learning to control my visions?

I tried to summon an active vision of Shaun, will him into existence. I pictured his intense green eyes, the dark hair always sliding down his forehead. It hurt to seek him out in this way, to try to visualize him as clearly as I could.

My phone buzzed on the table, startling me. I checked the screen, saw the name *Javi*, and breathed a sigh of relief.

Hearing his voice gave me a strange shot of confidence. He sounded measured, like always. It was comforting. Solid. But as I told him about meeting with Shaun, about everything, I felt the bottom slide out from under me a bit more.

"Mary's mom is coming over for dinner," I finished. "We hope she might help me find a way to convince my dad not to talk to Shaun."

"When? Tonight?" he asked.

"Yes. Why?"

"I'll be there."

"What?"

"I told you I would help you, so this is me. Helping you. As promised."

Freya didn't know what to expect. In the ten years since its publication, her dad's novel—*the* novel—had mutated and evolved in her imagination. When she was twelve, it felt like a thing with a fuse and faulty wiring. When she was a teenager, it was a spider in the corner of the room that would leave you alone as long as you didn't look at it. Now, in her twenties, she wondered if there was another perspective she could discern through the fog.

Freya started reading *Kuya* on the airplane coming to Toronto from Winnipeg. She told herself she'd just relax and watch a movie, but she could sense the book in her bag at her feet, as if it were vibrating at a frequency she could actually hear. Once they hit cruising altitude, she snapped off her seatbelt and pulled out the book. She placed it on her lap, looking at it. It was the paperback edition, well worn, the corners soft and white from years of Winnipeggers paging through it. The cover was black, with a photo of Okanagan Lake in the middle. It was an eerie photo, desaturated just enough so that the lake and the mountain behind it seemed to be one glassy object.

Dad's name was printed in white serif font in the top black bar, the novel's title in the bottom black bar. She stared at his name for a long time. It had been a while since she'd seen it in print. It seemed almost like a person with its own character.

Freya noticed the person seated next to her was eyeing her quizzically. She coughed and flipped to the first page even though she wasn't ready to begin.

The first thing that struck her was how lyrical Dad's writing was. She'd never heard him speak that way, but then again, she was sure most writers didn't speak the way they wrote. It was just like the books she'd had to study in high school English or Canadian Literature classes—which made sense. Her dad was a well-known Canadian writer, after all.

She stared out the plane window, letting the fact of his fame sink in as her gaze passed over the clouds. What would have to be different about her, about Dad, for her to appreciate who he was? Who was he really? Canadian writer Brian Tanangco? Or Dad, the guy who would take a different route home if he had a bad feeling, who'd snuck her sips of coffee when she was six?

Freya shook her head. She needed him to be Brian Tanangco if she was going to read this book. If she thought of him as Dad, she wouldn't be able to do it.

She read for the rest of the flight home. She read in the cab home from the airport. She read all the next day, all weekend.

Kuya was about the intertwined lives of a young man and his sister, two first-generation Filipino kids growing up in 1960s Kelowna. Victor and Janet. The boy was obsessed with books and the girl was in love with nature. Their conflicting lives eventually forced them apart.

Victor, the narrator, was obviously a character heavily influenced by Brian himself. Freya recognized immediately that he was named after her grandfather. He was sensitive, stubborn to a fault, prone to long periods of thought in which he was nearly insensible to the world around him, lacking the self-awareness to realize when he was clearly fucking up. Freya wondered if the way Victor was written was a sign that Brian was more self-aware than he'd ever let on.

Early in the book, Janet sparked like a wire. Even as a child, she seemed happy to exist in her own little world, one nobody could approach. But Victor understood, he was fond of her. He loved her, let her be the way she was. There was nuance in the portrayal of Janet's childhood.

That all changed once they became adults. The sections detailing Janet's—Judith's—sudden move to Ontario, her troubled marriage, and especially her battle with alcohol, were unflinching. Her story became less and less fictional, and Brian didn't take the opportunity to write a different ending for her.

Freya could see why her aunt had been upset by it. Why Mary was upset by it. She herself felt angry and awestruck at the same time. Why had he written it? What had he gained from telling

Judith's story? What did people feel when they read it, gossip disguised as elegant prose? Why had she never read any of her father's work until now?

On Sunday evening, Mary called her. They talked about Elliot, the new semester, Freya's visit to Winnipeg in general. After half an hour, Mary cleared her throat. "Did you read the book?"

Freya picked up the novel, flipped it over to look at the small black-and-white photo on the back cover. Dad: the way he was after Mom died, when it was just the two of them, before she was old enough to be the support he probably needed.

There was so much Freya wanted to talk about. Too much. But one thing jumped out at her, something that hadn't occurred to her in all the days she'd spent with the book.

"We're not in it at all. In that world, we don't exist."

The moment I saw everyone—Javi, Mary, and Elliot—crowded into the small TV room with Aunt Judith, I began to regret our plan. There was a definite tension in the air; it was almost claustrophobic.

"So," Elliot said from the floor, where Zeus was using his right leg as a pillow, "everyone has a drink? Is anyone hungry?" His arms were wrapped around his one dog-free knee. I could tell he was feeling unsettled. We both liked the peace of our homes, the just-rightness. We had that much in common. I gave him credit for being so agreeable with so little warning. He was surprising me more and more.

"It's fine, dear," Judith said tersely from the couch. The last to arrive, she'd greeted us all politely, but had eyed Javi warily. Since then, we'd just been sitting around not talking. I didn't know how to speak to her. Earlier, Mary told me they still hadn't talked about the fact that we knew she was paradextrous. Well, too late now. We'd have to do it later. Or maybe never, depending on how tonight went.

I tried to gather my courage while Javi ate. Mary had felt bad making Javi drive all the way to Solingate, even though it'd been his idea, and had all but forced a plate of leftover longsilog on him when he'd arrived. He'd protested, but his words died on his lips once he'd smelled the longanisa. Watching him save the sausage to eat last, I mentally scored one for the Filipino team.

As if reading my mind, Javi snapped his gaze up to me, giving me a grin around his mouthful of food.

I shifted in my armchair and took a deep breath. I had to say it all, right now, or I never would.

"Thanks again for coming, Aunt Judith. I know Mary told you we wanted to talk to you about something. Not about me this time. It's about my dad. I was hoping you could give me advice on how to get him to change his mind once he's decided on something."

My aunt guffawed, and my stomach dropped to my ankles.

"Good luck. Once your father sets his mind to something, no matter how long ago or how ill-informed, he won't let it go. He thinks his way is the only way and there is no arguing with him about it. Hell, not even arguing—there is no civilly discussing it with him. Believe me, I've tried. I spent my whole life trying to get through to him—he's my brother. I tried even after what he did to me. We used to be so close. I thought we understood each other. But the things he used to say about people like us—"

Aunt Judith stopped, three words too late. I knew exactly what her next thought was: she was wondering if she had just outed herself. The swell of empathy and love I felt for her in that moment made me desperate to fill the silence, to show her that she really was like us.

"Here's my problem," I said, my heart racing. "Someone from our support group, Shaun, is going on TV to share his story. He wants me to do it with him. I told him no, but he won't listen. I'd given him a fake name, but he still found out who Dad is. He thinks he can change my mind by telling Dad about me, to show me that I don't need to be afraid to reveal my skill to the world. I need to get to Dad before he does and convince him not to listen to anything this guy has to say."

Judith watched me, and in her evaluating gaze I saw so much of Mary.

Judith shook her head. "I'm sorry, Freya. Brian won't listen. I know he loves you, but when it comes to vekers, he sees nothing but red."

"Fuck," Mary muttered.

I dropped my head into my hands. "I was hoping you wouldn't say that."

"There must be something else you can do," Judith said.

"There is, but it's ridiculous. Our backup plan is to track down Alan Y and ask him to warn Shaun off. He's Shaun's hero."

"Have you heard from Cassandra?" Javi asked.

"Nothing yet." I caught Aunt Judith up: "A friend of ours found out where he might be hiding, but not an exact address. What are we going to do, fly to Maine and somehow chase down dozens of leads across that state, plus Vermont and New Hampshire?" I shook my head. "That'll take forever. Shaun could be in touch with my dad before we even land."

"I keep trying to think of a way I could use my skill to search for him." Javi set his now-empty plate onto the coffee table, arranged the knife and fork. It was his turn to explain. "I can sense other para-dextrous people. Like finding a homing beacon. But Alan Y lives in the States, and I don't have that kind of range."

I slumped back in the armchair and sighed. Maybe there was a Plan C. I already had practice living with a fake name. I could move somewhere else. Maybe leave Canada altogether. England was nice, full of remote villages I could escape to. Far away from the one Alan Y came from, of course.

"I can help," my aunt said quietly.

"What do you mean, Mom?" Mary asked.

Judith shifted on the couch and squared her shoulders, lifting her chin in that defiant Mary way.

"I have my own skill. I can use it to help Javi find Alan Y. Right now."

Alan Y was the scariest thing to ever happen to me.

I was only eight when the news came out about him, but I remember it so clearly.

"Judith," my father said. "Come here. Watch this."

The news talked about him like he was a nuclear bomb heading right for us. I can still hear the tones of their voices, the fear. They showed a school picture of him. I remembered thinking he could have been any kid in my class. This was the scariest person in the whole world? A little kid?

But my parents were terrified. Mom cried. They kept me and Brian home from school the next day. Ours wasn't the only family to keep kids home. Maybe Alan Y really was a nuclear bomb.

Everyone became suspicious of each other. Of people they'd just met, of people they'd known their whole lives. Mom wouldn't let me play with the girl across the street because she "acted weird." Everyone was jumpy as hell and getting swept away by it.

Your father started parroting what our parents said about Alan Y. Picture a ten-year-old kid on the couch with his parents every evening, leaning forward and absorbing the news. It was too much for me. I would get on my bike, go anywhere I could be alone.

Brian and I used to play and talk. He used to be my friend. But after Alan Y, we lost that connection. Sometimes I would see a flash of the person he used to be, but it would disappear if I got too close.

We left Winnipeg that year and moved to Kelowna. I hated it. In Winnipeg, my parents knew other Filipinos, we were part of a community that we didn't have to explain ourselves to. But in Kelowna, we stuck out. The only other Asians we knew were Chinese and even though we couldn't relate to them, everyone grouped us together as one unit. Brian took it hard. He wanted to fit in with the white kids, to prove himself to people who couldn't tell him apart from the rest of "us," who did things like tease us because we couldn't use chopsticks. He wanted to prove himself to everyone. Everyone except for me.

Thankfully, Kelowna had places for me to escape. There was a field near our house that was empty and overgrown and full of trees. I spent a lot of time there. It was quiet. I could be quiet for hours if I wanted to.

When I was ten, a new girl moved to town. Nancy. She was pleasant and happy to talk to anyone who talked to her first. So I talked to her. She was my first real friend in Kelowna, and I clung to her desperately. We went everywhere and did everything together.

One day, we were climbing trees and I slipped and fell. I'd never fallen out of a tree before. I landed weirdly and sprained my ankle. Nancy knelt down next to me and took my hand. I don't remember what she said, but I remember a wash of relief and calm. The pain let up. I felt dopey, unable to stop smiling.

Nancy stood up, and her eyes were huge. She got on her bike and rode away, and I limped home.

Nancy was away from school for a few days. When she came back, she pulled me aside at recess. She started crying and begged me not to tell anyone what had happened when we were climbing trees. She and her father had moved around so much because people had bullied her for what she could do. She didn't want to move anymore because she liked Kelowna and she liked me.

I asked her what she meant. She said, "When you fell out of the tree. I talked to you and made you not afraid anymore. It's a trick that I can do sometimes. I try to help people, but they sometimes get scared instead. Please don't tell anyone."

Don't tell anyone? Of course I wouldn't tell anyone! This was fantastic. A secret my best friend and I could share.

Over the years she developed her skill. We tested it, found the limits. Now and then it would slip out without her meaning it to—she was such a good person, always trying to help people and be kind to them. She'd talk to someone in her specific tone of voice and they'd feel calmer. But afterwards they'd get suspicious because they knew there was something unnatural about the interaction.

We were a unit, her and I. We did everything together, didn't care about anyone else. She never became very popular, but she didn't seem to notice the way I noticed.

In high school she did become friends with a couple of other girls, and she told them her secret. I warned her against it, but she thought I worried too much. It turned out I was right. These girls weren't really her friends like I was. They were just excited to have a pet veker. Sometimes I overheard them whispering about her behind her back, calling her a freak, but they'd take hours of her time whenever they were stressed about a test or a relationship—or anything at all. Sometimes they faked being upset just to see if Nancy's ability would still work on them—some of them liked the drugged feeling of happiness Nancy gave them. Nancy was so sweet and trusting that she never saw it. I had to knock one of the girls on her ass for them to finally leave Nancy alone.

Just before graduation, our class took a weekend trip to Vancouver. It was part educational, part celebratory, and I was thrilled. I'd never been to Vancouver before. It was amazing. Kelowna could fit into Vancouver seven times. Everything felt energized and electric. Nancy and I were going to go to the same university, but we decided to try to have as much fun as possible on our last high-school trip. We were lucky enough to be assigned to the same hotel room, and we barely slept, we were so excited. We made so many plans for our free hours over the weekend. We were eighteen and about to start our real lives and we couldn't wait.

The day after we arrived, a portion of our class was scheduled to go on a short sightseeing tour. We met up with our group at the Gastown Steam Clock, right in the middle of everything. Everyone cheered when we saw our small chartered bus coming up the street. Nancy hooted and clapped beside me, and I grabbed her arm in excitement.

I felt something strange, something I'd never felt before. It was a sort of warmth, different from the regular warmth of skin. It came from within, and hotter. But without burning. Curious, I gripped Nancy's arm tighter, focusing my attention on the heat. Like straining to focus on a lone voice in a crowded room. All my awareness was pulled toward it. Suddenly, it flared.

I immediately pulled my hand back, but it was too late.

Nancy screamed and began clawing into her own hair. I grabbed her again to try and calm her down, but she screamed louder. Then she broke free of me and ran into the road, right into the path of the bus. She died instantly. I saw the light go out.

Whatever happened to Nancy, I knew it was because I'd been the last person to touch her.

I shut down. My world stopped. The next thing I knew I was back home. The police asked questions and I answered without knowing what I was saying. I was in a haze for weeks. I didn't attend prom, I didn't attend graduation, I didn't attend anything. I stayed home. My parents and brother tried to console me, but that only enraged me. My best friend, the only truly good person I could think of, was dead. And somehow I had killed her.

I don't remember when the answer came to me. I just know that I couldn't stop thinking about the strange sensation I'd felt when I last touched Nancy. But when the answer came to me, I just knew it was true. I could feel it inside me, the way I could feel my breath or my heart. I didn't have to test it. I knew.

The warmth I was drawn to inside of Nancy was her ability. And when I reached out for it, that was when she'd lost all control.

That was how I'd killed my best friend.

I was a veker.

As soon as I knew, I became paranoid that other people knew too. That they could see it just as obviously as I could. A rumour came out that Nancy's accident was drug-related, and I hid behind that. So long as everyone believed Nancy was a hopeless drug addict, nobody would suspect me.

After graduation, I took up with Oscar. He was someone I knew from before the trip, a year older, already in university but not attending many classes. I never told him my secret and he never seemed to notice. I didn't go to the university I'd planned to. Instead, I took Human Resources classes by correspondence from a school in Vancouver. When I wasn't with Oscar, I was at home. I started drinking. First socially, with him in bars, then on my own in bars if he wasn't around, then alone at home, locked in my room.

When I drank I could feel the monster inside me settle down in a corner. I could almost forget it was there at all. I didn't care about anything except putting it to sleep.

I survived this way for a couple of years. By some miracle, I completed my course and got a certification. I started fitting in. I socialized. I had friends, or at least, people I could have fun with. My parents could tell I was drinking a lot, but I was working and bringing in money so they didn't much care, as long as I came home every night. They never liked Oscar, so I hid him as much as possible. We went out more, drank more.

When I was twenty-one, I lost my job and didn't immediately start looking for another one. I was having too much fun, and besides, Oscar had a good job and he paid for us. I didn't need money.

After three months, my mother confronted me. Suddenly I was too old to still be living at home. What would people think? This wasn't the Philippines. I couldn't live with my parents as long as I liked. Brian had already graduated university, whereas I sat in my room all day with my little vodka bottles. Mom sounded so disappointed, so profoundly hurt by the person that I'd become, that I just unravelled in front of her. I confessed and told her the truth about Nancy's death, and that drinking was the only way I knew to keep it from happening again.

I wanted her to gather me in her arms and tell me it would be okay. I wanted her to tell me that she loved me and she would help me. Instead, she screamed at me until she lost her voice. She threw things at me. Then she threw me out of the house for good.

Oscar and I left Kelowna, left BC altogether. He knew people in Toronto through work, so that's where we went to build a life. I never heard a word from my parents ever again. Brian and I talked on the phone sometimes and exchanged polite letters now and then. From these conversations I understood that Mom had kept my secret, at least from him. She told him only that I was a loser drunk who was getting into too much trouble to live at home anymore.

Over the years, your father's letters came more rarely. Camilla wrote to me as well, but she never opened up to me. When you were born, she called me from the hospital but we didn't talk long. I got my first photo of you six months later. I remember your fluffy dark hair and my brother's eyes.

Oscar and I got married. Of course we didn't invite anyone. Our witnesses were two of his coworkers. We left city hall and came home and got drunk. I found a job in an office where people left me alone. We got by. It was good. I was safe.

When I discovered I was pregnant, I was shocked—but I was also over the moon. A little baby, a little person to protect.

I decided I had to stop drinking. I went to a program that helped me quit. As soon as I was sober, I felt my ability stirring again. I knew I had to be more vigilant. I avoided handshakes and other contact. I kept my guard up. But otherwise, I was happy and healthy and going well. I was still fitting in, in a way I never had before.

When I was eight months pregnant, I went out for lunch with a coworker. One of our colleagues came into the restaurant, one I hadn't seen in a while, and I was happy to see him. He reached out to shake hands and, without thinking, I reached back.

I felt a warmth in him, just like I'd felt in Nancy.

He let go of my hand and looked at me. Then he pulled me a few steps away. A few seconds later, a waiter tripped and dropped a tray of scalding soup exactly where I'd been standing.

After lunch, he followed me out of the restaurant and demanded to know what I'd done. How I had known about his ability. How I had made his awareness powerful enough to anticipate a future event. He wanted me to help him develop his ability.

He was too intense and the conversation was too public. I turned and walked away as quickly as I could. He followed me for a few steps, then gave up. I kept going though. I didn't return to the office that day. I got permission to take maternity leave early. Then I quit. I never wanted to see that man again.

When Mary was born my life opened up, unfurled into something beyond me, beyond my ability. My entire existence focused on her. I was obsessed with her. I wanted her to have a perfect childhood. I wanted her to be smart and talented and happy and free and not take shit from anyone. I wanted her to be safe. Most of all, I wanted to keep her safe from me. Every time I touched her and felt no unnatural warmth pulling my awareness to her, I felt gratitude I didn't deserve. I had my guard up every time I hugged her, comforted her, bathed her, put her to bed, dressed her. I had to. I couldn't risk it.

I wanted her to grow up knowing only school and sports and music and art. Nothing about the monster her mother was. I didn't even care that her father worked so much that she barely knew him. I started drinking again, just a little, enough to keep the monster quiet again. But I was keeping her safe.

Once you had a cousin, Camilla became interested in me again. She started writing to me more and more. We talked on the phone sometimes. You girls were the only thing we talked about. We wanted you to become friends. As soon as Mary could string basic sentences together we made you talk to each other on the phone regularly, even just for a minute. You remember Mary's first visit to Kelowna when she was six. Oscar had to work as usual, but that was okay with me. I didn't want him there. I didn't want fights and snide comments and sarcasm. I wanted to be with my daughter, and I wanted her to have a good time with her cousin.

Going home was a bad idea. My father was dead and my mother refused to see me, but I was still terrified I would run into someone I knew. My favourite bar was still open, and I ended up visiting it more than I should have. Camilla came with me once, on the pretense of a girls' day out. We started to talk about things other than our girls. She was trying, I could see. But as I kept ordering drinks, I could see by the look on her face that I'd pulled myself out of her reach too.

I vowed never to go back to Kelowna. I loved Toronto. It was loud and big and nobody knew who I was there, nobody cared.

A year after that visit, Brian called me. He told me he'd just taken a camping trip with his family, and how on that trip he'd remembered the ghost stories we told each other when we were little. He told me that he missed me. I missed him too; I'd missed him for most of our lives. When he told me he was thinking of a new book,

I was supportive. I was supportive when he told me it would be loosely based on our childhoods. I told him it was okay.

But in the ensuing months, I grew paranoid. What if his book brought Nancy's death back to light? What if someone pieced together what'd really happened?

I tried to talk to him about this, but of course I couldn't tell him the truth. I could only sit there while he wrote whatever he wanted, treating my concerns as minor annoyances. As if I wasn't his own flesh and blood. Why couldn't he understand that I needed him to stop? That I was scared?

But he'd never tried to understand me. For all the characters he developed in his work, he never wondered if there could have been something more to why I drank, why I'd left home. To my brother I was just a drunk, a failure. Someone to pity. And that's how everyone who read that book would see me.

When your mother died, I was distraught. Even though we didn't talk as much as before, she was the only one who still spoke to me. I'd gone almost my entire adult life not being able to talk to my brother. Oscar and I were on the verge of separating. Tenuous as my relationship with Camilla was, at least we'd had one.

I regret not going to her funeral. But that can't be changed now. I refused to return to Kelowna, and Brian never gave me a chance to explain why it was so difficult for me. But maybe being able to talk face to face would have helped. Maybe it would have changed things.

Two years after Camilla's death, the book was released. One of Brian's former friends recognized himself in a chapter about high school and didn't take kindly to the way Brian used a private conversation as a plot point. He put two and two together and got his revenge by calling the local paper. My life fell out from under me again. It spread like wildfire. Everyone gossiped about us, everything got too much. I had nobody to help me with it. Oscar left me and Mary. I had to work more. I drank more. Mary started to pull away. She and I fought. By the time she left to go to university in Winnipeg, I'd halfway written her off too. My beautiful, intelligent girl, headstrong like her mother. When she returned home, I resented her. She was smarter—she could have gone anywhere, could have gone so far away.

I decided then that it was better for us to hate each other a little. She couldn't get too close to me. It was the only way to keep her safe.

"Holy shit," Mary said.

Aunt Judith had shared so much. Too much. I couldn't focus. I didn't know what to do. I wanted to stand up and scream and tear down the world for her. I wanted to hug her. I wanted to go back in time and try to protect her.

"Mom—" Mary said.

"It's okay."

"It's okay? Mom, all the things you just told us—"

"Not now. Please. I know you have a million questions. But not now. I want to do this thing before I lose my nerve."

"You don't have to. We can find another way. Right, Frey?"

I opened my mouth to answer, snapped it shut. A question tugged at me.

"Aunt Judith. You say you can reach toward people's skills, amplify them. Does that mean you've always known about me?"

"I knew." Her expression was unreadable.

"You never said anything. All this time."

She shook her head slowly, her gaze direct, "You have a right to your secrets, honey. Like I have a right to mine."

I caught Mary's eye. In all my life I'd never seen her like this. Eyes big, deathly still.

"We have to do it now," Aunt Judith said, "After all I've told you, can't you see why I want to do this for you?"

Mary nodded slowly. I released a shaky breath. We were really doing this. Javi shifted next to Aunt Judith on the couch, straightened his spine.

"Ready?" I asked.

He looked at me and I could see that he wasn't exactly ready, but he was resolved. He gave me a small nod and took a deep drink of his coffee.

"Are *you* ready?" he asked Aunt Judith gently. He was nervous, I could tell, but the amount of respect he was showing my aunt made me grateful once again for his presence.

Instead of answering him, she fixed Elliot with a glare that was more parental than I had ever seen from her. "If anything goes wrong, even a little bit, I want you to pull me away. Understand?"

Elliot gave her a placating expression. "I'm sure it'll be—"

"Do it!" she snapped.

Javi flicked another glance in my direction, worried now. I found myself leaning forward, as if proximity would help reassure them both.

"Okay," he said, and rolled up his sleeve as if he were giving blood.

My aunt placed her hand on his forearm and closed her eyes. Javi did too. After a few moments, he winced.

"Javi?" I asked, half-rising from the armchair. He shook his head quickly and waved me off.

There was a long silence. He squeezed his eyes tightly shut, and his hands gripped his knees so fiercely that his fingernails turned white. "Wait... I'm there... I think... It's hard to focus..." He clutched at his head with his free hand and gritted his teeth. His left nostril began to darken with blood.

"Javi!" I flung myself across to him to grab his shoulder.

An older man sat in a sunny room, staring at the television screen in front of him. Gary Quick. Alan Y.

I could feel something coming off him, a heat that pulsed, nearly tactile. But no, it was coming from... us? I realized I could still feel the nubby fabric of Javi's sweater against my hand. Somehow, he was in the room with me and Gary Quick. Not a vision of Javi but Javi himself.

I stared at him, marvelling at how I could make out every pore on his face. The folds and wrinkles in his skin as he squeezed his eyes shut, the twitch of the muscles in his brow as he opened his eyes and looked at me. Could I hear his breathing? Could he hear mine? I clenched my fingers around his shoulder. The world was fuzzy but Javi was solid, warm, his skin yielding beneath my hand. My lips formed a question in his voice.

Alan turned slightly, as if he'd heard a noise. He looked at us. No, through us. We were there and not there. He was a cat sensing an unseen danger. I read something sinister in his eyes.

Then he was gone. I fell backwards onto the floor, cracking an elbow against the coffee table. Javi was pale, and with a shaking hand, he wiped the blood from his nose. My aunt was hunched over, resting her elbows on her knees. Elliot, stopped mid-stride, dropped his hands with a relieved sigh.

"What happened?" Judith asked me in a rough voice.

"I think I had a vision. I saw Alan Y." I turned to Javi. "You were there too."

He released me. "I could sense you with me," he said, "when I found him. I actually sensed all the way to Vermont. It didn't make sense. I felt like I was everywhere, and I could find anyone." He shook his head. "There are fewer of us out there than I thought."

"How did you know it was him?" Elliot asked quietly.

"It's hard to explain. I could just tell. It's like he was sending out a beacon, and I just had to tune in. And then when Freya showed up, I was sure."

"Do you know where he is?" Mary asked, passing Javi a tissue.

"Yes," Javi said. "He's in Burlington, reasonably close to the Canadian border. Won't take me long to get there. As soon as I update Cassandra, I—"

"Us," I interrupted. "Us to get there."

Aunt Judith sat back up and looked around the room. The colour was beginning to return to her face. "Mary," she said. "You said the guest bedroom was ready for me? I think I'll have my dinner there, if it's okay, and then go to sleep. We can talk more later?"

She stood. Javi stood too.

"Thank you," Javi said. "We appreciate everything you've done for us. I hope you're okay."

"I'll be fine. I'm just too old for this. Mary, how firm is the mattress in your guest bedroom? You know I won't be able to sleep a wink if I can feel the springs."

Freya's four years of studying history, learning old stories and studying old lives, were done.

Dad, in town for graduation, flew home the morning after the ceremony. Freya knew he was going to leave early, but it still felt significant.

He'd assumed she would come back to Kelowna after graduating, as if her time in Toronto were a diversion, a month at a friend's country estate in a Jane Austen novel. Even made a joke about it: "Okay, you've made your point, you can come home now."

Back from the long, traffic-hindered cab ride from the airport, Freya felt a strange pang. Nostalgia for something that wasn't even over yet. Her apartment was her own. It wasn't U of T residence. Nobody was going to kick her out now that she'd graduated. Yet, standing in the entryway, she felt as if she were looking in on a past version of her life.

She sighed, tried to push down the waves of emotion running through her. Guilt for not going back to Kelowna, to Dad. Annoyance for feeling that guilt, though she was twenty-two and in charge of her own life. Regret for not having more of a post-graduation plan than to get a reliable office job.

Freya flopped onto her bed and looked out her balcony door at the roof points across the street. A black bird flapped onto her balcony railing, looking at her with seeming curiosity. Was it a crow? A raven? She could never tell the difference.

The goddess Freya wove the strands of fate. This Freya had a whole bunch of strands right now but didn't know how to weave them.

"What should I do now?" she asked aloud.

In response, the bird flew away across the street.

Freya moved to her closet and rummaged around in her storage bins. Once she'd found what she was looking for, she nestled back into bed, blankets tucked securely around her crossed legs, and pulled her old tarot cards out of their well-worn cardboard packaging. Freya slid the cards from one hand to the other, remembering the day her mother had given them to her as a childish distraction from a weird dream.

Her very first prophetic dream, and she'd told Mom about it openly, freely, without wondering whether she should.

Freya gasped. Of course she'd told Mom. It hadn't occurred to her before today.

She squeezed her eyes shut. Neither of them knew, at the time, what the dream meant. What the next one would do. How it would change everything.

She remembered what Dad had said to her at the airport just a couple of hours earlier: "Your mom would have been so proud." Mom should've been there to see her graduate. Maybe if Freya wasn't who she was, her mom would have been.

Freya shook her head. She flicked through the cards until she found the one she was looking for.

The Moon. All dark blues and greys, water and fields. Two wolves sitting by a stream, howling at a perfect yellow moon. The image always reminded her of her first-ever vision. She used to sleep with the card under her pillow for good luck.

A few cards later came the one that hurt to see. The Queen of Cups, with her thick blond hair. Freya remembered how she'd looked to it for comfort after Mom died, as if the card contained Mom's essence.

And why couldn't this card be Mom? Not literally, of course, but why not? The thought struck her as funny, but she didn't laugh. She ran her thumb along the Queen of Cups' braid.

Mom had told her that the cards could give her something to think about when she was having a problem. Now, maybe the cards could help her find direction.

She slid out from the covers, grabbed her laptop, and brought it to bed. She went to Google and thought for a second before typing: *How to read tarot?*

Cassandra met us at the airport before our flight. Somehow, Javi's information from our shared vision had been enough for her to arrange a meeting between us and Alan Y. Or rather, Paul Baxter, the name he was currently using.

"I have a contact connected to him," she explained. "She would've never revealed his location to me, or his assumed identity, but when I told her that you'd located him in Burlington, and that you were going to try to find him, she agreed to set up a meeting. Contingent on my being there as well."

She stopped there, and I didn't push her. I expected she wasn't too pleased at the prospect of giving up her weekend to go on a wild goose chase. However, I knew Javi shared my relief at not having to blindly search Burlington like a couple of dollar-store private investigators.

The flight was short and—despite the TSA agent's extra scrutiny of Javi before waving us through—we had a reasonably quick time at customs on arrival. Still, we were exhausted and starving by the time we checked in at our hotel, then went to a nearby restaurant for lunch.

Burlington, Vermont, was all decked out for Halloween. The trees of pedestrian-only Church Street were wrapped in orange-and-black streamers, ghosts and witches dangled from the bare branches. Jack-o'-lanterns sat in shop windows. From my seat at the restaurant's front window, I watched people bustle around, setting up bouncy castles, folding tables, PA systems.

We ate our lunches slowly, in silence. Something about the way we were going about this was still nagging me, so when Casandra pushed her plate away, I sipped my water and cleared my throat.

"So this friend of yours—" I began.

"Oh, she's not my friend," Cassandra said, holding up her hands. She sighed. "In fact, she kind of hates me."

"Hates you?" I couldn't help saying. The thought of even-keeled Cassandra inspiring ire in someone was pretty hard to believe.

Our server appeared to clear our plates, and Cassandra ordered coffee for all of us.

"She's not my friend," she repeated, "but I did her a big favour once, almost twenty years ago. When I was working with the Brain and Memory Institute. She'd published an article that sent our community in a tizzy. The Munich paper she was working for didn't want that kind of attention from vekers, so they cut her loose, and didn't support her amid the backlash. Kevin and I decided to help her. His career was just taking off and protecting journalistic integrity was something he took more seriously than almost anything. Still is. We set her up with his lawyer, who knew someone in Stuttgart who could help her. The whole thing worked brilliantly. All her problems went away."

Somewhere in the back of my mind I heard the distinct reverberation of a shoe dropping. "What was the article about?" I asked.

"It exposed the laboratory torture Alan Y experienced as a child," she replied.

Unsanctioned medical research. That was the term I'd heard watching the news with Dad; I thought of the intense look on his face all those years ago. I didn't know then what the words meant, but the phrase had always stuck with me. *Torture* fit better.

"You're friends with *her*?" Javi cried.

"As I said before, we're not friends," Cassandra said. "Anyway, now she and I are square, and I hope I never have to contact her again."

I swallowed, glancing at Javi. There were only four days until his television interview. He still wanted to go through with it despite everything that had happened between me and Shaun. He said it was too important not to. But talking about the Alan Y exposé reminded me what Javi was getting himself into. Because of that article, Cassandra's contact had lost her job, and Gary Quick had to go into hiding for a second time.

Cassandra checked her watch and frowned. "Half an hour. We should get going."

"Do you think he'll show?" Javi asked, looking suddenly as nervous as I felt.

"He'd better. If not, we lose our only chance."

Alan Y wanted to meet us in a neighbouring town called Shelburne. It was only about a twenty-minute drive, but when we arrived, I jumped out of the car, intent on stretching my legs.

Javi lowered his head toward me as we walked. "What's your plan?" he whispered.

"We need to convince Alan—Paul?—that Shaun is dangerous and that we need whatever help he's willing and able to give us. Exactly what I'll say, I don't know. I hope Cassandra can do that capable talking thing she does."

Cassandra was walking purposefully ahead of us down the quiet residential street we'd parked on, toward the bar Gary Quick had requested we meet at. A favourite haunt, maybe? A place where he felt comfortable? Or maybe a place where nobody knew him.

"What about me?" Javi asked.

"Say whatever you feel comfortable saying. Just don't say nothing. I don't want him to think you're our bodyguard or—"

"—that I have something to hide."

He'd spoken with such certainty, as if he already knew how Alan Y would react to him. Was this what Javi's skill did? Could he understand people like us better, after years of being able to feel us under his skin?

Cassandra had stopped to contemplate a large white house typical of the sort we'd seen a lot of during our short time in Vermont. High pitched roof, shuttered windows, large covered porch. If not for the sign in the window that read, modestly, *The Covered Bridge*, I would've thought she was just admiring the architecture.

"Strange place for a bar," she muttered, and led the way up the creaky porch steps. For a moment, I wondered if maybe it was Alan Y's house, and he was somehow tricking us. Trapping us.

I didn't have time to let my imagination run away with me, however, because as soon as we entered I saw that it really was just a regular bar. The walls were a deep red, punctuated by paintings of roosters, but the space was brightly lit and filled with tables in cozy clusters of twos and fours. To our right stood the bar itself, gleaming polished wood with relatively modern pendant lights casting a deep orange glow. Seemed nice enough. Quiet.

I slid a hand into my back pocket, felt the familiar smoothness and contours of the card I'd brought with me. Two of Wands. Upright it meant possibility, a plan. Reversed it meant fear of the unknown. A talisman that could apply either way.

"Shit, there he is," Javi whispered.

Already? I'd been counting on a few minutes to choose the best table, compose myself, at least get in a mouthful of beer.

But Javi was right. I followed his gaze to the corner of the room where a bespectacled man with grey hair sat leaning on his elbows, watching our entry. He was wearing a collared shirt under a plum-coloured sweater. He looked like my high school English teacher—not like the most important paradextrous person to ever exist.

I remembered my vision, the sinister look in his eyes.

Be careful.

He stood as we approached and accepted Cassandra's handshake. She introduced Javi, saving me for last. He considered me, letting the handshake go on a beat too long. We sat.

"Shall we call you Paul?" Cassandra asked. "Or would you prefer Gary?"

A tiny relaxation of the facial muscles at the latter, a tiny nod.

"Thank you very much for agreeing to meet with us," Cassandra continued. I was happy to relinquish the lead to her. "I know it's a terrible imposition. I appreciate your time, and I can promise you that anything we discuss will not leave this table."

"So what you're saying," he said, lifting his chin slightly, "is that you'll make sure to bring any reporters back to this exact table later to tell them everything we talk about."

A pit formed in my stomach. Of course he was already suspicious. Too suspicious.

Cassandra blinked, a smile frozen on her face, as she tried to think of what to say next.

Gary gave the tiniest of chuckles. His face lit up behind his smudged glasses. "It's a joke, love," he said quietly. We exhaled as one.

A server came to take our drink order, and within three minutes I had my long-awaited glass of beer in hand. I tried not to take an overly large first gulp, much as I wanted to. Cassandra sipped at her wine next to me, smiling neutrally at Gary. He in turn smiled neutrally back at her.

Javi was leaning forward on his elbows, staring into his pint glass, and it took me a second to recognize why. I wondered if it had been a mistake to let him sit next to Gary. But then again, no spot at this table would lessen any discomfort his skill was causing him to feel right now, sitting in the presence of *the* Alan Y.

As I opened my mouth to ask Gary if he liked Vermont, he looked right at me and said, "You're the one who's behind all this then, are you?" It wasn't accusatory or angry, not exactly, but I felt so far off my guard that my mouth went dry. I had to take another sip of beer before answering him.

"Yes. And believe me, coming to you is a last resort."

"I should hope so. I'm not exactly thrilled to learn that I've been tracked down, as you can probably imagine."

I swallowed, waiting for Cassandra to smooth things over, but she appeared to be taking this as an opportunity to nudge me from the nest. I tried a different approach.

"How much do you know of why we're here?"

"I know only that you've been threatened by someone and want my advice."

So the bare minimum. Which made sense, since Cassandra had threaded the information through a third party—a journalist, no less.

I took another fortifying sip of beer, then began sharing everything about myself. I had to. He needed to see me as I really was. And besides, while I was sure he wasn't the first person ever to exist with skills, he was still our poster child. Our figurehead. I felt I owed him that much.

"So you can see the future, can you?" he said finally. I couldn't read his tone at all.

"In a sense, yes."

He turned to Cassandra. "And you? What's your party trick?"

"I can remember everything I've ever read."

"Fascinating. Is that ever painful for you? Physically?"

"No, not anymore. I used to get migraines, blurred vision. But I learned how to partition it, and the side effects went away."

He considered Cassandra for a second, then turned to Javi, who twitched as if he'd been shocked.

"Javier?" It sounded so strange to hear Javi's full name. So formal.

"I can sense people who have skills."

"Can you now. Well, that must be a pain in the ass."

Javi looked at me briefly, without seeing me. He was fidgeting, drumming his fingertips on his glass and shifting in his seat. I'd never seen him like this.

Gary leaned back in his chair and surveyed the room. The light from the window caught the small hairs sticking up at the crown of his head, so grey and thin as to almost be translucent. His hairline had receded considerably from the last photo I'd seen of him. He hadn't been wearing glasses then either. He used to look stern, hard. I tried to reconcile this older face to that younger man, that beaten-down, given-up man. Now, you'd never be able to tell just by looking at him exactly what he'd been through.

"Now, don't worry," he said drily, as if he thought he knew what we were thinking, "the drugs they put me on, well, let's just say they served to erode the strength of my skill over the years. The worst I could do to you now is make you a little sleepy."

"I'm sorry that happened to you," I said. As soon as the words left my mouth, I regretted them, their hollow sound.

"Don't be," he said. "I don't need your pity. If anything, you should be afraid. Afraid for yourself, of the possibility of everyone poking into your life, trying to see how you're broken. My life should be your worst nightmare."

"It is."

"What I don't understand," he continued, "is how I can possibly help you. Or why I should, to be honest. Who's to say you won't sell me out the first chance you get? I know, for instance, that your husband is a journalist." He jabbed a finger at Cassandra.

"He is," she said, "but he's been married to me for eighteen years without making me or my group into a headline. Besides, it wouldn't do me any good to make an enemy out of our mutual friend."

"No, I suppose not." He scratched his chin, waved our server over and ordered us another round before I could protest. He turned his attention to Javi.

"What about you?"

Javi glanced at me again. "I have a nice, comfortable life. There's no need for me to sell you out. I'd have nothing to gain from it."

Gary made a sound, a small, cynical laugh. "I still don't know why I should bother," he said after a few moments. "I've already had to uproot my life twice. I don't want to have to do it again."

"This guy, Shaun," I said, "he's—"

"Unhinged," Javi muttered.

"He's an extremist," I said. "He's got this vision of a better world for people like us, and he wants to drag us all into it, whether we want to go or not."

"What's wrong with a better world for people like us? Why shouldn't we want that?"

"I do want that," I said so quietly I could barely hear it myself. "But not if it means I don't get to control my own life. To Shaun, I'm just a means to an end."

Gary eyed me. In that moment, he looked ten thousand years old. "I've known people like Shaun before. People with grand ideas and grander words but fuck all in the way of compassion or follow-through. I had to go into hiding like some criminal just because the world felt I owed them my story. And you three seek me out when I don't want to be found, when I've finally relaxed, and tell me the world hasn't changed one bit. It still wants more from me." He sat back, his upper lip curled like a snarling cat. He exhaled a long breath, and when he spoke again his voice was flat, "Tell me what you have in mind."

Amy was angry and Freya didn't blame her. Having the wrong audio tour descriptions for the latest exhibition was a huge fuck-up.

Amy paced the small distance of the museum's meeting room, then pinned Freya with her glare.

"You must have recorded the wrong thing," she said, "You were supposed to read the descriptions for the Quaker quilt exhibition, not the Japanese sashiko exhibition. The Japanese quilts aren't coming in until two months from now."

"I did record the Quaker descriptions. I remember them very clearly." Freya swallowed her words here, not sure if she wanted to make Amy angrier by telling her that she knew the difference, since it was unlikely that the mid-nineteenth century Quakers used traditional sashiko embroidery.

"You need to pay attention or else we all look bad."

Freya fumed. She was one hundred percent sure the files she'd marked as ready to load onto the audio guide system were the right ones. Not to mention that approving the audio tour wasn't her job to begin with. Freya's title was Curatorial Assistant, not Assistant to the Curator.

Of course, Curatorial Assistant meant something much different from the job ad she'd read a year before. In addition to helping digitize and maintain the collection, updating the website, and doing guided tours, she was also liaising with researchers and researching exhibition content. She hadn't realized she'd been taking on more and more of Amy's work until it was too late.

The meeting ended and Freya's blood was still boiling. Amy brushed past on her way to another meeting. It seemed like all Amy ever did was have meetings. It was a wonder the quilt museum was able to hold exhibitions at all.

And of course, half an hour later, Amy's cheery voice came floating up over the wall separating their cubicles. "Freya, I remember what happened with the audio files. I wanted to check your pronunciation of Moriguchi's name, and when I was done listening, I forgot to put the Quaker files back on the system. Isn't that funny? Brain fart! Make sure you double-check the Quaker files are loaded now."

Freya felt the anger rise again. She left her desk, more to clear her head than anything. She could go down to double-check the humidity levels in the exhibition room, make sure the lighting on the large quilt was even enough.

She felt the tension melt from her shoulders as she entered the room and wandered over to the temperature controls. It was quiet here, a domain she understood. A small group of people were examining the large quilt, making muted conversation, pointing out features of the design to each other.

Even though this quilt was over a hundred and fifty years old, Freya felt a sense of pride over it. It was the centrepiece of the whole exhibition. Made up of over fifty blocks featuring bright green leaves bordered by a crisscrossing red pattern, it was in beautiful condition. She'd helped the conservation team carefully clean the quilt when it arrived, and she'd loved the ritual of it. Wearing the right equipment, using the correct detergent, treating the quilt reverently. They'd discussed the different stitches of the design as they worked, shared the stories of how all the various quilts had been passed down through the generations to end up at the museum. Even though she'd let the others do most of the talking, Freya had luxuriated in it. She'd imagined the group of people who had likely made this very quilt a century and a half ago, gathered around it, talking and telling stories.

"Excuse me. What do the inscriptions on this quilt mean?"

Pulled out of her reverie, Freya looked at the group of people standing by the large quilt, watching her with expectant curiosity. She was happy to respond because she remembered the answer from the washing day.

"With quilts like this, people often inscribed important names and dates, and sometimes verses. Sometimes they were connected to an important event or they were given as gifts. Actually, sometimes the people named in these inscriptions weren't the people getting the quilt at all. It's fun trying to work out who the recipient is based on these inscriptions."

A loud cough behind Freya made her jump. She turned to see Amy behind her, a grimace on her face. Or was it a smile? She turned to the visitors and pulled her smile even tighter.

"Will you excuse us please? So sorry." She led Freya away by the elbow, and when they were not even two steps away, she hissed, "Don't talk to the visitors about the quilts. We have trained people for that. You need to go look at the bug traps, make sure the new ones are working properly. Then we need to get to that planning meeting. It'll run late, so I hope you don't have anything planned tonight."

Two hours later, the planning meeting was over, and Freya was paranoid it had ended because everyone could hear her stomach grumbling. Still, it wasn't that late in the day. She could still restore some semblance of the relaxing evening she'd planned.

As she followed the stream of co-workers leaving the meeting room, she heard Amy's voice behind her. "I forgot!"

Freya's stomach dropped. "Forgot what?"

"I finished a book yesterday and the author has the same last name as you! Brian Tanangco? Do you know him? Are you related?"

Freya twisted the strap of her messenger bag in her fists. She was hungry, overworked, resentful, and exhausted. There was nothing in the world she wanted less than to have Dad flung into the mix.

"No," she heard herself say. "Not related. Must be a coincidence." She turned and left the room, her ears burning. Had anyone else heard?

Once safely home, Freya threw her leftovers in the microwave and stared at the plate of food as it rotated unevenly.

Fuck this job.

What was it worth, all the ducking and reacting and fixing she had to do at work? And now she'd actually denied that her father was her father. He'd never find out, and it had stopped a conversation she didn't want to have, but she somehow felt cursed by the act.

What was she doing at the museum? She wasn't fulfilled by it. Every attempt to engage with the historical aspect of it was blocked, which must signify something. She wasn't building a career unless it was as a sponge for shitty treatment. She hadn't diverted the course of her life for this.

But the problem was that she didn't know what else she could do.

Her meal finished, Freya pushed the plate aside and crawled into her bed, retrieving her tarot deck from her nightstand. She shuffled the deck, focusing on the question, *What the hell do I do now?*

She pulled the Ace of Pentacles. Over an arched doorway with flowers on either side, a hand emerged from the clouds holding a pentacle, a star within a circle. It kind of looked like a coin, and in fact, Freya knew that in some decks the pentacles were called the coins. What did the Ace mean? She tried to remember. Beginnings. An invitation to create something new. Turning dreams into reality.

Freya smiled. It wasn't clear exactly what those beginnings could be, but what was clear was that she was done with Amy, done with all of it. Amy asking her point-blank about Dad was just the sign she'd been looking for. She might have been willing to grit her teeth through being treated like a lackey, but no way in hell was she going to stay in that environment and be constantly scrutinized for signs of being Brian's daughter.

It was a start.

She pulled out the Moon card, slid it under her pillow for good luck.

The first thing I did when I woke up was check my phone. Nothing. No missed calls from Dad. We still had time to put our plan into action.

My head throbbed. Probably residual exhaustion from the trip to Vermont, the excitement of talking to Alan Y, the trip back. I'd given Mary an update as soon as I was home, but not even her excitement and rapid-fire questions could prevent me from falling asleep on the phone.

I slid out of bed and shuffled into the living room in search of my tarot deck. I needed clarity, to calm down, before I did what needed to be done.

I decided on a simple spread. I shuffled the cards and chose four: one to represent the dilemma with Shaun, one for my current path, one for new insight, and one for guidance on what to do next. I flipped the cards over slowly, trying not to think too much about each one individually as I did so. I wanted to consider them as a whole.

The Fool. Seven of Swords. Temperance. The Tower.

An interesting combination. The Fool was a card of boundless optimism, unlimited potential. Courage, blindly following a course heedless of the risks. Temperance, the card I'd drawn to represent new realizations, was the Fool's counter—it was all about testing the waters, trying different options and finding a new way forward. My current path was represented by the Seven of Swords. Deception and betrayal, the acknowledgement of sometimes necessary deceit, and exercising caution.

The first three cards painted a picture of cunning and risk, and being careful not to make mistakes. Temperance also could suggest balance and synergy of a different sort: putting trust in others and working together. Shaun? Alan Y? Someone else?

I passed my index finger over the final card. The Tower. I'd felt a little jolt when I'd pulled it. In client readings, the Tower was met with almost same amount of fear as the Devil. It did look intimidating—a tower on fire, lightning above, crashing waves below, people falling or jumping from the windows. But the Tower was a card of change. Major upheaval, but the strengthening kind. I considered it a card that called for bravery—probably the most difficult-to-access sort of bravery though.

My phone buzzed then, almost as if it'd been waiting patiently for me to finish. It was a text from Alan Y—no, Gary. I was going to have to get used to that.

Are we doing this? Let me know.

Terse, succinct. Kind of like the man himself.

I sighed. I hadn't even begun to set those particular wheels in motion. I needed to move my ass.

I replied.

Calling him now.

It was a lie, sort of. I needed a cup of strong coffee before I could do anything. Annoyingly, making that cup of coffee didn't take nearly as long as I'd hoped it would, and then I had nothing left to do but to call Shaun.

My heart leapt, then sank, when he answered. His voice sounded flat, primed for another argument. I had to give the performance of my life despite my urge to unleash a stream of invective that would make Mary blush.

"I'm sorry," I said. "I don't like the way things ended on Wednesday."

"Neither do I," he said. And then nothing. He was waiting to see what I would say next. Crafty bastard.

"I've been thinking about it a lot since then and you're right. I need to be more honest, more brave. I've decided I want to do the interview with you after all. I'm not ashamed of who I am. In fact, I'm proud of it. I should thank you."

"Thank me? A few days ago, I got the impression you were going to throw me into the river."

I produced a laugh that, thank god, actually did sound as charming and ingratiating as I'd hoped it would. "I hope we can put that misunderstanding behind us."

"Are you serious about doing the interview?" he asked suspiciously.

"Yes. Dead serious. And there's something else. Are you busy today?"

"I have a bit of work to do, but it won't take me all day. Why?"

"I was hoping you would come over. I know it's a long way, but I think it'll be worth it."

"Why?"

I paused, as if considering. "Okay, I'll level with you. I got in touch with Alan Y."

"Shut up."

"I'm serious. He's the biggest reason I changed my mind. I was asking people for advice on what to do, and it turns out I actually know someone who is in contact with him. I took a chance and called him, and he's just the sweetest, chattiest man. We really hit it off. I told him all about STEP and he thought it was great. And then I told him about the work you're doing to help the paradextrous get more rights and fairer treatment. He was over the moon about your work."

"Really."

"Totally. He's had a lot of time to think about the way he was treated. The way we're treated. He told me he's ready to start speaking out more, getting more involved. When I heard that I thought, if Alan Y isn't scared anymore, why should I be? Anyway, he wants to talk to you about your ideas. So I told him we could video chat today. I wanted to do this for you. As a kind of peace offering."

"What? What?" He was so excited that he was starting to squeak.

"He just texted me and said he's ready whenever we are."

"Why not come here?"

"My car's in the shop. And getting to Toronto from Markland on transit would take forever. He's only free until about noon."

"Maybe you could give me his contact info?"

"Oh no, he wouldn't like that. He's still technically in hiding, you know."

"You're right. Fuck it. I can work later. This is so cool. I'm leaving in fifteen minutes, okay?"

When we hung up, I felt nauseated, thrilled, dirty, proud.

I had just finished drying my hair and dabbing on some makeup when Shaun buzzed in. I'd considered not making any sort of effort at all, but a small yet insistent part of me won out.

Making an effort turned out to have the desired effect. When I opened my door, Shaun blinked a couple of times at me before clearing his throat to say hello. For my part, seeing him again triggered a twinge of wistfulness, but it was quickly stamped down by the reminder that I had a plan, one that had to be followed precisely.

"Something to drink?" I asked. "I was thinking of coffee myself. I was out late last night." *Let his imagination run away with that little lie.*

"Sure, sounds good. How are you?"

I shot him my brightest grin over the coffee maker. "You know, I feel great. Talking to Alan Y was just... it changed me. Maybe you'll see when you talk to him."

"Is he calling soon?" He sat on the couch, leaned back, then stood again and moved to my armchair. I breathed a silent sigh of relief that I'd remembered to throw a cloth over my now-splintered dining table.

"He's waiting for our call. Oh, I'm done with that, by the way." I nodded at the book he'd lent me, which was waiting on the coffee table. He picked it up and looked at it briefly, turned to me, then dropped his gaze to the cover. In another life, he would've asked me what I'd thought, and we would have had a lively discussion about it. In this life, I couldn't bring myself to detach the book from the person who'd lent it to me. I would never finish it.

As the coffee maker gurgled to life, I set up my laptop on my desk. "I'll call him now and you guys can get to know each other while I finish with the coffee. I hope you don't mind if I sit in."

He sat at the desk, obviously trying to tamp down his excitement. I almost felt sorry for him.

I opened the chat app and soon enough, Gary's face appeared onscreen.

"Hi, Alan!" I chirped. We'd agreed to stick with Alan. His idea. He hadn't explained why and I hadn't wanted to ask.

"Hi Freya, so good to see you again, love," he cooed.

I couldn't help a grin. His demeanour seemed worlds away from the Gary I'd met in Vermont.

"Alan, this is Shaun Wyatt. I hope you two can chat for a bit while I finish making coffee."

I returned to the kitchen and busied myself, taking my sweet time. My hands shook. What if Gary had a change of heart at the end? What if he was swayed by Shaun and agreed to help him instead? I sighed and squared my shoulders. There was nothing I could do at this point. I had to put my trust in the reclusive, bitter, betrayed man I'd only known for a few hours.

I rummaged in my cupboard for some cookies and pretended like I wasn't eavesdropping. It was really incredible, listening to the two of them talk. Even though I'd only had one—albeit very long—conversation with Gary, I recognized his particular way of revealing only what he wanted to reveal. It had been frustrating to talk with him, but I couldn't help but admire his reticence. It was something I'd never mastered despite my own years of hiding away.

They started discussing Shaun's early life, how he'd come to discover his own skill. Shaun was pouring his guts out to his idol, much like I'd done in Vermont, and Gary was making sympathetic noises and saying things like "I understand that completely," as if they'd really made a connection.

I felt a wash of something approaching sympathy for Shaun. But then I remembered my vision, his cruelty. His cold determination to reveal my identity despite my refusal. My hands stopped shaking.

"What did I miss?" I asked. I placed a tray of cookies and coffee on the desk and pulled a dining chair next to him.

He was clearly annoyed that I'd interrupted, but he brushed it off. "I was just boring Alan with my life story," he said.

"Not at all," Gary said. "I quite enjoyed it. You remind me a lot of myself."

"I do?"

A brief pause from Gary, then I could sense the gears turning again.

"Well, any child who doesn't have an easy upbringing with regards to their skill, as you call it, is going to grow up disillusioned at the state of the world in that respect."

"Oh, totally. It's shaped the way I think and what I believe."

"And what do you believe?" Gary asked. I noticed his smile slip a fraction.

"The time to be passive and make nice is over. I don't know if you've heard, but the Dutch government has been compiling a list of people like us. Who knows what might happen if the pendulum swings in the wrong direction? Canada could be headed that way unless we stand up and take action, demand more rights and better treatment. I want the paradextrous to organize officially, protest, petition our government—whatever's necessary. I've got an interview on TV in a few days and I'm—" he caught himself and glanced at me, "we're going to take that opportunity to tell our stories, to speak out. I believe that there are thousands of Canadians like us who should be speaking out but are afraid. I think those people need to look past their fear."

"Better for them to go public and make a statement," Gary agreed quietly.

"That's right. A quiet life is a luxury regular people have," Shaun said. "We don't have that option. Not when so many of us are going through difficult times. It'd be dishonest to our people to live as if we're normal."

Gary's face darkened and he inhaled sharply.

I opened my mouth and spoke quickly, before he could. "Thank you for helping me to see the light," I said, "both of you."

Thank every god past, present, future, fictional—Gary's face broke into a wide grin. He was back.

"Well, I'm sorry, kids, but I have to go," he said. "I've got an appointment. But Shaun, it was lovely to meet you. We should keep in touch."

"Really? I'd love that! It's too bad you're in the UK and can't watch my interview when it airs. But once it's online I can send you the link."

"Sounds great. Well, thanks again, Freya, and we'll talk soon. Bye now."

And he disconnected. Gone. Silence filled the room. Shaun looked like he could float right off the chair, through the roof, into the galaxy itself. I felt something inside me trembling, threatening to burst out. Whether it was vomiting or cheering, I couldn't say.

"It's perfect!" Freya said, opening her arms wide. "Isn't it?"

Mary grinned. "It's so much bigger than your last place! You have a balcony!"

"Forget the balcony, I have a bedroom! With a door! Look," Freya ran to the room and closed and opened the door, as if to prove to her cousin that it was real.

In the empty space, their voices bounced off the walls. It smelled like fresh paint, a fresh life.

"And your landlord was okay with the fact that you don't have a job?" Mary asked, settling into a cross-legged position in the middle of the main apartment space. Freya joined her on the floor.

"Surprisingly, yes. I had a bank statement showing that I had enough saved up for the next few months and that seemed to be okay. It's nuts how much cheaper rents are in Markland than in Toronto. I'd barely saved anything, but I can live here for a little while before I have to start worrying."

"Have you been looking?"

Freya shook her head. "A bit. But everything I see makes me stressed."

"Not every place will be like your last job though."

"I know. And I know a job doesn't have to be perfect. It's just—" she sighed. "I got a history degree because I like learning about the way people used to live. I halfway thought I could find some sort of related job after I graduated. But once I found that job, it felt like a mistake. I don't know what interests me. And I don't want already settle for good enough at twenty-three, you know?"

Mary nodded. "Believe me, I know. I'm already scared shitless of graduating."

Freya didn't know what else to say. But maybe Mary didn't want advice or sisterly reassurance. What mattered was that they were together, talking about life as they always had, and the words weren't as important as being able to say them.

"Let's go get lunch. There's a coffee shop down the street that looks cool. And you probably need some food after helping me move all of this." She gestured toward the small pile of boxes in the corner of the living room, all she'd brought from her studio apartment. The only piece of furniture was the dining table. She wanted a fresh start for everything else. A good omen for starting a new life, she thought.

They walked down Freya's new street, kicking through piles of autumn leaves like kids.

"It's so cute here," Mary said in awe. "All these great old buildings, and the river is so close. I had no idea this place was so cool. And I've lived my whole life practically around the corner."

"Doesn't it feel so much more me than Toronto? I feel like I can just relax here. Spread out a bit. And everything I need is nearby."

"I get it. Living in Winnipeg has made me really appreciate smaller cities. So much more chill and easy."

"Maybe you and Elliot can move here after you graduate."

Mary grinned, ducked her head to let her hair fall in front of her face.

Freya laughed. "I will never get over seeing you get all giggly like that! I'm glad Aunt Judith is cool about you two living together now."

"Telling her in person at Thanksgiving dinner was the right way to do it. I'm glad you made me."

"Well, I also needed you to come home so you could help me move. Kill two birds with one stone."

"All your stuff fit in the back seat and trunk of your car. You didn't need my help."

Freya slung an arm around Mary's shoulder, said nothing.

The coffee shop was exactly what Freya hoped it would be. Small, but not so small that she'd be squished in with other people. Quiet, with good music playing. Cozy armchairs, comfortable tables. A place she could see herself relaxing in.

Relaxing after doing what, she had no idea, but right now it didn't matter.

They settled in with their food and drinks, enjoying their sandwiches and the silence. Then Mary's eyes lit up, and she gestured to Freya's purse while trying to quickly chew her mouthful of sandwich.

"Your tarot cards," she said. "Did you bring them? Why don't you do a reading for me? Help me figure out what to do after I graduate."

Freya laughed. "Shouldn't I be trying to figure out what to do with my own life?" But she pulled out the cards and cleared some space on the table. She handed the deck to Mary and told her to think of a question while she shuffled.

"Now, pick out a card without looking and put it on the table."

Mary did. It was the Tower.

"Holy shit, that looks terrible!" Mary said. "It's on fire! Are those people jumping into the water?"

"It looks bad but it doesn't have to be," Freya said, sipping her coffee. "This card suggests major transformation. Sometimes the kind that changes a whole life."

"Bad? Or good?"

"It depends. Sometimes a major change is re-evaluating things you've believed all your life, realizing they might not be what you believe now, and moving forward from that. Your foundations might break, but they can be rebuilt."

Your foundations might break.

They can be rebuilt.

Freya stopped talking.

I pull the Tower card. I pull the Queen of Pentacles. I pull the Chariot. I pull the Moon. The images dance together, showing me a story I don't understand. But as I speak, it comes together. The person I'm speaking to sends me a wave of relief, comfort. I have given them answers. Answers that come to me in dreams. I look at my face in the screen. I wake up.

"...wrong? Can you hear me? Freya."

Mary was shaking her arm. Freya blinked at her. She took a deep breath, smelling the food and the coffee, anchoring herself to the waking world.

"I think I just remembered a vision," she said. "But it was weird. It was about me. I was doing a tarot reading for someone. And it wasn't you." She squeezed her eyes shut, trying to grab the images before they drifted away. "I was doing a reading for someone else. But I didn't get the answer to their question from the cards. I got it in a vision."

Of course.

"I can use the cards," Freya said.

"Use them?"

"To help people. And if my ability kicks in, then I can really help them."

It just worked. Freya felt missing pieces sliding into their right places. What if she could just live her life here, in this new place, doing what she was good at, doing what she liked?

She looked down at the Tower. The lightning and waves attacking the structure.

"I have no idea where I even start though," she said. "How the hell do I do tarot readings for a living?"

She remembered Dad's photography career, the tiny studio in their first house, the bigger studio he'd rented later. She didn't want people coming to her home. She didn't want to sit across from a stranger and practice harnessing a weird skill. How would she get paid? What would she tell people she did for a living? Everyone would think she was a weirdo.

The foundation bristled with cracks.

On their walk back to her apartment, the cool autumn breeze cleansed the idea from her brain. It was silly for her to think she could step out onto the ledge like that and not immediately be blown into the waves below. Freya and risk didn't see eye to eye. Much safer to keep on doing what she'd always done. She'd find an office job in Markland. Maybe even a job at a gallery or something. She could learn to cope. It'd be fine. Most other people did. Why should she be any different?

Back home, she rummaged through boxes in the kitchen in search of her utensils. She still needed to sort out a bed and living room furniture. There was so much to think about. Too much to think about. Maybe moving had been a mistake.

"Freya. Look." Mary sat on the floor, leaning against the wall. Freya's laptop sat open on her outstretched legs. "What do you think of this?"

"What?" Freya knelt down next to her.

Mary spun the laptop around. "Them."

Oneira, the site was called. *Get answers from trusted visionaries with tarot, astrology, runes, and more.*

"Web chat?" She chewed her lip, considering. That might work. Nobody coming into her private world. The work would be more contained. Just her and the cards.

"They're hiring," Mary said, "and it says here no special technology is necessary. Just a good internet connection."

Freya looked at her cousin. "Is this a little off the wall?"

"Of course it's off the wall. But does that make it wrong?"

Freya thought of the Tower.

Major transformation. The kind that can change a whole life.

"It'll be okay," Mary said, gripping my wrist.

We were backstage in the television studio, sitting in a green room. I wished Javi was with us. I thought we'd have time to strategize when we arrived, but he was immediately whisked away.

Shaun was nowhere to be found either, but he'd texted me that he was going to arrive early and would see me on set. He really had no idea what we were up to. In all my years of keeping secrets, this felt like it should be second nature. Instead, I felt like I was going to vibrate apart.

Mary repeated herself. "It'll be okay."

"What makes you so sure?" I asked her.

"You're doing what you have to do."

I stood and paced back and forth, turned up a television displaying the station's broadcast, which at the moment was an English documentary about dangerous Victorian household items. On any other day I would have been interested, but today the sounds and pictures washed over me, meaningless. Suddenly, our plan seemed as stable as smoke. Too many things could go wrong. Too many strands of fate left to weave.

A knock at the door. A producer poked her head in, looking for all the world as if we should be thrilled. The interview was starting.

Mary changed the TV to the live studio feed, grabbed my hand as I sat down.

I'd seen this show a couple of times before and had always been impressed by it. The host, Christian Iseman, had an air about him, calming but perceptive. I hoped this boded well for Javi and for our plan.

The set was minimal: a desk, a blue-grey wall, and a small TV screen currently showing the show's logo. Javi and Shaun sat side by side, with Christian sitting behind his desk like he was at the head of the table at a cheerful Thanksgiving dinner. A third, empty chair stood next to Javi—a chair that was meant for me.

Mary squeezed my hand tighter.

They were making small talk. Shaun looked like he was having the time of his life. Javi, on the other hand, looked like he wanted to disappear through a trap door. Either they'd used the wrong shade of foundation for his skin tone or he was actually pale. For a moment, I wished I was right there to support him.

"Okay," Christian said, suddenly all business. "Remember the things we went over earlier. Relax and try to ignore the cameras."

"What did they go over earlier?" I asked.

Mary shushed me and turned her attention back to the TV screen.

"Shaun, tell us about your ability. Or, as you call it, your skill."

"Basically, I can read people's emotions," Shaun said. "With a touch, I can interpret what you're feeling in the moment. I've been using this skill to help people make decisions by being honest with themselves. For example, if I sense that someone has an overbalance of anger, I can bring that to their attention and help them work through it."

"So you're a sort of therapist then."

"No, nothing like that. But people find my input useful."

"So, if you were to touch me right now, you could guess what I was feeling? Sort of like a mood ring?" Christian said this in a chummy, familiar way, and I couldn't tell if it was the thrill of being on TV or Christian's charisma, but Shaun laughed.

"Not quite. It's something I can control. It doesn't happen every time I touch someone. And you'd have to give me permission before I go ahead. When I was younger, it was much more difficult to control. I had to learn."

"And that's the reason you're championing greater rights for people with skills? To ensure people with burgeoning skills get the help they need?"

"That's part of the reason, yes. There is also the issue of too much prejudice toward the paradextrous, both individually and at an institutional level. The Dutch government, for one example, has been exploiting a loophole that forces people with skills to disclose it on census reports. There's an advocacy group there trying to fight them on this, and I'm working to drum up support for them."

"Thank you, Shaun. Javier, you're a member of an organization called Support Tools Empowering the Paradextrous, or STEP. Can you tell us what you do?"

Shaun looked sharply at Javi. He'd respected Cassandra's request to not to talk about STEP. However, he had no way of knowing that in Vermont, she had given Javi express permission to act as the group's official representative—a designation I knew Shaun would have wanted for himself.

It was only the first surprise we had in store for him.

"Yes," Javi said, and I could see the slight adjustment of his shoulders, his expression. He was steeling himself. "For the past three years, we've been a resource for people like Shaun, who need help understanding their skills, and offering other support."

Almost imperceptibly, a muscle in Shaun's jaw twitched. Javi had just implied Shaun needed help. He wouldn't like that.

"And what sort of help do you offer?" Christian asked.

"Paradextrous people come to us because they're afraid. They're treated with suspicion or violence. Sometimes they have trouble understanding their skills. We offer advice, coping strategies, investigate third-party assistance, or even just give them a chance to relax and be around people who know what they're going through."

"Which is exactly what I'm trying to do too," Shaun interrupted, trying to wrest back the spotlight. "I'm pushing for us to tell our stories, to be less afraid of our unique gifts. We can help people like nobody else can."

Christian continued. "It sounds like you both are making great strides in helping to improve understanding of people with skills—paradextrous people—and make the world a better place." He then turned toward the camera. "Our next guest is someone who knows, perhaps better than most, the issues that paradextrous people have had to deal with."

Shaun nodded along. I knew he was expecting me to join them on stage any second. The smug, certain look on his face made me feel like I was windmilling my arms at the edge of a cliff.

Instead, Christian launched into a summary of Alan Y's early life, the infamous incident in 1972, and the impact that event had on people with skills. The feed then cut to a short montage of news headlines from the seventies and eighties, including a couple of vox populi sound bites from back then. I'd heard some of them before, but their vehemence and anger still made me cringe.

"After the break," he concluded, "we are privileged to welcome to the show—in his first public appearance since 1990—Gary Quick, the man known as Alan Y."

Someone in the studio called for them to stop filming and prepare for the next shot, and someone else placed a glass of water on the table by the empty chair. Gary came into the shot to sit next to Javi, and then the camera panned out to include Shaun. He'd gone completely white.

Gary sat with his arms crossed, eyes fixed on the table in front of him. He looked as uncomfortable as I'd ever seen a person look.

I only felt a little guilty at Shaun's reaction. Gary, on the other hand—I felt terrible for making him do this.

"He wanted to come, Frey," Mary said, as if reading my mind. "He didn't have to do this. He chose to."

Christian leaned toward him and asked, barely audible, "Gary, are you still okay to do this?"

A quick nod, a brief moment of eye contact. Christian nodded and signalled off-screen that they were ready to start again.

"Welcome, Gary. Let me just say, personally, it's great to see you. You look well. What have you been up to these days? I understand you were a Yorkshire Dales guide back in your home country of England."

"I was, yes. I liked it well enough, but I moved to America to be closer to family."

"And things are going well for you?"

"I have peace and quiet. Which is the best I could ask for, really."

"Now, I know you're not here to rehash your past, which is a painful story that has been told on countless occasions. So what prompted you to re-enter the limelight tonight?"

"This young man right here," Gary said, nodding toward Shaun, who looked at him with huge eyes.

"Shit, here it is," I muttered.

I had no idea if Gary was going to go along with our plan. I hadn't even been sure he was coming. When we were arranging for him to fly in, his texts gave me nothing I could interpret in my favour. I still had no idea if he liked me or hated me. This interview was either going to tip my way or ruin my life.

"You're a supporter of Shaun's initiatives?" Christian asked.

Gary scoffed. "Shaun doesn't have any initiatives. He does have initiative, though it's not working for him as well as he thinks it is."

Christian's polite smile tightened a bit, but ever the professional, he asked for clarification.

"I do agree with Shaun on one topic: the Dutch government forcing hundreds of people to reveal their skills against their will is a crime. But what you're doing, Shaun, is no better."

Shaun tensed up. "What do you mean?"

Gary turned to Christian. "I've spoken to a young woman Shaun has been hounding—no, harassing—to publicly reveal her skills despite her insistence that she doesn't want to. He's even researched her personal life and tracked down her family's private contact information in order to reveal her secret to them."

"I did not!" Shaun cried.

"Okay, we're done," Christian said to someone in the studio.

Shaun stormed off the set, and Christian shared a few stern words with Gary. Javi and Gary then got up and walked off-camera, leaving Christian alone and looking furious as producers flapped around him.

The green room door flew open. Shaun filled the doorway, fire coming from his nostrils.

"I know you were behind this," he shouted.

Mary leapt to her feet. "Hey, back off, you fucking shithead!"

I stood and faced him full on. I was surprised by how unafraid I felt.

"I had no choice, Shaun. I live my life how I think is best and I'll fight for that in any way I have to."

"You lied to me about everything!" he shouted.

Gary and Javi appeared in the hallway behind him.

Gary, whose life had been ruined because the world only saw him as Alan Y, the monster. He'd been just a scared little boy.

I thought of Aunt Judith, how my father had taken it upon himself to tell her story without seeming to care if she wanted it told, or without even knowing her real story.

"I wasn't lying," I told Shaun. "I said I was going to tell my story and I am. But the way I want to. Nobody else gets to tell it for me."

Gary blinked at me, nodded. "My story's run its course, but why don't I give you an opening?"

I caught Javi's eye. "No time like the present," he said. "I'll get a producer."

Shaun turned and took a couple of steps to follow Javi down the hall, then whirled back around to face me. He stared at me, his fists clenched. I could feel Mary tense beside me, ready to spring. "After everything we've shared, you still don't get that I was just trying to help you." He stormed out.

Mary looped her arm through mine. Javi returned, leaned against the door frame, looking at me silently. It's over, the look said. It's okay. I nodded. For the first time that evening, I took a deep breath.

Christian appeared at the door, looking like someone who had just screamed into a pillow.

"You're Freya Tanangco, I assume. We have an hour before our next guests arrive, so we need to get this started now. Let's get you to makeup and then we can go over your talking points before we begin. Gary, I trust you won't go off-script this time?"

He was gone, and the producer appeared in his wake to usher us along.

My stomach fluttered. I thought I'd have more time to prepare. I thought maybe we'd book an interview in a few days, a month. Was it really happening now?

"Ready?" Gary asked.

And if it's true that she started a war, think about how she helped to end it. She brings Vanir wisdom and seiðr magic to the Aesir. She unites them. She changes their fates forever.

I took a deep breath, squeezed my cousin's hand. Like Javi had said, no time like the present.

"I'm ready."

Nine-year-old Freya stretched her legs as much as she could in the back seat, trying to get comfortable with her book. Mom turned around from the passenger seat with a slight frown.

"I thought you were sleeping back there," she said. "I think you should stop reading now. It's getting dark and we're almost there."

"It's not dark! I can see just fine. Don't worry."

Mom frowned again but reached over the back of her seat to give Freya's leg a pat. "I'm glad you like the book."

Freya raised a thumbs-up, already halfway back in the book's world. She pulled the blanket higher up around her neck, tucking it under her chin. Had it been four hours already? The campsite seemed like it was still so far away. She evaluated the stack of books next to her on the back seat. Would they be enough for the weekend?

Dad must have seen her in the rear-view mirror because he laughed and said, "Don't worry, honey, I promise you won't get bored. We can go swimming tonight before dinner, and tomorrow we can go fishing."

"I want to bait the hook this time."

"Of course!"

"Brian, no," Mom said, smacking him lightly on the arm.

"I was younger than her when I learned. It'll give her confidence. Plus, she's not as accident-prone as you."

Another smack, but this one followed by a small giggle. Freya turned back to her book.

The campfire was hot, almost too hot, but she was so close to the end of her book to move. Mom sat down in a camping chair, folding her legs and cradling a cup of wine. She leaned forward to look at Freya's book. "Is this the same one you were reading in the car yesterday?"

"No, I finished it this morning. This is the next in the series."

"What's it about?"

"Someone loses a cat and the new girl gets in trouble for it. But then someone blackmails her!"

"Blackmail! Wow, that's pretty intense."

"It's not like movie blackmail, don't worry. It's funny blackmail. Anyway, I think I know who did it."

"I bet you do. You always figure it out. Tell me later, okay?"

"Dinnertime!" Dad said, carrying the platter of barbecued fish to the picnic table. Freya's stomach growled. Mom slung a tablecloth over the table and pulled Freya down next to her, gave her a kiss on the head. They ate fish and rice and salad. They talked about the fishing they'd done that day and planned their hike for the next. Freya insisted that she could walk farther than she had last year, and she wanted to see cooler animals than before. Dad had his notebook with him and scribbled in it, sometimes mid-sentence.

"This reminds me so much of when I was a kid," he said. "I used to come here with my family when I was your age."

Freya leaned against her Mom's arm and rolled her eyes in an exaggerated way. She'd heard this story a million times—she'd heard all of Dad's stories a million times. About all the books Dad would bring along and all the leaves Aunt Judith would collect for him to press in the pages of those books. How many fish Aunt Judith caught compared to him, how high she climbed in the trees. Mom and Freya listened and laughed at the usual parts. Mom then talked about her own childhood, the forests in Norway, her family cabin in the summers. The smell of campfire blew around them and the world was so dark, just the stories and the fire and the tops of the trees that swayed against the stars.

It was late when they went to sleep, later than Freya's bedtime at home. Dad bundled up extra blankets underneath and around her, until Mom said she looked like an egg in a carton. She started to drowse while Mom and Dad set up their own sleeping bags, but woke up a little when they got in. She sleepily stuck out an arm from her nest toward Mom and gave her a couple of pats just to make sure she was there. The low murmurs of their voices swept her up in a wave between awake and asleep, dipping down into dreams, then surfacing into wakefulness in the tent.

Dad was talking about a new book idea, using the stories he'd told her over and over again about his childhood, about her grandparents and about Aunt Judith, about Winnipeg and Kelowna. She always thought Dad's novels were supposed to be fiction, like her books about lost cats and mysteries. But this time Dad was talking about things that were true.

Mom shifted in her sleeping bag, clasped Freya's hand in her own and gave her a little squeeze. Dad was still talking in a murmur, and Mom answered him in a voice pitched low so Freya wouldn't hear, but she did.

"I think if you feel you need to write these stories, you should. It's important that you explore what's pulling at you. But are you sure Judith will be okay with it?"

Dad sighed. "If she even notices. I'll change enough that it won't be obvious it's her. I just can't leave her out of this story. She's my sister. My story isn't my story without her."

"So tell me again when your interview will air?"

I laughed. Mary knew full well when it would air—she'd talked my ear off about it the whole drive home from the studio. "Tomorrow evening, with web and print articles by Cassandra's husband the day after. Parts of Javi and Shaun's interview are going to be shown in the same episode, but my segment will be the longest."

"And your segment was mostly you? They didn't overlook you to focus on Gary?"

I shook my head. Despite the confrontation that had taken place before my interview, Christian had been nothing but kind and considerate. I'd told him bluntly that I didn't want to talk about my father, that I'd wanted my story to be about me. I had no desire to villainize Dad or make him seem like a negligent parent. Gary, for his part, remained mostly silent during the interview, deferring to me often.

"I wonder if I'll ever hear from him again," I said. "He left as soon as the interview was over, pretty much without a word."

I felt a wistful pang. He wasn't Alan Y to me anymore, spectre of my childhood. He was just Gary, a paradextrous person trying to live his life like I was. Maybe now that a spotlight would be on someone else instead of on him, he could finally really rest. I found myself wanting to know what he was going to do in the years to come. I felt a strange need to be a part of it somehow. It seemed wrong to never speak again.

Mary chewed a mouthful of spring roll thoughtfully. She adjusted her position on the couch and the precarious balance of the plate on her legs. "Do you remember when I basically bullied you into joining STEP the last time we had Chinese?"

"You had an uphill battle trying to get me to listen to you."

"But that's the thing about hindsight, right? I mean, I definitely could have handled it better. I just really love you, you know, and I was afraid of what was happening to you. I couldn't protect you." She trailed off, cleared her throat, and put her plate down heavily on the coffee table.

But she had protected me. Even when she'd felt her most helpless, she'd inadvertently given me the most support I'd ever had. In just a few weeks, I'd learned more about my brain than I had in the eighteen years since it'd first gotten away from me.

I thought of Cassandra, steady and curious, certain in her guidance. Javi, who'd immediately accepted me, stayed patient as I dug in my heels on my way to trust. For the first time ever, there were people like me in my life, on my side. Unafraid.

I opened my mouth to respond when Mary's pocket buzzed. She leaped up, fishing her phone out of her pocket.

"Who's that?" I asked.

In response, she hurriedly pulled on her shoes and flew out my front door. I stared after her. What on earth was she doing? I went out onto my balcony and leaned over the railing as far as I dared. The early November air prickled my skin and a gust of cold wind flung my hair around. I couldn't see anyone of note outside. I hoped she wasn't planning anything over the top.

The sound of my door opening jerked me out of my reverie. It was Javi. "Can you hold the door for a second?"

"Oh no. Javi, please. The interview was good but I need some peace and quiet. If this is some kind of surprise party—"

He snorted. "You absolute dork. Look." He gestured behind him.

I poked my head out of the door to see Mary holding up the other end of a small dining room table.

"What the hell?"

"Okay, move it or lose it," Javi said. I jumped out of the way and held the door open for them.

"My mom lost her mind when I told her your table broke," Mary said as she shuffled inside. "She knocked on all her neighbours' doors until she found someone with a small table they were willing to part with."

"This is so nice of her! I should call her and say thanks."

"Don't worry about it, it's no trouble. Though I think this might be the last spontaneous kind gesture either of us will get for a while. I don't think she enjoyed her little foray into the world of *you two*."

"Well, not everyone has to do what I did," I said. I made a mental note to talk to Mary in a few days' time about finding resources for Judith. I could invite her to STEP, but maybe there was something else for her. I just didn't want her to be alone with her skill anymore. I'd make sure, at least, that she could count on me. I knew what it was like to be alone and scared of yourself.

Mary and Javi flopped onto the couch, and I followed close behind with bottles of beer and fortune cookies and the rest of our fried rice. In the ensuing silence, interrupted only by quiet sipping and crunching and chewing, I felt myself relax for the first time all day. But then Javi made eye contact with me, and I knew my peace was short-lived.

"Has he contacted you?" he asked.

"No. You?"

"Who? Shaun?" Mary asked, frowning.

Javi nodded. "He called me when I was on my way here from Judith's place, demanding to know my involvement in the whole thing. I didn't say much, don't worry. But he sounded deflated. I pulled over and let him rant at me for a while. He said he might go to Amsterdam to see if he could help that advocacy group he keeps talking about."

"Holy shit," Mary said. "The weaselly shitwaffle does have a tiny shrivelled heart."

I laughed, but it mingled with a small puff of relief. Relief over the fact that Shaun no longer seemed interested in my situation, or relief that he was actually doing something productive, I couldn't tell.

"So are we all still on for dinner at Cassandra's tomorrow?" I asked them. "I'm looking forward to hearing about this new idea she has for STEP."

"I'm in," Javi said, "but I need to leave by eight. I've got a date."

"Ooh," Mary and I cooed in unison.

"Yeah, yeah, get lost," he said, laughing. "I've already cancelled on her once because of you. So don't let me down this time, Tanangco."

He looked happy, at ease. I'd never let him down, not on my life.

"Cross my heart." I turned to Mary. "Is Elliot still thinking of coming?"

"He is," Mary said. "He wants to make sure STEP is good enough for you."

I was so charmed by the sentiment that I couldn't even laugh at Elliot's intense lateness in expressing it.

"Well," Javi said.

"Well," Mary replied.

"Well," I said.

We all stood, but I didn't want them to leave. Once they were gone, there'd be nothing left for me to do but the scariest thing I'll ever have to do. Scarier than the interview. Maybe even scarier than living through my mother's death.

I shifted my stance, felt for the corner of the Queen of Cups in my pocket.

They must have read the conflicting emotions crossing my face, because before I knew it, we were locked in an awkward three-person hug, Mary's head jammed firmly in Javi's armpit. And then we were laughing so hard we couldn't breathe. I felt good. I felt light as air.

We untangled ourselves and spent a few minutes playing Tetris with the tables—moving the old one out to the hall, the new one to the vacated spot. The new table actually worked better for my space than the broken one had. Still, I felt a strange pang as I watched Mary and Javi carry it around the corner of my street and out of my life. A tether to another world, another person, now cut.

Then I was alone, with my new table, my old apartment, and the phone.

Before I could think, overthink, anything, I picked it up and dialed. I didn't know what time it was in Kelowna, but I didn't care.

"Hi, Freya," he said.

And at the sound of his voice, even though I had been expecting it, I felt tears prick my eyes. He sounded so happy to hear from me.

"Hi, Dad."

ACKNOWLEDGEMENTS

To my agent Kelvin Kong, thank you for being in my corner, and for everything from career advice to food and photography chats.

Endless thanks to Bryan Ibeas, Leigh Nash, Julie Wilson, Megan Fildes, Andrew Faulkner, and everyone at Invisible Publishing for your insight, guidance, and commitment. To Bryan, my editor, special thanks for giving me the confidence to weave in the stories I used to hold close to myself, believing it wasn't my place to tell them. Salamat po, kuya.

To the Semi-Retired Hens: Teri Vlassopoulos, Julia Zarankin, and Lindsay Zier-Vogel, thank you for your bottomless belief and wisdom, and for being the best writers' group in recorded history. And Teri, I'm honoured by the strength of your confidence in me over decades.

I am grateful for the many friends who have helped bring this book to life. Kiitos to Susanna Kaapu—without your love, support, and long chats about everything, this book wouldn't have been written. Thank you to Pamela Clark and Jake Dorothy for simply being the wonderful friends you are, and to Amy Brenham and Sonia Dorothy for letting me pick your brains for random research questions.

Thank you to my parents, Kaarina and Michael Marcelo, for believing in me sometimes more than I did. To my brother James Marcelo, thank you for a childhood spent reading X-Men comics together and discussing the worst superpowers someone could have, which evidently lodged in my brain more than I realized.

And to my husband Jason Garner, thank you for more than I can ever express.